The Case of EINSTEIN'S VIOLIN

William L. SULLIVAN

Published by the Navillus Press
1958 Onyx Street
Eugene, Oregon 97403

www.oregonhiking.com

Printed in USA

The Case of EINSTEIN'S VIOLIN

William L. Sullivan

Navillus Press
Eugene, Oregon

"Of course Einstein's ideas helped bring about the end of World War II, but what devilment might have been loosed if, instead of an atomic bomb, his theories had led to the creation of a gravity bomb?"

—Dr. Fritz Wenger, "The Red Cross and the Broken Cross" (Venice, 2007)

THE ENVELOPE PLEASE
(Ana)

Now I can say this: Sometimes you need to put yourself in Harm's way, even if she is the kind of person who sells the skeletons in your closet on eBay.

I might still be a high school German teacher drilling irregular verbs if Harmony hadn't persuaded me to break into my mother's house.

My old key didn't fit, and Mom must have switched the hide-a-key when Monty moved in. I just stood there on the dark porch, musing out loud that we'd have to go back to the hospital.

"Ana! Your mother's in surgery." Harmony put one hand on a hip and tilted her head. "Back in high school, how did you sneak into the house after a late date?"

"I never did that."

"Come on." She took a pen light from her purse. "The kitchen window usually works."

Soon we were creeping through the bushes like burglars behind the big Victorian house on College Hill. To my surprise, the kitchen window really was unlocked. Harmony clasped her hands as a stirrup to give me a boost.

When I heard a thump inside the house, I called, "Hang on, Einstein!"

"Who's Einstein?" Harmony asked.

"He's the real reason we're here." I squirmed down to the counter, unfolding my legs as stiffly as a butterfly trying to emerge from a cocoon. Finally I swung my feet to the floor. Then I found the kitchen light and unlocked the back door for Harmony. By that time an ancient Siamese cat was tottering up to an empty food dish. He looked at me and emitted a long, demanding meow.

"This is Einstein?" Harmony asked. "We're spending the night here to take care of a cat?"

"A very special cat. I got him when I turned ten. Now he's so old he needs a pill three times a day. I hope you're not mad."

Harmony bent down and petted the old cat gently. "Poor old guy. Medicine's no fun, is it?"

Up until that moment, I don't think I entirely trusted Harmony as my friend. After all, we had met only three months before, at a local women's support group called DANCE. The group's name stands for Divorced And Now Challenging Everything, but I was still too busy getting my feet on the ground to jump up and challenge everything at once.

Harm had just ditched a manipulative hunk named Leo, and I had just been left, again, by a randy wanderer with the name of (Why didn't I see this coming?) Randy. Eventually, I supposed, Harmony and I would be in the market for upgrades, but after you've burned your fingers on one stove, it's refreshing to take a little breather, and look around for some sisterly friendship, before warming up to the next fire.

Not that Harmony and I are much alike. To be sure, we were both thirty, and we both taught school in Eugene, Oregon. But Harm is a natural beauty, with wide brown eyes, a dimple in her cheek, and a blond ponytail that cascades casually out the back of a baseball cap. She grew up with hippie parents who make wooden toys on a commune behind Spencer Butte. As a child she was granted all the liberties in the world. The resulting innocent freeness has become a mysterious part of her attraction, from the way she shrugs with one shoulder to the way she chooses improbable combinations for a double-scoop ice cream cone.

Harm is irresistible to men, but she has a dangerous streak. Sure, she teaches kindergarten, but she also has an advanced belt in Aikido.

As for me, I'm happy with my roundish face, brown eyes, and mid-length brown hair, even though it tends to frizz out on either side. When I want to turn more heads than Harmony I write freelance articles for *Eugene Weekly*. Still, I couldn't help but envy Harm's adventurous style and her way with men. I'll admit I was lonely since the divorce. I told myself I wanted to lose ten pounds before I tried dating again.

It wasn't any easier knowing that my only living relative had just checked into McKenzie-Willamette Hospital to remove a lump in her breast. I didn't want to think it might be cancer.

"Where are the pills?" Harmony asked.

I blinked. "What?"

"Einstein's pills. Where does your Mom keep them?"

"Oh. They're in the dining room cabinet. By the wine."

Harmony turned on a chandelier in the next room. "Wow. Where did your mother get all the antiques?"

"The house used to belong to my great aunt Margret. Margret was confused about many things, but she understood antiques. When Mom inherited the house she wanted to modernize everything. I talked her into leaving the dining room alone."

Harmony was halfway to the cabinet when she paused beside an oak buffet. "Hey, here's a letter for you."

"But I haven't lived here for years." Curious, I picked up the envelope. There, neatly penned in my mother's looping hand, was the inscription, *For Ana Percey Smyth.* I turned it over. Written in large letters across the sealed flap were the words, *TOP SECRET! To be opened by my daughter in the event of my death!*

For a moment I simply stood there, stunned. The formality and the finality of the envelope made me fear for an instant that Mom really might be dying. I felt cold and a little queasy.

"What is it?" Harmony asked.

I held out the envelope in reply.

She read the words and bit her lip. "Damn. I'm always barging around in other people's business. This time I've gone too far."

"No, it's not your fault. My mother can be melodramatic. She probably leaves a letter like this every time she goes to the hospital."

Harmony handed back the envelope. "Any idea what's in it?"

I turned it over in my hands, wondering. Knowing my mother, the most likely message would be a maudlin farewell. Or some ghastly, detailed funeral instructions.

Or perhaps a photograph? That thought made me tempted to open it, despite the envelope's instructions. When Mom remarried, she burned our family photo albums. The only pictures I had of my father were memories, and they grew fuzzier every year.

"It's too small for a will, I suppose," Harmony mused. "But it might have the key to a Swiss bank account."

I laughed. Harmony really couldn't stop herself from prying. "I'd like to know as much as you, but it doesn't seem right to open it now, when Mom's in surgery."

"Did I say you should?"

"I think we need to give Einstein his pill." I set the letter decisively on the dining room table and took a medicine bottle from the glass cabinet.

"All right. You hold him while I pop in the pill." Harmony took the bottle and paused. "But tell me, why do you call him Einstein?"

"It's a long story." I gently picked up the old Siamese cat and settled in a plush chair. The cat blinked and purred. "We called him Kitty when I first got him. That was a hard year, when I was ten. I'd just lost both my great aunt and my father. I think Mom gave me a kitten to try to soften the blow."

Harmony pulled a chair beside me and opened the medicine bottle. "How did it happen, losing both your father and your great aunt at once? Were they in an accident?"

"No. Margret died of pneumonia that January. No one was very surprised. She was ninety-six and hadn't been entirely right in the head since she moved here from Germany after the war. Still, she and I had sort of become best friends, and I was crushed. Then Dad died just six weeks later. He was on a business trip to Europe."

"Was he in a dangerous business?"

"He sold perfume. He and Mom ran a little shop in the Atrium mall called Scents And Sensibility. Maybe you remember it? Anyway, he was in Greece shopping for essences of some sort when Mom got a phone call saying he'd died of a heart defect. Just like that, at the age of forty-two. I never saw him again. Mom thought it would be too traumatic for me, so she went to Greece to handle the arrangements alone."

"How awful. You should have been allowed to go."

I shrugged. "Yes, I should have. Instead I got a cat."

Einstein stretched and yawned wide.

CHAPTER 1 ~ ANA

"Harm! That was your chance to get a pill in his mouth."

"Oops. I got distracted."

I held up the cat's head, but he didn't seem about to yawn again, and I wasn't in a hurry to force open his jaws, knowing he'd put up a fight. I went on with the story. "Anyway, we named him Einstein because of where he slept."

"I guess I don't follow."

"When my great aunt died she left everything to my mother and me. Mom got the house and I got the contents of the attic."

"How strange." Harmony leaned back a little. "And what was in the attic?"

"Just the knickknacks of an old lady. When I was small I used to go up there with her. She'd invent the craziest stories. For example, there was a ratty fur coat she said she'd worn dancing with the King of Sheba."

Harmony snapped her fingers. "I know! You said she understood antiques. Maybe there's a Ming vase up there worth a fortune."

I shook my head. "We checked. Mom had an antique dealer appraise everything. All the valuable stuff was downstairs. Nothing in the attic is very old, and it's all in terrible condition. For years Mom's been after me to pack it up and get rid of it."

"Oh." Harmony frowned. She scratched the cat's neck. This time his tail twitched. "You still didn't explain about the cat's name."

"When he was a kitten he'd go up in the attic and sleep in Einstein's violin case, so I called him Einstein."

"I suppose this violin was another of your aunt's knickknacks?"

"There's no violin. It's just a case. Margret said she'd gone to school in Switzerland where Albert Einstein taught, and that later she'd somehow bought his violin case. It's probably not Einstein's at all. It's just an empty case where a cat liked to sleep."

"Fair enough." With that, Harmony pinched open the cat's jaws and popped a pill down Einstein's throat before he knew what was happening. Suddenly a telephone rang, and claws, teeth, and fur seemed to be everywhere.

A moment later the cat had vanished. But the phone was still ringing. I looked at it warily. Could the doctor be calling from the hospital already? Maybe the surgery really had discovered breast cancer.

The phone rang again. This time Einstein joined in, meowing

miserably at the back door. Finally I took a breath, crossed the dining room, and picked up the receiver. "Hello?"

"Uh-hm—"

"Monty, is that you?" From the way he cleared his throat, I knew it had to be my stepfather. "Monty, how's Mom?"

"Uh-hm, I'll be staying here tonight anyway. Um—"

"Monty?" I raised my voice, but the only reply was the maddening sound of a telephone being fumbled and dropped. Monty had always been rather dim. My mother must have married him for his looks. He has broad shoulders, a square jaw, and teeth as white and even as kitchen tiles.

Harmony watched from across the dining room, frowning with her eyebrows. Einstein meowed again, louder.

"Ana?" Finally Monty was back on the line.

"Hello? How is my mother?" I demanded.

"Uh, fine."

"Then it wasn't breast cancer?"

"Huh? Uh, no. Is that what she told you?"

I let out an exasperated breath. "She told me she was going in for surgery to have a lump removed."

"Well, uh, sort of."

"Sort of what?"

There was a pause on the line. Then Monty said, "She sort of decided she wanted to take out the, uh—"

"The *what?*"

"Uh, you know. The, uh, implants."

I stood there, my mouth open.

For once, Monty began speaking with some speed. "Remember the ones I got her for her birthday? After we got married? Anyway, she'll be home tomorrow, I think. I'm staying here, though, so it's great you're at the house and all. Thanks, Ana."

In a daze, I replaced the phone. My mother was going to be all right—that was a relief. But I felt angry, too, as if she had kicked me in the shins. Mom hadn't told me the whole truth about her surgery on purpose, so she could wring out a few extra days of guilt and sympathy. It made me think again about the mysterious envelope. If Mom had known she didn't have cancer, why had she left a letter for me?

"Well?" Harmony asked.

CHAPTER 1 ~ ANA

Einstein gave a prolonged meow. Mechanically, I went to open the back door.

"So it wasn't cancer?"

"No, she'll be home tomorrow. Without her breast implants. Apparently Mom's going back to a B cup." I turned the doorknob and Einstein streaked out into the night.

"A B cup?" Harmony put her hands on her hips. "If Monty expects us to baby sit a cat while his wife resizes her boobs, I think we're entitled to charge the going rate."

"What's that?"

Harmony opened the glass door of the cabinet. "A bottle of their best pinot noir."

I couldn't help laughing at Harmony's gumption. "I think you're right." I found a chrome corkscrew and a pair of long-stemmed crystal glasses.

Harmony twisted the corkscrew in place, popped the cork with a flourish, poured the glasses full, and clinked hers against mine. "Here's to—"

"Not to my mother. This isn't the first time she's lied to me. You think I'd get used to it, but it still hurts."

"Do you still love her?"

I contemplated the ruby liquid in my glass. "Yeah. But she's been trying to make me worry about her all my life. Everything's always about her. I'm ready to cut myself loose from dear old Mom."

"Bravo! Your sisters at DANCE salute you. Here's to—" She clinked her glass again and paused, waiting for me to choose the words.

"Here's to making our *own* dreams come true for a change." I solemnly closed my eyes and drank half the glass in one go. The dark, rich wine seemed to blossom inside me with the warmth of evening sunshine, chocolate, and cherries. When I opened my eyes the world really did look different—somehow more under my control.

"So what's the first step in making our dreams come true?" Harmony asked.

"That all depends on what they are," I said. "Go ahead, you start. You've listened to my problems all evening. What's your innermost desire?"

Harmony narrowed her eyes as she considered. "To find the perfect tiramisu."

"Yes!" I laughed. "Goal number one should always be dessert."

"It's no easy quest." She raised a finger. "I also need to find the one man in the world who knows how to make it."

"Even better. Sounds like a challenge."

"It's nothing compared to the challenge you've got," she replied. "How do you expect to write a murder mystery if you aren't willing to kill anybody?"

I flushed, thinking about all the first chapters I'd let her read. "There must be other readers out there like me."

"Grisly." Harmony shook her head. "You're going to need gore on every page if you want to quit your day job."

My festive mood faltered. It was true that my teaching position involved more work every year. The elective German classes were fine, but budget cuts had forced me to teach sophomore English instead for two hours a day. There was talk that I'd have to teach social studies next year as well. And class sizes had crept up to forty. The kids were great, but I dreamed of quitting so I could work on my writing full time.

What made it worse was that Harmony seemed to love everything about her kindergarten job. She even seemed to enjoy substitute teaching at the local Aikido center, in a class mostly for men. Perhaps it was her way of looking for the perfect tiramisu.

"The trouble with all the mysteries I start," I said, "is that I'm not as good a liar as my mother. Or Randy, for that matter—he was a pro. I'm too cautious to dive into the really big fictions. Where's drama when you need it?"

Harmony took a sip of wine. "Maybe it's in an envelope right here on this table."

I sat forward. "I thought we agreed I shouldn't open the envelope."

"That was before you declared your independence from a vain, scheming mother." Harmony gave me a one-shouldered shrug. "I wonder what she wrote in there?"

"Well, I doubt she wrote me the opening paragraph of the next Miss Marple." Still, I really had been wondering. Unleashed perhaps by the wine, my curiosity was beginning to stalk the envelope like a jungle cat circling its prey. Why did I keep thinking it had a photograph of my father? Perhaps this was the one sin I couldn't bear letting my mother carry to her grave: burning my memories of Dad.

Harmony said, "I suppose you could steam it open and reseal it later."

No." I set down my wine decisively. "I'm not going to sneak around behind my mother's back."

Harmony looked at me sideways.

With sudden courage I reached across the table. "I'm going to rip the damned thing open so she knows exactly what I've done." Before I could change my mind I tore the flap with my finger. Then I turned the envelope upside down and tapped, now almost certain that a photograph of my long-dead Dad would drop onto the desk.

To my surprise, nothing came out. When I looked inside, I found only a small slip of paper with a short note:

Forgive me, baby. Your father is not exactly dead. We're divorced. He's at the monastery of Saint Nicholas on Milos, Greece. If you want to know more about the crazy side of your family, ask him.

Love, Mom

GREEKS BEARING GIFTS
(Harmony)

I've never seen somebody turn so white. After Ana read that letter the paper quivered in her hands.

But then blood began rushing back to her face. Ana's hands were still shaking, but I could almost hear the strength come roaring back into her, like some kind of holy fire. Her mother had left a landmine of a farewell letter. Ana had taken the full force of the blast and was still standing.

And now I'll have to admit it: This is the kind of grit that drew me to Ana from the first, even during those first wobbly-kneed sessions with the divorce therapy group. In a world of rubber women and plastic men, Ana is iron.

Amazingly, most people don't see this. What they see is a quiet, intelligent, organized woman who shies away from conflict. Even Ana underestimates herself. She pooh-poohs her strengths. Sometimes she blames herself for troubles caused by others. But if she believes in her heart that something is wrong—stand back!

"So is it the opening paragraph of your next novel?" I asked, like a complete idiot. No wonder people have trouble taking me seriously. Even at life-changing moments like these I sometimes open my mouth and am amazed at the words that pour out. Who is this mindless, blond hippie chick I hear talking?

Ana handed me the slip of paper. "Mom says my father is still alive."

CHAPTER 2 ~ HARMONY

I read the note and whistled softly. In my own family people talk too much. They tell each other their feelings. Then they tell each other how they feel about each other's feelings. Sometimes it drives me nuts. I was fascinated to be peering into the window of a family that snarls over red meat—a family where a mother would cover up a divorce by telling her only daughter that her father is dead.

"This is hot stuff, Ana. Do you think she's lying?"

"She's been lying to me all my life." Ana stared at the table. "Damn her anyway. She wouldn't even let me have a picture of him. I can hardly remember his face."

"Perhaps she wanted to protect you from him after the divorce."

"From a Greek monk? What the hell was she thinking?"

I shrugged a shoulder. "Maybe he became a monk to atone for some crime."

Ana shook her head. "I was old enough when he left to know him better than that. He was one of the most considerate, quiet men in the world. My God, I can't believe it. He's still alive."

"So why hasn't he sent you a postcard from Greece in all these years? Even monks can write." I poured the rest of the bottle of wine into our glasses.

Ana frowned at the wine in her glass. "I don't know. I remember he used to make a big fuss about my birthday. He'd even buy me ice cream on what he called my un-birthday, six months later. In winter, when I wanted to go sledding, he'd drive to the mountains with me and Rags and watch all day while Rags did flips off the ski jump I built."

"Sounds like he started out as a normal Dad."

"I guess he was gone a lot in the evening, but that's only because he took the hours at the perfume shop that nobody else wanted, not even Mom." Ana stopped and set down her glass, as if struck by an obvious thought. She looked down, her face reddening.

"What is it?" I asked.

"I bet they were cheating on each other."

"Who? Both of them?"

Ana closed her eyes. "I don't know. Probably just Mom. She's the liar. I didn't see it as a kid, but now that I think about it, she wasn't even very sneaky. Whenever Dad worked late at the shop Mom would dress up and go out, leaving me to play in the attic with great aunt

Margret. They always took business trips separately. When it was my mother's turn, she'd come back tanned to her bikini line."

"Maybe your Dad found out, and that's why he left."

"More likely, she got tired of dodging him and told him to get lost. And to think I've been stuck with her ever since." By now Ana was fuming. "All these years Mom's been portraying herself as some needy, neglected widow, when in fact she's nothing more than a deceitful, egocentric, vain—"

"Hold it, hold it," I interrupted her rant. "This is the same mother you were all teary-eyed about fifteen minutes ago, right? Now you're clenching your fists like you're ready to strangle her."

Ana looked down at her white-knuckled fists. She took a deep breath and slowly unfolded them.

"That's better. You don't like grisly murders, remember? Besides, you don't have enough facts yet to murder anyone, much less write a novel. You need to do some research first."

"Research?"

I leaned forward. "You've got a real mystery on your hands, Ana. What happened to your father? Who are you going to ask?"

The answer seemed obvious to me, but Ana lurched off in a different direction. She grabbed the telephone and started punching buttons.

"What are you doing?" I asked.

She ignored me for a moment. Then she said, "Monty? Oh hell. No, this isn't a wrong number. I'm trying to reach my mother, Winona Smyth. Goddam it, yes, it's an emergency. I don't care. What about Monty Perkins? He's staying in her room, and he's not sedated, unless he's drunk. What? Oh for—"

She slammed the telephone onto the table.

I waited.

She glowered at the telephone. "The hospital won't let me talk to either of them until tomorrow. When Mom wakes up I'm going to nail her to the wall. I wonder what she'll say? And Monty—how much does he know?"

"Not much, I'll bet." I put my hand on Ana's wrist to calm her down. "There's somebody else who knows more."

"Who?"

"Your Dad, of course. Call him and ask what happened."

Ana's eyes betrayed an instant of fear. But then she took a deep breath. "I guess it hadn't really sunk in. He's still alive."

I gave a one-shouldered shrug. "All you need is his number."

"Maybe we can find it on the Internet." Ana led the way into a side room. Pictures of houses on the walls told me this must be the office where her mother and Monty ran their real estate business. Ana sat down at a desk, moved the mouse to wake up the computer from its screen-saver sleep, and typed in the search words "Milos" and "Greece." Before long, as I watched over her shoulder, Ana was clicking through a tourist website. There were pictures of semi-tropical beaches, ancient marble ruins, and whitewashed hilltop villages.

"Wow," I said, and before I could stop myself, "Nice vacation digs."

"Wait, here it is." Ana had found a map of a horseshoe-shaped island with a label on one tip, in Greek letters and in English, "Monastery Saint Nicholas." When she clicked on the label a page popped up with a small picture of a white fortress-like building atop a seaside crag. Below a paragraph of Greek text were the words, "Monastery Saint Nicholas, founded 312 AD. Miraculous icon of the virgin, relic tongue of the saint, catacombs. Open Tuesday-Saturday 11-13h."

"It's the sunny shrine of Saint Nick," Ana marveled. "I wonder what Dad would be doing in a place like that?"

"And if you called, would Santa's relic tongue tell you about the mysterious side of your family?"

"There's no phone number or address. Look, here it says they don't have telephone service at all. The only access is by donkey path." Ana frowned. "Without an address I can't even write him. We're back to square one."

My mind was racing. "No, I've got it."

Ana looked at me skeptically. "What?"

"Simple. Let's go to Greece!"

Ana just laughed.

I laughed along with her. We both needed to release some of the evening's tension. But when the silence of the old house had seeped back into the room, I asked, "Well, why not? I'm going to Italy next month anyway. Remember? To protest at the globalization conference. If you go to Greece I can catch up with you there."

Ana shook her head. "Harm, you're something else. We don't even know if it's true that my Dad's in Greece. And besides, I'm broke. All Randy and I had to split were his debts. If I flew off to Europe the credit card people would own me."

"No problem. You can let your family pay for it, the same way I am. That's the beauty of it."

"What on earth are you talking about?"

I laid it out for her with my hands. "Remember those tie-dyed pajamas my parents gave me?"

"No."

"Well, Mom said she'd gotten them back in the 70s from Jerry Garcia, the guitarist, you know? Anyway, I went online and found a PR photo of the Grateful Dead where he's actually wearing them. So I put them on eBay and sold them to a guy in Wisconsin for $1000."

Ana was quiet for a moment. "How did your mother get Jerry Garcia's pajamas?"

"Look, I don't know. It doesn't matter. The point is, you've got a fur coat and a violin case and a bunch of other stuff in the attic. If we sell it on eBay, it could pay for your trip too."

Suddenly a small, ghost-like face appeared in the lower corner of the office window. I pulled back with a start. The face gave Ana a silent meow.

Ana opened the window and gently lifted the old Siamese cat to her lap. "What do you think, Einstein?" she asked, stroking the cat's neck. "I'm not sure we should sell anything. But maybe Margret left us a clue upstairs. Something I didn't understand when I was ten. Should we take a look at our old haunt?"

Posters of Care Bears and My Little Ponies glared at us from the walls of Ana's old upstairs bedroom, as if they thought she ought to become a child again and move back in. With a great creaking of coil springs, Ana lowered a trap door from the ceiling and unfolded a retractable staircase. The smell of dust, old paper, and wood wafted down from the black hole over our heads. I shivered.

Einstein climbed the stairs to the attic first, his eyes black and his ears pricked. Next Ana ventured up into the darkness.

"Isn't there a light?" I asked, my voice a little shaky.

"Yes, I'm looking." Ana pulled a string and a bare bulb clicked on among the rafters.

CHAPTER 2 ~ HARMONY

Why was I so frightened by Ana's attic? As I scaled the steps I kept imagining bats were going to fly into my hair. At the top there was hardly room for me to stand up. A pair of planks ran the length of a peaked gable. Dusty boxes and trunks stood stacked to either side.

I looked around and sneezed.

"Gesundheit," Ana said. "Remember to walk only on the boards or you'll fall through. There's nothing but plaster lath between us and the bedrooms below."

"This was your inheritance?" I said. "Bizarre."

"I thought it was pretty special at the time. Margret and I used to pretend the attic was a gateway to the fourth dimension."

"Seriously?" I waved a hand before my face, trying to clear a cobweb.

"The fourth dimension is time, you know. We pretended we could travel at the speed of light and end up in any age we chose. Often as not, she'd be a little girl in a medieval castle." She looked away. "People said she was a little crazy, but to me it was just magic."

"Here's the fur coat," I said, taking the plastic cover off a brown, knee-length jacket on a hanger. "Do you suppose it's genuine mink?

"Fox, I think."

"If you tried to wear this in Eugene, animal-rights activists would probably throw paint at you. But on the Internet we might get $500."

"We're not selling anything," Ana objected. "We're looking for clues about my father. Or about my great aunt, for that matter. That whole side of my family history is pretty much a blank."

I opened the front of the fur and looked at the label. "Here's something. Isn't this in German?"

Ana read the label. "*Pelzmodehaus Ulm, Bahnhofstrasse 29.* It's from a fur fashion shop in Ulm. I think that's in southern Germany, near Munich."

"Well that shows she probably did come from Germany."

"That much I know. She taught me German nursery rhymes. She always had a bit of an accent."

I cocked my head. "If she was German, why was her name Smyth? Did she marry?"

"Not that I know of. My Dad was her nephew. I guess she must have changed her name when she came to America."

"You guess? And why was your Dad brought here by his aunt?

What happened to his parents?"

Ana raised her shoulders. "I've puzzled about these things all my life. Before I was ten, no one would talk about it. After that, there was no one to ask."

For a while we flipped through boxes of books. Finally Ana shook her head. "No letters, no photographs, no old documents. What good is a nearly complete set of *World Book Encyclopedias* from 1957?"

I peered into a different box. "I wonder why everybody saved old copies of *National Geographic*?"

Ana held up a pair of ragged sandals from a trunk. "The same reason people kept their worn-out shoes, I guess. To remind them of all the places they might have gone."

I peered around a corner toward a smaller side gable and whistled. "Wow. This is weird, but it might just be our jackpot."

"You mean the shrine?" Ana came up beside me to look.

Dozens of brightly colored garden gnomes stood grouped about an open, rectangular violin case like munchkin mourners at a corpseless funeral. Behind them a beveled glass mirror in a massive, carved wooden frame doubled the throng of statues. Arcs of paisley curtain fabric and aluminum foil draped from the rafters on either hand.

"When I was a child I thought my great aunt's shrine was the most elegant thing in the world." Ana voice's had a catch in it. "She was the queen of a fairy castle. And now everything up here just looks pathetic. The clutter of a senile mind."

"What—"I groped for words. "What was this a shrine to?"

"*Weisheit*," Ana said.

"To what?"

Ana covered her eyes with a hand. "Wisdom."

"Look, maybe we should just leave—" I stopped short when I realized tears were running down Ana's cheeks.

"Are you OK?" I asked, proving once again that I am a complete idiot. Ana turned away, sobbing into her hands.

Why hadn't I seen this coming? All day long my friend had been through an emotional wringer, first worried that her mother was in surgery for cancer, then outraged that her mother had lied, and then shocked to realize her father was still alive. I had only made things worse by encouraging her to confront the ghosts in her attic.

I put my hand on her shoulder. "I'm sorry, Ana. We don't have to dig through everything tonight."

She shook her head. "No, no, you're right." She wiped her eyes with her fingertips. "Let's get rid of this junk. There aren't any answers about my father up here."

"Maybe you should wait a while."

Ana knelt down and picked up one of the gnomes. She managed to give me a smile, her cheeks still damp. "Hey, we'll make a fortune, selling treasures like this on eBay."

I laughed with her, and it felt good. "The market for gnomes has been a little weak lately. How on earth did your great aunt get them all anyway?"

Ana turned the ceramic figurine in her hand. It was a grinning woodsman, about six inches tall, with a hand-painted red cap, a white beard, blue trousers, and a stubby black ax over his shoulder. The other gnomes varied from three to twelve inches in height. They represented a broad range of gnome activities. One jolly man pushed an empty wheelbarrow. An old woman with an apron wielded a rolling pin. Others squatted, laughed, or smoked pipes.

"She got them as birthday and Christmas presents." Ana had a faraway look. "It's all she ever asked for. We'd order them from catalogs, and my parents always brought them back from trips abroad. Garden gnomes are a little hard to find in America, but you see them in backyards all over Europe."

Suddenly she turned to me in earnest. "Let's get rid of it all. There really was some craziness in my family, and I'm ready to see it go. Besides, you're an eBay expert. Do you think we can make enough for a plane ticket to Greece?"

I looked at the gnomes in the shrine with a more calculating eye. "Well, maybe somebody else out there has been collecting gnomes too. I could lump them into lots—men doing things, women doing things, and the ones that just stand there and grin. We might make $300."

"You're kidding."

"I probably am. The mirror is a surer thing. And hey—what's this bottle in the violin case?" I picked up a small blue vial.

"Oh, that's Cloud Nine, a perfume my Dad invented."

I pulled the stopper. Suddenly I felt like I was drifting into another world. "It's *wonderful.* Why don't you use it?"

"I don't like perfume." Ana shrugged. "I guess because I grew up in a perfume shop."

"But this stuff is amazing. It makes me feel all light-headed."

"Keep it, then."

"Really?"

"Sure. Now what about the violin case?" Ana held it up skeptically.

I replaced the perfume stopper and set the bottle aside with the gnomes. Then I took the violin case and turned it over, examining the scuffed leather and the brass latches. "Well, it looks old enough to be Einstein's. It's a little strange that it's not shaped like a violin on the outside."

"Margret said most violin cases were rectangular back then. That gives them room for hidden compartments." Ana opened the case. The plush green velvet inside had the shape of a violin. She lifted the lids of three side compartments to show they were empty.

"It's awfully beat up," I said.

"I know. I asked about it at a violin store once. There are thousands like it. I think we started pretending it was Einstein's because it has the letters AE on it."

"Seriously?" I inspected the worn letters on a brass plate on the side.

"OK, or possibly it's AF."

"It's hard to tell."

"There's also an Italian label inside, under the cushion. Maybe you can read it." Ana removed a green velvet pad inside the main compartment.

I guess if Ana's the German expert, I'm the Romance specialist. My kindergarten is in the River Road neighborhood, a part of Eugene where nearly half the schoolchildren have Mexican parents. I use Spanish a lot, and can get by in Italian or French.

"It's from a music shop in Siena." I put the cushion back and faced Ana. "Listen, the violin case will only sell if we can hype it as Einstein's. To make the story work we need something more to go on. How much do you know about Einstein?"

Suddenly Ana's Siamese cat emerged from the shadows and stood among the gnomes, ears pricked.

I laughed. "I meant the physicist, not the cat. For example, do you even know if he played the violin?"

"Oh yes," Ana said. "Not professionally. Just to help him think. Wait, I'll show you a picture." She walked across the attic and returned with the E volume of the encyclopedia.

"What happened to his violin?" I asked.

"I don't know. It's probably in a museum somewhere." Ana held open the book to a black-and-white photograph of a slightly stooped old man with disheveled white hair, a bushy moustache, haunted eyes, and a violin.

I took the book and read, "Albert Einstein, born March 14, 1879 in Ulm, Germany." I looked up and arched an eyebrow. "Ulm—that's the same place your great aunt got her coat."

"But his family moved to Munich before he was a year old and he never went back."

"Oh." I read farther. "He moved to Italy at the age of 15. Milan, not Siena, unfortunately."

"He could have ordered the case from a different part of Italy."

"Maybe." I continued reading. "Then he went to school in Switzerland at 16, took a clerical job in a Swiss patent office in 1902, published his special theory of relativity three years later, and became a professor in Zurich in 1909." I skimmed the rest of the article. "After that he accepted a university position in Berlin in 1914, fled Nazi Germany in 1933, and taught at Princeton until his death in 1955."

Ana sat down cross-legged beside me and sighed. "I guess there could be hundreds of old violin cases with as good a claim to be Einstein's." The cat climbed onto her lap, kneaded her jeans a few times, and curled up.

I waved my hand at the ranks of gnomes. "But look at this shrine. Your great aunt obviously believed the violin case was authentic. I'm sure there are other collectors out there who wish they had something that belonged to Einstein—even if it's just an old box. All we need is the right story." I leaned forward. "What exactly did your great aunt say about how she got it?"

"Almost nothing. Just that she'd bought it because she'd known him as a girl."

"Did she say anything more about it at all?"

Ana hesitated. "There—there was a rhyme she taught me that went with it. Sort of like a nursery rhyme, I guess, except—"

"Except what?"

"Well, it was mostly mathematics."

I stared at her. "You mean a formula? She found a mathematical formula in the case? But that's the perfect story!"

Ana was shaking her head. "No, no, no. There wasn't anything in the case, and it wasn't $E=mc^2$, if that's what you're thinking. It was just—" her voice trailed off and she looked aside.

"Well? What was the formula?"

Ana shrugged apologetically. "This will sound silly, but Margret made me swear never to tell anyone. Besides, she said it was only the first half of a formula."

I rolled my eyes. "Terrific. Look, she's been dead for years and we're trying to sell this stuff. Surely you can tell people about it now."

She bit her lip. "I'm sorry. Margret and I were very close. She said I could only tell the rhyme to—" Again she paused.

"To who?"

"To the burgermeister of the gnomes."

I held my hand to my mouth, but a muffled laugh leaked out anyway.

"What?" Ana demanded.

I almost blurted that this was the craziest thing I'd heard all night. Instead I managed to give my usual one-shouldered shrug. "So I'm guessing there aren't any burgermeisters in your attic?"

Ana shook her head.

"All right." I put my hand on her arm sympathetically. "I'll just say the case comes with the legend of a lost formula. That's true enough. And who knows what fish it might catch?"

A GAMBLE IN GERMANY

Thirty-six hours later and half a world away, in the dark, paneled dining hall of Schloss Klingenstein, the Baroness von Hohensteuern turned her wheelchair to face police commissioner Meyerhof. "Wolf," she said, "It is kind of you to step out of retirement for me." Her fine hair was white and her shoulders bent with age, but her large, dark eyes and prominent cheekbones showed that she must once have possessed great beauty. And although her German was excellent, she spoke with a faint French accent, the coquettish souvenir of a foreign past.

"The baron was one of my oldest friends," the commissioner replied, inclining his head slightly toward her. He was perhaps a few years older than the baroness. His wire-frame glasses seemed precariously perched between bushy white eyebrows and an equally bushy moustache. But the energy with which he held his thin body straight suggested strength and confidence. "I asked at once to be involved in the investigation. It is all the more important to me because my granddaughter is still relatively new to her position."

The baroness lifted an eyebrow. "I am not sure I approve of young women entering the profession of the criminal police. Don't you also find it—unfeminine?"

"The public's view on these matters has changed from our day, baroness. Certainly Rosi was determined to undergo all the necessary training. I could hardly object that she wanted to follow in my field."

"No, of course not." The baroness nodded.

The commissioner covered her hand with his. "I assure you every possible avenue is being pursued. Rosi has launched an interagency search of police and government records on two continents. If there is anything to be learned, she will discover it."

The baroness sighed and looked out the deep-set leaded window to the estate's forests and the red tile roofs of the village in the valley below. "Gerhard was in such pain those last days that I expect his words were only part of a waking dream."

"Undoubtedly. Still, you are perfectly right to—"

A soft knock at the door interrupted his words.

The baroness turned, irritated. "Come in."

The door opened a crack, and the balding head of her secretary leaned in.

"Herr Weiss," the baroness snapped. "You must know after all these years that I do not bite."

"It's just that the baroness asked not to be disturbed."

"So I presume this is important. Out with it."

The secretary stepped inside. "I wanted to report, baroness, that my son had a moment's spare time and was exploring on the Internet."

"Honestly, isn't he supposed to be chiseling or whittling something? After all the years of schooling I paid for."

"Sculptors are not busy with commissions every day of the week," the secretary objected. "Peter was searching the Internet, hoping to be of service to you, and he found this." He spread several sheets of paper on the worn, wooden dining table beside her.

The baroness took her spectacles from her pocket and examined the first sheet. "This appears to be a gathering of garden gnomes, Herr Weiss."

"It is an estate sale in America," the secretary explained, quickly shuffling the other papers to the front. "Here they are offering a violin case that they claim once belonged to Albert Einstein. And here is a fur coat brought from Germany by the same woman, now deceased. Notice the label."

"It's from a shop in Ulm."

"More precisely from a shop in the *Bahnhofstrasse*. That portion of the city was destroyed in the Allied air raid of 1944. Obviously the coat must be at least that old."

CHAPTER 3

The baroness put down her glasses and looked at the commissioner. "Does your Rosi know of this?"

The old gentleman demurred. "I doubt she would find it worth pursuing. An estate sale of garden gnomes in America?"

The baroness turned back to her secretary. "Did the advertisement mention the name of the deceased?"

"I'm afraid, baroness, that the woman was described merely as 'great aunt Margret.'"

The baroness pursed her lips at this news and looked out the window again, as if the decision she faced might be resolved there. At length she handed the papers back to her secretary. "Buy it, Herr Weiss."

"Even the gnomes, baroness?"

"Just the coat and the case. If they look genuine, I'll want more research done."

The commissioner protested. "Really, this is too much. There's no need to launch a wild goose chase on the basis of some crackpot computer sale offering. The police are undertaking a proper, methodical investigation."

The baroness laid her hand on his sleeve. "Yes, Wolf. But I am just enough of a crackpot myself to want my own investigation as well." She turned to her secretary and asked, "How is Peter's English?"

The secretary looked baffled by this sudden change of topic. "Excellent, baroness. My son spent a year in Cambridge."

"Then this may be an opportunity for him to make himself useful, if he is not too busy with his other commissions."

"But—" the secretary stammered. "Surely you wouldn't send him to America! Such a delicate matter would require the utmost secrecy and finesse."

The baroness looked out the window, thinking. "Yes. It is hard to decide who would be less competent for such a task, young Peter or the police. I think, though, that I would rather gamble on the artist."

RAGS AND RICHES
(Ana)

I had just finished writing the first paragraph of another murderless mystery when my cell phone jangled loose with Schubert's "Erlkönig." I glanced at the screen, saw that it was my mother, and angrily buried the phone under my backpack.

I took a deep breath and concentrated on the soothing view from my secret woodsy nook along Eugene's Willamette riverfront bike path. A crook-necked heron glided upriver, a reflected gray double S. A kayaker spun above the rapids and slipped down a glassy green chute into the whitewater. A fluff of cottonwood seed broke clear of the riverside trees and sailed up into open sky.

For the past week I had struggled to overcome my anger. My mother had lied to me about my father for twenty years. Worse, she didn't seem to have answers for my questions. All that she would admit was that my father was alive in Greece. What was I supposed to do with a mother like this?

When a muffled version of "Erlkönig" began again, I reluctantly pulled out the phone. "Hi again, Mom."

"Baby?"

"Are you feeling better yet, Mom?"

A strangled noise came out of the cell phone. "Better? How can I recover from major surgery when half the world is trying to break into my attic?"

The wording of the call was much like the others from her in the past two days, but a new note of desperation put me on a higher level of alert. "You've only had the two calls, right? From Japan and Slovakia?"

"No! Now it's the police or the KGB or something. I think they were from Switzerland, for God's sake."

"What did they want?" More concerned now, I folded my laptop closed. At first I'd written off my mother's complaints as imaginary—more of her melodramatic lies. But now I was beginning to wonder.

"The same thing. A secret formula, or at least the story of crazy aunt Margret."

"What did you tell them?"

A moment's silence on the cell phone suggested that Mom was gasping for words, like a drowning man for air. "There isn't anything to tell! Baby, what on earth have you done?"

I switched the cell phone from one hand to the other, at the same time mentally shifting to damage-control mode. "Mom, all I did was to start cleaning out the attic. You've been bugging me about it for years. It was Harmony's idea to add the story about the formula, not mine. I can't help it if there are strange people out there on the Internet."

"Well, why are all these strange people calling me?"

"I don't know." I really didn't know. Harmony and I had used my mother's computer to post the auction offerings during that long and giddy night, but the Internet site was supposed to be confidential, and I certainly didn't remember giving out Mom's telephone number.

The auction itself had netted only $650. To be sure, bids had flown back and forth with astonishing vigor, especially for the violin case, but after Harmony and I had packaged up the violin case, the fur, and the mirror, and sent them off to various parts of the world by express mail, there had definitely not been enough left to finance a trip to Greece. In the meantime I had become so curious about my father that I was nearly ready to dive into the murky waters of credit card debt to fly to Greece anyway. When I had confronted Mom with her letter, her response had been so evasive ("Ask me again after I'm really dead") and suspicious ("Your father simply lost interest in me, so we divorced") that I wanted to know the truth.

"I can't take this anymore." The sound of Mom's voice broke into my thoughts, bringing me back to the Willamette riverbank in early summer, with an alienated and desperate mother inside a small plastic cell phone. "Baby, it's time for the bottom line. You've got to do a garage sale."

I pressed the phone closer to my ear, hoping to make sense of what I was hearing. "I'm sorry, Mom. I thought you said 'do a garage sale.'"

"I don't care if you do it or have it or just plain hold it. You can even use my driveway; that would probably be simplest. But I'm telling you, I don't want crazy aunt Margret's stuff in this house any longer. You've got two weekends to get everything out of my home. Do you understand?"

I wasn't sure I did understand. "Mom, are you saying I should clean everything out of *my* room too?"

"No—" Mom quickly replied, but the word trailed downward into an awkward pause. Meanwhile the heron circled back, spread its gargantuan wings, and landed on stilt legs in the smooth arc of green water above the rapids. "No, of course not, Ana. You've always had your room."

It was rare that Mom called me simply by my given name, instead of Baby or Sweetie or at least Ana dear. I closed my eyes, trying to absorb the meaning of it all. I had demanded my independence, and here it was. But now I realized that loss was the other side of the coin I had flipped. What had my anger accomplished, really? I certainly hadn't won a clearer picture of my nebulous father. All that now seemed certain was that Harmony and I had unlocked a dungeon of demons by cleaning out the attic on the Internet. And now we would have to try finishing the job with a garage sale.

Several days later I saw my father again in a dream. I wasn't sure when the dream began, but eventually I noticed that Rags was there. Rags—the brindled mutt that had shared so many adventures with my Dad and me long ago. Rags was curling up at the foot of my bed, just as he always did when Dad came up to my room to invent another bedtime story. Rags cocked his head so that one shaggy ear flopped down and the other stood up, as if to listen all the better.

"What would you like in your story tonight?" Dad asked, slowly taking form in the darkness beside me.

I tried to see his face, but the shadows were deepest there. When I hesitated, uncertain and a little fearful, his large, smooth, reassuring hand emerged from the dark and stroked the hair from my forehead.

His soothing voice melted out of the night. "Or don't you want a story after all?"

"Rags," I said quickly. Suddenly I felt nine years old. A simple happiness enveloped me like a fuzzy bathrobe. This was no ordinary dream. It was a gift—a chance to relive an important, half-forgotten evening with my father.

Dad's voice chuckled. "Yes, of course. You always have to have Rags in the story. What else?"

"And the secret door—and the magic perfume."

"Are you sure?" Dad's voice sighed in the darkness. Rags cocked his head the other way and began to wag with anticipation.

"This time tell what really happened," I said.

"I always do," Dad reassured me. "Just the way I heard it from Rags."

"Daddy! Rags can't tell stories."

"No, not like he used to. He's a lot quieter now that you've grown so big. But do you remember when you were a very little girl, and he discovered the secret of the pet door?"

I shook my head, because I really had forgotten most of the story. I certainly did not want to dispel the dream. "Please tell me."

"The story starts out a bit scary, you know."

"Tell me anyway."

"Well, it all began when you were very small, still in preschool and the black dust began to fall. Remember?"

I shivered. I felt as if a cold wind had blown a curtain aside, revealing a dangerous window onto a landscape of memory. My mother said I'd imagined it all because of my father's frightening stories, but it had seemed real. In those early years, black dust had polluted nearly all the world with a faintly sour smell. The worst of it had been the dust on my hands. The preschool teachers made us wash our hands before snack each day. Most children didn't want to wash up, but I would scrub and scrub until my hands were red. Even then, the dust was still there, black in the creases of my fingers, like the day after finger painting. When I held my hands to my face the sour, dead smell made even cupcakes taste wrong.

"Where did the black dust come from?" I asked.

Dad shook his dark head. "That's what you asked Rags long ago. But he wasn't sure. At first he thought it had rubbed off from newspapers and money. Then he thought it might be the mountain trolls, burning coal to make iron for weapons and railroads. Finally he decided to ask the Great Dane on the mountain behind Tamolitch Lake. The Great Dane was a wise old dog who could see many things others could not."

As a grown woman I would have laughed at Dad's invention. But I wasn't thirty years old anymore. I clutched the covers to my chest and asked, wide-eyed, "What did the Great Dane say?"

My father held up a hand to urge patience. "It was a long trip to Tamolitch Lake. Rags had to swim many rivers and find his way through ancient forests. When at last he reached the lake he had to climb a rocky crag to an old lookout tower where the Great Dane kept his watch over the world below. When Rags crawled up to the lookout, panting, with burs and twigs in his fur, the Great Dane looked at him and said, 'You have traveled far for a city dog. What do you want?'

"'It's Ana,' Rags panted. 'The little girl down in Eugene. She's worried about the black dust that's settling everywhere.'

"'Ah, the dust. Yes, it is troubling,' the wise old dog agreed.

"'Ana wants to know what's causing the dust. Is it rubbing off from newspapers and money?'

"'Not most of it, no. When people's hands get gray from newspaper they can wash them and they'll be clean again.'

"'Then is the dust coming from the trolls' coal mines in the mountains?"

"The Great Dane laughed. 'Don't be silly. There are no trolls. And the gnomes down in the caves don't burn enough coal to matter.'"

I interrupted, "Are there really gnomes?"

Dad shrugged. "That's what the old dog told Rags."

I thought about this a moment, and then returned to my original question. "What caused the dust?"

"The Great Dane chewed on his paw a while, something he always did when he was worried or thinking hard. Finally he said, 'I'm not a physicist.'"

"He said that?"

"Stop interrupting!" Dad objected. "The Great Dane said, 'I'm not a physicist, but I think the black dust is from the glue that holds everything in the world together. Normally we don't notice the glue, because we take it for granted that the world won't fall apart. But once things start to go wrong, the glue begins to turn to dust. Even then, only a few people have the wisdom it takes to see the warning signs and smell the decay.'"

My heart was beating faster now, even though I knew this was a dream. "Is there anything that will stop the dust? What's gone wrong that's making everything fall apart?"

"Rags asked the same questions," Dad reassured me. "And that's when he learned that the pet door could also enter onto a secret world, between the inside and the outside ones, where—" his voice trailed off into a buzz.

"Where what?" I asked, desperate to know about the secret world. Dad had stiffened and was melting into a bright rectangle against the wall, his voice now only an insistent, repeating buzz.

When I realized I couldn't return to my father, at least not tonight, I opened my eyes to the sunny window, lifted my hand to the bedside table, and squeezed the alarm clock silent. Seven thirty. Saturday morning. The day I had agreed to sell my memories in the driveway of my mother's home.

By the time I got there, Harmony and my mother had already unpacked a dozen boxes on card tables in the driveway. An overcast sky gave the morning a gloom that portended rain or worse, but half a dozen cars were already parked in front of the old Victorian house. Although the sale wasn't supposed to start for another half hour, diehard garage sale shoppers were already lurking about, trying to peer into boxes. I was in a bad mood, partly because I now realized I'd left my purse lying on the living room table in my apartment. All I'd remembered to bring were my keys and two boxes of magazines.

"You're too late," Harmony chided cheerfully. She and Mom were sitting side by side, putting price stickers on a small army of ceramic gnomes. I don't know why it bothered me that the two of them seemed so chummy. After all the trouble Mom's deceptions had stirred up in my life, I thought Harmony should show a little more outrage. But Harmony can't help liking people.

"I'm too late for what?" I asked.

"Your mother's already sold your family Bible."

"Really, Harmony," Mom objected. She had begun arranging hats and shoes on boxes. "You make it sound too ruthless."

I set down my magazines. "I didn't even know we had a family Bible."

Mom shook her head. "We didn't until last night. This good-looking Australian Mormon missionary came to the door, giving away leather-bound Bibles decorated like Gutenbergs. All you had to do was fill out a questionnaire about your genealogy. Apparently they've got Mormon kids out collecting names of dead people to save. Sort of like the middle school kids selling magazine subscriptions. If they sell enough they win a free trip to Disneyland, or heaven, or whatever."

"So you accepted a Bible from this Australian guy and then you turned around and sold it?" I was still in the process of repainting my mental image of my mother. Every brush stroke made her less attractive as a parent. There she stood, posing in a mohair sweater to show off her new, less ballistic profile. Her hair had been cut too long, dyed black, and pulled to one side, revealing a white forehead that had been wiped clean of wrinkles and expression by injections.

"Don't look at me like that," Mom objected. "It's not like I sold our ancestor's souls to some cult. I only knew the names and dates for my side of the family anyway. And I ended up making ten dollars for the cash box."

Mom leaned over to get a sheet of price stickers from Harmony. Suddenly my mother stopped, closed her eyes, and took in a short, pained breath.

"Mom! Are you all right?" Although I had often seen my mother give this kind of melodramatic gasp, and she had never really suffered a stroke, I couldn't help a flutter of fear. "What is it?"

Mom let out her breath slowly, her eyes still closed. "Harmony's perfume. I haven't breathed that scent for years."

Harmony looked up brightly. "Isn't it heavenly? We found it in the attic. Ana said I could try it."

"Cloud Nine." Mom opened her eyes and nodded. "It's not very attractive to men, but who cares? It makes you feel light all over, like you've lost five pounds. Max was a genius in the laboratory. It's the one thing I miss about him."

"Oh?" I let acid drip into my voice. "Well I've missed a lot of things about Dad."

Suddenly Mom returned to the shoes she had been sorting, and she frowned. "I hope you're not serious about going to Greece to look for him."

"Why not?" I began sorting my magazines, trying to look like I didn't care about the answer to my next question. "Were you just kidding about him being there?"

"No, he's there all right. It's just that— " Mom seemed to search for words. "Well, to be honest, Max was never very stable mentally, and I doubt he's any better now. He had a terrible impact on you as a child."

"How can you say something like that about my father?"

Mom shrugged. "It's the truth. He was nuts, and you were starting to go over the edge too, after being around him. You remember the counseling sessions I paid for? All that hand washing and the talk about dust? I almost went broke, trying to get you well. I can't believe you want to put yourself at risk again, after all I've done for you."

Infuriated, I put my hands on my hips. "After all you've done for me? You practically murdered my father."

Harmony held up her hands. "That's enough, both of you. Ana, you need to know your mother has been here since seven o'clock, setting up the sale."

I didn't look down. "Thanks, Mom."

Mom lifted her head slightly, as if to show she had won another round. "Here's something else you should know, Ana. If you go off to Greece, you can pay for your next round of counseling yourself. I tell you, I've been trying for years to clean Max and his crazy aunt out of my life. These telephone calls have been a recurring nightmare."

"Have you gotten more calls?"

"Not me, thank God. Now I guess the Internet people are plaguing poor Harmony instead."

I looked to my friend, surprised. "You've been getting calls too?" Maybe my mother hadn't been exaggerating about the strange calls.

"Just one, last night," Harmony said. "From the old Italian gentleman who bought the violin case. Since I was the one who shipped the box, he had my address. At first he thought I was you."

"What did he want?"

"He was very nice, actually. He said he wanted to call again tonight after the garage sale to talk to you in person."

"About what?" I asked, on my guard.

"Some sort of business idea. He didn't say exactly what, but he promised it would be worth your while. Anyway, I gave him the telephone number of your apartment."

"Harmony! I wish you'd asked me first."

"Hey, this guy might have a better way to earn money for Greece than holding garage sales. Do you want to find out about your father or not?"

My mother shook her head. "You two are getting mixed up in something bigger than you can handle. Some people have skeletons in their closet. Max has full-size dragons."

It was late afternoon, and our garage sale had reawakened with a final flurry of bargain hunters, when Harmony whispered to me, "There's something strange about that cowboy." She nodded toward a young man with a black vest and a new-looking, white cowboy hat. He picked up a frumpy women's sweater and inspected it with the intensity of a professional knitting critic. A moustache hid most of his mouth, but his eyes and nose were delicate, almost boyish. He stood out among the other shoppers—students in college T-shirts and women in baggy sweatshirts.

"Maybe he's buying a present for his grandmother back on the range," I suggested.

"I think he's creepy," Harmony said. "He's looking at everything with x-ray vision. And that moustache looks fake."

The cowboy peered into a lady's flowered hat, wrinkled his brow, and headed toward us.

Harmony slipped away, whispering, "He's all yours. I'll go let people know we're about to close."

The young man stopped in front of me, nervously turning the lady's hat over in his callused hands. "I beg your pardon. This is your estate sale?"

I looked him in the eyes. His accent was British, but with a clipped, alien cadence. He might be a foreign graduate student at the university, but then why was he dressed like a cowboy? "It's my sale. The estate belonged to my great aunt."

"Forgive me. I'm sorry to hear of your loss."

"That's all right. She died twenty years ago. All this stuff has been in an attic since then."

He held up the flowered hat. "Has no one put this on today?"

"Not that I know of, no." I shrugged. "It's about time for us to pack up. The hat's marked $1.50, but you can have it for a dollar."

"Yes. Of course, yes." He frowned, his thoughts obviously elsewhere, and withdrew a crisp hundred-dollar bill from his pocket.

I was in no mood to count out ninety-nine dollars of change. "Oh, forget it. Just take it." I waved him away, but he simply stood there, looking into my eyes, his lip quivering, as if he were working up his nerve to admit he had just run over my cat.

"Wait. The truth is, I'm not really a cowboy."

I laughed. "Yeah, I figured that."

He took off his cowboy hat and roughed up his dark, wiry hair. "I'm just— " He paused in mid-sentence.

"You're just what?"

"I'm just one of the summer students from the Czech Republic," he said, blushing slightly. "We're here to do a class in English. Our assignment this week is to write a story about something we buy at a garage sale, without letting people know we're Czech. I think I won't be scoring a perfect grade this time."

"I'm sorry," I said, embarrassed that my suspicion had caused him trouble. He was actually not a bad-looking guy.

"Maybe I can still get part credit," he added hopefully, picking up the woman's hat. "What did she look like, the one who wore this? Brown hair, like yours?"

I shrugged. "She was old, so it was white when I knew her. But I think she did say it used to be like mine."

"Brown eyes, like yours?"

"A little more hazel, maybe."

"Thank you. That will help me." He tucked away the hat with an air of finality, but before he turned to go he added, "I imagine she was once as beautiful as you, too."

I watched him go, shaking my head.

A gate slammed from the direction of the house. "Five o'clock," my mother announced. "I'll help you pack up. How did it go?"

Harmony flipped through the cash in the cigar box. "Not too bad, considering we'd already sold the best stuff on the Internet. We probably made $300. And we'll only have a couple boxes to take back."

"None of the gnomes sold, I'm afraid," I said, and added, "Don't worry, Mom. I won't leave any of great aunt Margret's stuff to bother you."

Mom gave me a strangely conspiratorial smile. "It's a good thing I sold that Bible bright and early this morning, huh?"

I looked at her askance. "What do you mean?"

"Oh, come on. I saw you making eyes at the missionary, like maybe you were going to get another Bible out of him."

"Mom, I honestly don't know what you're talking about."

"The Australian. I liked him better in his business suit, but the cowboy getup is cute too."

I stared at her. "Him? He's the one who gave you the Bible last night?"

"Handsome fellow, isn't he?"

"But—but he told me he was an English student from the Czech Republic."

"Uh oh." Harmony looked at us, her face paling. "I think we've got a problem."

My mother's eyes widened "Oh—my—God. I should have known. I've been trying all week to convince you something fishy is going on."

I hate it when Mom is right. "All right, so maybe this cowboy guy is up to something. But what?"

"That's the scariest part of all," Harmony said quietly. "We still don't have a clue."

LEAVING IN A FURY
(Harmony)

When I was growing up my parents didn't have a car. They took me everywhere by bicycle or bus. So when I finally broke loose, I decided to leave in a Fury.

OK, maybe my old, shoebox-shaped Plymouth lacks the lordly poise of a 1970s Thunderbird or the sexy squat of a 1960s Mustang. But it's decked out proudly with antique license plates all the same. The dashboard has nifty circular dials and space-age pushbuttons. A stick off the steering column controls the automatic shift. The front seat is a sofa of textured blue-and-white vinyl. A pair of fuzzy dice hangs from the rear-view mirror.

So yes, I'm Harmony. I grew up in a commune and didn't change my name. Even a recovering moonchild can only rebel so far. But at least now whenever I show up, I arrive in a Fury.

After the garage sale closed I drove Ana home. The Fury swung left onto 19th Avenue with a ponderous, boat-like tilt that sent the box of unsold gnomes clattering to one side of the back seat. "I suppose we should have been expecting a spy to show up," I said. "You know, after all those phone calls."

Ana shifted on the passenger side of the front seat as if she were nervous too. "I'd say he was a funny sort of spy. Certainly no James Bond."

"He was clever enough to trick your mother into writing down your genealogy. And he weaseled a description of your aunt out of you. That sounds like the work of a detective to me."

"But he was so young—and a bit goofy too, with the Bible and the cowboy outfit. Not blatantly malicious, if you know what I mean?"

I pulled into an alley, spraying gravel. The Fury bounced down a potholed lane between Dumpsters and telephone poles. "He's a spook, Ana, a spy. And from what you say, he doesn't even sound like a local one. What if he really is from Eastern Europe? Maybe he's working for a foreign government." I pulled into a parking spot between a board fence and Ana's duplex.

Ana got out and closed the heavy car door with a *ka-thunk*. "You saw my great aunt's attic. It's hard to believe that junk would interest anyone, anywhere. There must be something else important, something obvious that we're missing." She took out her house key, but then stopped short, as if she'd been touched in a game of freeze tag. "Oh, shit."

"What is it?" I asked. Then I noticed the door was already ajar, and fear began creeping up on me.

Ana pushed the door open to reveal a hallway strewn with clothes.

"Wow, you really need to do your laundry." Immediately I knew this was the ditziest thing I'd said all day. I hoped Ana would understand. Because I don't have her courage, my first response to danger is to sidestep it, or worse, to attempt a joke.

"Somebody's broken in." Ana's voice betrayed anger and hurt.

"Don't go inside!" I grabbed Ana before she could step through the doorway. "If somebody's in there, they could kill you."

"All right. Let's check the windows first." Ana led the way around her cottage, past the garbage cans and compost bin. She stopped at each of the windows, peering past the mini-blinds.

"Whoever it was must have picked the lock," Ana said when we got back to the front door. Before I could stop her again she barged inside, apparently immune to the fear I felt. "Hello? Anyone home?"

When nothing happened I followed her cautiously into the living room. All of the books from her shelves had been dumped on the floor. For some reason the burglars had pulled the furniture away from the walls. "Do you think it was Randy?"

Ana stopped. Because of all those divorce support sessions we'd shared, I could guess what she was thinking. There are a lot of reasons a man might break into his ex-wife's apartment. But Randy? This is a guy who winks at waitresses and thinks his Robert Redford moustache is sexy. A man who prides himself in his mini-golf trophies. If Randy had paid so little attention to her when they were married, why would he care now?

"No," Ana reflected out loud. "When Randy moved out he took everything he wanted. Absolutely everything."

"Well, whoever it was, they didn't want your TV," I said.

"Or my purse." Ana knelt down and picked it up from the papers on the floor. "Looks like they went through it, though. I guess they didn't think ten dollars was worth taking. Thank God they left my credit cards."

"You know, these were pretty sloppy burglars, when you get right down to it." I moved on to the kitchen. The cupboard doors stood open. Although the glasses and spices had been moved around, nothing seemed broken.

"I don't think they were burglars at all," Anna said. "They must have been looking for something. You know, the obvious thing we missed."

"OK, but what?"

"Something that belonged to my great aunt."

"Do you have anything of hers here?"

"Just her clavichord."

I looked at her sideways. "I give up. What's a clavichord? Don't tell me it's a collarbone."

"No, that's a clavicle. A clavichord is like an old-fashioned piano. I hope they didn't hurt it." Ana stumbled over the pile of clothes in the hall on her way to the bedroom. But the suitcase-sized keyboard was sitting there on the bureau with its lid open. Sheet music lay strewn across the floor, along with the rest of the clothes that had been emptied from her dresser drawers.

I picked up a carved teak box from beside the bed. "What about your jewelry?"

Ana looked through the box. "There wasn't much to begin with, but it all seems to be here."

I touched a finger to my chin. "I think I know who it was."

"Who?"

"That cowboy detective. He grilled your mother last night, and he grilled you today. Turning your apartment inside out was just part of his job."

Ana frowned. "Maybe. He certainly was nervous when he talked to me today. I suppose he could have been upset because he didn't find what he wanted here."

I picked up a mobile phone from the bedside table and handed it to Ana. "I think it's time to call the police."

"Not 911?" Ana asked.

"They'll just tell you to call the police."

Ana dialed the Eugene police department and explained about the break-in. Minutes of silence passed. I quietly collected the sheet music from the floor. Then Ana repeated her story more slowly into the phone, this time with a note of exasperation.

When she finally hung up, I asked, "Well? What are they going to do?"

Ana shook her head in wonder. "Not much. They can't send out a patrol car until tomorrow. In the meantime we're supposed to figure out what's been stolen. If nothing's missing, the insurance people don't care, so the police might not even bother to fill out a report."

"What!" I waved a hand at the disorder on the floor. "Isn't it a crime to wreck someone's apartment?"

"Well, there's breaking and entering, but the clerk didn't sound all that convinced. She wanted to know if someone had forced the door. Then she asked how many of my boyfriends have keys."

"Of all the nerve! What are you supposed to do?"

Ana shrugged. "Clean up the apartment, I guess."

"Wow. It doesn't make you feel very safe."

"Especially not when there's someone out there who knows how to pick my lock. I'm not sleeping here until I get a deadbolt."

"We can buy a deadbolt, but that's not much of an answer."

"No, it's not." Ana sighed, tossed the mobile telephone on the bed, and sat down beside it. "They might even try breaking into your apartment next."

"Mine?"

"If that detective knows about me, he knows about you. And he didn't find what he wanted here."

I sat down beside her, suddenly shivering. "You're right. Neither of us will be safe until we find out what's going on."

"And how are we supposed to do that?"

As if in reply, the mobile telephone beside her beeped.

I looked at the phone with a strangely ominous feeling. "Maybe it's the police?"

"No, the only one who calls me this time of day is my mother." Ana punched the mobile telephone's talk button. "Hi, Mom."

Ana's brow furrowed. Then she clapped her hand over the mouthpiece. "It's the Italian guy! Get the phone in the hall. He doesn't speak English."

"Yes, he does. He's probably just confused because you called him Mom." I fetched the phone from the hall and stretched the cord to the bedroom door, where I could watch Ana.

An elderly voice asked, *"Scusi. Con qui parlo?"*

I nodded encouragingly to Ana.

"Hello?" Ana said. "This is Ana Smyth."

"Miss Smyth! *Que bello*." The voice was gravelly and deep, but with an Italian lilt that peaked in the middle of each phrase. "My name is Nimolo. Dr. Enrico Nimolo. You sold me a violin case last week. I spoke last night with your friend, Miss Ferguson. Is this a good time to talk?"

Ana gestured silently at the mess on the floor and rolled her eyes at me. "Yeah, it's just great."

"I am glad to hear this," the elderly voice replied, and then gave a weak cough. "You see, it is three in the morning here in Italy. Your friend said this would be a convenient time for you."

I slapped myself on the forehead and mouthed the words, "I forgot about the time difference."

"I'm sorry, Dr. Nimolo," Ana said. "We've been having some problems here since we held the Internet sale. So, are you happy with the violin case we sent you?"

"Happy, yes. Relatively happy," Nimolo replied, and then added, "You say you have problems since the sale? What kind of problems?"

Ana gave a long sigh. "You don't want to know."

"Yes, I do."

Ana looked at me and shrugged. "Well, first we had people calling from all over the world. Then a detective showed up and asked questions. Now somebody's just broken in to my apartment and turned it inside out searching for something."

There was a pause on the line. Then Nimolo answered, sounding more tired than ever. "I was afraid this might happen."

"Why?" Ana asked. "Do you know who these people are?"

"When I saw your offering on the Internet I said to myself, two kinds of people will answer this notice from America. The good people who love Einstein, and the bad ones who chase after nonsense."

"What kind of nonsense?"

"Is it possible you do not know?" His voice rose so far with the question that it was easy to picture his hands rising to show incredulity as well. "Your advertisement mentioned the story of the lost formula."

"It was nothing but a story," Ana objected.

"Exactly so. No serious person would believe that Einstein would write a theory on a piece of music, lose it, and not mention it again. But once a story starts on the Internet, it never ends."

"This formula was supposed to be on a piece of music?" Ana glanced at me, and then we both looked at the sheet music I had collected from the floor.

"Yes, on a Brahms sonata for violin and piano. Einstein liked to play this piece with friends. The people who invent these Internet stories add details to make it sound possible. Now you have seen what happens. Some people believe anything." He paused again. "You don't have any sheet music by Brahms, do you?"

Ana covered the phone and looked to me. "I don't trust him. What if he's just looking for the formula too?"

I held up my hands. "He knows something we don't. Play along with him for a while."

Ana took her hand off the phone. "No, mostly I play Bach. I have a clavichord, and it doesn't have enough keys for the later piano pieces."

"A clavichord? I too prefer the early music. Since the baroque, composers have lost their sense for mathematics."

I put my hand over the mouthpiece and whispered, "Get him back to Einstein! We were just starting to get somewhere."

Ana sat up straighter on the bed. "Dr. Nimolo? Why did you say you thought only bad people would want the Einstein formula?"

"Einstein was a great man. He helped people to understand the universe, but he also helped to build terrible bombs. Now he has been dead for fifty years. His important work was finished thirty years before that. What type of person would believe a forgotten, eighty-year-old formula would be useful today?"

"I don't know. Who?"

The elderly man coughed lightly. "Only a bad person, I'm afraid. The study of physics has moved on. I know because this is what I do. I work with the United Nations' theoretical physics institute here in Trieste."

Ana raised her eyebrows at me.

I shrugged and whispered, "That's where I sent the violin case. I checked it out on the Internet. He really is a bigwig at the United Nations center over there."

Ana spoke into the phone, "Dr. Nimolo? I still don't understand why you would pay so much for a violin case."

He laughed. "I would gladly pay much more if I could be sure it was Einstein's. In my private life I am a collector of history. For many people this is a hobby. For some of us, it is a passion. I have the shoes Einstein wore as a boy, and the chair he used in Berlin. He was a great man who discovered a window into the universe. For me, even a violin case can be a window into Einstein." His voice dropped to a lower tone. "But I must be sure the window is genuine. This is why I call you."

Ana shook her head. "I don't know if the violin case belonged to Einstein. The advertisement in the Internet admitted that."

"Yes, but perhaps you could find out."

"How?"

"By asking your father in Greece."

For a moment Ana seemed bewildered that this Italian physicist knew about her father. She herself had learned only last week that Max Smyth was still alive. Then she put her hand over the mouthpiece and whispered angrily to me, "How much did you tell him last night?"

I raised a shoulder innocently. "He said he wants to help."

Ana took her hand off the mouthpiece. "Look, I don't know if my father has any more information about the violin case than I have. I don't know if he'll even talk to me. The Internet sale was supposed to raise enough money so I could go see him in Greece, but I came up about $1000 short."

"Of course." Nimolo did not sound surprised. "Since you talk about money, I will also talk about money. I paid you only $400 for the violin case because you had no proof that it belonged to Einstein. With proof, it would be worth $4000 to me."

"Seriously?"

"Possibly even more. This is why I am willing to make you a further offer."

"All right. I'm listening."

"I will give you $1000 and send a colleague to Greece to help you, if you agree to come to Trieste afterwards and tell me everything you find out about the case. But you must leave the USA very soon. Tomorrow if possible."

This time both Ana and I put our hands over our telephones simultaneously. "A thousand dollars!" Ana whispered.

I whispered back, "What's the catch?"

"I don't know. Probably that we're the most gullible people on the planet."

"Ana! Take the money and go."

"That's crazy! What if he's some pervert?"

I whispered back, "He's a famous physicist. You wanted a ticket to Greece, and here it is. Take it!"

"What about you? Maybe I should ask for $2000."

I shook my head. "My flight isn't for a week, and I can't leave earlier."

"Why not?"

I winced. "I've got this family thing coming up."

"What?"

"I'll tell you later. Just go!"

A muffled voice came out of the telephone. "Hello? Miss Smyth? Hello?"

Ana took her hand off the mouthpiece. "I'm still here, Dr. Nimolo."

"Well? And will you accept this offer?"

Ana looked about her at the mess in her apartment, left by an unknown and possibly dangerous intruder into her private life. Then she took a deep breath and said, "All right. I'm in."

ANOTHER STEP IN ULM

"Greece?" The Baroness von Hohensteuern twisted in her wheelchair to look back at her secretary, who was pushing her along a garden path. Behind them stood the square tower of the small, two-story castle, Schloss Klingenstein. "Peter wants to travel to Greece now? Do you know, Herr Weiss, how much this little adventure has cost me so far?"

"Yes, baroness, 2894 euros. As much as I am paid in a month." The balding man stopped to give a small shrug. As secretary, he did the bookkeeping at the castle. Since the baron's death, he also did the maintenance and the shopping and a great deal of the caregiving, especially when his wife was busy cooking or cleaning elsewhere in the castle.

"Don't stop here, Herr Weiss," she snapped. "We are going to inspect the museum."

"As you wish." He pushed the chair onward, past two concrete statues of knights in armor.

The baroness added in a low but firm voice, "I understand that you and Frau Weiss are underpaid. Believe me, I much preferred leaving financial matters to Gerhard, even though it is now clear that he had no talent for it. I am doing my best to take the matter in hand."

For a while they were both silent. The fine white gravel of the walkway crunched beneath the chair's hard rubber tires. "Look at this garden, Herr Weiss," she said. "Once this was the pride of the castle.

Today grass grows among the roses. Ivy is choking the beech trees. No one has raked the paths."

"Ramon does what he can, baroness, but he is officially retired and doesn't always understand your German."

"What I am pointing out, Herr Weiss, is that I cannot afford to hire a gardener who speaks German. I can't even repair the castle's foundation to stop the front wall from cracking. With all that needs doing for my little castle, how can Peter ask that I pay his way to Greece?"

"If you recall, baroness, I too originally doubted that he should be sent abroad."

"And? Have you changed your mind?"

The secretary leaned forward as he pushed the wheelchair up the gravel drive. At the top of the slope he paused beside a stone gateway to catch his breath before answering. "As you said, baroness, his investigation is a gamble. Ordinarily I would counsel against risk. But Peter is making progress. He is sending a hat with hairs that belonged to the person known as 'great aunt Margret'."

"A hat with hairs?"

"Yes."

The baroness twisted her thin shoulders so she could look at her secretary again. "Your son is sending me a hairy hat, and he believes this is progress?"

"A hair follicle could be used for genetic testing, baroness."

"Good God, of course." As her secretary pushed her past the museum entrance sign toward a large, half-timbered building, the baroness mused quietly, "But paying for a laboratory test might be throwing good money after bad. Wolf tells me the police investigation has found nothing."

"Then the new police officer has filed her report?"

"Wolf's granddaughter? Yes, she's convinced the baron was mistaken. She says we're being tempted by treasure tales. By a dying man's dream." She sighed and looked up at the half-timbered building before them. Each of its four stories had rows of crooked windows in a latticework of exposed posts and beams. Two rows of tiny gables peered from a long, sloping roof of motley red and brown tiles. "Sometimes I regret being such a sloppy representative of the Hohensteuern line. It comes of marrying in and never really studying their history, I suppose."

CHAPTER 6

The secretary began to object, but she cut him short. "No, Herr Weiss, it's absolutely true. In fifty-seven years I doubt I've been inside the museum five times. Now kindly tell me what you know about the building itself."

The secretary cleared his throat and repeated the story, much as he told it to visitors on the one day each year when the grounds were open to tourists. "The building dates to 1654, when it was built as a harpsichord workshop. In those days the Hohensteuern family was famous for musical instruments. The shop declined for centuries, perhaps because the family never made the transition to pianos. Finally it closed altogether before the Second World War. After the war a small portion of the building reopened as the town museum, with a collection of chairs, scythes, dolls, beer steins, and of course harpsichords. The city pays us a nominal rent of a hundred euros a month."

The baroness held out a withered hand toward the building. "Herr Weiss, this was once the source of the family's wealth. Why can't we do that again?"

"Build harpsichords, baroness?"

"No, no. The suburbs of Ulm have grown to our doorstep. We could rent space for restaurants and offices and shops. A historic building near the castle would be an attraction. Surely that income would more than make up for the baron's military pension?"

"It might be possible. But there would be a problem." The secretary wheeled her chair to the unused side of the building. He took a large iron key from his pocket and unlocked a massive wooden door. The arch-topped door creaked open to reveal a long, dark room, where cobwebs hung from crooked beams. The secretary gestured toward the room. "I suspect that renters would want electricity and plumbing."

"Doesn't the government pay for restoring historic buildings? The state or the city or something?"

"Yes, but renovations sponsored by the government require matching funds from the owner. A project such as you propose might cost a million euros or more. Your share would certainly be over a hundred thousand."

"I see." The baroness tapped her fingers on the armrest of her wheelchair, thinking. "In other words, we would need to find a treasure first."

"That would be one solution, baroness."

"And does Peter believe he will have better luck if he follows this Ana Smyth to Greece?"

"I think he has no illusions. The estate sale in America showed no sign of wealth, and the nephew in Greece lives in a monastery."

"Then where does he think the money is?"

"It is no longer merely a matter of money for him, baroness. Peter believes the girl is in danger."

"Danger?" The baroness looked up, alarmed. "You haven't told me about this. Danger from whom?"

"It seems that at least two other people are following Ana Smyth. Peter isn't yet sure who they are or what they want, but one of them has broken into her apartment. The fact that she is leaving for Greece so suddenly may well be related to her pursuers."

The baroness was silent for a long time. At length she said quietly, "Tell Peter to pack for Greece—and to keep his work secret until we know more."

GREEK IN A WEEK
(Ana)

I closed my copy of *Greek in a Week* in frustration and leaned my head against the jetliner's plastic window. It was somehow reassuring, watching the spidery night lights of cities string slowly across twilit Quebec toward Labrador. Learning Greek might be impossibly difficult, but at least tonight, for the first time in the twenty-four hours since I'd found my apartment door ajar, I felt certain I was not being followed. Even when Harmony had driven me to the Eugene airport in her Fury, I kept glancing out the back window, imagining that other cars might be taking the same turns. The missing Einstein formula was obviously valuable enough that even possessing a fragment had put me in danger.

Another source of unease was the travel arrangements I had received by email from the Italian physicist, Enrico Nimolo. At the airport in Greece I was to meet a certain Gilberto Montale, who would organize my visit to the monastery. Why was Nimolo going to the expense of hiring this tour guide? He didn't even sound Greek. Would it turn out that he was actually some sort of guard, or yet another detective? All in all, Nimolo's interest in the violin case seemed unnaturally intense, even for a passionate collector of Einstein memorabilia.

Below the red blinker on the wingtip, only a few star-like points now gleamed across a ghostly white landscape of frozen lakes and treeless hills, dimly lit by the pale pink glow of an aurora borealis beneath the deep blue of the arctic horizon.

I wished Harmony could have come with me. At least we had agreed to exchange emails and phone calls. I'd made sure we both had phones that could be switched to European service. Two weeks from now, after she'd finished protesting the globalization conference in Italy, we would meet in Athens. As it turned out, the "family thing" that had kept Harmony in Oregon was a reunion at a beach resort near Reedsport. Harmony's grandmother insisted that all her relatives meet for a long weekend each summer to do the things she had done as a girl. The family dug clams in the mudflats at dawn. They picked strawberries and baked shortcake in Dutch ovens over a beach fire. They slid down sand dunes into the bay. It sounded like fun, but it was only for Fergusons.

What was my family in comparison? I could hardly imagine carousing with a crowd of cousins while aunts and uncles sat beside a beach fire telling stories about the family's past. My own past seemed as dark and lonely as the emptied attic of my mother's house. If only my father in Greece would be able to turn on a light!

Still leaning against the window, I closed my eyes and let the drone of the jet engines roar in my head. Slowly I sank into a dim world where voices began separating from the rushing air. In the shadows I could just make out the hazy form of my father once again sitting on the end of my bed. On the quilt, a shaggy brown dog cocked its head and looked at me questioningly.

"What? You're already asleep?" Dad's voice asked.

"No, I'm awake, really," I objected, as insistent as a sleepy nine year old.

"I don't think so."

"Yes, I am. And anyway, you haven't finished the story."

Dad clicked his tongue from the shadows. "All right, then. But you might not like the way it ends."

"Just tell me. What did Rags find out about the black dust?"

Dad sighed. "You remember the Great Dane? He was the wise old dog who told Rags that the black dust is the glue holding the world together. If you're a dog, or a sensitive little girl, you notice the smell when the glue starts rotting and turns to dust. The Great Dane told Rags to look for help in another world where things were still all right."

"Is there really a world like that somewhere?"

"Oh yes, it's everywhere, all around us, but hidden. I suppose you could call it another dimension. The Great Dane said it was 'the space in between.' He said to look for an entrance inside the pet door."

"Margret used to say the entrance to the fourth dimension was in the attic."

"Did she?" Dad sounded vague, and he began to fade.

"Wait! Come back! I won't interrupt anymore. What did Rags find in the pet door?"

Dad cleared his throat and almost became visible. I thought I could see curly hair. "Rags climbed down from the Great Dane's mountain and traveled for two days back to Eugene, swimming to cross the rivers. When he got home he started to walk in through the pet door, but then he turned in a tricky sort of way. Instead of coming out inside the kitchen, he suddenly found himself in the space in between."

Rags whimpered and lay his head down on the bed.

"Rags remembers, don't you, boy?" Dad said. "It was frightening at first. The 'space in between' is not a world of hard, real things like chairs and walls. Instead it is a land of memory and dream. The distance from one thing to another is not measured in space, but rather in time. And the things you find there do not have hard surfaces. They are made of smell."

"Made of smell? How can that be?"

"Think of it as a gigantic version of our perfume shop," Dad explained. "Imagine closing your eyes and walking alongside the counters of Scents and Sensibility. It's like flying through the world on a magic carpet. In one moment you're lost in a flowery rain forest. Then you could be picking apples on a sunny summer day. Then it's Christmas, and you're baking cookies by candlelight."

I took a deep breath and nodded.

Dad continued, "It didn't take Rags long to understand, too. Dogs already see the world as a landscape of smells. The 'place in between' was a lot more dizzying than our world though, because after every few steps Rags fell through time to somewhere else. Eventually he found a place where the rotting smell was gone, in a time before things had started to go wrong. And that's where he found what the Great Dane had promised."

"The magic perfume?"

"Exactly. A small vial of special perfume. Rags held it tightly in his mouth. He found his way back through all the times and places to the pet door. He made another tricky sort of turn, this time in the opposite direction. Then he trotted across the kitchen to the dining room, lay down in the center of the spiral rug, and pulled the cork out of the vial with his teeth."

"Is that why the dining room doesn't have black dust?"

Dad shook his shadowy head. "It has the black dust just the same. The black dust is everywhere in the world. Even now."

"But the magic perfume!" I objected. "It was supposed to make the dust go away."

"No, Ana. The magic perfume can't fix the dust. It only hides it by covering up the smell."

"Oh." I felt disappointed. "Then Rags didn't really make everything right again."

"No. He just made it easier for you to grow up." A glow had begun to shine through my father, hiding his form with light. "Now that you're big you've covered up the black dust almost everywhere. I don't suppose you even think about it anymore."

I could only faintly remember those dark days. "I want to stop the dust. It's got to be stopped or everything will fall apart."

My father was gone in a ball of light, but Rags was still there, faintly floating just above the bed. "I can't do that, Ana," the dog said, his voice hollow.

"Then who can? Einstein?"

Rags laughed. "Once, perhaps. But now it's just you."

"Me?"

The light had become so strong that it drowned out the dream. Bewildered, I opened my eyes to the glare.

Outside the jetliner's plastic window, the sun was rising over the coast of Greenland. Tiny glaciers poured down between mountains to bays full of icebergs.

I had slept for an hour. Already this was the start of a second travel day, radically foreshortened as the world spun beneath. I was traveling through time toward my father.

The sun had tilted toward evening by the time my Olympic Air flight dropped through a cloudless sky toward a horseshoe-shaped island in the startlingly blue Aegean Sea. It had been easy to get a window seat on the nearly empty puddle-jumper from Athens to Milos. The main tourist season in the Greek islands wouldn't begin for another few weeks, and Milos was off the beaten track anyway.

After twenty-eight hours of travel I felt like a zombie, trapped in the same clammy clothes I had worn while still alive. But I couldn't tear myself away from the window. The barren cliffs that rimmed the island's bay were capped with white. Could the mountains be so tall that they still had snow in June? Gradually the white crystallized into cubic grains, like salt. Then I suddenly realized these were villages of whitewashed, angular houses, improbably jumbled together along cliffs and peaks. Pinkened on one side by the low sun, punctuated only by the stunning blue domes of churches, they might have been sky cities, gleaming at the gates of heaven. And then the vision was gone. A crazy quilt of dark fields rushed upwards and the plane jolted onto a sea of tarmac.

Fired with the adrenaline of anticipation, I made my way out the door and down a staircase to the runway. Nimolo had said my guide Gilberto would meet me at the terminal. I walked across the vast tarmac, waited until I could grab my blue backpack from a baggage trailer, and carried it through the door.

Inside the small, dingy lobby a crowd of perhaps a dozen men and women began frantically waving signs and shouting in a mixture of Greek and pidgin English.

"*Domatia!* Thirty euro! Swimming pool! *Orea!* Twenty-five!" The crowd pushed against a restraining cord, holding out signs with pictures of hotels, beaches, and whitewashed balconies.

Dazed, I looked beyond them to the building's front windows. There was no city bus, no train, nothing but a few cars in what looked like a vast desert. Where was this guide of mine, Gilberto? How was I supposed to recognize him? Maybe he wasn't going to show up, and I should get a room with one of these frantic hotel people—if that was really what they were. I certainly didn't want to be stuck at this airport overnight.

A tall woman leaned forward and shoved a brochure into my hand. "One people, *mono* fifteen euro!"

The brochure was a jumble of Greek letters. The shouting was an alien din. In growing alarm I looked around the small room. Even the directional signs were as unreadable as physics formulas, sprinkled with sigmas, gammas, and deltas. Suddenly a touch of panic tightened my throat. I'm a language teacher, for God's sake, and for the first time in my life I was in a place where I understood nothing.

Just then I spotted an old, rectangular violin case waving in the air among the signs. I smiled: Here at least was one message I could read. I handed back the brochure and made my way around the crowd. Then I held out my hand to the man with the case. "You must be Gilberto Montale?"

"You?" he exclaimed. "You are Signora Smyth?" He was a relatively good-looking man of medium build, perhaps in his late twenties, with black slacks and a blue shirt open at the collar. His black hair was a bit tousled and the shadow of a beard darkened his square jaw, but his eyes were a surprising gray-green. Ignoring my outstretched hand he set down the violin case, took me by the shoulders, and kissed the air beside my cheek three times—right, left, and right again. "Dr. Nimolo did not tell me you would be so—so young and charming. Welcome to Milos. Have you had a good flight?"

The air kisses did not put me at ease. In fact, they reminded me of my doubts about this tour guide. "I've been on four different flights. My head's still spinning." I glanced at the crowd of hotel people, who were already putting away their signs in disappointment. The few who had managed to snag tourists were herding them off toward minivans.

Gilberto held up his hands. "No problem. I have a room for you on the beach at Adamas, the main town. Very nice. We go there tonight, get something to eat, you get some rest, and tomorrow we start looking for your father. OK?"

"I guess that's the plan, yeah." Somehow the business of tracking down my father seemed more complicated and perhaps less sane now that I was really here, on an island somewhere in the Aegean Sea.

"Excellent." Gilberto picked up the violin case in one hand and took my daypack in the other. "Together we will find out about the case of Einstein. No problem."

I sighed. "Right."

I had never before seen a taxi driver who could chew gum, smoke a cigarette, honk his horn, and talk on his cell phone at the same time.

While careening through alleyways at breakneck speed the man held the cell phone in his right hand, talking in Greek with such animation that his other hand sometimes left the steering wheel too, illustrating his words with emphatic, grasping gestures. It looked as if he were frantically picking invisible grapes from the car's ceiling. Outside, a ragtag city rushed past the window, a jumble of ugly, four-story concrete buildings, striped with balconies and cluttered with TV satellite dishes.

A neon sign loomed atop a building: *ΤΡΑΠΕΖΑ ΕΛΛΕΝΙΚΑ*. The words seemed to echo from the "Monday" lesson in my Greek book. If *R* was spelled *P*, and *P* was spelled *Π*, then the first word was actually *trapeza*. But *trapeza* didn't mean trapeze, it meant something else—something trapezoidal perhaps, like a table or a—yes, a bank. Triumphantly, I leaned across the backseat of the taxi toward Gilberto and pointed to the sign. "That means Hellenistic bank, doesn't it?"

Gilberto grinned. "Very good. The Bank of Greece. You have been studying Greek?"

"A little. I'd like to be able to read signs. I don't know how far I'll get here with English and German."

"Not far outside of the tourist areas. In the monasteries they use only Greek and Latin. They have very old traditions. Agios Nikolas, your father's monastery, is the oldest on the island. No telephone, no road. Just a trail."

"Is my father really there?" I wondered again why he would have chosen such a remote spot.

Gilberto shrugged. "I asked yesterday about this. The monks adopt new names when they are accepted. They are all called brother. It is hard to tell who is there. Everyone says, you just have to go see."

"I suppose if my father's lived there fifteen years, he's learned Greek." I looked to Gilberto. "How come you know Greek, if you're Italian?"

"From family vacations. My grandfather was stationed in Greece when Italy occupied the country in World War II. Later he bought a vacation house in the Peleponnese. For me, as a child, it was like a second home."

The taxi swerved onto the sidewalk in front of a gray stucco building with the sign *ΧΕΝΟΔΟΚΕΙΟ ΑΦΡΟΔΙΤΕ*. The driver put away his cell phone, flipped his cigarette out the window, and went to get the luggage from the trunk.

I got out and stretched, trying to work the kinks out of my leg muscles.

Gilberto pointed up to the sign. "Can you read this one too?"

I looked up, blinking. "Xeno—"I started to sound out the letters, and then gave up. "I hope it means hotel."

"Very good," Gilberto said.

"Just point me to my room and I'll see you tomorrow."

"But it is only nine o'clock," Gilberto objected. "This is when the evening begins. I thought we would walk down to the harbor to eat."

"Not me." I shouldered my pack and gave Gilberto a tired smile. "Maybe tomorrow. I mean, thanks for meeting me at the airport and everything, but I need about a dozen hours of sleep."

"OK. No problem." He paid the taxi driver and led the way into the hotel.

The lobby was hardly wider than a hallway, with walls and floor made entirely of marble. A niche held a replica of the armless Venus de Milo, twisting coquettishly from an inadequately draped tunic.

A hunched clerk looked up from the counter. "Ah, you must be our American guest. Passport please?"

I fished the blue folder out of my purse. "Do you have a room with a private bath?"

"Yes of course." The man filed my passport in a slot. Then he handed me a key attached by a ring to a large piece of metal that resembled a brass doorknob. "Room 203, three floors up. Do you need help?"

Gilberto shook his head. "I know the way."

I followed him up a worn marble staircase. I felt a little uneasy that the clerk had kept my passport. I was also uncomfortable alone in a dim stairwell with Gilberto. I knew almost nothing about this man, and had no reason to trust him very far. After the third flight of steps he crossed the hall and stopped beside a door marked 203. I fumbled with the gigantic metal key ring, managed to open the door, and pressed a wall switch. No light went on. Even when I groped along the wall and pressed the bathroom light switch, the place remained a dark and frightening grotto.

"Give me the key, please, Miss Smyth." Behind me Gilberto stood silhouetted in the doorway, his hand outstretched.

For a moment I felt trapped, blockaded by a shadowy man in an unknown room. Did he imagine he would be staying in here with me? He hadn't actually said that he had booked a separate room for himself.

"The key, Miss Smyth." Gilberto repeated, his voice low.

I studied him warily, fighting back my fear. If he tried anything funny, I'd scream loud enough to break the windows. Slowly I held out the large metal key ring.

"Very good." Gilberto took the key ring and inserted its brass knob into a plug beside the door, just below the main light switch. Instantly the lights blinked on, revealing a small but tidy bedroom with a double bed.

"How did you do that?" I asked.

"My room is the same way. Greek hotels use the room key to connect the power. That way it is impossible to leave the lights on when you go. It saves them money. And don't try to take a shower too early in the morning. The water is solar heated. Shall I show you?" He stepped in toward the bathroom.

"No!" I held up my hands and practically pushed him back through the doorway. "Thank you, Gilberto, I'll manage on my own. Good night."

"Good night, then, Miss Smyth. What time shall I knock you up?"

I stared at him. "What?"

"Don't you want someone to knock you up in the morning?"

"You mean, wake me up?"

"Is that how you say this in America?"

I pushed him into the hall. "Don't wake me up at all."

"But the free breakfast ends at 9:30. You will miss—"

"Enjoy it by yourself. Don't expect to see me until noon. Goodnight." I dragged in my backpack, bolted the door, and sagged back onto the bed. For a minute I just lay there with my eyes closed, hoping my head would clear and everything would be simple. When that failed I rolled over, unzipped my pack, took out a little bottle of airline riesling I had saved from the flight, and drank a long pull. Then I lowered the room's blinds, stripped off my travelworn clothes, and walked naked into the bathroom.

To my surprise, the toilet, shower, and sink were all jammed into a single, closet-sized space. There wasn't even a shower curtain in the tiled compartment, just a drain in the floor. The toilet would obviously get wet if I took a shower—in fact, it almost looked like you were expected to sit there while showering. Stranger still was a notice posted on the wall. In four languages the placard announced that used toilet paper should NOT be placed in the toilet because of a water shortage on the island. I read this notice several times, even in German, to make sure the hotel really wanted dirty toilet paper in the wastepaper basket. Then I shrugged, used the toilet as instructed, and showered awkwardly with a nozzle on a hose. Only when I was done did I realize that the towels were now soaked, stacked on a dripping bathroom shelf.

In frustration I mopped myself off with a wet towel and lay down to dry on the bed's cover—a blanket in a white sheet bag. While I waited to dry I took the remote control from the bedside table and flipped through television channels. There were thirty, all in Greek. Game shows with heavily made up women in revealing outfits. Talk shows with heavily made up women in revealing outfits. And a dozen channels with American movies and TV programs dubbed into Greek. Even with an effort, the only word I managed to understand was *ke*, the word for "and". Tom Hanks sounded as if he was trying to speak Russian with an Italian accent. Long after his mouth stopped moving, polysyllabic words kept coming out.

Finally I zapped Hanks into a white dot, emptied my backpack on the floor, put on fresh underwear, and turned out the light.

When I crawled under the sheet bag, I almost hoped I might find Rags there.

A BACKSEAT DRIVER
(Harmony)

Driving back from the Eugene airport, I couldn't shake the feeling that someone was behind me. Perhaps it was because Ana had turned around so many times, looking nervously out the back window. For all that, Ana still hadn't noticed the white car shadowing us toward the airport. No doubt Ana had been looking for a cowboy. The white car had had two big redneck guys propped up in the front seat, like maybe they were Roseburg loggers out for a Sunday drive. Maybe they were. Probably it was nothing. After the weirdness of the international phone calls, and especially after seeing Ana's ransacked apartment, it didn't take much to creep me out. I felt like the whole mess was my fault, encouraging Ana to face up to her murky past. How was I to know ghosts were stacked in her closet three deep?

Perhaps too, I'd been thinking about what the cowboy detective didn't find when he broke into Ana's place. There was one thing we'd taken from the attic that was never in her apartment. We hadn't sold it at the garage sale or on eBay, either. This one thing was sitting right here in my purse like a ticking bomb. It was the blue vial of her father's peculiarly evocative perfume. We had found the bottle right at the center of her great aunt's attic shrine, inside Einstein's violin case. What did that mean?

At a stop light on Franklin Boulevard I punched my Fury into "park" and dug the bottle out of my purse. I unbuckled my seat belt, writhed halfway over the back seat, and stuffed the damn thing under the floor mat. Then I buried it beneath an old *Eugene Weekly*, a pair of fuzzy slippers, and a pizza box. The car behind me was honking by the time I punched back into drive, but I felt a little better, a little safer now.

As I boated on down the boulevard I let the engine growl, like a fearful animal warning others to keep their distance. I knew I should go home to pack for my family reunion, but I felt I owed Ana a little detective work first.

I swung off Franklin into the court of the Campus Inn, the biggest and poshest motel within walking distance of her apartment. They actually had a valet sitting on a folding chair by the door. I gunned the Fury past him, steered around to an empty parking lot behind the hotel, and parked in the far corner. Then I walked in the back door and made my way down a long, plush-carpeted hall lit with milky glass sconces. Ferns hung in the lobby beside a counter of black granite and cherry veneer. A middle-aged woman with a flat bow tie like a flight attendant gave me an uncertain look. "Can I help you, Miss?"

I crossed my arms in front of my chest, a sort of reflex to defend myself against the motel's wild hospitality and tacky opulence. I wanted to say, "Smile when you call me that, sister." But I knew confrontation wouldn't get me anywhere. "Oh, hi, I'm looking for a friend. He's about my age, maybe a couple years younger, not very tall, with dark hair."

"Just one moment please." She answered a telephone blinking on the counter. When she finally hung up and saw I was still there, she asked, "What is your friend's name?"

"Well, actually," I went on, wishing already that I'd gone with the tough-guy approach instead, "We met at a concert Friday night. He's got a little bit of an accent, you know, British or Australian? He's in town for three or four days and said I might find him here."

The woman screwed up her mouth. She made a pretense of flipping through a registration book. "Are you sure he said the Campus Inn?"

Then it hit me: Our cowboy would never have stayed here. "Actually, now that you mention it, I think it might have been the Campus Lodge."

"That would be next door, behind the Burger King." She pointed with a pen to the door. For once, she smiled.

The Campus Lodge was one of those cheap two-story motels from the 60s, with angled parking spaces in front of each lower room. The units upstairs had a railed balcony instead of a hall. I sensed at once that it was the kind of place our cowboy would choose.

The office was lit with an orange neon sign that read *OFFICE.* I slipped silently through the swinging glass door and surveyed the room's lone vinyl chair, the coffee pot on a side table, and the rack of tourist brochures. The place smelled as if mildew and Pine-Sol were wrestling on the carpet. As soon as I saw the receptionist I knew I'd do best with a hippie-chick routine. The young man wore dreadlocks and a tie-dyed sweatshirt. He was sitting hunched over a comic book at a back desk, lost to the world. I undid the top button of my blouse before I tapped the counter bell.

The clerk jumped up, startled. With his mouth partly open he looked me up and down. "Oh wow. Can I, like, help you?"

I gave him a one-shouldered shrug. "Maybe. I'm looking for a man."

"Yeah?" He swallowed.

"Yeah, about your age. Or maybe a couple years older." For a moment I held his gaze. Then I lowered my eyes and drew my mouth into a pout. "I can't believe he left without saying goodbye, after all the stuff he told me about the Country Fair." I gave a big sigh that puckered my blouse half open. "He had a touch of a British accent, you know? He'd been in town a few days, by himself, I think. I was hoping, if he stayed here, you could at least tell me his real name."

The clerk reddened. "I— I don't know. I'm not supposed to—"

"Please?" I could see he was softening, but I needed something more. "He collected hats," I said, taking off my baseball cap and shaking my head. The blond ponytail swung over my shoulder and splashed across my blouse. "Cowboy hats, old ladies' hats, I love that stuff. Don't tell me he's gone." I let the sweep of shiny hair slowly slip from the tautened fabric over my right boob.

"He's gone," the clerk blurted. "He checked out half an hour ago."

I let me eyes go wide. "Then his name wasn't really Jupiter?"

The clerk shook his head. "Sorry. Here he called himself Peter Weiss. I helped him with plane reservations out of Portland because he'd missed the flight from Eugene."

"Thanks." With a smile I turned toward the door, glad that I'd have some solid information to share with Ana. "Oh," I added, my hand on the door handle, "Did your Peter say where he was headed next?"

The clerk's mouth opened and closed silently.

"Weiss," I said. "Where's he going?"

The clerk managed a single word: "Greece."

As I walked out past the Burger King, my teasing mood quickly drained. The cowboy spy must be even shrewder than we thought. How could he have discovered that Ana was going to Greece? She had made the reservations with her laptop computer. She had told no one except me. And her mother, of course. And Dr. Nimolo. But why would either of them want Ana shadowed? Nimolo was sending his own man to escort her in Greece.

I needed to warn Ana. I wished I could contact her before tomorrow, when she had agreed to check her email at an Internet café. I wished I didn't have to go to my family reunion, and could instead rush off to Europe a week ahead of schedule.

I took a shortcut behind the Burger King to my car. But as soon as I saw it, a jolt of fear shot through me. While I was gone, a white car with an Avis sticker on the bumper had parked next to my Fury. It looked exactly like the car that had followed me to the airport.

My heart began beating way too fast. Of course it was ridiculous to think that someone had followed me back from the airport. And the cowboy detective had checked out half an hour ago, headed for Portland.

Nonetheless I approached the two cars as if they were dozing Rottweilers. I couldn't help imagining that some bogeyman was hiding in my back seat, drawn perhaps by the mysterious perfume under the floor mat. If I slid into the driver's seat, would a cord whip around my neck and yank me backwards? Or perhaps instead of a cord, a violin string?

People who are unfamiliar with my Aikido training assume that it has given me attack skills. But Aikido is not an aggressive martial art like karate or judo. It is defensive. Aikido is all about channeling an attacker's energy. How the hell are you supposed to channel the energy of a violin wire yanked around your neck from the back seat of a car?

If I were Ana, I might have marched up to my car and flung open the door. But I am not Ana. I sidled up to take a look in the cars' windows. Only when I was convinced that both cars were empty did I unlock my Fury.

I had just fired up the engine with a roar when I noticed a torn Mars wrapper lying on the passenger seat.

I hadn't eaten a candy bar in twenty years. Who the hell had been in my car while I was gone?

I punched "drive" and ripped out of the parking lot, tires squealing.

QUANTUM GRAVITY
(Ana)

It really was noon before I lifted a slat of the blinds and squinted out into the bright sunlight. I caught my breath at the view. Beyond my balcony were palm trees, a beach, and a turquoise bay where white sailboats lay at anchor. I pulled on jeans, sandals, and a short-sleeved white blouse. Then I locked the door behind me with the massive key ring and went downstairs to explore.

From the lobby I followed a marble hallway out to a white gravel terrace with a beachfront café. The bay seemed to glow green from within. I walked across the sand and put my hand in the water. It was a little cool for swimming, but two teenagers were splashing about and a dozen tourists were sunbathing on reed mats—including a topless, middle-aged woman who was nonchalantly rubbing sun block cream on her white breasts. In the other direction, where the beach became rockier as it arced toward the town's harbor, a cluster of old Greek men sat on a seawall beside their gaudily painted, red-and-green wooden boats, mending nets and smoking pipes. One of them scowled and shouted a few words in a complaining tone to the topless woman, but she didn't seem to understand or care.

"Welcome to Greece, Miss Smyth," a voice from the terrace said.

I turned around. Gilberto was smiling from a table in the striped shade of a palm. He was wearing an open shirt, white slacks, a white straw fedora, and sunglasses. Behind him a row of Venus de Milo statues and Mythos Beer lanterns separated the terrace from the next café.

"You certainly look like you have slept well. May I call you Ana today?"

I laughed, embarrassed that I had treated him so abruptly last night. "I suppose so."

"Very good. Let me order you something to eat. You must be hungry."

"I'm starved. What do people here eat if they miss breakfast?" I pulled up a blue wooden chair opposite him and opened a menu. To my relief the Greek listings were repeated in English, German, and French.

"We simply move on to lunch. At this café they specialize in whole fish." He pointed to a list entitled *psaria* on the menu. "You can choose from little fish, tiny fish, or very tiny fish."

"Whole fish? With heads?"

"Of course."

The thought of little fish staring up at me from a plate weakened my appetite. "I don't eat animals I recognize. What else is there?"

"How about a selection of *mezes*, vegetable dips with bread."

"Perfect." I closed my menu and waved a waiter to our table. I let Gilberto order the food. Then he ordered a cappuccino for himself. I added, "Also, a large orange juice and a coffee."

"*Cafe elleniko*?" The waiter asked.

I looked to Gilberto. "That means Greek coffee?"

He nodded.

"Okay, *cafe elleniko,*" I told the waiter. When he crossed something off his notepad I remembered that "okay" sounds like *okhi,* and that *okhi* means "no" in Greek. That had been the first lesson in *Learn Greek in a Week,* To make matters worse, *nay* meant "yes". It was very confusing.

"Wait!" I said. "I meant to say *nay*. You know, yes. *Nay, cafe elleniko.*"

The waiter shrugged and left. I wasn't sure whether I had succeeded in ordering coffee or not.

Gilberto looked aside and ran his hand over his jaw, a gesture I suspected was covering a smile at my expense. I was reminded of my doubts about him last night, and how little I knew about him. It was time to find out more. "So Gilberto, do you work all year as a tour guide, or just in summers?"

He took off his sunglasses and looked at me with his startling, gray-green eyes. Together with his white fedora, his eyes contrasted so dramatically with his tan face and unruly black hair that I felt a flutter of confusion. "I'm not a tour guide at all, Ana. I'm a physicist."

"What? I thought Nimolo said he was sending a guide."

Gilberto tipped his head. "I work in Dr. Nimolo's laboratory in Trieste. There are so few jobs for physicists these days, even those who graduate *cum laude.* I was glad to find a position with such a well-known scientist. Because I speak Greek, he asked me to accompany you here. For me, it is a free vacation."

"This laboratory of yours. It's run by the United Nations, right?"

He fidgeted. "It is a private lab under the—how do you say?—under the umbrella of the United Nations. They have an international research center in Trieste, with a cyclotron complex underground. Many physicists with private grants study there because of this facility. Dr. Nimolo is an expert at private funding."

"And what exactly are you studying?"

"Nuclear theory."

I frowned. I decided I might find out more about Gilberto by shifting the subject. "So how did you get into physics? Don't tell me it runs in your family."

"No, no. For me, it was the opposite." Gilberto put on his sunglasses and tilted back in his wooden chair. "I grew up in Sardinia. My father and grandfather were both with the *carabinieri* there, the Italian army police. They wanted me to join the *carabinieri* like them, not to study physics. My mother, however, she comes from a village in the Alps. She was proud I could go to the university. Me, I did not want to be with the army. Even for my year of required military service, I wanted to do alternative work in a hospital. But in Sardinia, the father is king."

His story made me feel more sympathetic to him. I too had been caught in a conflict between my parents. "What did you do?"

"In the end we compromised. I spent my military year with the *carabinieri* in Cagliari. Then I went to the university in Berkeley."

"Aha. That explains why you speak English so well."

He shook his head. "After a year I had to return to Italy. I finished at the university in Padova, but I was not happy there. I hope someday to go back to America."

At this point the waiter arrived with a tray. He spread a white paper tablecloth over the cloth one and fastened it on all four sides with little metal clips. The paper was printed in blue with a map of the island, a picture of the Venus de Milo, and the words *Café Aphrodite*. Finally the waiter set out silverware, an oil-and-vinegar bottle, a basket of bread, and our coffee.

I picked up my tiny, espresso-sized cup and tentatively sipped the thick, foamy liquid inside. I made a face. The coffee was a bitter, gritty sludge. "Oof! What do they put in this stuff?"

Gilberto laughed. "For *cafe elleniko* they leave in the coffee beans. The Turks ruled Greece for 400 years. They drove out the good Italian coffeemakers."

I cleared the taste from my mouth with a gulp of orange juice. Then I pointed to the picture of the Venus de Milo on the tablecloth. "And what's with all the Venuses? They're everywhere."

"Well, this is the island of Milos."

I tapped my forehead. "Of course—this must be where they found the original statue of Venus."

"Actually, Venus was her Latin name," Gilberto said. "The Greeks call her Aphrodite. People here don't like it when the tourists say Venus de Milo. It reminds them that the statue was taken by the French."

"It's in the Louvre, isn't it?"

"The Greeks want it back, but the French keep refusing."

"That does sound hopeless, trying to get a love goddess to leave Paris." I looked at one of the café's armless statues wistfully. I would have liked to see the original, the personification of love. It seemed I had the same luck with love itself, always missing the real thing. But right now, I needed to find a missing father.

"When can we go to my father's monastery?" I asked.

Gilberto moved the breadbasket and pointed to the map printed on the tablecloth. "We are here on the main bay, at Adamas. Early tomorrow morning we should take the bus up to Plaka, the old capital. We've missed the bus today. Then the next day we can take the trail from there to your father's monastery." His finger followed a crooked line toward the northern tip of the horseshoe-shaped island.

"It will take us two days?"

"This troubles me too," Gilberto admitted. "Dr. Nimolo thinks people may be following you."

I stopped short, my senses suddenly on high alert. "People following me? Who?" Had someone traced me to the airport after all? And if so, how would Nimolo know?

"Bad people. I don't know. People looking for quantum gravity."

"Looking for what?"

But the waiter had returned with a tray of dishes, and Gilberto motioned me silent by putting a finger to his lips.

"*Salata melantzana, tzatziki, ke elies,*" the waiter said, setting out dishes filled with lumpy green, white, and brown sauces. "*Parakalo.*"

As soon as he was gone I repeated my question to Gilberto, "What did you say people are looking for? Quantum gravity?" I felt I was getting closer to learning why the sale of Einstein's violin case had caused such a furor. But Gilberto seemed to be in a different world, his attention diverted entirely to the food.

"This one is made of olive oil and *melantzana*. Do you call them aubergines or eggplants in America?" He broke off a piece of bread, used it to scoop up some of the muddy green sauce, and slowly savored a bite. "Excellent. Definitely not from the supermarket. You must try it."

It was maddening, yet Gilberto seemed obsessed with cuisine. With a sigh, I dipped some bread in the sauce. It turned out that the eggplant sauce was surprisingly delicious. Or had I just been famished?

"The olive paste is supposed to be very salty," Gilberto said. He scooped up some of the brown sauce with a piece of bread and chewed it slowly. "Yes. It's hard to make wrong, if you start with good kalamata olives. The real challenge is *tzatziki*." He pointed to the white sauce. "Do you know it?"

"They have it in stores in Eugene," I said. "It's made from cucumbers, isn't it?"

"Cucumbers and garlic, grated together in fresh yogurt." Gilberto sampled this third sauce thoughtfully. Slowly his expression darkened. "No. No, this won't do. It seems so simple, *tzatziki*. But so often it is lifeless. We must order it again later, somewhere else."

When the bread was gone and the dips ran low, I pushed back my chair and looked directly at Gilberto. "All right, now I want to know what you meant about the gravity. Exactly what is it that all these people are looking for?"

Gilberto returned my gaze. "Quantum gravity? How could you sell Einstein's violin case and not know?"

"I'm still finding out how much I didn't know. Could you explain it, in simple terms?"

He shook his head and signaled the waiter for the check. "This is not something to talk about over an empty table. Why don't we walk down the beach? Do you like to swim? There's a very good swimming spot at the far end."

"I swim just fine, but I'd rather talk."

"Good. Get your suit and meet me on the beach in ten minutes. Then I'll tell you whatever you want to know."

I sighed. "All right then. In ten minutes."

"Gravity is the one force nobody understands," Gilberto said, carrying a bag over his shoulder as he walked barefoot down the beach. He was wearing his white fedora, an unbuttoned shirt, and a tight little swimsuit that looked as if it had been painted on with shiny blue nail polish. Obviously he was proud of his body, and I had to admit that his tight little hips and muscular legs were unsettlingly attractive. His chest was as narrow as Randy's, however, and only his face had a good tan. I couldn't help but remember how vain Randy had been about his silly blond moustache, as if that were the ultimate mark of manhood. I shut Randy out of my mind and returned to Gilberto.

"Didn't Einstein figure out what gravity was?" I asked. I held the front of my loose shirt closed to cover up my one-piece bathing suit. Harmony, I knew, would have come up with a far cleverer outfit for a beach in Greece.

"Not even Einstein was sure about gravity," Gilberto said. "It isn't electromagnetic. It's not normally a wave, although it can form waves. It's not made up of particles—at least none that has been found. So what is it?"

Almost to myself, I said, "Maybe it's the glue that holds the world together."

"Exactly, but how? For years Einstein tried to make gravity fit into a unified field theory. He wanted to explain all the forces of nature at once. Finally he suggested that gravity isn't a force at all. It's just a distortion of space and time."

I looked at him. "How would that work?"

He nodded toward a group of boys playing soccer on the beach. "Imagine the earth is like that soccer ball. If you kick the ball into a net, the squares of the net stretch out around it. Einstein said the earth distorts space and time the same way. He even said he knew how to prove it."

"And how was that?"

"He said if you watch closely during a total eclipse, the sun's gravity should bend the light of stars next to the sun. But he made this prediction just before World War I. For years nobody had time to do the experiment. After the war, in 1919, British astronomers finally watched during a solar eclipse. The stars near the sun really were in the wrong place. Einstein was right. Gravity bends light because it bends space. Within weeks he was world famous."

I thought about this for a while. "So he proved that gravity bends light. For me, that still doesn't explain what holds the world together."

"It didn't for Einstein, either. Space is curved, yes, but what causes it to curve? Maybe there really is a hidden force, a quantum of gravity."

"What do you mean, a quantum?"

"An amount. A unit. Light is made of photons, matter is made of quarks. Is there a quantum of gravity, a smallest possible amount? Maybe a particle, a graviton? Since Newton, people have theorized about quantum gravity, and every theory has been wrong. Physicists today laugh at the crazy theories. It is like astrology. Surely, they say, Albert Einstein would not have written a formula about quantum gravity. He was a famous man. It would be embarrassing for him."

"So if he did, he would have hidden it." I thought: Perhaps he would have stuffed it in an old violin case along with his sheet music. Perhaps my great aunt really had found an Einstein formula, and had taught me part of it in the form of a childhood rhyme. But then where was the rest of the formula?

By this time we had reached a quieter part of the beach, beyond the clutter of hotels and tavernas that straggled out along the sand from Adamas. I asked, "If Einstein really did write a formula for quantum gravity, and if it were correct, what would that mean?"

Gilberto shrugged. "What would it mean if we understood gravity the way we understand the atom? Theoretically, you could take it apart and put it back together. You could build an anti-gravity device. Or maybe bend time along with space."

I shook my head "This all sounds like something from an old science fiction movie."

"Exactly. Only science fiction fanatics would believe an old formula from the 1920s could be used for such things. But historians are also interested. People like Dr. Nimolo. For him, the formula would be important for understanding Einstein. That is why he is paying to research your violin case."

The beach finally ended at an outcrop of red rock that jutted into the bay. Gilberto took two mats out of his bag and unrolled them on the smooth sand above a high-water mark of shells, pebbles, seaweed, and plastic flotsam. Then he took off his shirt and hat. "Are you coming in?"

I hesitated. He was almost naked, a good-looking man standing there in the sun. Against my will, physical desire was beginning to gnaw at me, like the hunger after a skipped breakfast. "Maybe I'll just wade a bit."

"Oh, come on." Gilberto waded in past his knees and then dived forward. He came up dripping, shook his black hair to one side, and called, "See? It's as warm as a swimming pool."

"A poorly heated swimming pool, I'd say." I waded in slowly, stepping around seaweed-covered rocks to find sandy spots underwater. Once my legs were in the water they really weren't cold, but every wavelet that broke around my thighs brought a chill shock.

"Come on!" Gilberto called again. "You said you were such a good swimmer."

This taunt was too much. I gritted my teeth and lowered myself to my stomach. My skin felt like it was shrinking beneath my swimsuit from the cold. Then I carefully launched myself forward into a breaststroke. To my surprise, it was easy to keep my head high enough that my hair stayed dry.

"That's better," Gilberto said.

"I've never swum in the ocean before," I said between breaths. "In Oregon the Pacific Ocean is freezing cold. This isn't too bad. It's amazing how well you float."

"Salt water has a higher specific gravity. The Aegean has so much salt because water evaporates in the sun."

I couldn't help but smile. Gilberto analyzed everything like a physicist, even when we were facing each other, treading water in a Greek bay. His comically foreshortened legs kicked scissor-like against a rippled backdrop. Through the clear water I could make out yellow sand, an underwater boulder at the end of the headland, and small flickering shapes that must be fish. I was beginning to like Gilberto. Much of what he had said about Einstein confirmed what Nimolo had told me over the telephone. Perhaps it was just luck that our interests happened to mesh. Gilberto wanted to know about Einstein's history, while I wanted to know about my own family's history.

Suddenly I felt the urge to tease him, just a little. "If there really was an old Einstein formula," I said, turning slowly around as I treaded water, "Would it begin with F?"

"What?"

I completed my slow spin and faced him again. "You know, a formula. Would it begin with 'F equals something?'

He opened his mouth, but a wave caught him in the face, and for a moment he could only sputter.

I was enjoying his obvious confusion. At the same time, I felt a premonition that this could be a dangerous game.

When he could speak again, Gilberto said, "Then is it true?"

"What?"

"That your great aunt taught you a formula?"

Now it was my turn to gape with astonishment. "Who told you about that?" I had never told anyone about the childhood rhyme. Except Harmony. With a flash of dismay I remembered that Harmony had talked to Nimolo. The night before the garage sale the Italian had called her. They had talked about my father in Greece. Obviously she must have told him more as well. I seethed at the thought. Harmony was lousy at keeping secrets. A friend had no right to tell strangers such things.

"I'm sorry," Gilberto said. "I did not mean to make you angry."

I was mostly angry at Harmony. At Harmony and at myself.

Gilberto asked, "Do you not want to talk about the formula?"

I didn't want to answer. I didn't want to talk to Gilberto at all. I needed some time alone. I shook my head and set off swimming. I needed some space, and the bay was big enough to provide it.

No longer trying to keep my hair dry, I headed for open water with my best stroke, the Australian crawl. I had earned a badge once in Girl Scouts for swimming a mile. It had been arduous, swimming so far in an icy Oregon lake at Camp Cleawox. Here the water seemed to carry me like a dolphin.

The rush of the water in my ears was so loud I almost didn't hear the whine of the motor and the desperately shouting voice until it was too late.

When I finally looked up, gasping, the prow of the motorboat was already looming directly in front of me. I barely had time to take half a breath and dive for the depths.

THE FERGUSONS
(Harmony)

I paid two dollars at the bar of the Rusty Baitbucket and unfolded my laptop at the quietest table, in a back corner by the restroom door, to see if there was an email yet from Ana in Greece. Finally I would be able to warn her that the cowboy detective was named Peter Weiss, and that he'd followed her on a flight to Greece.

While I logged onto the bar's wireless network I could hear my cousins laughing at a rerun of "Survivor" on the big-screen TV across the bar.

The annual Ferguson family reunion had not been going well, and it wasn't just because of the drizzly fog outside. Last night, when the clan assembled as usual at Reedsport's Umpqua Palisade Motel, Grandma Ferguson had announced that this would be her last reunion. Obviously her rheumatoid arthritis was worse. She could hardly walk, and she took so much pain medication that she sometimes nodded off in the midst of a conversation.

Still, none of us was prepared for the bombshell our matriarch dropped. Grandma announced that she had had a really convincing dream about Grandpa. He had died of emphysema five years ago, but in the dream he was pretty peppy. Grinning and winking, he had told her she would be joining him soon. He said she'd die a natural death, in her sleep, in exactly two months. As a result, she declared that this weekend would be a celebration of her life—sort of a funeral in advance.

All the aunts, uncles, and cousins were silent for a long time as we digested this astonishing news. We exchanged glances of worry and alarm. Had Grandma gone bonkers? Finally Uncle Derek asked, "Have you talked with your doctor about this?"

Grandma looked at him evenly. "Don't you believe your own father?"

Uncle Derek was groping for an answer when Grandma smiled. "Of course you do. Now I want this last reunion to be just like always. The fishing, the clamming, the strawberry picking—everything Henry and I loved. I want you to do it all, and then come back to the motel and tell me all about it."

My email program finally appeared, but before I could log on, flashing boxes flooded the screen, screaming that I should track down my high school classmates. As I clicked them closed, my cousin Daren stumbled past toward the bathroom, his eyes slightly unfocused. "Harma-roo, what're you doing back here? They're about to vote Kathy off the island and give that goofball Ronald a bazillion bucks."

I didn't really blame my cousins. That morning my three uncles had dutifully taken their boats over the Umpqua River bar in search of striped bass, despite the rain and the choppy sea. My own parents had tried to beg off, pleading vegetarianism and sympathy for the wildlife. But the guilt proved simply too powerful, even for laid-back, tie-dyed toymakers from Eugene. So we all went fishing. Not only did we fail to catch fish, but Aunt Muriel barfed on the swivel chairs, and my Dad lost his wallet overboard. That afternoon when we tried to build a fire on the usual beach to dry out, the smoldering wood sent up such an enormous plume of smoke that a state trooper drove up in his Jeep to tell us driftwood fires aren't legal anymore.

I logged onto the program with the password "Tiramisu1" and waited again for the bar's sluggish wireless connection to slowly accept the transmission of eighty-seven new email messages.

Still, I thought, we Fergusons are a tough, outdoorsy bunch, and everyone might otherwise have laughed off the rain, the lack of fish, and the doused beach fire. The whole family had dragged back to the motel and told Grandma about their adventures over dinner. But then, after the strawberry shortcake, Grandma had handed each of the aunts and uncles a list of her twenty most prized belongings, from the Betty Crocker silverware and the mahogany table to the nearly complete set of crystal and the grandfather clock. Grandma said she didn't want anyone arguing about who inherited what after she was gone, so they should spend the evening deciding now. The cousins, she said, should go play Crazy Eights on the living room carpet, just as they had when they were little. Then Grandma sat on the couch and fell asleep.

I worked my way down the Inbox headings, deleting spam. I almost zapped the title "loose lips sink ships," too, until I saw it was from Ana. Puzzled, I clicked the icon and waited for the text.

Of course Grandma had hardly dozed off before Uncle Derek went ballistic, accusing Aunt Muriel of somehow already getting her claws into Grandma's half mile of Umpqua riverfront property. A bunch of old silverware, he said, was worthless junk in comparison. We cousins, meanwhile fled in my Fury and Barbie's Fiesta, caravanning into Reedsport to look for a bar. In the Rusty Baitbucket, where a grinning swordfish over the door holds a skin diver's swim fin in its mouth, I realized the Fergusons no longer were a family. Not like Grandma imagined. The old woman had held us together for years with the force of her will. Now my grandmother was pulling back within herself, gradually letting go. And her drifting progeny were wondering if they ever had been a family at all.

"Greetings from Greece." The email from Ana swirled me up and away.

> *Harm, I survived my first day on Milos, and I'm still shaking. Everyone says it was an accident, but I don't know. I wish you were here to talk about it. By the way, I can't believe you told Nimolo so much about me! What a rat you can be. It turns out Nimolo's guide for me here is a physicist named Gilberto. Also Italian, but he's young and the kind of guy you would probably call simpatico. Possibly even molto simpatico. He thinks I'm being followed by people looking for quantum gravity. It's a theory that most physicists apparently think is nonsense. I suppose that's why my apartment was searched. What I don't understand is why these people, if they have really followed me here, would try to kill me.*

"Hey Harma-roo, lemme buy you a Bud." My cousin Daren yanked me back to the Rusty Baitbucket by clapping a clammy hand on my shoulder.

I tried to smile. "I'm your designated driver, remember?"

"Oh yeah," he said, weaving off toward the plasma TV.

At once I returned to Ana's email, rereading the last startling sentence to make sure I had gotten it right.

What I don't understand is why these people, if they have really followed me here, would try to kill me. This morning when I was swimming in the bay a speedboat ran straight over me. At the last minute I heard a warning shout and dived, but it was so close I could feel the wash from the propellers whip my hair.

As I read this, I found myself clenching and unclenching my fingers so much that I flicked the touch screen and covered the text with a pull-down menu. Ana had nearly been killed. I felt a shiver of guilt. It had been my idea to sell the violin case, and it had been my idea for Ana to go to Greece. All that day, while I put up with the rain and my disintegrating family, I had hoped Weiss might have lost track of Ana. I had imagined her on a sunny beach sipping ouzo with her long-lost father.

Gilberto and I notified the police here, but it was hard to explain the problem in Greek. The police seem even less interested than they were in Eugene. We didn't have a good description of the boat and there weren't any other witnesses. Probably it was just an accident – the police say there are lots of drunk tourists in powerboats. They say swimmers get hurt by them every summer. Anyway, tomorrow Gilberto and I are moving to a village closer to the monastery. I hope Dad's still there, and that he's still Dad. Meanwhile, have fun at your family reunion, Harm. Gilberto and I are otherwise getting by all right here. The food is good, and the scenery is fantastic, but I envy you. Best, Ana.

PS – The Internet café is about to close for an afternoon siesta, so I'll catch you by telephone tomorrow night from Plaka.

I sat back, realizing that Ana was in more trouble than she knew. Yes, she had been followed to Greece, and yes, the speedboat incident probably was intentional. I felt frustrated and frightened, knowing I could do nothing more than warn her, in an email full of capital letters and exclamation points, to beware of the cowboy detective.

Another weird thing about Ana's message was the phrase she repeated three times: "Gilberto and I." Who was this "simpatico" physicist she was trusting so much?

It was only later that night, after I'd sent Ana the frantic email reply and had driven my drunken cousins back to the motel, that I began thinking about the perfume bottle in my Fury. Whoever had been in my car in Eugene hadn't found it—but was that because they were still looking for a mathematical equation on sheet music? Could the missing formula for gravity somehow be encoded in perfume? I knew it sounded weird, but as I lay awake in the dark motel room, fear began seeping in through the night, making my heart thump. Ana's father had developed Cloud Nine in his laboratory. We had found the bottle in Einstein's violin case. The mysterious scent, Ana's mother said, makes you feel like you've lost five pounds. What if the bottle in my car was in fact the missing thing everyone was looking for?

PLAKA
(Ana)

Festive strings of colored lights ringed the harbor of Adamas, marking a dozen different sidewalk tavernas. Gilberto picked up the menu from the outer table of the first café, but I pointed to a collection of bright red tables on the far edge of the stone quay. "Let's try over there."

"Taverna Takhemia. The Wishing Well. Why that one?"

"For one thing, it has the most people."

Gilberto shrugged. "Sometimes it works, this American method of choosing restaurants by following others. Or are you thinking, after today, you will be safer in a crowd?"

"A little of both." I led the way past the other tavernas to an empty table at the Wishing Well. Gilberto quickly stepped forward and held my chair. In Eugene, I would have rolled my eyes at this overly gallant gesture. But here, somehow, it seemed comfortable and natural. Then I flipped open the menu. "Oh no. It's not translated. And really, I'm not very hungry after everything that's happened."

Gilberto closed my menu. "Tonight you should forget your worry. You are with me. Please."

The intent look in his gray-green eyes did help distract me from my previous worry. Here was a different sort of danger—dining with a handsome man I'd known only for a day. I would need to be on my guard.

"How can I order, if it's all in Greek?" I objected.

He shook his head. "If you are going to choose a restaurant by its patrons, then the menu requires a different kind of translation."

"What do you mean?"

"Look around. Here is the real menu." He lowered his voice to a whisper and nodded slightly toward a table with two couples. The men wore sweaters over their shoulders and the women wore designer scarves at their necks. "They are French, you see? Probably from one of the yachts in the harbor. They ordered octopus, and are on their second bottle of wine. Translation: The wine is excellent, perhaps from Macedonia, but the octopus is tough."

This was just silly enough that I couldn't help relaxing a little. With a smile I leaned forward and whispered, "How about the two old men by the tree? How do you read them?" With black berets and wrinkled faces, the men were nipping on beers and playing cards.

"Milos is full of old Greek men," Gilberto said, "But for them to play cards like this in the evening, the taverna must be very traditional, and the price reasonable."

"Then that's another good sign about the menu?"

"Yes, we should try the *tzatziki* here. But the best sign is the family in the back. You see them?"

I had to turn slightly, pretending I was adjusting my chair. Along the street, three tables had been pushed together to make room for a large Greek group, ranging in age from young grandchildren to a jovial, elderly grandfather. In the street beside them, a toothless old man with an accordion was squeezing out Balkan tunes in a minor key.

"It's a family celebration with *souvlaki*, barbecued lamb," Gilberto whispered. "Perhaps this is the fortieth birthday of the man in the middle, the one with his back to us. His father has invited the whole family, three generations, you see? The meat must be famous in all of Milos."

"Is *tzatziki* the only vegetarian dish you imagine is on this menu?" I asked.

"Well, there's *briam*." Gilberto nodded to a young Greek couple at yet another table. "Look at them. On their first date, perhaps. Both very shy, and he can only afford baked vegetables for the pretty girl. *Briam* is sort of like lasagna with potatoes instead of noodles. For his sake, I hope it is very, very good here."

"That's what I want to try, too. *Briam*." Then I hesitated, tapping the closed Greek menu on the table. "Are you sure you've really translated the menu right?"

"I know how to find out." Gilberto waved a waiter to our table. "Do you speak English?"

The waiter nodded. "Yes, a little."

"We'd like to order some *tzatziki,* if it is fresh."

The waiter lowered his notepad with a hurt look. "Fresh? My mother, she makes *tzatziki* every day. Every day."

"Very good." Gilberto gave me a meaningful glance. "And a bottle of red wine. I suppose the house wine is from Milos."

The waiter shook his head. "Milos has many good things. But wine? Ours is from Macedonia."

"A bottle of Macedonian, then." Gilberto handed him the menu. "For dinner, I'd like the *souvlaki.* I believe the lady would like to try something that is new for her."

I pronounced the word carefully. *"Briam?"*

"Ah!" The waiter beamed. "Our specialty. To taste it is to fall in love."

Over the *tzatziki*—which really was noticeably crisper than at the Café Aphrodite—I couldn't help thinking about how everyone seemed to be more adept at solving mysteries than I am. Gilberto could read a closed menu. Harmony had connected the break-in at my apartment to the cowboy detective. I didn't want to think about how many times Randy had pulled the wool over my eyes. Above all, the near miss with the motorboat stood out as a warning flag. If I hadn't heard Gilberto's shout, I would almost certainly have been hit. I needed to start thinking more systematically, and soon.

"If people are looking for an Einstein formula," I said aloud, "I can see why they'd break into my apartment. But why would they try to kill me?"

Gilberto refilled our glasses with the heady Macedonian red wine. "Perhaps it is dangerous, being the only one who knows a certain formula? Gravity is a powerful thing. There may be people who want its secrets left unknown."

"But I don't know a formula!" Irritated, I turned aside. A large white ferry was steaming between the harbor's breakwaters. The old man with the accordion collected a tip from the large Greek family and moved on to play at the next taverna.

"No?" Gilberto asked. "Even though it starts with an F?"

I sighed. "My great aunt only taught me half of a formula. I was a child, and it was like a game." I looked out across the harbor, thinking. Perhaps if I made public how little I knew, everyone would leave me in peace. Of course that would mean breaking my promise to Margret.

I turned to Gilberto. "You said there was a story behind the formula. How did that story get started?"

"For many years it was just a story." Gilberto tossed a bit of bread crust into the bay. Small fish snapped at the crumbs, rippling the water. "A rumor, you would say. Then, about three months ago, a retired Swiss doctor in Venice published a book. It was a memoir about his life in Switzerland in World War II. He had treated many refugees and heard stories about life in Germany under the Nazis. One of the refugees was an elderly Jewish man who said he had found the formula for quantum gravity while in Germany."

Gilberto paused to wave away a young black African man who was going from table to table, selling music CDs.

"Where in Germany?" I asked.

"No one knows. The man had been shot in the lung while escaping to Switzerland in a boat across Lake Constance at night. A woman with a baby had helped him. The old man couldn't speak much and died the next day. Before he died he told the doctor that they were smuggling the formula out of Germany in the hopes that it might help the Allies."

"A woman was with him?" I thought of Margret. She'd always said that she left Germany several years after the war, but now I wondered. "Did he say who the woman was?"

"I'm afraid not."

"What about the baby? Was it a boy or a girl?" If the woman was my great aunt, I realized the baby must have been my father.

"The doctor saw the woman for only a few minutes. She was carrying a violin case. After she left, the wounded man said she had the formula in it."

"In the violin case," I said.

"Yes. On a sheet of music for a Brahms sonata."

The waiter arrived with our plates, and for a time Gilberto dedicated himself to his *souvlaki*. My *briam*, served in a small, steaming casserole dish, was a pungent blend of Mediterranean flavors: thyme, olive oil, garlic, and oregano. As I ate I mulled the story Gilberto had told me. It helped explain why Harmony's Internet sale had aroused such widespread interest, but the story also raised new questions. If Margret really did flee Germany with an elderly Jewish man, who was he? Was she a Jewish refugee too? She'd never mentioned anything about Judaism, or any religion for that matter. It also seemed unlike Margret to abandon a wounded man.

"*Parakalo?*" An old woman with a black shawl over her head was standing beside our table, holding out a bunch of red roses and heart-shaped lollipops.

"*Efcharisto.*" Gilberto bought a rose and presented it to me with a bow of his head.

I flushed—as much from the wine and the dinner, I told myself, as from Gilberto's chivalry. Meanwhile, the old woman moved on to offer her wares to the large Greek family nearby. The grandfather in the middle of the group, with smiles and small jests, bought roses for each of the women and lollipops for each of the children. I was glad I also had a rose.

"I was ten when I last saw my father," I said, as much to myself as to Gilberto. "A child that age doesn't ask questions about family. You just take for granted that things are the way they are." I held up my rose and breathed in the sweet, somehow nostalgic perfume.

Gilberto leaned closer. "To me, it is not important if we find out the truth about the violin case. That is Dr. Nimolo's concern. I think you have a more important reason to find your father."

The closeness of Gilberto—and his sympathetic words, and the rose, and the wine—left me with a sweet confusion I hadn't felt for years. I knew I should still be on my guard, but I wasn't. I couldn't help but enjoy the feeling that this sympathetic Italian man found me attractive. What should I say to him? I was grateful when a raucous drum and a whiny Balkan clarinet gave me a distraction. "Look, more entertainers."

Two men in shabby suit coats were sauntering along the row of harbor-front tavernas, playing for tips. The toothy, dim-looking drummer whacked a snare drum at his waist with such violence that wine glasses shook. His companion blared delirious Roma tunes on his clarinet. Their shtick, apparently, was to find a likely looking patron and play the clarinet directly into one ear, and then directly into the other, while the victim grimaced and the rest of the people at the table laughed. They spotted the large Greek family and promptly aimed their din at the grandfather.

Although I could not understand his Greek, I could read from his gestures what the grandfather was saying. Grimly the old man shook his head and held both hands in the air: "No, no. Not for me." The musicians paused at the sternness of this rebuke. But then the grandfather began to crack a sly smile. He pointed across the table: "Play your music for my son instead."

At once the table erupted in laughter. The clarinetist plagued the son in one ear and then the other until he finally came up with a coin. After that the musicians played a sweeter melody while the family clapped along and the grandfather settled the bill with the waiter. A few more tunes and the family party was over. They walked happily into the night, carrying roses and singing.

The telephone rang at 8:45 the next morning—way too early for my jet-lagged brain. When I picked up the receiver, all I heard was a click and a buzz. I fumed groggily for a minute until I remembered. I had agreed to take a bus to Plaka. This was the wake-up call I'd requested from the hotel desk.

Gilberto had told me the night before that a ride on a Greek bus was an adventure I should not miss. Wearily I showered, packed, and went downstairs to meet Gilberto in the breakfast room. I ate a roll with gritty Greek coffee. Then we lugged our baggage down the street to a city park. There were rows of pollarded willow trees, reduced by years of zealous trimming to bushy, ten-foot stumps. Beside a cigarette kiosk stood an old, dusty bus labeled *ΠΛΑΚΑ*. Inside, the area around the driver's seat had been decorated with icons of saints, silver crosses, rosary beads, basketball pennants, beer logos, and snapshots—a makeshift chapel to the things the driver held dear.

We stowed the violin case, my backpack, and Gilberto's suitcase in an overhead rack. "You take the window seat," Gilberto offered. We hadn't quite sat down when the bus jolted off around a corner. I was thrown against Gilberto's chest and would have landed in the aisle, but he caught me firmly.

"Sorry!" I gasped, pulling myself away and straightening my shirt.

I blushed—not because the bus had lurched me into Gilberto's arms, but because I found myself starting to like the security of being close to him.

The bus careened through Adamas for three or four stops, collecting several old women with groceries and a clutch of squealing schoolchildren. The driver beeped his horn incessantly at cars, cats, acquaintances, almost anything. He leaned out the window to yell "*Ya*, Nico!" to a friend. Then the bus barreled out of town into what appeared to be a dead-end desert canyon. When I squinted up at the sky, I was puzzled to see distant cars clinging to the cliffs almost directly above the bus. Then the bus swung around a hairpin curve carved into the canyon wall.

"We're going up there?" I pointed up the cliff.

"All of the old cities in the islands are up high. Protection from pirates. Hang on."

The bus growled into a lower gear and climbed through switchback after switchback, often swinging the windows within a foot of the cliff face. Below, the port city of Adamas shrank to a cluster of boxes washed up along an arc of blue bay. At the top of the cliff the bus stopped to let out an old man with a newspaper, even though I could see no house for miles—just endless rocky slopes with meandering stone walls and an occasional goat. Then the bus rocketed across an uneven plateau toward a white-capped peak. I remembered from my plane trip that the white was not snow, but rather a city.

"Plaka," Gilberto said, nodding toward the hill.

When the bus reached the jumble of white buildings the driver opened his window and folded the side view mirror flat against the side of the bus. Then he shifted down and threaded the bus into an alleyway only inches wider than the bus itself. Geraniums from the houses' balconies brushed the windows on either hand. Twice the bus stopped to wait for cars to back up into side streets or garages so we could pass. Once the bus itself had to back up to let a bottle delivery truck through. Finally the bus swung to a stop in a small stone plaza, wedged between a blue-domed church and an airy precipice. When the driver set the hand brake and opened the door, three or four passengers actually clapped. I joined them, relieved that we had arrived intact. The driver acknowledged the applause with a nod. Then he began straightening the icons that framed his front window.

"All roads end at Plaka," Gilberto said. He took down my backpack and hauled out his suitcase. He led the way to the low stone wall at the edge of the cliff.

I caught my breath at the view. Left and right, the square, white-washed houses of the city clung to the crest of a cliff that crashed hundreds of feet down into a hanging valley. Olive orchards and narrow farm fields lined the slopes in stone-walled terraces. Immediately beyond, another ring of cliffs dropped a thousand feet directly into the blue Aegean.

"Which way is the monastery?" I asked.

Gilberto pulled a map from his shirt pocket. After orienting himself for a moment he pointed to a headland that jutted into the sea. "Out at the tip of the island. About seven kilometers by trail."

"Their Internet site said visiting hours are only from 11 am to 1 pm. I suppose it's too late to go there today."

He nodded. "We'll have to start tomorrow morning early. Today we need to find a place to stay. There are no hotels in Plaka, but I'm told we can find rooms."

The wheels of Gilberto's suitcase thumped on the flagstones as we zigzagged through the crooked, unmarked alleyways of Plaka, searching with increasing frustration for lodgings. After fifteen minutes we had discovered only a pottery shop, two tavernas, a jewelry store, and a pastry shop. I wasn't entirely sure I could even find these again amid the labyrinth of white walls. Finally I pointed triumphantly to a tiny placard with an arrow and the English words, *BETTYS ROOM TOILET.*

Gilberto looked puzzled. "Do you need a toilet?"

"No, the sign's been vandalized. It must mean *TO LET.* Come on." I followed the arrow up a winding stone staircase to a small courtyard where an old woman was watering geraniums. Gilberto was still clunking up the stairs with his suitcase, so I asked the woman, "Betty? Rooms to let?"

The woman shook her head. "*Okhi.* Sorry. *Domatia* full." Then her face brightened and she pointed back down the stairs. "Maria's rooms? Maria my cousin?"

"Yes, fine," I said. "I mean *nay. Nay,* Maria's rooms. OK?"

"*Kalo.* I show you." She set down her watering can and hurried down the steps past Gilberto. For the next five minutes we followed Betty as she scurried through archways and down passages. "*Orea, orea,*" she urged us on. The sun was growing hotter, and the straps of my backpack were damp with sweat.

At length we had taken so many turns that I almost suspected we were being led around in a circle—especially when we reached a vaguely similar courtyard where a vaguely similar woman was watering geraniums. But the sign here said *MARIAS ROOMS.* The two old women hugged each other, speaking Greek so rapidly that even Gilberto shook his head. Then Betty bustled back the way she had come and Maria took over, urging us up one last flight of stone stairs with the mantra, "*Orea, orea.*"

On a balcony with a bright blue wooden railing Maria opened a door beneath a stone lintel inscribed with the date *1876*. The room inside had a surprisingly high ceiling, supported by crooked wooden beams. Maria opened a window and leaned across a two-foot-thick sill to throw open blue wooden shutters. "*Orea?*" she asked. "Thirty euros?"

I nodded. It was obvious that Maria had decorated the room herself. The style, I decided, was Yaya Retro. Crocheted doilies on dark wood desks. Shelves with ceramic pots shaped like dolphins and donkeys, each with a votive candle. Framed on the wall were a gilt icon of a saint and a print of a cherub surrounded by doves. But there was also a bed and a small bathroom with a shower.

"Do you have a second room?" I asked, and just to make myself clear I pointed to Gilberto. "He can't stay in my room."

When Gilberto translated this, Maria showed us a two-room apartment in the basement, with almost no windows, for thirty-five euros. Gilberto paid for both of us for three days in advance. "Unpack, take a shower if you like. Then we can get something to eat and find the start of the trail to your father's monastery."

I took out my cell phone, flipped it open, and frowned. "I'm supposed to call my friend Harmony tonight, but there's no cell phone service here. Ask Maria if there's a public telephone or an Internet café."

As Gilberto translated this, I could see the woman shaking her head. When she had answered, Gilberto said, "No one in town has an Internet connection. There is only one public telephone. It requires a special card that you can buy only during certain hours in a post office at the edge of town."

I sighed. "My father really chose the end of the world, didn't he?"

While I washed off the day's dust with a hot shower in my room, I began to worry about what I might learn at the monastery tomorrow. I was likely to meet the man I had known only when I was a child. In those early memories Max Smyth had been tall, kind, and funny. Was he still that man?

After Mom told me he died, I had entered a dark teenage tunnel with few memories. The emotion I recalled from those black years was a burning, suppressed anger. Why had my father left me? Everyone else had a Dad. I had a hole in my heart. I blamed him for my loneliness, my awkwardness, my lack of love. He became the ogre who made my life hell. Would he be that man?

In college my father had been a ghost who followed me on every date. Paul wasn't as funny as that hazy specter. Jonathan wasn't as tall, but at least he had a blue BMW motorcycle. Randy wasn't as kind, although I didn't see that until too late. I'd been in love with a phantom all along. Would my father be that man?

Or, worst of all, would he not be there? Every other doorway into my past seemed to have slammed shut. Detectives, physicists, and possibly even assassins were littering my life with mines. If Dad told the world that the formula in the violin case was nothing more than a fairy tale, perhaps my life could return to normal. Perhaps I'd even have a father again. Dad, and only Dad, had the map I needed to safety.

Late that afternoon Gilberto and I explored the start of the hiking trail. The route led behind Plaka's church and down a long stair between precarious-looking, unmortared stone walls. A few weary tourists stood in the shade, drinking bottled water, evidently on their way back from the monastery.

"What I don't understand," I said as we ambled through an olive grove, "is how my great aunt could have gotten any of Einstein's belongings at all."

"What did she tell you about it?" Gilberto was wearing his white fedora and mirrored sunglasses in the brilliant afternoon light. With his tan features and dark hint of whiskers he looked like a caricature of an Italian Mafioso.

"Just that she'd bought Einstein's violin case. She said she went to the school where he'd taught in Switzerland. Later, when he became famous, she wanted a memento. Where would she buy something like that?"

Gilberto paused at a fork in the trail. Then he set off between the olive grove and a field of spiny weeds, following white crosses painted on rocks. "Dr. Nimolo has thought about this too. He says this is not impossible. You see, Einstein had to leave most of his belongings behind on two occasions."

"Oh?"

"Yes. The first time was 1919, when he and his first wife, Mileva Maric, were divorced."

"I didn't know he was married twice."

"The first marriage was not happy. The woman was Serbian, from a village in the Balkans. She was brilliant, but unstable. They met in 1900 while they were both studying at the polytechnic school in Zurich. Three years later they married, despite the objections of both their families. They had three children. One died young and another died in an insane asylum."

"That's terrible! Don't tell me that's why he divorced her."

"I don't know. They argued about many things. Some say she helped him with his theories. Some say she kept him from his work. In any case, when he won the Nobel Prize for physics in 1919, he divorced her and gave her the prize money."

"All of it? Nowadays a Nobel prize is worth a million dollars."

"Even then it was a huge amount. He also left Mileva many of his personal belongings. Some of them she sold. After that, Einstein married his cousin. A quiet woman with no knowledge of science."

We fell silent as we passed a pair of Japanese tourists. They were trying to photograph a lizard, but every time they set up a shot, it scurried further along a stone wall.

When we were beyond them I brought Gilberto back to the subject of Einstein. "So it sounds like 1919 is a time when my great aunt might have bought the violin case. She would have been in her late twenties then. You say there was one other likely time. When was that?"

"In 1933. The year Hitler came to power. Einstein knew the Nazis might arrest him because of his Jewish background. He was lecturing for the summer at Princeton. At the end of the summer he sent a letter to the officials in Germany saying that he was not coming back. Within days the Nazis confiscated everything in his Berlin apartment. They sold it to raise money for war."

"Even his formulas?"

"That is an interesting question. For Nazi officials, Einstein's formulas were worthless. They didn't believe his theories because he was Jewish."

I couldn't help but smile. "There's irony for you. Because the Nazi leaders didn't believe Einstein, Germany's physicists never quite managed to develop an atomic bomb—the one weapon that could have changed their war."

Gilberto tightened his lips and looked away.

I wondered if I had said something wrong. It was a little hard to read his expression behind the mirrored sunglasses. Perhaps Gilberto did not like to be reminded that physicists created the atomic bomb. He himself was a physicist.

To change the subject I asked, "Do you know where on the island the Venus de Milo statue was found?"

"I'm sorry." He shook his head. "The government refuses to say. They are afraid people would start digging. You know, to find the Aphrodite's missing arms."

"That might be easier than finding a missing father." I stopped to pick up a reddish chip from a plowed field beside the trail. Now that I looked more closely, about a third of the rocks in the field were actually bits of broken pottery—recognizable handles, lips, and bases, perhaps from wine amphorae.

"Are you looking for a marble finger?" Gilberto asked, smiling.

"Puzzle pieces," I said, tossing aside the pottery chip. "Milos seems to be full of them."

PICKING UP THE SCENT
(Harmony)

When my phone rang I rolled over with a groan and fumbled until I found the receiver. "My God, do you know how early in the morning it is?"

"Well, it's seven in the evening here." The familiar voice crackled distantly.

Quickly I sat up on one elbow. "Ana!"

"There's a ten-hour time difference, so it should be nine in the morning in Oregon. Isn't it?"

I looked at the clock radio and groaned. "Oh, man, it really is. I didn't get to sleep last night until three, worrying about everything. Jeez, Ana, are you OK? Has anybody else tried to kill you?"

"Not today. Why?"

"Didn't you get my email?"

"I'm afraid not."

"Why?"

"Uh— " Ana's voice crackled again over the line. "Harm? You won't believe how hard it is to keep in touch out here. That Internet café I found never reopened, and now we're in a village out of cell range. There's only one public phone. It took half an hour to figure it out and now it's eating up all the money I put on this card. There's a meter reading 6.2, whatever that means— no, 6.0. We'd better talk fast."

"OK, listen carefully." I was wide awake now, and my heart was beating fast. "I checked the motels in Eugene. The cowboy detective stayed at the Campus Lodge under the name of Peter Weiss. And get this: The day you left he went to Portland and caught a flight to Greece."

"Greece? Are you sure?"

"You were followed, Ana."

"Oh, shit. How could he have known where I went?"

"That's what scares me. He has some way of tracking you. I don't think that motorboat thing was an accident."

"Do you seriously think this Peter Weiss tried to kill me?"

"Yeah, I do. Ana, I'm worried."

She took a long breath. "Why would he try to kill me? It doesn't make sense."

"Maybe your father knows something you're not supposed to find out."

"Well too bad." Ana's voice switched to a resolute tone that made me marvel. "Tomorrow Gilberto and I are going out to the monastery."

"Ana, are you sure you're not trusting this Gilberto guy too much?"

"What? No, I think he's OK."

"Ana, he's not just there with you on vacation. He works for that physicist Nimolo. Who knows what they're really after?"

"I've thought about that, Harm. I think he's just helping me find out about my family." There was a pause, and the phone clicked. "Damn. Only 2.8 left. I'll try to call again tomorrow night, to your cell phone. So how did your family reunion go?"

I groaned. "Terrible. My family's getting weirder than yours. Grandma says she's going to die August 23rd."

"What? How would she know that?"

"Oh, it's a mess. She's been talking to my dead grandfather. I explained it all in the email you didn't get." The phone clicked again. In desperation I sped up. "Look, Ana, I'm flying to Florence tonight for that protest thing. I'm still planning to catch up with you next week. We'll work out the details later. Meanwhile, I thought I could go check out the violin shop in Siena to see if they know anything about the case. Siena's only an hour from Florence by train."

"Good idea. They won't have the formula for quantum gravity, but they might know if Einstein really shopped there."

"Ana, about the gravity formula—" I hesitated, knowing how strange this would sound.

The phone clicked, and an electronic voice said, "*Deka sekundi*. Ten seconds."

"Ana, could the formula be in your Dad's perfume? You know, Cloud Nine? Could it *be* the perfume?"

"I don't think—"

"Oh, Ana, take care of yourself!"

"You too, Harm—"

The line went dead. I stared at the buzzing phone in my hand as if it were a time bomb. Time was running out. We needed answers if we were going to outwit the cowboy detective. Ana didn't seem scared, but I was frightened enough for the both of us.

AGIOS NIKOLAS
(Ana)

The next morning Gilberto brought coffee and croissants to my blue-railed balcony. Over breakfast I told him everything I knew about the cowboy detective.

"This Peter Weiss sounds dangerous, with his disguises," Gilberto said.

"How did Dr. Nimolo guess I was being followed?"

"I don't know." Gilberto frowned. "I think it was just what you say—a guess."

I shook my head, dissatisfied. "We need to find my father. I want answers, and that's the only place I know to start looking."

"*Bene, signora.*" Gilberto set down his coffee and looked at his watch. "We should leave soon. Bring a hat, sunglasses, and water. I'll bring lunch and the violin case."

"Why the violin case?"

"Your father has lived at Agios Nikolas for many years. He may need help remembering the history of the Einstein case."

I nearly added: After all those years, Dad may need help remembering me. The thought gave me butterflies in my stomach. My own mental picture of my father was still shifting from shadow to shadow.

"Can you be ready in five minutes?"

I nodded. The butterflies were not going away.

Soon Gilberto and I were drifting in a platinum sky. A high haze had slid across the sun, casting the sea, air, and hills in almost indistinguishable metallic shades of silver-blue. Still, the day was so bright that we needed hats and sunglasses. A white ferry on the horizonless sea hung suspended in the air, as distant and inaccessible as the monastery, shimmering before us at the tip of the cape.

We slowed down when the trail crossed a steep slope on the cape's edge. Above us, ancient stone walls created terraces for a few gnarled, dead trees. Below, the cliff vanished into haze.

"Be careful," Gilberto warned. "The trail's narrow here."

"Don't get so far ahead." My heart sped as I threaded my way past a seemingly bottomless gap. I could have been flying above an empty sky. I breathed more easily when the trail returned to a ridge of rocky fields.

The monastery seemed to be floating, ghostlike, where the cape dissolved into sky. Our trail descended through a corridor of crooked stone walls that partitioned the tip of the cape into countless gardens of lemon trees, vineyards, and olive trees. The scent of earth, spice, and salt hung in the warm air. A thirty-foot-tall whitewashed wall enclosed the monastery itself, hiding all but the tip of a blue dome and a stone arch with two bells. There were no windows and no signs. Beside the massive wooden entrance gate stood a donkey, methodically using its teeth to strip greenery from a spiny bush.

I looked to Gilberto. "I guess you're just supposed to knock." I lifted an iron ring on the giant door and let it drop. A boom rang out like the slow beat of a giant heart.

Gradually, silence returned. The donkey continued eating.

Then a small side door opened that I had overlooked. A young man with a cylindrical black hat leaned out, sized me up and said, "Ah, good. Now we have enough for an English tour. Come in, come in."

Gilberto and I followed him into an arched foyer with an old-fashioned cash register and a rack of postcards. Half a dozen tourists stood along a wall, examining a faded fresco.

The young doorkeeper stepped to the cash register. His black robe was tied at the waist with a tasseled cord that reminded me of a curtain tieback. A heavy gold cross hung at his neck. He smiled. "So that's sixteen euros for two adults. Or do you want just the short tour to the chapel?"

"Uh, actually— " I found myself at a loss for words. How was I supposed to ask about my long-lost father? Suddenly I wasn't sure I was ready to meet him face to face at all—not without knowing more about the monastery he'd chosen as his home.

Gilberto stepped forward. "Is there an American by the name of Max Smyth in the monastery?" Gilberto was still wearing his Mafia-style fedora and sunglasses. With his Italian accent and the violin case under his arm, he really did look like an actor playing a Casa Nostra hit man.

The young monk eyed Gilberto uncertainly. "We do not use worldly names. Even tours like this are an intrusion."

"It's all right," I said quickly, trying to avoid trouble. I didn't want to be thrown out for being confrontational. The closer we came to my father, the more cautious I had become. Perhaps it would be safest to scope out the monastery before attempting contact. I laid a fifty-euro note on the counter. "We'll take the full tour. For two."

The monk made change and slid the tickets across the counter. Then he nodded toward the rectangular case. "Would you like to check your—your baggage?"

"No, it's just a violin case," Gilberto said. Then he said to me, "We'll need it when we find him."

The monk asked, "You'll want to play a tune?"

"Look, it's empty." I opened it on the counter. "See?"

"Ah. So it is." The monk raised his hands as if to say he didn't want to know more. "Very well, then. Let's get started."

We followed him to a door at the far side of the entry. There he stopped and motioned us together. "OK, today we have a couple from Holland, a family from England, a Dane, an American, and—"

"I am Italian," Gilberto said.

"Yes. So it is. Let me know if anyone has trouble understanding my English. First I'll have to ask the women to wear these." The monk handed me a towel-shaped piece of fabric with a pattern of tiny brown polka dots.

The cloth seemed large for a scarf, but I knew Catholic churches in America sometimes required women to cover their heads. Evidently my sun hat wasn't good enough. I took it off and draped the cloth over my frizzy hair.

"No, madame." The monk stopped passing out the cloths. He pointed from my head to my jeans. "It is a skirt. Women cannot wear pants in a monastery."

I reddened. My visit wasn't off to a good start. I took the apron from my head and tied it around my waist instead. The two other women gave me sympathetic looks, perhaps because they might have made the same mistake if they'd been first.

"Good. Now we will start in the cloister." The monk unlocked a door and ushered the group into a pillared arcade that surrounded a square garden. "This is where the original church on Milos was built in the first century AD, and where Saint Nicholas founded our order in the fourth century. Today it is a place where the members of our order come for reflection, or to meet and talk. Most of the outer doors lead to workshops and dormitories that are off-limits to the public. If you'll follow me to the center of the garden?"

I paused to consider the ancient wooden doors along the arcade. If one of the doors opened and my father walked out, would I recognize him? What would I say?

"This is all that remains of our earliest history, at least above ground." The tour guide was pointing to what looked like an empty, Stone Age hot tub in the middle of the courtyard. He continued, "The church that surrounded this baptismal font was destroyed by an earthquake in 311, the year before Saint Nicholas arrived. You can still see the outline of the foundations, now used as a border for the monastery's medicinal garden."

I walked behind the group to the grid of raised garden beds. Each rectangle held a different herb, labeled in Greek and Latin. I recognized mint, dandelion, and rosemary, all in bloom. It was a peaceful, beautiful place. For the first time, I could understand why my father might be attracted to such a well-ordered world, far from the trauma of cities and divorces.

Beside the garden a monk in a brown, hooded robe stood at an easel, sketching the plants and the blue-domed chapel beyond. I wondered for a moment if this could be him. But the sketch looked professional—far better than my father had ever drawn—and the monk's hood kept his face in shadow.

"This way to the chapel, please." The tour guide held open a large wooden door. I noticed that Gilberto took off his fedora and made the sign of the cross on his chest before entering. It occurred to me that he must be Roman Catholic. I envied him his faith. Church had been not been a part of my own childhood. Eugene was a secular town, far from any Bible belt. If my father had been religious when I was growing up, he had kept it to himself.

The hall inside was lit only by ranks of candles and by a circular hole at the top of the dome. Even after I removed my sunglasses, it took my eyes a while to become accustomed to the dark. The dome itself was dark blue with gold stars. The chapel had neither chairs nor pews. Instead there were wooden niches along two walls where the monks apparently stood during services. Elsewhere the walls were crowded with gilt paintings of flat-looking saints. A screen hid most of the main altar. An old woman in a black veil knelt before a smaller altar in a nook to one side. As I watched, the woman stood up and kissed the ornate silver frame of an icon on the altar.

"The miraculous icon of the Virgin Mary brings many pilgrims to the monastery each year," the tour guide told the group in a low voice. "By tradition, some crawl the last half kilometer on their hands and knees."

The old woman lit a candle, stood it in a sand-filled tray among a cluster of other tapers, and made her way past the tour group to the gate.

The English man behind me said, "The icon doesn't look miraculous."

"But it is," the monk said. "It was painted in 800 AD and then lost for a thousand years. In 1823 the abbot had a vision that an icon was buried in an undiscovered chamber of the catacombs beneath the chapel. When the monks dug where he directed, they found both the chamber and the icon. Since then the icon has helped many people. The tokens surrounding it are offerings of thanks. It is said if you offer a candle, the Virgin will answer your prayer."

Now that I looked closer, I could see that the icon's frame was actually composed of thousands of silver tokens. Some were in the shape of a heart or a baby. Others were shaped like a house or a leg. A few had Greek letters pressed into strips of silver foil.

When the tour guide moved on to the main altar, Gilberto dropped a coin in a box and took two candles from a table. He lit one and set it in the sand before the icon. Then he gave the other to me. The candlelight flickered in his gray-green eyes. "For your prayers, Ana."

I held the candle in my hand, unsure what I should do. Did Gilberto consider this a religious ceremony, or a romantic one? The thought of a closer relationship with him was both tempting and disturbing. I found myself reminded of the time Harmony had poured two glasses of my mother's wine for a toast. Was it only two weeks ago that I had said, "Here's to making our own dreams come true for a change"? Now that wish seemed narrow. I closed my eyes and thought: *Help me choose the right dream.*

When I opened my eyes and lit the candle, I could feel Gilberto watching me from the side.

"Are we still all together?" The monk craned his head to count the tour group. "I'll have to ask you to stay closer when we descend to the crypt." He took a ring of keys from a fold of his robe and unlocked a door beside the main altar. Gilberto and I joined the others filing down a dimly lit circular staircase. At the bottom, in a vaulted chamber carved from the rock, stood an elaborate gold altar flanked with stone sarcophagi. Three elderly monks with square white beards emerged from a passageway, nodded to the tour guide, and climbed the stairs behind us. I had time to study each of the faces as they passed, but was disappointed to see nothing familiar in them. Would my father have grown a beard like this, I wondered? He would be sixty-two. How old that sounded!

"The crypt of Saint Nicholas is the original entrance to the early Christian catacombs of Milos. The monastery expanded this chamber in the tenth century to house our order's greatest treasure, a relic of the saint." The young monk held out his arm to the altar. Now that I looked closer, I could see that the altar's elaborate gold rays and leaves radiated from an apple-sized glass globe. Inside the glass was what looked like a withered brown slug. With shock I realized that it was in fact a mummified human tongue.

"Crazy!" The teenage son of the English family made his first statement of the tour. "It's a piece of Santa Claus."

"*Allemal*. The original *Sinter Klaas.*" The Dutch woman leaned forward to inspect the glass globe. "How is it that children believe this saint brings them presents on December 6?"

"You mean on December 25th," the English father corrected.

"In Scandinavia, it is December 24." The Danish tourist smiled. "Perhaps it is easier for him to cover the world in stages."

The tour guide held up his hands with a patience that showed he had heard such comments before. "For 1700 years people have told of

Saint Nicholas miraculously bringing gifts to those in need. Today, I think he is sometimes helped by parents?"

The group laughed.

"Still, the saint has performed many genuine miracles over the years." The monk pointed to an icon of a long-faced man labeled *AΓIOS NIKOΛAS.* "The name Nicholas means 'one who conquers evil and does good.' The saint was born in 270 AD to wealthy parents in Patras, a Greek city on the coast of what is now Turkey. His parents died while he was studying to be a priest. Instead of using his inheritance for himself, he gave it to orphans, the unemployed, and the poor. Later he became bishop in Myra. When famine came to that city he fed the people from a single bag of wheat. Everyone ate all they wanted, and yet the bag was still full. After his death, the saint continued to appear to people in need, bringing gifts, quieting storms, and guiding the lost."

The tour guide laid his hand on one of the sarcophagi. "Here on Milos we try to follow the saint's example. We turn no one away who is in need. We give guidance to those who come seeking direction. We study and pray so that we might conquer evil and do good."

In the silence that followed, I considered that my father might have chosen this monastery because of its tradition. The monks here were used to granting refuge to people in difficult times.

Suddenly the English teenager asked, "Have you got the rest of Santa Claus in that box?"

Gilberto and the boy's parents looked shocked. The Danish tourist hid a smile.

The young monk seemed unruffled. "These boxes hold the remains of the monastery's abbots." Then he leaned forward to the boy. "I think you will be interested in the next part of the tour. We're going to the catacombs where we're still excavating skeletons."

"Crazy!" the boy said.

The monk led the way along a passageway and down a stone stair. He spoke over his shoulder, but his voice echoed in the tunnel. At the back of the group, I could understand only a few phrases. "Persecuted by the Romans . . . caves dug from a layer of soft volcanic ash . . . unlike the cemeteries of the heathens . . . members still researching . . ."

"Crazy!" An exclamation echoed up the stair.

When I emerged from the tunnel my heart nearly stopped. At the far end of the chamber, in a rectangular excavation, an old, white-bearded monk was looking up at me from a jumble of half-buried bones. It was as if he had finally stepped into the light from one of my dreams. At a glance I recognized the brown eyes, the prominent nose, the thin lips, even the look of uncertainty that haunted his wrinkled features.

"Dad?" I knelt beside the pit and looked him in the eyes. "It's me, Ana."

"Ana?" His voice was gravelly and faint. "Ana is dead."

"Is that what you thought?" I asked. "I don't know what Mom told you. She's lied to both of us. For years I thought you were dead too. That's why I've come to Milos, to try to find out the truth."

The old man dropped his archeologist's brush. "No. You can't be Ana."

"Dad! It's been twenty years. It's really me. I need to talk with you."

Most of the tourists were still clustered around the tour guide, listening to an explanation of the spread of Christianity. Gilberto, however, noticed what was happening and came up beside us.

The old man jerked his head up to look at Gilberto. "Who is this?"

"I'm a friend, Mr. Smyth," Gilberto said gently.

"No. No." The old monk shook his head. "My name is not Smyth. I am Brother Mikonos. How do I know anything you say is true?" His voice was now so loud and agitated that the tour guide turned to see what was wrong.

"Dad, please calm down." Obviously Brother Mikonos was my father, but he seemed so old and fragile that I feared for his health. His mouth stood half-open, his brown eyes narrowed. He looked so distressed that I wondered if he might really be insane.

"Brother Mikonos," Gilberto said, holding out the violin case. "Here is proof that this is your daughter. The violin case from your aunt's attic."

Suddenly Brother Mikonos' eyes went wide. "This case follows me like a curse!"

The young monk who had served as tour guide took Gilberto by the sleeve. "Perhaps we should go now, *signor*?"

"It's all right, Dad," I said, ignoring Gilberto and tour guide. "They'll take the case away. I'm sorry. We didn't know."

Brother Mikonos looked at me, his hands shaking.

I could sense my father's fear, his uncertainty, perhaps even his shame? In another moment I might be ordered to leave, and I would lose my chance to reconcile myself with him. I'd known he might not recognize me after all these years, but it still hurt. I had only one chance left, a gamble I'd planned as a last resort.

"Rags," I said. "Do you remember our dog? Will you tell me what happened to Rags?"

A calm spread over Brother Mikonos' features like a wave. He closed his eyes and put his hands on the gold cross at his neck. For a long moment he was silent. When his eyes finally opened, they had the look of a different person—the solemn man I had also known as a child, late at night when he had sat on the edge of my bed in the dark.

"Ana," he said simply.

I let out a breath of relief. "Yes. Can we talk?"

"Not now, Ana."

"Why not?"

He shook his head, and his white beard swayed. "Not here. Go."

"Dad!" Tears of frustration began to well up in my eyes. Here he was, the father I had lost for so long. The one man in the world who might have answers about my family's past. And yet I might as well have been talking to the shadowy father I'd seen in my dreams—the man who faded away if I pressed him too far.

"Please, Dad," I said, holding my voice as calm and quiet as I could. "I need you."

He took a long breath. After a moment he gave me an almost imperceptible nod. "Tomorrow. In the cloister garden. By yourself. Now go."

"But Dad—" I began, bewildered. Was he really going to send me away and make me hike to his monastery a second time?

"Tomorrow! Alone." He raised his hand toward the tour guide, who was leading Gilberto and a cluster of confused tourists up the stairs. With a voice that echoed through the catacombs, Brother Mikonos commanded, "And don't bring back that damned case!"

BURNT IN SIENA
(Harmony)

P*ericolo Del Morte!*

Signs with skulls and crossbones were riveted to each of the metal power poles my train passed, warning people in Italian: Danger of Death!

I was supposed to be preparing for the course in non-violence I would teach in the morning at the campground outside Florence. Jetlagged protesters came to these conferences from all over the planet. Students, workers, weirdos, and vagabonds—all of them united in their determination to halt corporate globalization. Perhaps only one percent of them planned to smash windows and throw rocks at policemen. In English, Spanish, and whatever Italian I could manage, I had made it my job to give training sessions for the protesters, convincing them not to pick up anything heavier than a banner or a flower.

I should have collapsed in my room at the hostel long ago. It was past midnight, Oregon time. But I was too nervous to sleep. At this very moment Ana was on a desolate Greek island with a suspicious physicist, trekking through the wilderness in search of a reclusive father, while an assassin named Weiss somehow tracked her progress. She had promised to call my cell phone in two hours. In the meantime I had decided to do the only thing I could to help: I'd taken the train to Siena to track down her violin case.

A grinning young Italian man slid into the seat opposite me. "*Scusi*, are you tourist? Please, I can help."

I covered my eyes with a hand and sighed. Before setting out from Florence I had concealed my blond hair in a dowdy bun, put on Leo's old wedding ring, and donned the frumpiest sweatshirt I owned. But in Italy, it was no use. Everywhere I went, boys, men, and even doddering grandfathers leapt up to help me with my bag, with a door, or with a train schedule. If I let them so much as touch my pack they followed me around like panting hounds. As if I needed another domineering chauvinist in my life! Leo had been more than enough. Why had I imagined that the unpossessive, honest man I wanted would hail from the land of tiramisu?

"This is your first visit to Siena, yes? I tell you the history."

I uncovered my eyes and took the measure of yet another eager, dark-eyed man. With his black silk shirt and his hair slicked up into a shiny black crest, he looked like a married electrician getting an early start on a night on the town.

"The ticket in your pocket says Poggibonsi," I pointed out. "If you stay on the train after the next stop they'll throw you off."

"Ha," he scoffed vaguely, as if brushing aside an invisible conductor. "The cafés in Siena are much better. I can show you authentic Italian coffee, yes?"

"And authentic tiramisu?"

He looked puzzled for a moment. "Or grappa? You know grappa?"

Why do women in Italy bother to wear perfume to attract men, I wondered? Certainly as a blond foreigner I seemed to exert more pull on stray males than a large moon. Perhaps Cloud Nine would have reduced my effect on these people. The few times I had tried Ana's perfume, it really had lifted my spirits without noticeably interesting men.

Of course now that I thought of the blue vial in my purse, I began to worry. If the people chasing Ana knew I had a secret formula, even in the form of a perfume, would they start chasing me?

"Siena is very beautiful, but the streets are small and confusing. I can show you the Duomo, the Campo, everything."

"Can you show me this?" From my sweatshirt pocket I unfolded a photo of Ana's violin case label.

The man's eyebrows lifted unevenly. "Uh—"

"It's from a music shop. Somewhere in Siena." By this point I had decided I could use a little backup. "My name is Harmony. What's yours?"

Alessandro was actually quite helpful in locating the music shop. The place was little more than a hole in the wall of a crooked alleyway, marked by a small sign, *Strumenti Musicali*. For some reason that Alessandro tried in vain to explain, the entire neighborhood was decorated with banners of snails.

I walked into the music store and asked the white-haired shopkeeper whether Albert Einstein had once bought a violin case there. In reply the old man reached under the counter and pulled out a pistol.

I reeled backwards in terror. Something hit my head, and the world seemed to come crashing down.

When the chaos subsided I found myself lying on the floor, surrounded by a pile of music CDs. The elderly shopkeeper hurried up and knelt beside me with a small glass of clear liquid.

"Here, drink some grappa," the old man urged me in quavering Italian. "I am so sorry to have frightened you. Your friend just turned and ran out the door — I don't know where."

"Probably to Poggibonsi." I managed a fiery sip of grappa, but the room still spun.

"*Santo cielo*. Do you think?"

I nodded grimly. So much for Italian heroes. "I don't think he'll be back."

The shopkeeper helped me to my feet. "It's just that I've had so much trouble these past two weeks. Almost every day strange men come into my shop demanding to know about Albert Einstein. Twice I've had to call the *polizia*. Now I keep a gun, but I never dreamed someone would, you know — " He waved an arm to demonstrate how I had keeled over against his rack of CDs.

"Yeah, I'm pretty amazing in a pinch." I ran my hands over my face. "Sorry abut the mess."

"Oh, this is nothing! The ones last week, these two big Italian men with accents from up north, they tore my whole shop apart."

The thought of Mafia thugs rampaging in the shop did not make me feel safer. I dreaded the question I had to ask next. But I didn't have much choice. "So did Einstein really buy a violin case here?"

The shopkeeper threw his hands up in despair. "Yes, yes of course!

This is not a big secret." He pointed to a large sign I hadn't noticed on the wall behind the cash register: *ALBERT EINSTEIN BOUGHT A VIOLIN HERE ON APRIL 9, 1898*.

"I don't know about the case," the man admitted. "I assume he bought a case, yes, but his violin, that has been the pride of our shop for a century. Of course when he was famous he had a Stradivarius, but our violin was the one he played when he did his most important work."

I unfolded the picture of the violin case label. "The case was kind of a strange shape, just rectangular, you know? Not shaped like a violin?"

He nodded. "All of ours were rectangular back then. Leather, with green plush inside. We got them from a factory in Germany."

Then the case Ana and I sold on eBay really might have belonged to Einstein. If I had known that earlier, we could have charged ten times as much. "What about the other people who came into your shop in the past two weeks? What did they do when you told them Einstein bought his violin here?"

He lifted his shoulders. "Some of them, they just went crazy. The two big men, one of them held his hand over my mouth while the other picked up every violin in the shop, looking inside like he was going to find something there. Then they took all the sheet music by Brahms— only Brahms! Why Brahms? It's enough to make an old man keep a gun behind the counter. And now all I have done is to frighten a beautiful young woman."

I put my hand on his arm. "I'm fine, really. I'm just sorry I caused you more trouble."

He took a deep breath and shook his head. Then he looked up at me. "You have a Spanish accent. Are you a tourist?"

"I'm American, actually. But yes, a tourist."

He ran a hand over his white hair and gave me a crooked leer. "Perhaps I can help you? I can close the shop. Then I can make for you authentic Sienese coffee. Right here in my private office. OK?"

Call me suspicious, but I suggested sampling Sienese coffee someplace a little more public. We ended up sitting under a café umbrella on the Campo, a vast semicircular plaza that tilts toward the town hall's bell tower. The setting sun lit the black-and-white-striped tower with a warm orange glow.

The café's tiramisu was a soggy disappointment, but the white-haired shopkeeper proved to be a gentleman after all. He sighed as he told me about his grandchildren, who refused to take an interest in his shop. "Today it's all boom boom boom from electronic music players made in China. In Einstein's day this was one of the finest shops in Tuscany."

"What happened to his violin?" I asked.

He shrugged. "I wish I knew. Perhaps then these strange men would stop—"

Suddenly the Mamas and the Papas began playing "Monday, Monday" in a chorus of electronic beeps from my purse. "Oh my God," I said, fumbling with the clasp.

"What is it?" he asked.

"It's my friend Ana."

PAY PER PET
(Ana)

As soon as Harmony and I began exchanging news of our adventures on the telephone, I knew we were going to run out of time again. I had bought a 20-euro phone card, the most expensive one available in the Plaka post office, but now the office was closed and the telephone's meter was gulping euros like candy.

Harmony applauded when I told her that I had found my father at the monastery. I gasped when she told me about the shopkeeper who pulled a gun on her. She tried again to convince me that I was being followed by the murderous cowboy detective, and I tried to explain that we had seen no sign of trouble yet in Plaka.

"Damn, we've only got a minute or two left on my phone card," I said.

"Then let me talk to Gilberto."

"To Gilberto? Why?"

"Just give him the phone," Harmony insisted.

I handed Gilberto the phone with a shrug. "She wants to talk to you."

Gilberto put the receiver to his ear. He nodded for a while, frowning. Then he said, "*Si, capisco,*" and gave the telephone back to me.

"Harmony?" I said quickly. "We're almost out of time, but I—." There was a click as the telephone's meter turned to zero, and the line went dead.

"Damn." I shook my head at the amount of money the crazy

telephone had swallowed. "Well, at least now we know the violin case probably did belong to Einstein." I looked up at Gilberto. "Why did Harmony want to talk to you, anyway?"

"She is an interesting one, this Signora Ferguson."

"What do you mean by that?" I felt a twinge of jealousy. I didn't want Harmony to be interesting. How did she manage to beguile men, even when she wasn't there?

"Your friend informs me that you are a martial arts expert. She says you will rip off both my arms if I mistreat you. I will look like the Aphrodite."

I smiled. Of course, it was Harmony who was the Aikido expert. But I saw no need to correct Gilberto.

"Is it safe for me to invite you to dinner?" Gilberto held out an arm cautiously.

I hooked my arm in his and set off through the alleyways of Plaka.

A three-year-old boy toddled across the taverna's terrace toward our table, proudly carrying a basket of bread. His little sister lugged a plastic bottle of mineral water, her tongue sticking out from the effort.

"*Efcharisto!*" Gilberto accepted the bread with a bow. I rescued the bottle of water before it could slip from the little girl's hands. The two children beamed and ran to hide behind the skirt of the waitress by the kitchen door. At a table beside the door, a grandfather was trying to entertain a whiny baby in a booster seat.

"It's cute to see them all helping out," I said.

"Seven o'clock is too early for most guests. The taverna owners are still dealing with their own family." Gilberto poured us each a glass of the carbonated water. "And what about you? Are you glad to have found your father?"

I sighed. "Yes and no. In some ways he's so familiar. In other ways he's a complete stranger." I dipped a piece of bread in a dish of olive oil and balsamic vinegar. "I guess it's hard, trying to clear up twenty years of misunderstandings. I feel like I need him more than he needs me."

"In what way?"

"I've never had much family. I'm afraid if I don't ask my father some important questions now, I'll never find answers. Like how he wound up in Oregon. And why he left." I looked across the terrace to the distant cape's cliffs, tinged with red against the evening sky. "It must be different for him, out in the monastery. The people there have become his family now. They all have a daily routine. Any uncertainties are answered by the abbot, or by prayer. My father's life there has been neatly ordered for years. Until today."

"That was my fault." Gilberto frowned. "I shouldn't have come with you."

"Nothing's your fault. Who could have guessed a violin case would upset him that way?"

I still found my father's reaction puzzling. I couldn't remember him mentioning the violin case before. To my knowledge, he had never even gone up to Margret's attic shrine where the case was kept. I wondered how much he knew about the formula.

Gilberto held up his hand. "I don't care what Dr. Nimolo says. Tomorrow, we leave the violin case behind. I'll wait outside the monastery. You go talk to your father alone. Ask him the questions you need. This is what is important now."

His tone was so sympathetic, and his words were so generous, that I was tempted to hug him. But at that moment the waitress arrived with our dinner, and Gilberto's attention shifted to the food.

"I ordered vegetarian, as you said," he centered a platter of grilled vegetables between us. "Still, this dish should have the smoky flavor of *souvlaki*. And of course, *horiatiki*. You must already know the country salad?"

I studied the salad bowl before me critically. "It's different from the Greek salads we get in Oregon. At home we crumble the feta cheese instead of leaving it in one big slab. And we always use lettuce."

"Lettuce?" Gilberto looked shocked. "How could there be lettuce? *Horiatiki* has only four vegetables. Tomatoes, cucumbers, onions, and green peppers. *Basta*."

A faint meow came from beside the table. "Oh look, it's a kitten!" I reached down to pet the skinny gray cat, but it ran away. After a few feet it turned and watched, curling its thin tail around its paws. "Here, kitty," I urged. The cat didn't move.

Gilberto smiled. "I think it is what I call pay-per-pet."

"A paper pet?"

"No, pay-per-pet. It's like pay-per-view. You know, on cable TV.

In Greece the street cats come running as soon as you are served your food. But if you want the full show, you have to pay."

"Is that allowed in a restaurant?"

Gilberto shrugged. "Usually."

"I almost wish we had some fish."

"Try some bread in olive oil. We're the first dinner guests. The cat looks hungry."

As soon as I held out a sop of bread the cat started purring loudly. While it ate, I petted its gray fur. The skinny tail stood up like a question mark. Then the bread was gone, and the cat bolted back into the shadows.

For the rest of the evening, the cat appeared only when new customers were served. I noticed that it no longer accepted bread. The cat vanished entirely after someone gave it a large fish head.

When I finished the last of the grilled zucchini, I sat back with a glass of mineral water and looked at Gilberto. I was still trying to figure him out. "You said your family was from Sardinia. That's a long ways from Trieste. Do you visit them often?"

"My parents moved to the Alps last year. I think my mother was homesick. They bought a *rifugio*, one of these small hotels in the mountains. Still I have time to visit only twice a year. Dr. Nimolo has no family, so he works most evenings and weekends in the lab. He thinks the rest of us should always be there too."

I worked up my courage and said, "That must leave very little time for a social life. Do you have a girlfriend?"

He sighed. "I had a girlfriend at the university. After I moved to Trieste, she said it was too far away. I think she's met an archeologist who works in Macerata."

"I'm sorry," I said, although I wasn't. I liked Gilberto's company, and I savored the idea that he was unattached.

"Someday, I want to make my own schedules. I want my own lab, at a university where I can teach."

"I suppose it's hard to get a position like that."

"Very hard. To get your own lab, you first have to publish a paper about important research. And the only way to do the research is to have your own lab. A person like me can never win." He shook his head and looked away.

Now I did feel sorry for him. I signaled the waitress and took out my purse to pay the bill.

Before I could take out the money, Gilberto's hand covered mine. "No, Ana. After working so many nights in Trieste, it is a pleasure to make Dr. Nimolo pay for a beautiful evening like this with you."

On the way back to our rooms, Gilberto held my hand so that I would not stumble on the dark flagstones. But how could I fall? I felt as if I were soaring through the starry streets in the company of this debonair Italian. He paused at the stairs in Maria's courtyard. For a long moment I looked up into his eyes. Then he ran his fingertips along my cheek—a thrilling, delicate stroke—and kissed me lightly on the lips.

"Good night, Ana" he said. "I hope you find everything you are looking for in Greece."

BROTHER MIKONOS
(Ana)

Although Gilberto had kissed me the night before, I was glad he didn't mention it in the morning. I needed to concentrate on what I would say when I visited my father again.

Almost in silence, Gilberto and I hiked out along the cape trail toward the monastery. I found myself constantly looking around, checking to see who else was hiking that morning. There were half a dozen tourists—mere dots in the distance, too far away to know if one were the cowboy detective in disguise.

The light was different today, with a blue sky that brought the landscape back to earth. A blinding white sun cut slate shadows from the few gnarled olive trees. Below the cliffs the blue-green sea shone like polished jade.

Gilberto stopped in the shade of a rock where the trail led past gardens toward the monastery. "I'll read a book here until you come back. Good luck, Ana."

I steadied myself with a deep breath and set out toward the portal. This time when I banged the door's iron ring, the side door opened almost at once. A monk I had not met before asked, "Miss Smyth?"

I hadn't been this nervous since I'd been called before the school principal in the third grade. That was the time I had been asked to explain why I had screamed in class. No one had understood the terror of a pencil sharpener that suddenly opened, spilling black dust on my hands. Would my father understand why I had come to Greece?

"Brother Mikonos is this way." The monk gave me an apron. Then he led me through a different door than we'd used on the tour the day before. After passing through several chambers we reached the pillared cloister. The monk bowed and retreated back through the door, leaving me alone. Ahead I could hear the echo of a familiar, low voice. When I walked along the row of stone arches I noticed two figures standing on the far side of the courtyard garden. The brown-cowled monk was at his easel again, now painting his drawing with watercolors. Beside him stood my father, in the black cylindrical hat of the Saint Nicholas order. He pointed with a trowel to the painting, saying, "Yes, or even a brighter purple. The mint should look as vibrant as it smells."

I stepped onto the gravel of the courtyard's central path. At once my father spun about, his eyes narrowed, his features tense.

"It's all right," I said, as calmly as I could. I didn't want another scene like the one yesterday in the catacombs. "It's just me, Ana. Just me."

He set down his trowel and held the cross on his necklace with both hands. Ignoring me for the moment, he walked quickly to the empty baptismal font in the center of the garden. Then he waved his arm, indicating that I should come sit in one of the sunken stone seats.

I hesitated before joining him at the font. His changes of mood worried me. When I arrived he had been calmly critiquing a painting. At the sight of me he had become a fearful stranger. When he motioned again for me to sit down, I took the plunge. And it really did seem like a plunge, this long step down into the ancient stone vessel. It was like stepping back in time to an age when Christianity was not a church at all, but rather a dangerous, secretive cult, whispering through the caves of the Aegean islands.

My father placed his hand on top of my head, closed his eyes, and muttered a prayer in a language I did not understand. When he finally opened his eyes, I saw at once that he was back. This was the calm gaze of the father I had known as a child.

"Ana," he said, lowering his hand. "I have missed you."

I leaned over and hugged him, overcome with relief. I wanted to say, "I've missed you too," but the words dissolved in tears. All I could do was bury my face in the black robes at his shoulder and sob.

Finally he held me at arm's length and wiped the tears from my cheeks with his long sleeve. "Come, I need to work in the garden. If you like, you can help and we can talk."

I nodded. The lump in my throat was still so large I could not speak.

He pointed to one of the raised beds. "We'll start by clearing the weeds out of the thyme. There's an extra trowel and apron on the bench."

I tied on the apron, glad that he had given me something to do. This was the familiar father who had organized household chores on Saturdays, assigning me to clean my room or trim the walk. With a trowel in my hand, I knelt on the other side of a raised bed from my father and set to work on the overgrown thyme between us.

After a few minutes he asked, "Did your mother ever tell you how we met?"

I shook my head.

"She'd come to buy perfume. I worked in the old Bon Marché department store in downtown Eugene. That was before the store moved out to the mall. I think I was the only man they ever hired to work the perfume counter. It's always the heart of a department store, you know. Right in front of the entrance, almost blocking the escalators. No one goes anywhere without breathing the scent of seduction."

This was not quite the story I had come to hear, but I was so happy just to be working near him, listening to his voice, exploring the past, that I nodded encouragingly.

"I was perfect for that counter," my father continued. "I had a special talent. I didn't just smell the scents, I *saw* them. Even now, although they are fainter, every scent has its own distinguishing color. Mint is purple, honey is a dusky green, and thyme is a pale yellow, like faded paper. For years I thought everyone could see the colors of scents." He paused and looked at me. "Can you?"

I shook my head. He had never told me about this ability before. But I dimly remembered him inventing a bedtime story long ago, where smells had shape.

"I'm sorry. It is a great blessing." He returned to his work. "Most people have a color too, you know. Usually it has nothing to do with the color of their skin or their hair or their clothes. It's the color of their presence, their persona. You don't exactly see it, you just know it's there." He looked into the air at nothing for a moment. Then he continued with his story. "Colors made my work at the perfume counter easy. When a pale blue woman asked which scent she should wear, I knew immediately what it had to be. Rose petals. And I was always right. No one sold as much perfume as I did. Of course I didn't care about the sales. I was just glad to make the colors come out right."

"What color do you see in me?" I asked.

"Shiny royal blue," he replied without looking up. "The exact opposite of your mother. She was a sort of smoky wine red, the color of wet leather and crushed cloves. It's a peculiar scent, really, and we didn't have it in the store when she first came in to ask my advice. I made her come back the next week so I'd have time to order several bottles and mix them at home in my laboratory. In doing that, I created my own worst temptation. When your mother wore that perfume she was irresistible to men, even to me."

I could remember the odd perfume my mother had worn when young. I hadn't really liked it, but then I wasn't a man. "I'm afraid she doesn't wear it anymore."

He sighed. "She was a beautiful woman. But so materialistic! Somehow she squeezed $50,000 out of Margret to start our own perfume shop."

"Margret paid for Scents and Sensibility?"

"Oh yes. Even the name was her idea. Your mother handled the accounts. I handled the stock. It was the 1980s and Eugene was full of hippies. Half the people who walked into the store really were the color of sandalwood and patchouli. It was easy at first, easier than at the Bon Marché. Then gradually the people changed. There were foreigners from the university and young people with colors I'd never seen before. Bright pink, lavender, khaki. I had to travel to find perfumes to match. Your mother thought I was wasting money, flying to India and Greece. Maybe I was. We argued more and more. She started taking expensive trips of her own for no reason at all. Just to get even, I suppose."

I looked down, ashamed. "She might have been seeing other men. Maybe that's why she asked you not to come back from Greece."

My father's muscles tensed. He slowly pressed his trowel down into the soft bed until only the handle stood above ground. "I knew she was dating other men. That is not why she told me to stay away."

His voice had an ominous quaver that made a chill run up my spine. Still, I couldn't stop myself from confronting him. "Then why didn't you come back? You abandoned me. What could Mom possibly have said that would make you leave your family?"

"Your mother said I was crazy. That everyone on my side of the family was crazy. That I was making you crazy too. She said doctors had warned her that you might commit suicide if I tried to contact you again."

"What! Is that why you never wrote?"

"I did write," he said, enunciating each word. He gritted his teeth and added, "The next time your mother called, she told me you were dead."

I stared at him, horrified. "How could Mom do that to us? Do you know what she told me? That you died of a heart defect. A heart defect!"

I stabbed my trowel into the dirt beside his. "*She* was the one with a defective heart! For twenty years she made each of us believe the other was dead, so she could marry someone else and do whatever she wanted. If anyone in our family is crazy, it's *her!*"

I regretted my outburst almost at once. My father's hands were trembling, and his eyes had taken on the look of a haunted man. He stood up, sat on the stone bench, and slowly rocked.

"I'm sorry," I said, sitting on the other end of the bench. I wanted to put my arm around his shoulder to comfort him, but I was afraid touching him might upset him still more. "I shouldn't have raised my voice like that. I'm angry at Mom, not at you. You probably came to the monastery to get away from that kind of stress."

My father took several long, deep breaths. His hands were still shaking, but the tension in his face began to ease. "No, don't apologize. It's important to say the unspoken things. The monastery is not meant to be a place to escape from the world, but rather to see it more clearly." He ran a hand over his face. "I have something to tell you about our family. A confession about our history. I would guess it is what you came all this way to hear."

It was, but now I wasn't sure I wanted to find out after all. I felt as if I had pushed my father to the brink of a dark edge. Maybe it was better not to know what demons were lurking down there in the shadows.

"Come closer," he said.

I scooted over on the bench, leaving only a few inches between us.

He clenched his hands before him. "Aunt Margret was not Aunt Margret."

"What do you mean?"

"Margret. She was not my aunt."

"Who was she then?"

"She was my Oma. My grandmother."

This unexpected revelation stopped me cold. "Wait. You're saying Margret was my great-grandmother? Why wouldn't she have told me that?"

"People have different ways of hiding. Especially from things inside themselves. My grandmother was trying to escape a memory. A night of fire, when I was very young. We never talked about it, of course."

"Was this when you were in Germany?"

"I suppose so. There were no words then." He closed his eyes and began rocking again. "A roar. Perhaps a house, I don't know where. I wanted my father. Grandmother held me, but I could feel her terror."

I shivered. I pictured a fire, the trapped parents, and a baby rescued by a distraught grandmother. The picture explained why Margret had fled far away, to America, trying to escape the memory. Perhaps it even explained why Margret had become a "crazy aunt." But then I remembered the story I had heard from Gilberto. In that version, a woman and a baby had been escaping Nazi Germany with an elderly Jewish man who had been shot.

I asked, "After the fire, did you leave Germany in a boat? A small boat on Lake Constance?"

"I don't remember."

"In your memory, was Margret wearing a fur coat?"

"Maybe. Yes, I think so."

I braced myself and asked the question I feared might blow up in my face. "Was she carrying the violin case?"

My father clenched his fists. "You don't know about the evil, do you? What was inside that case?"

"All I ever saw was an empty case." I chose my words carefully, afraid that a misstep might send my father lurching over the brink. "Until just a few weeks ago I didn't suspect there had been a formula inside."

My father lifted his head. "A formula!" He laughed out loud—a bitter, hard laugh.

I drew back. "You mean she didn't smuggle a formula out of Germany in the case?"

His laughter died. "Oh, she called it her formula, all right. Einstein's formula of wisdom, she used to say. But the only thing I ever saw in that case was money."

"What!"

"Gold, jewelry, coins. When we arrived in America that case was stuffed with evil. She used some of it to buy the house in Eugene. Some of it started the perfume business. Everything her money touched went wrong."

I was still trying to grasp the meaning of this news. My father had seen the case full of treasure, long ago. What had become of the money? Now that I thought about it, Margret had never worked, yet our family had never scrimped. We had lived in one of the largest houses on College Hill. "But—where did the money come from?"

"The evil of money is powerful." My father's face grew dark. "As a child I sometimes wondered if she had rescued the money from the flames instead of rescuing my parents."

I drew in my breath. I had known Margret well enough that it was impossible to picture her making such a cold-blooded choice. "No. She was a loving, wonderful woman. She might have been a victim of tragedy, but not a cause."

My father sighed. "I've come to believe this too. In the end, I tried to fight the evil. I remember being angry when she left me nothing in her will. But now I know this was a gift. She wanted me to be free of the temptation that had followed her. She led me to the lesson of Saint Nicholas."

"Is that why you chose the monastery?"

He pointed to the baptismal font. "Here I washed away the sin of greed. Here I found a haven."

I looked down. "I wish you weren't so far away. Now that we've found out about each other, you could come back to Eugene."

"This is my home, Ana. I work in the catacombs, sorting the past. I work in the garden, tending the future. This is how I hold my world together, from dust to dust. This is all I want now."

A bell chimed twice from the arch beside the chapel. My father stood up. "That is our call to prayer. I'm afraid it is time for visitors to leave."

"Already? But we've just started talking." I wasn't ready to go. Surely there were questions I had forgotten to ask. Everything I had learned about Margret and the violin case had only made me more confused. "Perhaps I could come again tomorrow?"

My father shook his head. "Let this be our good-bye, Ana."

"No!" I hugged him tightly, clutching his robe. "I won't let you abandon me again."

He let me stay like that for a long time. Gently he stroked my hair. "I've never abandoned you in my heart, Ana. All these years I've loved you, and I always will. I'll always be here. But you still have so much to do with your life. You're the one who needs to move on."

"I don't want to move on. I want you."

"I understand." He put his hands on my shoulders and looked at me from arm's length.

"Then I'll come back tomorrow?" I said.

"No, Ana, you mustn't. Not next week, not next month. Perhaps someday, after your spirit has settled."

"But—"

He shook his head, more firmly this time. "I've told you what I know. You've heard a difficult confession. You are old enough to make up your own bedtimes stories about Rags now. Please. I need my peace."

He stepped back and gave me a small bow. "May the spirit of Saint Nicholas be with you, my daughter." Then he turned to the cowled monk at the easel and said, "Brother Pietro, I'm afraid this must be the end of your visit as well. God bless."

My father walked across the courtyard and joined the procession of monks slowly filing into the chapel. With their identical black robes and cylindrical black hats, he was already indistinguishable.

I felt as if I had lost my father a second time. But there was something else about his words—something troubling that I couldn't quite place. I watched as the monks filed into the chapel. The door closed behind them. When the echo of a chant rose from inside, I sighed and began walking back across the courtyard where the cowled monk was putting his brushes away.

Was it the way this monk moved his arm as he packed his art kit?

Was it simply that I had grown more suspicious in the past weeks? Or was it that my father had said he was a visitor? Now, with a jolt of fear, I noticed that the picture on the easel did not merely show the chapel courtyard. It also depicted a young woman sitting alone on a bench. Why had he drawn me? With a sudden conviction I rushed forward and pulled back the monk's hood.

In the instant before he could turn away I recognized the young man's startled face and his dark, wiry hair. "You! The detective!"

The young man dropped his art box and bolted across the courtyard.

"Wait! Stop!" Without thinking, I ran after him.

He ducked into one of the doorways along the courtyard's arcade. It was only after I had rushed through the doorway that I paused. The unfamiliar room had three closed doors. Which way had he gone? And what would I do if I found him? Did I really want to confront the mysterious cowboy detective alone? To be sure, I wanted to find out why he had followed me here from Eugene. Who was he, behind his many disguises? Was he really the one who had almost run me down with a motorboat at Adamas? If he wanted to kill me, this remote monastery would be full of opportunities.

More cautious now, I slowly opened the middle door. Silent rows of benches and tables in the room beyond suggested that this must be the monastery's dining hall. Dust motes hung in the blue light of a single cross-shaped window of colored glass. A fly buzzed past, spiraling toward an arched stone passage. I followed it into a large, dark kitchen that smelled of smoke and sour milk. Cast-iron kettles stood before a huge tiled oven. Above a stone drain board hung a rack of knives. One of the knife rack's slots was empty.

I backed away from the kitchen, my heart beating faster. I wished Gilberto had not insisted on waiting outside the monastery. When I was back in the dining room I heard the distant clunk of a door latch. I turned with a jerk and stared into the ghostly blue shadows. Suddenly I wished that I had thought to take one of the kitchen knives myself. But something told me not to go there. Instead I ran headlong across the dining room to a different door. It opened onto a chamber with desks. Yes! This was the room I had seen on my way in that morning. With relief I hurried to the entrance hall with the familiar postcard racks. The front door was standing ajar. I stepped outside into the blazing light of the afternoon sun. If the detective had come this way, he was already out of sight.

"Gilberto!" I called. There was no answer. Where was he? I hurried past the stone walls of the gardens. When I reached the rock where he had said he'd be reading a book, there was still no sign of him. The bare rock radiated heat in the relentless sun. My shirt was already damp with sweat.

"Gilberto?" I called again.

This time I heard a distant, "Hallo, Ana!" When I shaded my eyes I could make out a figure waving a book on the far side of trail's steepest slope. "Over here!" he called. "The shade is better!"

With a sigh I set out across the slope. This was the same part of the path I had disliked the day before. Now, although I tried not to look down, I couldn't help but glimpse the waves washing along the cliffs almost directly beneath the trail. In the middle of the slope the path narrowed to a mere ledge.

Suddenly I heard a cry from above. I pressed against the rock, looking up. Far above, at the top of the slope, a stone wall was slowly crumbling. Already pebbles were bouncing loose, arcing into the sky.

"Run, Ana!" Gilberto called, hurrying toward me on the trail.

How could I run? The ledge was so narrow I could hardly edge forward. I inched ahead as if on a balance beam. A rumble above me began to grow. Small rocks hit the ledge on either side.

"Run! Now!"

I held my breath and ran toward Gilberto. Behind me an avalanche of boulders thundered down the cliff. He caught me in his arms and pulled me against the cliff face. The sea below bloomed white. A cloud of dust swirled in our faces.

I closed my eyes and held tight.

TIRAMISU FLORENTINE
(Harmony)

I love it when men cook. Ana and I have that in common. But if the man is cooking tiramisu, I'm helpless.

Tim wasn't much to look at, just a pimply *American Herald* reporter covering the mob scene on the streets outside the globalization conference. That afternoon an armored battalion of riot police had showed up out of nowhere. When, to everyone's surprise, the protesters did not respond by throwing rocks, Tim had interviewed me about what had gone right. One thing led to another, and I had ended up in his Florence apartment, coddling a glass of red wine while he fixed dessert.

"So, what is it about globalization that's so bad?" Tim asked from the kitchen. "I mean, free trade makes everything less expensive, doesn't it?"

From my sling chair in his tiny living room I could hear him whipping cream. I answered loud enough for him to hear, "Yeah, toys and underwear are cheaper if they're outsourced to China, but look at what you lose."

"What?"

"Community. Local jobs. Social justice."

He leaned out from the kitchen to look at me. "God, you're beautiful when you say that."

I ought to get mad when men talk stupid like this. But mostly I'm just embarrassed for them. I've said more than my share of stupid things myself. In Tim's case, though, I couldn't help thinking that his tiramisu had better be good. "Don't you care about local jobs?"

"Sure, I'm a journalist. I'm just lousy at sewing underwear. Who wants a job like that?"

"My parents make wooden toys on a commune in Oregon."

"Jesus Christ. Really?"

I didn't answer. Now I was pinning all my hopes on the tiramisu.

"Ta da!" Tim announced, carrying a casserole dish out of the kitchen amidst a cloud of sweet smells. "Up you go."

"Up?"

"It's a joke at my newspaper office. *Tira mi su* means 'pick me up.'" He set the dish on the coffee table, fetched dessert plates, and served up a rectangle of Italy's layered heaven.

I tasted a forkful and looked at the ceiling. Something was wrong. Something was very wrong.

"Can you guess my secret ingredient?" Tim asked.

"No. What is it?"

"Twinkies!"

"Twinkies?" I stared at him, aghast.

"Neat, huh? I found them in a supermarket by Boboli Gardens. The Italians use some sort of cookie, but Twinkies make tiramisu way moister. I layer them with cottage cheese, instant coffee, and rum. What do you think?"

I looked at my watch. "Oh my God, I just remembered."

"What is it?"

I had to think fast. A protest meeting? No, too late at night. A state dinner? Too unlikely. Better to go with the truth. "I'm expecting an important call from a friend in Greece. She really needs my help. Thanks for everything, Tim, but I'm afraid I'll have to eat and run."

It was two miles from Tim's apartment to my hostel on the Viale Michelangelo, but I was glad for the chance to get out and walk, just to clear my head. I hadn't eaten a Twinkie since the Halloween party when I was twelve. Why was I such a lousy judge of men?

In a few minutes it would be eight o'clock, the time Ana had said she'd call. The sun was dying in a disgusting orange haze, but Florence was starting to wake up for the evening *passeggiata*—the downtown parade of shoppers, diners, showoffs, and people-watchers.

As I passed the Mercato Centrale waiters were arranging fan-shaped cloth napkins in wine glasses on the sidewalk tables for dinner. Sure, there were gangs of leering Italian boys standing around with their slicked-up hair. But there were also plenty of Italian girls in short leather skirts and clonking heels to distract them long enough for me to get by.

I was just crossing the piazza in front of the Duomo, the giant red-domed cathedral, when the Mamas and the Papas beeped from my cell phone.

I punched a button. "Hey, Ana. How'd it go with your Dad?"

Ana told me about her talk in the monastery. Pretty intense stuff. I started getting alarmed when she told me about the rockslide that almost knocked her off the trail into the ocean. "Another accident? Wow, Ana, I don't think one person can be that unlucky. Even you."

"I know." Her voice sounded small and less certain. "At first I thought it must have been the cowboy detective, but now I'm not sure."

"Wait a minute." I stopped in my tracks, beside the Duomo's big square bell tower. "You've seen the cowboy detective? Peter Weiss?"

"Well, here he's been calling himself Brother Pietro. And instead of a cowboy outfit he wears a brown robe like a monk. But yeah, it's him."

"A master of disguise." I let irony drip from my voice. "Why don't you think this chameleon spy is the one who set off the rockslide?"

"Because he could have attacked me anytime he wanted. He'd been in the monastery for two days, painting a picture while I talked with my father. When I got suspicious and pulled back his hood, he ran away. Anyway, I'm not sure he could have gotten to the cliff in time."

"So who tried to kill you?" To work off my nervousness I started walking again, down a pedestrian street toward the Palazzo Vecchio, downtown's other big square tower. The little street was crowded with people. The weird thing was that most of them seemed to be talking on cell phones too.

"I don't know. It might have been another accident."

I sighed. What would it take to convince her these weren't accidents? "All right. Next point. You talked with your father while the detective was listening. The guy heard everything. What did the two of you learn?"

"A lot, really. It turns out my great aunt Margret wasn't my great aunt. She was my great-grandmother."

I whistled softly. "I'm not sure I'd want to be a direct descendant of Margret. She sounded like she was, well, at times, a fruitcake."

"Granted, she was eccentric," Ana admitted. "But I don't think all her problems were genetic. Margret might have gone off the deep end because of a shock she got in Germany."

"What kind of shock?"

"Dad says he remembers her saving him from a fire as a baby. Probably a house fire where his parents died. Margret and he survived, but it must have been traumatic."

"Ugh. Grim. I suppose she saved the violin case from the fire too?"

"Possibly. But here's the clincher. Dad doesn't remember seeing sheet music in the case. He says it was stuffed with money."

"What!" I stopped again and dropped my voice to a whisper. Although I had reached the Uffizi's piazza, and no one was close enough to hear, the arched colonnades were full of troubling shadows. "Did you say money?"

"Right. Gold, jewels. You know, treasure."

"Bizarre." I puzzled over this for a moment. "If other people know about this treasure story, that could be the real reason you're being followed. The detective thinks you're going to lead him to a treasure. That even explains why he ransacked your apartment. Now that he's heard you and your father talk, maybe he'll give up."

"Then you don't think anyone cares about the formula? All they want is treasure? If that's true, they wouldn't have any reason to kill me."

"Maybe." I set off along the Arno's riverbank promenade, the darkest part of my walk so far. "Still, Greece doesn't sound like it's a very safe place to vacation."

"You're right, Harm. I'm ready to move on. Besides, I've done all the research I can do here. Dad told me he doesn't want to talk to me for a while. He said something about letting my spirit settle first." Her voice faded.

"Ana? Are you all right?" I heard a rustle of cloth, as if she were wiping aside tears. I couldn't imagine a father shutting himself away from his only child. What a blow that must have been for Ana!

Ana's voice returned, nearly as strong as before. "Gilberto and I have to go to Trieste to report to Nimolo anyway. Maybe if we stop at Venice, you can meet us there."

"Venice? Look, Ana, maybe it would be safest if we all just went home. You've got enough material now that you can write a terrific mystery novel."

"Harmony! You were the one who said I should go looking for answers. So far all I've got are more questions. My grandparents died in a fire somewhere in Germany. My great-grandmother somehow showed up in America with a baby and a violin case full of money. If I write a shaggy dog story about that, no publisher on earth will print it."

"Yeah? And where are you going to get more answers?"

"Maybe in Venice. Gilberto said—"

"Gilberto!" I interrupted. Maybe it was the shadows along the riverbank that made me so jumpy. I should have followed the streetlights across the Ponte Vecchio, even though it was out of my way. "You're always talking about Gilberto. I don't trust him."

There was a pause. Then Anna said, "Why not?"

"For a bodyguard, he seems amazingly inept at keeping you out of trouble. Where is he now?"

"At our rooms, cooking dinner."

"Well, *buon appetito,*" I said. "Call me tomorrow. And let me know if he knows how to cook up a decent dessert."

A FORMULA FOR ROMANCE
(Ana)

When I walked back from the pay phone through the alleyways of Plaka it was that eerie hour of evening, caught between day and night, when the sky still faintly glows but the streets are dark. I shivered and walked faster. Maybe I really was taking unnecessary risks, going out alone at such a late hour.

I was glad when I saw a candle in the kitchen window of Gilberto's apartment. He answered the door with flour on his apron and an empty wine bottle in his hand.

"Welcome to *la cucina Montale.*"

I nodded toward the empty bottle. "You've already drunk all the wine?"

"But of course not. I got two bottles, one full Montalcino de Toscana for us and one empty Vino de Milos for the pasta." He closed the door behind me and began rolling out pasta dough on a flour-strewn counter, using the empty bottle as a rolling pin.

"You got an empty bottle to roll out the dough? Why not just use the full one?"

He looked at me doubtfully. "Oh, Ana. Think of the wine. How can it perform at dinner if it is dizzy? A good wine is like an athlete. It needs to rest first." He waved a floury hand toward a bottle on the table. "I uncorked it a few minutes ago to catch its breath. Perhaps you could pour us some?"

While I fetched wine glasses from the cupboard Gilberto cut the dough into thin strips. He draped the strips over his arm as if he were putting tinsel on a Christmas tree branch. Then he dropped the noodles one by one into a kettle of boiling water. "There!" he announced, pushing a button on his wristwatch. "We now have 165 seconds until dinner."

I couldn't help but smile. He was an impassioned chef, but still obviously a scientist.

"All right, let's see if we can set the table in 159." I spread a cloth on the table while Gilberto fetched the plates. Then he stuck the candle from the window into the empty wine bottle and set it in the middle of the table. When his watch beeped he forked up two platefuls of noodles. Then he poured on a simmering red vegetable sauce from a skillet and sprinkled the top with pungent green basil leaves.

"To your health," Gilberto said, clinking his glass with mine.

"And to yours." I watched him over the rim of my wine glass. He closed his eyes as he drank, the candlelight highlighting the shadows on his chin. It seemed as though I had known him for months instead of just days. In the glow of the wine I remembered Gilberto swimming in the clear water of the bay, kissing me on the apartment step, holding me on the trail. Perhaps it was the sense of danger that had stretched time and brought us closer. Even now I felt the thrill of risk, invited into his apartment for a candlelight dinner, not knowing how the evening would end. Harmony asked about my relationship with Gilberto every time she called. She said she didn't trust him. Could it be that I had actually made her jealous?

"Aren't you hungry?" he asked.

I snapped out of my reverie, blushing. "Oh! I'm starved." I wound a forkful of noodles in the sauce. Never had I tasted pasta quite like it—a blend of brilliant, clear flavors. "This is wonderful! Where did you find all the ingredients?"

Gilberto smiled. "The pasta has only three ingredients, and the sauce five. But if each is fresh, the taste should ring like church bells."

For the next few minutes I let the bells ring. When I finally sat back from my plate, I breathed a contented sigh. "That was perfect. I guess I'd forgotten to eat anything since breakfast."

"This is no surprise, on such a busy day. First you talk with your long-lost father. Then you narrowly escape a rockslide." Gilberto mopped up the last of the sauce on his plate with a piece of bread. "I am curious about your talk with Signora Ferguson. Did she instruct you to rip off my arms?"

"Possibly." I was enjoying my sudden reputation as a martial arts expert. "She thought I'd learned enough from my father that I should leave the dangers of Greece and go home."

"And what do you think?"

"I think we don't know diddly squat."

Gilberto stopped, a piece of bread halfway to his mouth. "Diddly squat? Is this something we should know?"

I smiled. "Yes. It means we don't know anything substantial. I have no idea what part of Germany my great-grandmother came from, or how she showed up in America with a treasure in a violin case. I only know half of a formula, and I've no idea what it means."

Gilberto put down his bread. "Do you think your father can tell us more about these things?"

I shook my head slowly, reminded again of the sadness and loss I had felt when my father said goodbye. "No, he made it clear that he doesn't want to talk to me again for at least a month. And to tell the truth, I'm not particularly keen on hiking out that steep trail again."

"Then if we want more answers, they are not on Milos." Gilberto stood up and walked across the room to the violin case. He flipped the latch and opened the lid. "I wish this case could talk. It has seen many things we want to know. Now I don't know where to turn."

Candlelight flickered on the case. "How about Venice?" I suggested.

"Venice?"

"Yes. Remember the Swiss doctor who wrote a memoir about the war? You said he lives in Venice. If we could talk with him, he might be able to tell us more about Margret's escape from Germany. Even knowing the precise date would help."

Gilberto looked at me sideways. "Are you suggesting that Dr. Nimolo should finance another trip?"

"It wouldn't exactly be another trip. We're supposed to go report to him in Trieste anyway. Venice could be a stop along the way."

A smile spread across Gilberto's face. "*Brava!* We tell Dr. Nimolo that the only flight we can get is to Venice. Then, before we go on to Trieste by train, we tour Venice looking for clues. I think I will enjoy this plan."

"Do you know Venice?" I had always thought of Venice as a

romantic destination, and the idea of visiting it with Gilberto gave me goose bumps.

"Ah, there is no place like it. Towers and cathedrals and palaces, all floating in the sea. A city where the laws of physics stand on their head. Just the place to track down a formula for gravity." Gilberto unfolded a sheet of music from the bottom of the violin case. "You see? I have already started."

I stared at the paper in his hand, astonished. It was a Brahms violin sonata—the same piece of music the Swiss doctor had said would be in the violin case. And the margins were in fact scribbled with mathematical formulas. "Where did you find this? It wasn't in the case when I sent it!"

"You can blame Dr. Nimolo." Gilberto chuckled. "He had me buy a copy in a music shop. He thought it might help your father's memory. Does it look familiar?"

The music didn't, but parts of the formulas did. Most of them began with an F. "Who wrote the formulas?"

"I worked on them while I was waiting for you at the airport. Quantum gravity is not a subject physicists study much, but I wanted the music to look authentic, so I made something up." He looked down. "Of course, I am no Einstein."

"Why do so many of the formulas start with an F?"

He shrugged. "F stands for force. It's the usual abbreviation for gravity. The same way that E stands for energy."

"As in $E=mc^2$?" I asked.

"Exactly. Energy is mass times the speed of light squared." He poured the last dribble of wine from the bottle and clicked my glass. "Matter is nothing more than compressed energy, waiting to be released. A simple explanation. Beautiful."

I finished my wine, thinking. "Do you think it's possible that Einstein invented something that clever about gravity?"

"It's hard to tell." He took a mechanical pencil from his pocket, drew a line across the top of the music sheet, and laid the pencil in front of me. "You know German. How would Einstein have written the words 'quantum gravity?'"

I thought about this for a moment, and then wrote *SCHWERKRAFTQUANTUM*. It was all he had asked me to do, but I could feel his curiosity. What did I have to lose by writing down the half of the formula that I knew? He was a physicist. He would know if it really might be part of an Einstein formula, or if it was just a nonsense rhyme Margret had invented. I wrote "F =" and paused. It seemed silly that Margret had made me promise to keep it secret. That was so long ago, when I was a child. Now I knew that Margret had been lying to me all along about being my great aunt. And Gilberto had been so attentive, showing me the island, ordering for me at tavernas, cooking pasta for me from scratch.

"I suppose it's getting late," Gilberto said, standing up and stacking the plates.

I dropped the pencil. "Wait!" I looked up, as startled as if I had been caught passing notes in class.

"What?" Gilberto stopped and turned.

What could I say? That I didn't want the evening to end yet? That he should grab me and whisper something seductive in my ear? I had to say something, and fast. "At least you have to let me do the dishes. That's been a rule in my family as long as I can remember. Whoever does the cooking doesn't have to wash up."

I took the plates from his hand, carried them to the sink, and started running the water. I was trying to act calm, but inside I was angry with myself. How had I managed to ruin the evening so thoroughly? Last night Gilberto had kissed me. Tonight, despite candlelight and wine, I had managed to foul things up by rambling on about the least romantic things imaginable—dead great-grandmothers and physics formulas.

I shot an angry squirt of dishwashing detergent into the sink. Maybe I should have asked my father what perfume would make me irresistible to men. My mother had been a knockout in wet leather and ground cloves. But I was the opposite—what had my father said?—a shiny royal blue. Did that mean I could have gotten Gilberto's attention with wet cloves and ground leather? Why couldn't I charm men the way Harmony did?

I had just turned off the water faucet with my fist when I felt a gentle touch at my back. Gilberto slowly slid his hands around my waist. He held me lightly from behind and whispered with his lips in the hair beside my ear, "Let's do the dishes tomorrow, Ana."

I dropped a glass into the sink with a splash. "Tomorrow?" Couldn't I think of anything better to say than that? I should throw him on the bed and tear off his shirt, but I suddenly felt paralyzed, afraid I would do something wrong yet again.

"This is our last night together in Greece." His hand slipped slowly inside my blouse, having somehow unfastened a button.

Should I pull his hand away? No! Yes. I should have worn a sexy lace bra instead of one with a strap held together by a safety pin. No! Say something quick. "Do you like royal blue?" What nonsense, but now it was too late to take it back!

"Mmm. I love blue. Tomorrow in Venice, let's get a room with a view of the Grand Canal." He nuzzled closer to my ear, caressing my earlobe with his lips.

I felt as if I were melting into a puddle of gooey dark chocolate. Had he said "a room", instead of "two rooms"? I could feel the pressure of his chest against my back, the warmth of his thighs. I lifted my dripping hands and touched them to my own blouse, where his fingers had found their way to the undersides of my breasts. "That will be wonderful, Gilberto." At last, something that made sense. "A room on the Grand Canal. Yes."

In the morning church bells rang through the sleepy Greek village. The lace curtain cast a beaded shadow across bare shoulders on the bed. The dishes were still not done. And at the top of the paper in the violin case was the penciled notation,

$$F = \frac{Gm_1m_2}{r} +$$

A REPORT TO ULM

"Are you saying the girl has left Greece?" The baroness set down her fountain pen and pulled herself straighter at the castle's writing desk.

"It seems Miss Smyth has vanished altogether, baroness," Herr Weiss replied, standing in the doorway, his hand over the mouthpiece of a portable telephone.

"Incredible. How did your son lose track of her?"

"Peter reports that he broke a rib in an altercation with two of her pursuers."

"Oh." The baroness bit her lip. "I am sorry, Herr Weiss. I shouldn't have put Peter at risk like this. Is he going to be all right?"

"He will have to wear a brace for a few weeks, baroness. He has a great deal of other news as well. Would you like to speak with him?" He held out the phone.

"Yes, of course." She took the phone. "Peter? I'm so sorry. I hope you're not in pain."

Peter's voice sounded tired. "A little, but I'm managing."

"Who are these people attacking you?"

"I don't know, baroness. They spoke German with a strong Swabian accent. Two thugs, rolling rocks down a hill at Miss Smyth. When I tried to stop them, they jumped me. After the fun was over I had to walk seven kilometers back to town."

CHAPTER 19

"Good God. You have seen a doctor?"

"Yeah, he says I'll be able to get back to my sculpture before long. But while I was in the medical clinic Miss Smyth caught a flight to Athens with this Italian person, Gilberto Montale. He seems to think she'll tell him a lost Einstein formula. All I know so far is that she didn't use her return ticket to America." Peter's voice sounded frustrated and a little desperate. "She could be anywhere by now."

"Peter, I'm beginning to suspect your interest in this Ana Smyth has become personal."

"Personal? Yeah, I'd say. After following her halfway around the world, watching her get misled and almost killed, you start to worry about her."

The baroness sighed. "This is all such a mess. And probably pointless."

"What do you mean? Have you gotten the results of the DNA test? You did have the hairs from Margret Smyth's hat analyzed, didn't you?"

"Yes, but we haven't heard anything conclusive yet. Commissioner Meyerhof is handling it for me as a personal favor. He thinks I'm wasting his time."

"You're not, baroness," Peter said. "Yesterday I overheard a conversation between Ana and her father, the monk. He told her that Margret Smyth was not his aunt, but rather his grandmother."

"Really." The baroness did not sound impressed.

"There's more. He remembered a fire in Germany when he was a baby. He thinks his parents died in a burning house, and that his grandmother Margret saved him."

Now the baroness raised her eyebrows with genuine interest. "A burning house? You don't think he was actually remembering the air raid in Ulm?"

"That's exactly what I think. He also remembered the violin case Margret took out of the country, but he said he didn't remember seeing sheet music in it. It was stuffed with money. Gold, jewels, the whole lot."

"The treasure." The baroness mused silently for a moment. "Then perhaps the baron was right. Not all of his relatives were lost in the war."

"Exactly. Instead, one of them is lost right now—and her name is

Ana Smyth." Peter lowered his voice. "I need to spend more money to go after her, baroness."

"More money?" The baroness groaned. "How do you propose to find her, with a broken rib and no idea where she's gone?"

"I haven't checked all the airlines in Athens yet. In any case, I've got a hunch she'll show up in Trieste. That's where this Gilberto Montale works."

The baroness covered her eyes with her hand. "All right, all right. Go after the girl if you can. But try not to take any more risks. And don't go sneaking around undercover anymore. If you find her, bring her here."

"To Schloss Klingenstein?"

"Yes. It's time she learned who we are."

BENVENUTO A VENEZIA
(Ana)

I called Harmony as soon as Gilberto and I left the Marco Polo International airport. She didn't answer, so I left a message that I was on the shuttle train to Venice and (at last!) back in cell range. I think my voice betrayed how much I was looking forward to seeing her again. We had a lot to talk about, especially after last night with Gilberto. Not only did our relationship look promising, but I had been relieved to learn that my half of the Einstein formula, if that's what it really was, had no value by itself.

Suddenly the rundown buildings outside my train window vanished. A beach flashed past. Then the train launched itself across open sea. Marveling, I pressed my cheek against the window. Waves crashed along the boulders of a causeway. Seagulls circled above fishing boats. Far ahead across the water a thin lavender silhouette shimmered: Venice.

"Why would anybody think to build a city out in the ocean?" I asked, almost to myself.

Gilberto leaned closer to look. "Visigoths," he said.

"What?" I flushed at his closeness and the scent of his aftershave.

"Once Italy was full of raiders. Sometimes I wonder if anything has changed." He leaned back in his cushioned seat, took out his cell phone, pressed some buttons, and began speaking rapidly in Italian.

Why is it so annoying when *other* people use cell phones? I can't understand Italian anyway, so I watched out the window as the silhouette grew. Venice didn't look nearly as romantic as I had imagined. An industrial area on one side had oil tankers and cruise ships. The largest building was a concrete cube marked with a blue *P*—evidently a parking garage for the cars that drove to Venice on the expressway beside the train tracks.

Gilberto was still on the phone, making his third call, as the train pulled into a rundown station where the tracks split into a dozen dead-end spurs. When I began wrestling my backpack down from the overhead rack, Gilberto finally folded his phone. "Here, let me get that for you."

"I can manage." I swung the pack onto my back. "Who have you been calling?"

"Calling?" He looked at me blankly.

"On your telephone."

"Oh, that." He lifted his suitcase and the violin case out of the rack. "The hotels in town are mostly full. I could only get a place on an alley near the Rialto. I also found the Swiss doctor, but he doesn't answer his phone."

"That's just great." I wondered what had become of the romantic room he had promised, overlooking the Grand Canal. Was I just imagining it, or was Gilberto cooler toward me today?

"At least we have the doctor's address," he said. "It's close enough to our hotel we can try walking there tonight."

The lobby of the Venice train station was as drab as any I'd seen in Europe. I perked up, however, when we walked out the front door. Instead of a noisy street full of car traffic, the plaza opened onto a boat canal. No trucks, no taxis, not even a bicycle. Pigeons scattered as Gilberto led the way down the plaza steps past clusters of tourists. Ahead, a footbridge arched across the canal to a crooked wall of balconied houses, standing shoulder to shoulder with a domed church.

"It'll be rush hour soon. Let's try to catch a *vaporetto.*" Gilberto hurried to a crowded railing where a bus-sized ferry was docking. "Number 13 to San Marco. It should stop at the Rialto. Come on!"

I just had time to squeeze aboard before a crewman closed a metal gate behind me and unlooped the boat's tether rope. The engine chugged and the deck canted as the boat swerved out into the canal. I nearly staggered onto the lap of a businesswoman in a pin-striped skirt. "*Scusi!*"

CHAPTER 20 ~ ANA

"Over here," Gilberto said, waving me on through the crowd on the deck. "We'll have to get out on the other side in a few stops."

Barges putted past with loads of roofing tiles, Coca-Cola cases, and garbage bags. A speedboat marked *AMBULANZA* whined past, rocking our ferry bus. Side canals opened to fleeting views of gondolas bobbing at striped posts. I wished I could get out my camera, but the boat was too crowded to take off my backpack. When I managed to make my way to Gilberto I said, "They do everything here by boat. I love it."

"It's easy to love Venice." Gilberto picked up his bags and nodded toward an elliptical footbridge arching across the Grand Canal. "Come on. This is our stop."

The dock was almost as crowded as the boat. As I pressed through, I asked Gilberto, "Is it always this busy?"

"Just at five o'clock. Every afternoon the city empties. People go back to the mainland where it's cheaper to live."

"I guess you were lucky to find a hotel at all." I was still letting go of the room he'd promised with a view. The street leading to the Rialto bridge was lined with kitschy tourist booths selling cheap watches, hand-blown glass beads, silk scarves, leather handbags, and T-shirts.

Gilberto asked directions in Italian. Then he led me down a dark side alley beside a narrow, foul-smelling canal. A cat hissed, defending a pile of discarded spaghetti it had found on the cobblestones.

Our hotel was a dingy tenement with so much stucco flaking off the walls that the few remaining patches of pink looked like a gigantic skin rash.

I might have forgiven Gilberto for all of this, but when the clerk gave him two separate keys—keys for rooms on different floors!—Gilberto handed one of them to me with a matter-of-fact tone. "Let's meet back down here in half an hour."

I felt like slapping him in the face. Had our night together in Plaka meant nothing? I didn't want to believe that his attentions had merely been a ploy. Too many people had lied to me lately.

"Did I say something wrong?" Gilberto raised both his hands, as if I were a sheriff and he were at gunpoint.

I aimed the key at him, thinking he was lucky it didn't have a trigger. "This isn't the way I pictured things last night."

His hands stayed up. "The nice hotels were full. I promised to help you find out about your family. I thought you wanted to go talk to the Swiss doctor."

"Is that it?" I demanded. "Is that all you have to say?"

"No." He lowered his hands. "I'm sorry. I care about you, Ana. Believe me, I do. Don't rip off my arms because we have separate rooms. I think it's best for now."

"You do? Well that's good, because now I definitely want my own room." Furious, I went up to my room—a dark cubicle with a single bed—and cried. Not because he'd deceived me. I didn't know what to believe. Maybe he was telling the truth. It's just that everything I did seemed to make my life more confused.

An hour later I had patched myself up well enough that I felt I could go downstairs to face him. Or maybe I'd just go find the mysterious Swiss doctor on my own. I hadn't decided.

Gilberto was sitting there in the lobby, hanging his head like a bad dog that's been told to go home. He caught sight of me and jumped up. "Ana. Please. Let me explain."

I walked past him. When he followed me outside I turned and said, "All right. I'm listening."

"I know you want to rush, Ana. Some things need to hurry, it is true. We need to find out about the violin case and your family very soon. You were followed to Greece. I worry about your safety." He shook his head. "But love? You cannot rush a relationship. It's like a flower—you cannot force it to bloom. Please, do not turn me away."

I sized him up, trying to decide whether this was an apology, an excuse, or a pledge of devotion. Maybe he was right—our relationship needed time, but our other investigations couldn't wait.

"Do you have the address of the Swiss doctor?" I asked.

He handed me a slip of paper. "Let me come with you, Ana. Please."

I let Gilberto come with me. Without talking much, we walked out to a booth by the Rialto, where he bought us slices of pizza margherita. Then, following a city map that showed more corners and blind alleys than a labyrinth, we stumbled around for twenty minutes until we found a door with five buzzers beside it. The top buzzer had a brass plate with the name "Dr. F. Wenger".

Gilberto reached for the button, but I caught his hand. "No, this is my job." I pressed the buzzer and waited.

After a long time an old man's voice crackled from a grated speaker. *"Ist da jemand?"*

I'd been hoping for German. The doctor's name suggested that he came from the northern, German-speaking part of Switzerland.

"Herr Dr. Wenger?" I asked.

There was no response. But I noticed a slight hum from the speaker that suggested he was still listening. "Dr. Wenger, this is Ana Smyth from America. I've heard about your book and was hoping I could ask you a couple of questions. It's about a violin case—"

"Nein, nein, nein!" The old man's voice interrupted angrily from the speaker. "I don't know anything about Einstein! I don't care about formulas!"

"But Dr. Wenger—"

"That's all! Now go away! Just go away!"

I sighed, disappointed. Obviously the same people who had harassed the violin shop owner in Siena had been here as well. I could hardly blame the old doctor for defending his privacy. Still, it was a letdown to come so far for this kind of rejection. The doctor really might have had some answers.

I was turning away when I noticed Gilberto silently pointing toward the speaker. Then he made a strange hand motion, as if his hand were a sock puppet trying to talk.

That's when I realized that the speaker grill was still faintly humming. The old doctor might be listening.

"Dr. Wenger, I'm the great granddaughter of the woman who took the violin case out of Germany."

The hum continued.

I added quietly, "I brought the case with me to Venice."

The speaker hummed for another few seconds. Then it squawked, "Do you have it with you now?"

"No, but it's at my hotel and I—"

"Bring it tomorrow at ten." There was a click, and the hum stopped.

CLOUD NINE
(Harmony)

Last night after Ana's call from Greece I got more and more frightened. Walking alone on the dark riverbank, I kept imagining that someone was following me. Finally I turned around, ran all the way back to the crowds at the Ponte Vecchio, and paid fifteen euros for a taxi to take me the final mile to my hostel.

Of course this morning the whole taxi thing seemed like a ridiculous waste of money. Besides, I soon had other stuff on my mind. After breakfast a whole squad of police marched through the protester's campground, clubbed a few guys randomly with nightsticks, and hauled forty people away to a makeshift concentration camp in the old fortress behind the train station. I spent all day going from one police office to another trying to find out what was going on. The media reporters were just as confused.

It didn't help that there were four different kinds of police here—the *carabinieri*, the *polizia*, the *milizia*, and some other *guardia* thing—all with different offices and different uniforms. By afternoon, however, everybody was starting to figure out that the raid on the campground was total bullshit. So the police got together and held a big press conference at the *questura*. That's the police headquarters near the university. By then everyone was talking about new demonstrations and sympathy strikes.

Of course Tim was at the press conference for the *American Herald*, and of course he interviewed me again. Then he wanted to give me a ride home.

Of course I turned him down.

So here I am again, alone, walking home through downtown Florence in the twilight. Just like last night. The déjà vu is so potent I check my cell phone to see why Ana isn't calling.

It turns out my cell phone must have been switched off during the confusion of the day. So I check my messages, and there's Ana on the train, all excited about going to see Venice. I don't know why she isn't scared, considering how often she's nearly been killed. In fact, she sounds so damn cheery that I begin to wonder how her dessert with Gilberto turned out. Maybe I'm a little jealous after my lousy evening with Tim. Anyway, I put the phone away without even trying to call her back.

By this time I've reached the colonnaded courtyard of the Uffizi, where the shadows scared me last night. Someday I've got to see the art museum here—they have an amazing room of Botticelli paintings. But there's a three-hour line and I'm running out of money. Unless I can find more Jerry Garcia pajamas to sell on eBay, I definitely shouldn't keep paying for taxis.

So I hurry through the colonnade to the riverbank promenade. Giant spotlights are trained on the Ponte Vecchio so tourists can see the old bridge's quaint shops reflected in the Arno. But the only lights on the promenade itself are dinky iron lamps every hundred feet. Bats flit across the sky. Somewhere across the river a man is laughing like a monkey. Metal jangles from the pavement behind me—maybe a bicycle tipping over. I start walking faster, and my heart speeds up.

I'm almost to the streetlight at the Ponte Alle Grazie when a man jumps out from behind a parked car and grabs my arm.

I scream.

Of course I scream. I'm scared out of my skull.

But I also duck, hook his chest beneath my shoulder, and leverage his momentum with a simple Aikido throw. The guy must weigh two hundred pounds, and with Aikido, every ounce is suddenly working against him. He lands with a thud on the curbstone.

"Jeez, are you all right?" I ask, like a nitwit. I'm too panicked to come up with anything better, much less in Italian.

Before I have the sense to run away, a second goon comes charging out of the shadows at me with a stick.

He has a big stick, yes, but bigger is not usually better in the world of Aikido. I spin to one side to let the club whoosh beside me through the air. Then all I have to do is assist, guiding his arm down to the ground, where I snap it back with a crunch.

There is another scream.

This time it's not mine.

I'd only meant to dislocate his shoulder. But from the sound of it, I've broken the dope's collarbone. "*Idioto! Stupidoso!* Look what you made me do," I sputter at him in broken Italian. This is not the kind of conflict resolution I've been teaching at the conference, and I'm pissed.

"*Scusi, donna. Scusi,*" he whimpers, clutching his shoulder.

Now I can see he's hardly twenty years old, with a crewcut and a tank-top shirt. "What the hell are you doing? You could get yourself killed, attacking women at night."

Suddenly a voice behind me stands my hair on end: "*Tengola. Andiamo!*"

I whirl around. How could I have turned my back on the first attacker? The big goon is limping as he humps away, but I can see he's carrying something in his hand. Something small and blue.

"*Scusi,*" the boy says again, running past me with his face screwed up in pain.

Then I see the remains of my purse, strewn across the pavement where the first attacker dumped it. My passport is still there, and my wallet. But the blue vial of Cloud Nine is gone.

The two muggers are staggering away with the perfume formula from Einstein's case. Perhaps it is the one thing Ana needs most. How can I stop them?

For an instant I wish Aikido wasn't just a defensive art. If I were to rush at them, I would merely be a 120-pound woman throwing myself blindly at two large, violent men. All of the advantage would be theirs. Of course I could try to provoke them into attacking me again. Then if they were stupid enough, they might land upside down on the sidewalk again.

But I can't do that either, despite all my anger. And it's not just because I'm afraid they'll pull a gun. Attacking them is not an answer. How many times have I told protesters that aggression always ends up making things worse? None of my anger, none of my outrage is going to win back Cloud Nine. Not by force, and not tonight. Nonviolence works, but it's slow, and it's never easy. At first, all you feel is defeat.

And so I lower my head, pick up my scattered belongings, and walk slowly back to the hostel, choking back tears of humiliation and fear.

DOKTOR WENGER
(Ana)

The Swiss doctor flipped the latch of the violin case, opened the lid, and lifted out the scribbled sheet of Brahms music. "So this is the Einstein formula that caused all the trouble?"

I hedged. "Actually, that's a reconstruction. The formula itself has been lost."

Dr. Wenger shot me a sharp look. "You said this was the case I saw in 1944. Were you lying?" He was surprisingly tall for a man in his eighties, with a shiny bald head and thick, black-framed glasses.

"No. The formula's gone, but I think it's the same case." I met his gaze for a moment before turning aside. The doctor's study really did overlook the Grand Canal, but the windows had hand-blown panes that distorted the boats below to ugly fish in a murky aquarium. "My great-grandmother said the case belonged to Einstein. It has his initials, and it came from the same shop in Siena where he bought a violin."

"This proves nothing. When exactly did your great-grandmother leave Germany?"

"I don't know." The doctor's questions were hitting me like blows. I wished Gilberto had come along for support, even if he couldn't speak German. "Sometime in the 1940s, I think."

The doctor closed the case. "You are lying, like all the rest."

"No!" I turned to face him. "Two days ago, in Greece, I talked to my father about it. He said he was very young when he left Germany—too young for him to speak. He remembers a terrible fire that probably killed his parents. My great-grandmother must have rescued him. She left Germany with my father, the violin case, and a fur coat."

"A fur coat?"

I nodded.

Dr. Wenger lowered himself into a red leather chair beside a desk. "I did not mention a fur coat in my book."

"The coat my great-grandmother had was knee-length, with a black collar."

The doctor motioned to the left with a finger. "Look to the side."

"Why?"

"Just do as I say! Turn your head toward the light."

I didn't trust him, so I kept an eye on him as I turned. He studied me for a moment against the window.

"Yes," he said quietly. Then he reached for a silver box on his desk. "I don't suppose you smoke?"

"No."

"Americans never do anymore." He lit a cigarette, leaned back, and blew smoke toward the shadows of the ceiling. "In the war the Red Cross actually distributed cigarettes as if they were medicine. Shameful, really."

Sensing that he'd dropped his confrontational tone, I sat down on a straight-backed chair opposite him. "You saw my great-grandmother wearing the fur coat, didn't you?"

He nodded. "You have the same haunted look in your eyes. Somehow beyond fear. It's not something one forgets."

"Tell me what happened. Please."

He fired another volley of smoke at the ceiling. "I was interning for the Red Cross in Rohrschach. It was December 18, 1944. I had to get up early to open the clinic. When the fog lifts on cold mornings like that, Lake Constance looks as flat as a sheet of steel. I remember hearing the drone of an airplane—probably a lost Allied bomber trying to get out of Germany. There was a distant popping sound, too. Nazi flak gunners across the lake in Friedrichshafen."

He tapped cigarette ash into an elegant dish made of blue-and-red glass swirls. "Every morning I dreaded finding a line at the door. Wounded pilots. Refugees who'd escaped across Lake Constance. That day there was a woman in a fur coat—your great-grandmother, I suppose. She was carrying a small child and a violin case. And there was an old man with his chest wrapped in bloody rags."

"Was my great-grandmother hurt too?"

"No, not that I could tell. She was bringing in the old man to have him treated for a gunshot wound."

"Who was he?"

Dr. Wenger shrugged. "I don't know. They must have crossed the lake together in a boat. The only name I could get from him was Ephraim. As soon as I took him into the emergency room the woman gave me a thousand-Reichsmark note and left. I never saw her again."

"What happened to the old man?"

"There wasn't much I could do. He'd been shot in the lungs, maybe twelve hours earlier. With a large-caliber police pistol, obviously at close range, so it wouldn't have been the marine patrol. He died the next day."

I drew in my breath. "Could this Ephraim have been a relative of mine? Maybe my great-grandfather?"

Dr. Wenger was already shaking his head. "The woman and the old man were entirely different. She was maybe your age, with expensive clothes and a stylish fur. Her speech, her manner—everything suggested wealth. The old man was poor. At least seventy, with a trace of a Yiddish accent and the clothes of a factory laborer. He even called her 'the Lady.'"

"Then he could talk?"

"Just a word or two at a time, and just that first day. Every syllable was an agony."

I leaned forward in my chair. "What did he say?"

A thin plume of smoke wavered as it rose from the cigarette in the doctor's hand. "He said the Lady would end the war. The fact that she had saved him from the Nazis, he said, was unimportant. The Lady was going to save everyone. She was smuggling a lost Einstein formula for quantum gravity to the Allies. The formula was in the violin case. He said it would allow the creation of a gravity bomb."

A chill ran through me. I felt I was being pulled into territory that was far too dangerous for a high school German teacher. "Did you believe him?"

"Not at the time. I wrote it off as a delusion caused by shock. Now I'm not so sure."

"What would a gravity bomb do?"

The doctor crushed the stub of his cigarette in the glass dish. "Who knows? But after seeing the effects of the atomic bomb, I don't want the world to face another of Einstein's inventions. You really don't have the formula?"

I shook my head slowly, a little frightened by the thought that I did know half of a formula—and that I had given it to Gilberto. "From what I've heard, no one believes in quantum gravity anyway."

"Who told you this?"

"A friend. A physicist."

Dr. Wenger looked at me steadily. "An old friend? Or was this someone you met recently? Perhaps since I published my book this spring? You do realize that I've been locked in this building for three months to protect myself against physicists seeking violin cases?"

I didn't answer. But a chill of terror ran through me.

By the time I left Dr. Wenger's house, I felt hunted. Fingers of fear were closing like a cold hand at my throat. I tucked the violin case tightly under my arm, but it might as well have been a bomb, ticking so loud that everyone could hear. Strangers turned to stare at me.

I hurried through the crowded labyrinth of Venetian alleyways, no longer sure if any place would be safe. Gilberto would be waiting for me where I'd left him, in a café by the Rialto bridge. But could I trust him? I really had known him only a week, and he had been strangely distant since we left Greece. If only Harmony were here! She was supposed to meet me in Venice as soon as she could get free, but she hadn't been answering my messages. Was she in trouble too?

I stopped at the near end of the Rialto's arched bridge to catch my breath. What I wanted most of all, I suddenly realized, was to unravel the mystery of my great-grandmother. Perhaps that was the key to everything. Who was this well-to-do German lady who became Margret Smyth? She had escaped to Switzerland with a baby and an elderly man named Ephraim. How difficult that must have been, at night, across Lake Constance! Why had Ephraim been shot? Why had Margret vanished after taking him to the clinic? And what was in the violin case she carried? Was it a formula on a sheet of Brahms music, as Ephraim believed? Or was it the treasure my father recalled?

I took a deep breath, forcing the fear back into a corner. Yes, I needed to square a few things with Gilberto. But then the answers I wanted were probably somewhere in Germany. I would—

Suddenly I was thrown to one side, bumped by a boy with a shaved head. A blade flashed in the sunlight and he was off, running across the bridge. Incredibly, he hadn't hurt me or the violin case. But my purse! The cut straps of my purse were flying behind him as he ran.

While I regained my balance I wanted to shout "Stop, thief!" but I was too shaken to know which language to use. Meanwhile a big, rough-looking tourist nearby shouted, *"Ach, Scheisse! Halt d'n Dreckbub da, Günther."*

To my amazement, another big German tourist at the far end of the bridge jumped out, grabbed the boy, and threw him to the ground. Then the two German men converged on the young thief and began pounding him with their fists. After what seemed like ages the boy finally scrambled away, bleeding.

The first German picked up my purse. He held it out to me, but turned his face aside.

In other circumstances I might have offered to reward a hero for rescuing my purse. But these vigilantes had been far too brutal. Is that why they were hiding their faces?

"*Danke,*" I told them.

"Ach. Nix danke. Scheisse," the man said. Then the two of them shambled away, keeping their faces down.

When I told Gilberto about the purse snatcher, he slapped his forehead.

"You had your passport in a purse on the Ponte di Rialto? Promise me, you will never do that again."

The café was starting to fill up for the midday meal. A television blared the news from a corner of the ceiling. The bartender was making me a cappuccino and a panino. I was ready for both. "Where am I supposed to keep my passport, if not in my purse?"

"In your bra. Or a pouch inside your pants. Anywhere but your purse." Gilberto was nipping on a cup of what he called *caffè corretto,* with a shot of grappa. It may have been the correct sort of coffee for Venice, but I thought it had far too much alcohol for lunch.

"What bothered me most were the men who caught the thief," I told him. "They kept trying to hide their faces. They were like—I don't know—big dumb German tourists."

"Well, we get a lot of big dumb German tourists. I'm just glad that detective hasn't followed you here from Greece. What was his name? Peter Weiss."

I frowned. "Yes. We seem to have shaken him off our trail."

"He is a dangerous one, with his disguises." Gilberto shook his head. Then he suddenly pointed to the television screen. "*Madre di dio!* The TV says *Harmony Ferguson.* Isn't that your friend?"

I looked at the television and my jaw dropped. It really was Harmony! Her mouth was moving, but I couldn't understand a word. "What on earth is Harmony doing on Italian TV?"

"She's beautiful!"

"I know, I know. But what is she saying?"

Gilberto watched her a while before he answered. "She has a strange mix of Spanish and Italian, this Harmony. *Dio mio!* She could be in the movies."

I felt myself flushing red with anger and jealousy. "Gilberto! What is she saying?"

"Oh. It seems the police have beaten up some protesters in Florence. She says they're completely innocent. And you know what? It's hard not to believe someone who looks like her."

I wanted to punch him. Of course I'd seen other men go goofy after looking at Harmony. Maybe I'd been foolish to think Gilberto would be different.

The television news switched to a soccer game. Gilberto turned to look at me. "The bus drivers have gone on a sympathy strike until the police release the protesters. The *autostrada* is blocked with checkpoints. Florence is a mess."

"I bet that's why Harmony hasn't been answering my calls." If my friend was too busy to call, she probably wouldn't be coming to Venice anytime soon. I would be on my own with Gilberto for a while.

"Ana." He said my name so earnestly that I flinched. "I know the last few days have been difficult. You have been worried. I am getting more worried too. We need to trust each other. Tell me about your meeting with Dr. Wenger. What did you learn about your family?"

At this point the bartender brought my cappuccino and panino, so I had a moment to consider how much I wanted to tell Gilberto. After a few bites I said, "I found out that my great-grandmother fled Germany with an elderly Jewish man."

"Yes, we already knew that. Who was he?"

"I don't know. He wore the clothes of a laborer, but she was wearing a fur. I wonder—"

"What?"

"My great-grandmother's fur had a label from a fashion shop in Ulm. I wonder if the shop's still there?"

"Do you remember the address?"

"Yes. We took a picture of the label before we sold the coat on eBay. It was *Bahnhofstrasse 29.*"

"Then we can check it on the Internet. If this shop still exists, I think we should go to Germany. I would like to help you find out about your family."

I set down my sandwich, surprised and a little suspicious about his offer. "I think I'd like to go to Germany."

"But first I'm afraid we have one required visit to make."

"Oh?" My suspicions increased.

"Have you forgotten? Dr. Nimolo is expecting us at the laboratory in Trieste."

STRIKE TWO
(Harmony)

"Am I the only one who thinks SMART cars are dumb?" I asked Ana, steering around Porto San Gallo's traffic circle while I held the cell phone to my ear. Apparently Ana was in some romantic café in Venice, cozying up for lunch with her boyfriend Gilberto while I jumped from crisis to crisis. "It's like driving a glass egg, you know? Except the other drivers are trying to make omelets."

"You won't believe this, Harm, but we just saw you on Italian TV."

"Yeah, here I am, trying the save the world from itself."

"Shouldn't you pull over when you're on the phone?" Ana asked. "And how did you get a car anyway?"

"I borrowed it from a bad date named Tim. Don't ask. It's just that everything's on strike until they free the protesters." A kook on a motor scooter cut in front of me, juggling a guitar, a girl, and a cell phone. A policeman stood to one side, ignored by everyone, waving a little circle-tipped baton as if he imagined he was actually conducting this circus. I headed around Porto San Gallo one more time, trying to find a good exit street.

"Are you all right?" Ana asked. "I've been worried."

I swerved off onto Viale Lavagnini, following a pointer for the train station. Trucks and mopeds loomed up through the curved windows of my little motorized egg. "Well, it hasn't been all roses. Last night a couple of guys jumped me."

"Harm!"

"The bad news is, I think I broke a collarbone."

When I heard Ana gasp, I quickly added, "One of *their* collarbones. Not mine."

"Oh. That figures. What's the good news?"

"There isn't any. They stole the bottle of Cloud Nine. I'm sorry, Ana."

"Don't worry about it. It was just perfume."

I couldn't believe her calm. "Ana! That stuff might be a coded version of the Einstein formula."

"How on earth could it—"

"I don't know. Why else would someone steal perfume and leave the rest of my purse behind?"

That stopped her. Meanwhile I hadn't been paying enough attention to the signs, so I wound up sucked into a tunnel behind the train station.

Ana asked, "Were they German?"

"Who?"

"The two guys who jumped you."

"No, Italian. Why?"

"Because I just had *my* purse stolen, and two creepy German men returned it."

I blinked as my little bubble-car emerged from the tunnel. "That's weird, Ana. And scary. I guess bad news really does come in twos." What were the odds that we'd both face purse snatchers within twenty-four hours? I wondered why her marvelous Gilberto hadn't been on hand to save her.

"Bad luck comes in threes, Harm."

"What?" I pulled onto a street to the right, trying to circle back. Another tunnel loomed ahead.

"Never mind. I talked with the Swiss doctor who mentioned the violin case in his book."

"What did you find out?"

"He really did see my great-grandmother in World War II. He said she looked like a wealthy lady. She had just escaped across Lake Constance with a baby and an old Jewish man."

"OK, so the baby would have been your father. Who was the old man?"

"I don't know. I'm thinking the answers must be in Germany, maybe in Ulm where she bought the fur coat. But first Gilberto and I have to go to Trieste."

"Oh, yeah. You promised to report to Nimolo."

"Harm, you've got to hurry up and come to Venice. We need to talk."

I pulled out of the tunnel and veered to the right, toward a cluster of flashing police lights at the back entrance to the fortress. "Haven't you heard, Ana? The railroad workers are striking in sympathy with the bus drivers. You can't even get a rental car. Until the police let the protesters go, it's gridlock all over Northern Italy. No one's going anywhere."

While policemen waved me to a stop I could vaguely hear Ana in the background, apparently talking with Gilberto.

"Harm?" Ana said. "With the strike, Gilberto thinks the only way out of Venice is by boat. There's a private ferry line to Trieste. He says we should go there tomorrow. Then you can meet us in Trieste as soon as the trains are running."

A grim-looking policeman tapped on my window with a nightstick.

"Just a sec, Ana." I cranked down the window and flashed the policeman my brightest smile. "*Ciao!* I'm with the legal defense team? For the demonstrators?"

The policeman's expression softened. "Just a security check, signora. Could you step out of the car, please?"

I unbuckled my seat belt and took off my jacket "Look, Ana? I've got to go. But you might as well take that ferry. I'm pretty sure they'll release the demonstrators by tomorrow. Then I'll meet up with you in Trieste. Just give me a call, OK?"

I folded the phone and stepped out of the car. Then I swung my ponytail and clasped my hands behind my head, giving the policeman another great smile. If there was one thing I knew how to do, it was to pass a security check. Nonviolence, I've learned, always works best.

TRYST IN TRIESTE
(Ana)

That night my father looked more worried than I had ever seen him. "Rags is missing," he said, sitting at the end of my bed.

"Missing?" For a horrible moment I thought I was still awake. I had been tossing in this bed for hours, alone in the dingy Venetian hotel room. I had listened to distant bells and fighting cats, all the time thinking about Dr. Wenger's warning, about Harmony's attackers, and about the 9 am ferry that would take Gilberto and me to a physics laboratory in Trieste.

"It's not like Rags at all. He said he'd be back two days ago." My father's face was ashen, lit by a streetlamp outside my window. I could make out every wrinkle around his eyes and every hair of his white beard. This was not the father of my childhood, I realized, but rather the anguished monk I had seen last week in Greece. How could I be sure this was a dream?

"Dad," I said, "Rags is imaginary. Real dogs don't talk. You and I made him up when I was a kid."

"Rags is older than you think, Ana. That's why I'm so worried that he's gone."

"What do you mean, 'older than I think'?"

"He's from the night of fire." My father stood up and stepped to the window. The bluish light on his robe turned him into a ghostly wizard. "There is more between heaven and earth than we were meant to know."

"Where did Rags go?" I asked.

"To find the cave of the gnomes. The Great Dane called on everyone to help. The glue that holds the world together is failing. The black dust is turning to white."

"What does that mean?"

"Time is short. Rags is lost." He looked at me, but he was already fading. "Help me, Ana. Help us all."

After a restless night I found myself on a rust-streaked ferry churning into the teeth of an Adriatic rainsquall. My romantic visit to Venice had been a disaster. That morning a storm tide had left the canals overflowing with what looked and smelled like raw sewage. Gilberto had seemed preoccupied, strengthening my doubts about our relationship. The city itself was a dismal gray maze. I was glad to leave it behind.

A tourist brochure I found on the ferry's cafeteria table made Trieste sound even less inviting—an industrial backwater, lost on the fringe of the old Iron Curtain.

"It's better than that," Gilberto said, sliding in beside me on the cafeteria bench.

"What is?"

"Trieste. Tourists never go there, but there's something genuine about it you don't find in Venice."

I looked at him. "The hotel in Venice gave me genuine nightmares."

"I'm sorry." Gilberto looked out the streaked plastic window at the gray waves. "Perhaps you won't want to stay in my apartment in Trieste. It's not fancy either."

A few days ago I would have jumped at this invitation to share his apartment. Now I wasn't so sure. If I hadn't committed myself to this visit by accepting Dr. Nimolo's trip to Greece, I wouldn't be going to Trieste at all. Gilberto and I looked out the window for a long time without speaking.

By the time the ferry sailed beyond a white lighthouse and began angling past the oil tankers in Trieste's gigantic harbor, I was thinking about the two forces that held the world together: gravity and love. Both had obviously puzzled Einstein, a man who divorced his first love and married a cousin. My own father had been drawn to my mother by mistake, apparently, because he invented the perfect perfume for her. What kind of physics attracts bodies so powerfully? Certainly, in the galaxy of love, Harmony was a supernova. Any man who strayed within her pull seemed doomed to orbit her. I know that caused her problems. But by comparison I felt like a mere asteroid, barely able to deflect the trajectories of the comets that came whizzing into, and out of, my life.

"A euro for your thoughts?" Gilberto asked.

I looked down, stalling. Finally I said, "If the taxis are still striking, I hope you have a car."

"I have an old Saab at my apartment, but we won't need it. Dr. Nimolo is sending a Mercedes to meet us."

"Sounds like we're getting the VIP treatment."

"Only for you, I'm afraid." Gilberto tightened his lips. "Before we arrive, I have something to confess."

"What?" I looked at him, a little alarmed.

"I think I gave you the wrong idea, Ana. The truth is, I'm not an important physicist. I have met Dr. Nimolo two times. Only famous scientists work with him in the cyclotron. New people like me have to work in little rooms, doing calculations. You shouldn't waste time on me, Ana. I am nobody."

The obvious sincerity behind his words began to melt through my suspicions like a warm wind through frost. "You're an important person to me, Gilberto. And you know what? I'm not a famous high school teacher either."

He smiled with relief. "Maybe someday you will be. And by then? Maybe I'll be more famous than Nimolo."

"Tell me about this Dr. Nimolo. What's he like? The one time I talked with him on the phone he sounded like a gentleman."

"Oh, he's a gentleman." Gilberto frowned slightly. "But he's very old, and he has something in his eye."

"Something In his eye? Like what?" I suspected Gilberto had missed something in his own translation.

"I don't know. When you meet him tomorrow, maybe you can tell."

Suddenly a loudspeaker started whining in Italian. People began gathering their belongings for departure. Gilberto took the violin case while I shouldered my purse. The straps were uncomfortably short since I'd had to tie the cut ends together. We joined the throng crowding down a metal staircase to the cavernous car deck. Cars and buses growled awake, puffing acrid blue clouds of exhaust. Slamming doors echoed down the metal hall. While Gilberto and I grabbed our baggage from a pile by the wall, giant hydraulic pistons began tilting up the entire prow of the ship. Seagulls screamed. The ship engines rumbled, and a froth of white water seethed up around the pilings. Then a metal apron lowered onto the dock and we joined a swarm of foot passengers surging ashore.

While Gilberto and I were walking up the dock, a long black Mercedes with tinted windows pulled alongside the parking lot's bollards. Its headlights flashed and its trunk popped open. Then a heavyset Italian man in a dark suit stepped out of the driver's door. I noticed he limped slightly.

"*Montale? Bene. Andiamo,*" the big man said.

Gilberto cast me an uncertain smile. "I guess this is our chauffeur. I'm not used to this kind of service."

"Neither am I," I said.

The driver stowed our bags in the trunk. Then he held the back door open for us. When I slid in I noticed a second man in the passenger side of the front seat. He was young, with a shaved head and sunglasses. An ill-fitting suit coat bulged over his shoulders.

The car was spacious, but I still felt confined—somehow trapped by these taciturn drivers. As we rode through Trieste Gilberto pointed out statues and pillared buildings, perhaps even an ancient Roman theater. I found it hard to pay attention. When we stopped in the parking garage of a supermarket at a modern shopping mall, the two Italian men stayed in the front seat with the engine running. Gilberto tried to win my enthusiasm about the things he was buying for dinner, but all I noticed were the empty spaces, the tiny shopping carts, and the jumble of Italian signs. Then we were back behind tinted windows, motoring through a district of ten-story concrete apartment buildings.

"Here we are, Capodistria 11," Gilberto said, fumbling with a key. "Remember to ring flat 6e if you need to get back in. The management hasn't changed my mailbox, so it still says G. Brunetti."

We rode a creaking elevator up to Gilberto's apartment, three simple rooms with a balcony facing factory smokestacks and a small church.

"The church is Slovenian orthodox," he said. "The Slovenian border is just seven kilometers away, and most of the people in the villages are Slavic."

I leaned over the railing and looked down at the laundry lines, birdcages, and lounge chairs on the balconies below. When I straightened, I noticed that my palms were black with a fine layer of soot. I closed my eyes for a moment, fighting back a dark memory. "There's dust on your balcony."

"I know. The oil refineries make the air dirty. I don't know why they built apartments in an industrial area. Until I get a promotion, it's all I can afford." Gilberto pointed to a low building near the church. "That factory was a rice processing plant before the war. The Nazis used it as an extermination center for Italian Jews. They trucked the bodies up to limestone pits in the hills near the border. It's a museum now."

Why did I go make a bed for myself on the inflatable mattress in the den? Yes, I was shaken by the black dust. Yes, I was worried about tomorrow's meeting with Dr. Nimolo. And yes, I was beginning to realize that my attraction to Gilberto had become a weak force—perhaps more physics than chemistry.

But what really bothered me was the view from Gilberto's bathroom window. Before bed I'd called Harmony and learned that the protesters were still in jail, and that the trains still were not running. Then I'd gone to wash up. On a whim I had I stood on tiptoe beside the toilet to look out the little window. Far below, still parked on the street in front of the apartment building's door, was the black Mercedes.

RESULTS FROM ULM

"Rosi who?" The Baroness von Hohensteuern paused, telephone in hand. "Oh yes, of course. Wolf's granddaughter. It's just that your voice sounds so young for a policewoman." She cleared her throat. "I understand you're marrying Dieter Braun, Klingenstein's next mayor. I suppose congratulations are in order."

"Thank you, baroness. The wedding and the election won't be until fall, but so far everything is going well."

"He's rich enough, it ought to. So why are you calling?"

The policewoman's voice faltered. "Actually, baroness, I'm calling to let you know the results of the genetic test you requested."

"Yes, I remember. The hair from the suspicious American hat. And what have you learned?" The baroness leaned back in her wheelchair, surveying the oil paintings of Hohensteuern ancestors on her office wall.

"It's not a match." The voice on the phone was curt.

"Not a match? What do you mean?"

"Just that. The DNA from the two samples is entirely different. Whoever wore that hat is not related, even distantly, to your departed husband."

"I see."

"Our database records seem to connect the American woman to a missing housewife in Böblingen, but we still don't—"

"Thank you very much." The baroness cut her short. "You needn't continue the search on my account, officer. Good-bye." She hung up the telephone, and her eyes narrowed. Then she called with a surprisingly loud voice, "Herr Weiss!"

A moment later her secretary peered in from the kitchen door, his hands in wet rubber gloves. "Yes, baroness?"

"We have been deceived."

"I beg your pardon?"

"Deceived, Herr Weiss! The hairy hat has nothing to do with our family. There are no lost Hohensteuern relatives wandering around, not in Greece or anywhere else."

"Are you certain? Peter seems confident that—"

"Nonsense!" The baroness slapped her hand on the oak telephone table. "The DNA doesn't match. If anything, this 'Margret' person appears to have been some missing housewife from Böblingen. Swindlers have been at work here, Herr Weiss."

"Yes, baroness."

"Peter's entire trip has been a colossal waste of time and money. Order him to come home at once."

The secretary lowered his head and began pulling off his gloves. "I'm afraid that may be difficult, baroness."

"What? Speak up!"

"I'm sorry, baroness, but I can't contact my son right now. He's, how do I say this? He's out of touch."

"Good God, Herr Weiss. Where on earth is Peter?"

"That's just it." The secretary lifted his shoulders. "He's gone underground."

NIMOLO'S CAVE
(Ana)

I awoke to terrible screams. Unlike the Pacific seagulls I knew from Oregon, the Adriatic things outside Gilberto's balcony did not sound like birds at all. They swooped at each other with the raucous, subhuman howls of souls in anguish—as if I were hearing echoes from the old rice factory beside the Slovenian church. While I pulled on my jeans and a short-sleeved shirt, the gulls mimicked the barks of a madhouse kennel. Then they switched to the laughs and gurgled screams of deranged Verdi tenors.

Overnight, black dust had settled on the railing where my hand had wiped it clean.

Gilberto and I finished a breakfast of bread, cheese, and coffee. Than he took the violin case and we walked outside, where the men in the black Mercedes were still waiting. To my surprise, they appeared clean-shaven and refreshed. Either they had left the apartment unguarded, or another carful of goons had spelled them.

"How much do you really know about Dr. Nimolo?" I whispered to Gilberto in the back seat of the car.

"He's probably the most famous physicist in Italy," Gilberto whispered back. Why were we whispering, I wondered?

"Nimolo was one of the co-founders of the International Center for Theoretical Physics, back in the Cold War," Gilberto continued. "He helped collect the brightest scientists from around the world. He brought them here to Trieste, on the edge of the Iron Curtain. Back then the goal was to beat the Russians in the arms race."

"Is that what you're working on now? Nuclear bombs?"

"No, no. It's all theoretical these days. I'm using string theory to project the effect of antimatter on quantum black holes."

"Really?" I didn't have a clue what he was talking about. Not a glimmer.

"I know it sounds exciting, but mostly I just do calculations."

"What does Nimolo use the cyclotron for?" I asked.

Gilberto shrugged. "That's not my specialty. It's a particle accelerator, you know. Nimolo is a genius at winning grant money. He's at the front edge of research."

"Then why is he so interested in Einstein?"

That made Gilberto tilt his head uncertainly. "I guess it's a hobby. I know he picked me to help with your trip because I speak Greek."

The Mercedes bounced on a pothole and swung uphill, onto a two-lane highway through the woods. The more I listened to Gilberto, the more I believed he was telling the truth. The problem was, I suspected he didn't know the whole story. I'd have to get that from Nimolo himself.

The car reached the top of a long hill and turned left into the first of perhaps a dozen parking lots that curved along the side of a vast, circular three-story building.

"So that's the cyclotron," I said.

"No, it's just the office building where I work. But it also serves as the entrance to the particle accelerator."

"What exactly is a particle accelerator, anyway?"

Gilberto looked at me with surprise. "You don't know?"

I shook my head.

By then our car had stopped in front of a walkway. Gilberto got out and held the door for me. As we walked toward the building, I noticed our drivers left the Mercedes at the curb and followed behind us. The larger of the two men was definitely limping.

"We call our cyclotron the *Sincrotrone*. It's a ring-shaped tunnel five kilometers in diameter." Gilberto swept his hands in a circle to suggest the tunnel beneath us. "Inside is a super-cooled vacuum pipe surrounded by liquid nitrogen. The tunnel goes through limestone rock and natural caverns almost to the border of Slovenia."

"But what does the cyclotron *do?*"

"It smashes atoms, of course." Gilberto tucked the violin case under his arm while he held open the building's door. "It accelerates protons almost to the speed of light. Then they are fired into a tank. When they hit an atom, they break apart the—how do you say?"

"The glue that holds the world together." I looked about at the foyer's curving counters and floor-to-ceiling glass windows. The building must have been daringly modern when it was built in the Cold War, but now it just looked tired and heartless. There was a low hum and a faint chemical smell, like a dry-cleaner's shop. It made me shiver.

"Exactly. The atomic bond. Then you are left with quarks." Gilberto smiled to an Asian girl in a blue suit behind the reception counter. " I need a visitor pass for a guest of Dr. Nimolo."

"He's expecting you in laboratory Z-1." The girl gave me a holographic card on a necklace. She asked to inspect my purse, looked inside, and handed it back without commenting on the cut straps.

"I've never been back as far as the Z labs," Gilberto said, clipping a photo ID badge on his shirt pocket. "It's a bit of a walk. Could I show you my office first?"

I nodded absently. "Why does Nimolo want to talk to me anyway? Haven't you already told him everything we found out about the violin case?"

"Not everything." Gilberto set off down a hallway. As we walked along, several of Gilberto's colleagues stopped to greet him. They seemed to come from all over the world—a physicist from Pakistan, a mathematician from Nigeria, a manager from Korea. Everyone spoke English, apparently the lingua franca of the physics field. The only Italian we saw was a janitor wheeling a trash bin—not counting, of course, the two men behind us from the black Mercedes. They followed us like evening shadows.

Gilberto's office was small but well lit. The place seemed surprisingly cluttered for a man so fastidious in a kitchen. Facing backwards on his desk stood a snapshot of a girl with long black hair, a pair of skis, and a fuzzy white parka. His erstwhile girlfriend from Padova, I assumed. More puzzling was a small black-and-white photograph of a balding man with jowls.

"Who's this?" I asked, nodding to the portrait.

"Oh." He put the ski girl in a desk drawer, reddening. "I haven't seen her for six months."

"No, I mean the man."

"Him?" Gilberto looked at me, apparently puzzled. "That's the Great Dane."

I opened my mouth, but could find no words. Hadn't I heard that name in a dream?

"That's what I call him anyway. Niels Bohr was the Danish physicist who explained how atoms work."

"And that's why you keep a picture of him on your desk?"

"Not just that." Gilberto hesitated. "For me, it's a reminder of the problem with my work."

"What do you mean?"

"You said it yourself, Ana, when we were in Greece."

When I shook my head to show I didn't recall, he explained. "Physics can bring many dangers. During World War II, physicists on both sides were working on an atomic bomb. Niels Bohr had an argument with his friend from Germany, Werner Heisenberg. Bohr had to choose whether to help the Nazis or leave everything behind. He left everything behind."

"*Basta, Montale. Presto!*" The gruff voice of the big Mercedes driver interrupted from the office doorway. Gilberto argued with him angrily in Italian for a moment before throwing up his hands.

"What does he want?" I asked.

"He says Dr. Nimolo is getting impatient." Gilberto stopped and looked at me. "I don't know, Ana. I have a feeling there's something wrong about this."

"You don't usually have gangsters at your door as escorts?"

'No." Gilberto lowered his head. "I feel like all I've done is take you to dangerous places. I don't really know what Nimolo wants. I just know this doesn't feel right. Maybe we shouldn't go."

I took a long, steadying breath. Fear had been building inside me all day, with the black dust, the Mercedes drivers, and the atom smasher in its cave. Knowing that Gilberto was afraid made it all the harder to stand my ground. But the closer I got to Dr. Enrico Nimolo, the more I sensed this was the heart of darkness I needed to understand. How else was I going to find answers to the terrors that had been following me?

"No," I said, picking up the violin case. "I promised I'd report to Dr. Nimolo. Let's go."

And so we walked to an elevator, accompanied more closely now by the Mercedes men. Gilberto waved his ID badge and the doors slid open. In silence we rode down five floors, past three basements, to a level marked only by a star.

In this lower hallway the hum was louder. Bare light bulbs in metal cages lit the ceiling at twenty-foot intervals. A draft ruffled my frizzy hair with the stale scent of damp cement.

"I don't even know which way the Z labs are," Gilberto admitted.

The big Mercedes driver grunted and led the way to the left. The younger man with the shaved head followed just behind us. After several turns we reached a high-ceilinged corridor with a four-foot pipe on steel trestles. Draped with icicles, giant bolts clamped the pipe's segments in place. Left and right, the pipe's corridor extended into a dim distance.

"The cyclotron." Why did saying this world out loud give me a tingle of fear?

The big Italian grunted and tilted his head to the right. We followed him in silence, walking beside the pipe for what seemed like ages. Finally we reached a closed portal with a sleepy-looking security guard in a military uniform. After checking our passes, he touched a control panel of blinking green lights and the heavy door slid aside.

Beyond the portal the corridor opened into a natural cavern as large as a gymnasium. Giant tanks, catwalks, and machinery on tracks dwarfed the pipeline ahead. Work lamps hung from the cavern's ceiling among stalactites. Limestone rock formations dripped to either side, as if a giant gluepot had exploded, spattering the walls. Everything about the place made me want to turn and run—to escape to daylight and fresh air.

"Over here, Montale!"

Dwarfed by the cavern's machinery, four elderly men in green lab coats were using an electric hoist on an overhead track to move a ponderous black container the size of a semi truck. As Gilberto and I approached, a stooped, bald man manipulated a control switch that dangled on a cable from the hoist's motor. By deftly alternating the use of a red and a black switch, he positioned the giant container beside a tall, cylindrical tank.

"*Perfetto.*" The old man turned toward us, smiling broadly and extending his hand. "Welcome to my laboratory. I am Nimolo. Enrico Nimolo."

I'll admit I'd been curious ever since Gilberto said Nimolo had "something in his eye." In fact, his eyes looked perfectly normal—light brown, surrounded by wrinkles. With a prominent nose and a small mouth, he looked like a grandfather, or perhaps a beardless gnome.

"I'm Ana Smyth," I said, shaking his hand. "Thank you for helping with my trip to Greece."

"Think nothing of it. I see Mr. Montale has preserved both you and the violin case. It is good to have young physicists on the staff. Those of us in the lower labs are—how do you say? Rather long of the teeth." Nimolo shared a chuckle with his colleagues. "May I offer you a *caffè americano* before we talk?"

When I hesitated Nimolo said, "I make it myself from a secret formula." He grinned and whispered, "Kona coast, Hawaii."

"All right, then. I'm just afraid I don't have much news about the violin case I sold you."

"Maybe more than you think." While the other scientists collected folding metal chairs Nimolo stepped to a table full of laboratory equipment. He unstacked several ceramic beakers and began filling them with black liquid from a stainless steel tank.

"What do you mean, 'more than I think?'" I accepted a beaker of the brew, but waited until Dr. Nimolo had sipped from his own before I sampled mine. It tasted good, with a transparent, wake-you-up twang.

"Well, how much have we learned about the case so far?" Nimolo began ticking off points on his fingers. "We know it came from the shop in Siena where Einstein bought his violin. We know your great-grandmother brought the case from Germany in the war."

"But I don't know who she really was, where she came from, or why she left," I put in. "Most importantly, I still don't have any proof the case belonged to Einstein at all."

Nimolo smiled. "Except for the formula."

I shot a withering glance to Gilberto. "Did you have to tell him that too?"

Gilberto winced.

"Of course he did." Nimolo said. "After all, that was Mr. Montale's assignment."

Anger and revulsion brought me to my feet. I gave Gilberto a glare that made him recoil as if slapped. "Is that what I was for you? An *assignment*?"

"No." Gilberto looked down. "Not since the first day, Ana, I swear."

I turned my glare on Nimolo. "Well, half of a bogus formula won't do you any good."

"Bogus?"

"Wrong. Made-up. The formula was a fairy tale my great-grandmother taught me as a child."

"The first half is definitely not bogus." Nimolo glanced to his colleagues and smiled. "It is Newton's law of gravitation."

"It is? Gilberto told me it was worthless by itself."

"By itself, yes. Einstein's genius is that he thinks the formula is incomplete. A second half exists. Presumably it describes gravity at the quantum level."

"Why do you want it, anyway?" I demanded. "You said yourself Einstein's work is eighty years out of date."

Nimolo touched his fingertips together. "You have to understand, Miss Smyth. In Einstein's day he did not trust his own work on quantum gravity. You see, it suggested there should be black holes."

"So? Everyone knows there are black holes." Even I knew this much. Black holes were collapsed stars or something.

"Yes. Einstein called them 'singularities.' Like everyone in his day, he thought they were physically impossible. Now we know they come in many sizes. Powerful ones in space. And microscopic ones, right here." The old scientist gestured around the room. "The Big Bang created many little black holes. Most of them did not last long. They are hard to detect because they have so much gravity that even light cannot escape. They are simply black."

"Ana," Gilberto began, "Let me—"

"Just shut up." I cut him short and turned again to Nimolo. "You still didn't tell me why you want the formula."

Nimolo held his hand out toward the cyclotron. "Ask the *Sincrotrone*. When we split atoms, energy is missing. Where does it go?"

He left the question hanging for so long that I finally asked, "Where?"

"Perhaps to create tiny black holes? We think it is the same with atomic bombs. Everywhere, nuclear tests are making miniature singularities. Gravity holes in the fabric of space-time."

Gilberto began to object, "I haven't read anything—"

"I told you to shut up." I turned to Nimolo. "What you're saying is, the glue that holds the world together is breaking up."

"*Veramente,*" Nimolo said. "Unless we do something, gravity could reach a critical point. Then space and time collapse. That is why we need the entire formula. If we understand how gravity works, we can control a singularity." He pointed to the container dangling from the hoist. "This device is designed to hold a stable black hole, where we can study it."

Gilberto looked amazed. "A stable black hole?"

Nimolo nodded. "Do you know what that means? We can repair the damage to space-time, yes. But a black hole is also a portal to another universe. It is a door into time itself. Inside our laboratory we will have the key."

The old man squinted at me with his right eye. "Miss Smyth, we need your help. Look at us. Dr. Kockler and I were students in Heisenberg's laboratory when the Allies beat us to the atomic bomb. Dr. Yevshenko and Dr. Kaczinsky were forced to work for the Russians, always a step behind the Americans. I helped them to escape, to give them another hope. Now people call us the Immortals, but we are old. Quantum gravity is our chance to change the world of physics."

Although much of Nimolo's jargon had gone over my head, I did understand two things: He wanted to keep the universe intact, and he wanted to win yet more fame for himself. The problem was that Nimolo's boastful tone had set off warning sirens in my head. How much of what he'd told me was true? Despite the way Gilberto had treated me, I turned to him for a second opinion. "What do you think?"

Gilberto threw up his hands. "I think I don't work for Dr. Nimolo anymore."

"Why?"

"Dr. Nimolo is famous. But Ana, I've never heard of this damage to space-time. The danger I see is trying to put a black hole inside a box. Then I think there are several possibilities. If the black hole is large, it might swallow the box and then the whole world. If it's small, it might collapse. The explosion could destroy everything."

Nimolo looked at him evenly with his left eye. "Yes, we know these risks. But what is the alternative? To let gravity fail?" He turned to me. "This is why, Miss Smyth, I am making you another offer. It is like the first one, but more important."

"What's your offer?" I was trusting him less all the time.

"Your great-grandmother came from Germany. I can help you discover your past. I will pay for your trip, and for a guide, if you tell me what you learn. All I need is the second half of the formula."

"No," I said, making up my mind. "I don't know where the second half of the formula is, but I wouldn't give it to you if I did. And I'm certainly not trusting another of your guides."

"*Bene, signora,*" Nimolo said in a low voice. "Then I have other ways."

He snapped his fingers. The drivers of the black Mercedes pulled pistols from their suitcoats. They aimed the muzzles at Gilberto and me.

Gilberto covered his eyes with his hands. "*Dio mio.*"

"Dr. Nimolo?" I asked. "How is this helping?"

He stood up and faced me directly. There really was something unsettling about his gaze. A slight squint made his right eye smaller than his left.

"Miss Smyth, I think you need to join us in the Hall of the Immortals."

For a terrifying moment I thought he was about to order the gunmen to kill us. Instead he motioned us forward. The gun barrels prodded us toward a doorway in the rock wall. Nimolo waved his hand. When nothing happened, he kicked the door and it slid aside. In the smaller cavern beyond, spotlights revealed glass cases along the rough limestone walls.

"This is our window onto the world of genius." Nimolo spread out his palms. "Now do you understand? Here is Heisenberg's typewriter. Newton's rocking chair. Einstein's childhood shoes. And here—" he took the violin case from Gilberto, "is a table reserved for the case of Einstein's violin."

He was insane. If I hadn't been certain before, I knew it as soon as I saw the altar to Einstein. I wished I were back in Margret's attic, playing out one of her harmless fantasies in front of her tinfoil shrine.

"Do you have anything of Niels Bohr's?" Gilberto asked.

"The Danish traitor?" Nimolo scoffed.

At this point I noticed a surprisingly familiar blue bottle on a glass counter. I picked it up, bewildered. "This is my bottle of Cloud Nine." Suddenly my fear gave way to a searing flame of anger. I glared at Nimolo. "You had someone attack my friend to steal it!"

He lifted his shoulders. "You don't understand what it is."

"It's my father's perfume."

"And who is your father? A monk, I suppose?"

"Yes, he is."

"Where did he go to school?"

The question stopped me.

Nimolo laughed. "Maximilian Smyth spent two terms studying astrophysics at CalTech in 1967. Did you know that?"

I shook my head, taken aback. Why hadn't I been told he'd studied science?

"Before your father flunked out, he was arrested for leading an anti-Vietnam protest."

"How do you know this?"

"School records. Police reports. I had my people check. Your father transferred to a Christian college in Eugene for six weeks. Then he quit and built his own laboratory. Cloud Nine may be more than it seems."

"Like what?"

"Perhaps the trigger for a gravity bomb? I'm having it analyzed to find out."

"No you're not." I held up the bottle, about to throw it against the wall.

"No dramatics, please, Miss Smyth." Nimolo nodded to the younger of the two men with guns. "Take it from her."

As the young guard reached up for the vial, I noticed him wince slightly. Suddenly I realized this must have been Harmony's attacker—the man whose collarbone she'd broken. Sensing an opportunity, I swung my arm down onto his shoulder.

The young man crumpled to the ground with a groan.

Gilberto looked at me wide-eyed. "*Dio!* You really must have a black belt."

"No, I'm just angry." I slung my purse at the other guard's hand and sent his pistol flying into a glass case. Then I ran for the door.

"Stop her!" Nimolo commanded.

Before I was halfway across the main cavern the guard at the portal woke up enough to draw a large gun.

"Oh, shit." I panicked, changing direction. I headed toward a tank as cover. Along the way the hoist's control cable practically hit me in the head. I grabbed it, trying to swing to safety, but of course that maneuver didn't work. All I did was flip the switch, starting a motor overhead. Meanwhile a bullet slammed into the tank beside me with a bang. Liquid spurted from the hole.

"Don't use firearms in the lab!" a scientist in a green coat shouted. "You've hit the nitrogen tank. Shut off the valve."

By this time the big Mercedes driver had limped up to join the chase, but now instead of going after me he reached down toward a valve at the bottom of the tank. As he knelt, a spurt of the liquid splashed a white streak across the back of his suit coat. Suddenly the big man arched backwards with a horrific cry. He vaulted onto the floor, clawing at his clothes with curled fingers.

Overhead, the hoist rumbled forward, moving the truck-sized container toward the tank and the cyclotron beyond. One of the elderly scientists fumbled with the dangling control switch. "It doesn't work. It seems to be jammed with ice."

Everyone stopped as the giant container clanged against the tank. The big cylinder tilted slowly to one side, leaking a fog of liquid down a seam.

"Get out of the lab!" Gilberto cried. "Everyone, out!"

Before we could reach the portal the tank tipped loose and burst. A wave spilled across the floor behind us with a deafening hiss. Icy fog roared up the corridor, surrounding everyone in a freezing blizzard.

Amid the shouts I heard Gilberto somewhere to one side calling, "Ana? Ana?"

"Don't let her escape!" Nimolo's voice came from behind.

"The *Sincrotrone!*" another voice cried.

I ran blindly onward, gasping for breath in the cold wind. Twice I slipped and fell on icy dust. Then I noticed the gray outline of the cyclotron's supports and I ran on, following them. Finally the freezing fog thinned, but I was hopelessly lost. Hallways seemed to branch off in all directions. The voices behind me were growing louder. Which way should I turn?

"This way!"

I looked down the largest hall and saw the Italian janitor holding a door open with his trash bin. "What's in there?" I asked.

"Rags."

"What?" I stared at him, confused. How could anyone but my father know about my imaginary dog? Despite the janitor's unfamiliar black hair, large nose, and black-rimmed glasses, I wasn't entirely sure I hadn't met him somewhere before.

"Hurry!"

I followed the janitor through the door just as another blast of cold wind swept down the hall.

When the door clicked behind us it was suddenly so dark and quiet that it took me a minute to sense what kind of place I was in. The air had the sweet, clean smell of soap. The room was so small that I could feel shelves on two sides.

"Where am I?" I whispered, uncertain who or what would answer.

"In the janitor's closet," the man's voice replied, but without as much of an Italian lilt as I had heard at first. "Put these rags under the door to stop the ice. Where is it coming from, anyway?"

"A liquid nitrogen tank I knocked over." I felt towels pushed into my hands. The only light came from a crack below the door, where white dust was blowing in. As I stuffed the rags into the crack, blocking both the ice and the last remaining light, I said, "Thanks for helping me hide. By now half the people in the building are probably after me."

"I was afraid of that." His voice was low, but changing in a disturbing way.

"You were?" I stared into the darkness, trying in vain to see his face. "Who are you?"

"First we should talk about who *you* are." The man's voice now had lost all of its Italian tone. What remained was a semi-British accent I remembered only too well.

I reached frantically for the door handle. But I didn't dare go outside either—back into a nightmare of white dust and armed guards.

God help me.

I was trapped in a closet with the cowboy detective.

ESCAPE FROM TRIESTE
(Ana)

"You!" I held my arms in front of me in the dark, as if this would somehow protect me from my nemesis, the relentless detective who had pursued me at every step of my journey, from my mother's garage sale to my father's Greek monastery to the sub-basement of an exploding Italian cyclotron. How had he managed to do that?

"What the hell do you want?" I demanded.

"I just want to help you."

He must have been reaching out to me with his hand, but somehow he missed my arm and connected with my left breast. I slammed down hard with my elbow and punched into the darkness.

"Ow!"

There was a moment's silence.

"Ach, was," he mumbled. "I think you gave me a fat lip."

"You're German?" I asked, nonplussed.

"Yes, and so are you. That's why I'm trying to help."

Now I was really lost. "Wait a minute. Aren't you the Australian missionary who gave my mother a Bible?"

"Yes."

"And the Czech cowboy who bought a hat from me at the garage sale?"

"Yes, yes."

"And the Italian monk who painted me on Milos?"

"Yes, of course. But I'm not the one who broke into your apartment or tried to kill you."

"Oh?"

"No, those are some different Germans. Two big stupid guys. I don't know who."

I thought about this a while before I answered. "Prove it."

"Well, I can't prove they burgled your apartment, but when they tried to run you over with a motorboat at Adamas, you must have heard me calling out to warn you."

"Wait," I said. " Gilberto was the one who warned me."

The voice sighed. "Your Gilberto friend was swimming the other way. I was up on the headland trying to keep an eye on you. Anyway, how could I know about the warning if I wasn't the one who shouted?"

That was in fact puzzling. "What about at the monastery?"

"In Greece I wasn't supposed to let you know who I was. So when you recognized me at the easel, I ran away. On my way back to Plaka I spotted the same two guys. They were knocking down a wall at the top of a cliff. I shouted to let you know."

It was true that Gilberto couldn't have been the one to warn me about the rockslide. I mused aloud, "The voice came from the top of the cliff, where the rockslide began."

"Right. So when the two German guys heard me they beat me up. I had to walk back to Plaka with a broken rib. It still hurts."

Parts of his story were starting to fit together. But there were still some huge holes. "How have you been able to follow me?"

"I just guessed about Trieste. Before that, every time I lost track of you I followed the two German guys. Somehow they always seem to know where you are."

"But you're a detective, right?"

"Not usually." The voice sighed again. "I'm a sculptor."

"What?"

"I'm a sculptor. My name—"

"I know," I interrupted. "Your name is Peter Weiss."

His voice rose with incredulity. "How did you know that?"

"Shh!" I could hear muffled footsteps running through the hall outside. Gilberto's voice called out, "Ana? Ana!"

An hour ago I would have rushed to Gilberto's side. But he had lied to me when it mattered most. Harmony had been right not to trust him.

When the sound of footsteps died away, Peter whispered, "How do you know my name?"

"You left clues all over. Who sent you anyway?"

He sounded tired. "The Baroness von Hohensteuern."

"A baroness? Why?"

"She thinks you might be her second cousin, or niece, or something."

I caught my breath. "What makes her think I'm related?"

"It's a long story."

I folded my arms. "I'm listening."

"Well, the baron died last month. Near the end he said his aunt might have survived the war after all. Her name was Marthe von Hülshoff-Schmitt. She owned the Einstein house in Ulm. We thought she'd been killed in the air raid of 1944. When you auctioned Einstein's violin case on eBay and mentioned a 'great aunt Margret' I started to get suspicious. The baroness asked me to go check, but to keep undercover until we knew more."

I was still trapped in a dark closet, but suddenly it seemed as if light was pouring into the mysteries of my family's past. "And where in Germany is the Hohensteuern family from?"

"Klingenstein," the voice said. "Schloss Klingenstein, just outside of Ulm. Maybe you want to go there and see for yourself?"

Before I could answer, the rumble of a distant explosion shook the darkness. The shelves rattled, and the rags popped loose from the crack beneath the door, swirling up a cold cloud of white dust.

"What on earth was that?" Peter asked.

"I don't know, but I think we'd better get out of this building soon. The problem is, guards with guns are looking for me. Any ideas?"

"I'm a janitor, aren't I?" Peter's Italian accent had returned. "What if I take you for a little ride in my trash bin?"

A minute later I had jammed myself into the wheeled plastic garbage can. Peter hastily covered me with rags and began trundling me down the hall. When I lifted my head I could just peer out a crack at the side of the lid. White dust still swirled past the caged lights. Somewhere a two-tone siren began to wail. A woman in a white coat ran past.

"Hey!" a man's voice called out. "Where do you think you're going?"

"Up to the ground floor?" Peter said.

I wished he could sound a little more convincing.

"What's in the bin?"

"Rags?"

My heart was thumping like a drum. I pulled the rags tighter over my head.

"Idiot," the other voice said. "You don't take garbage in the staff elevator. Go to the X hall."

We trundled back down the corridor. I was shivering from the close call. After what seemed like ages, I heard the whirring of an elevator. Then the garbage can's wheels bumped over several steps, jolting me from side to side.

"Stop right there!" The voice was female, but she bellowed like an Army sergeant.

"What?" Peter said.

"The building's locked down. Take garbage out tomorrow."

"If that's what you want," Peter said. "But by tomorrow this load is going to smell pretty bad."

Once again we were rolling. I jolted down another step. Peter flipped open the lid and whispered, "Hurry, let's go."

I blinked around at what appeared to be a loading dock. He was just helping me out when the woman with a sergeant's voice called out, "Stop right there!"

Peter and I leapt from the dock and ran along the edge of a parking lot. "Where's your car?" I asked.

"No car. There's a strike. All I could get was a bicycle."

"Terrific."

Peter stopped at a bike chained to a tree. While he fiddled with his keys, the Army lady was closing fast. Finally he threw the lock aside and jumped on the bike. I sat awkwardly on the back rack, hugging his waist while I held my knees in the air. Behind us the Army lady put on one last spurt of speed. But Peter was pedaling hard, and because the parking lot tilted downhill, we began pulling away. As we turned onto the highway, I saw her stop and pull a phone from her belt.

"Nice work!" I said, giving his waist a squeeze.

"Do you think they'll send someone after us?" Peter asked.

I thought about the destruction I had left behind in Nimolo's laboratory. "Yeah. Maybe not the entire Italian military. But most of it."

CHAPTER 27 ~ ANA

By now the highway had steepened and we were zooming down through the woods. Peter asked, "Do you want to go to Klingenstein?"

"I don't know." Everything was happening too fast. A few minutes ago Peter Weiss had been my enemy. Now he was helping me escape. "I just want to go someplace safe."

"Well, the castle's a lot safer than here. And if you want answers about your great-grandmother, that's a good place to look."

"But how can we get out of Trieste? The Italian trains aren't running."

A bee zinged past us. Then another. Puzzled, I turned around. The black Mercedes was bearing down on us from behind.

"They're shooting at us! Do something!"

Peter looked over his shoulder. "Hang on."

We swung through a tight corner at the bottom of the hill and barreled into downtown. When another bee buzzed past, Peter tilted hard to the right, bumping across a strip of cobblestones into a pedestrian shopping zone. A flower lady jumped aside, strewing us with daisies. An old man yanked his dachshund out of the way, cursing.

Peter shouted to me over his shoulder. "There's an old city tram up to the Slovenian border. Do you have a passport?"

"That's about all I have. My purse was stolen for a while in Venice. Since then I've been keeping my passport in a pouch in my shirt."

"Perfect." Peter pedaled another few blocks, zigzagging through alleys. Then he pulled up beside a ticket booth. He paid for two fares. We left the bicycle and got onto an ancient blue streetcar. After a minute a yellow tractor chugged up the track behind us, bumped into our streetcar with a jolt, and began pushing us up the track. The rails quickly steepened to a precarious pitch. Views out the tilted window soon stretched across the red tile roofs of the old town to the blue harbor, dotted with white sailboats. I felt as if this tram was taking me away from the dangers in Dr. Nimolo's laboratory. But I knew the thugs from the black Mercedes would eventually realize where we had gone.

"Your purse." Peter folded away his black-framed glasses and peeled off his large nose. The face underneath was boyish—the same handsome, innocent look that had struck me when I first talked with him at the garage sale in Eugene. "Tell me again what happened to your purse."

"I lost it in Nimolo's cave when I threw it at a guard."

"Before then. You said it was stolen for a while?"

"Yes, in Venice. A street thief cut the straps and took off. I only got it back because two big German tourists beat the kid half to death."

Peter raised his eyebrows at me. "Two big German tourists?"

I stopped. "What? You think they're the ones who've been following me?"

He sighed. "I may not be much of a detective. But I've got to wonder why these two guys always know where you are. And why they beat up a thief to give you your purse back."

I thought about this a moment. "A homing device. They must have planted some kind of homing device in my purse."

"Was the purse in your Eugene apartment when they broke in?" Peter asked.

"That's right. I'd left it by mistake the morning I went to the garage sale. They could have put something in it then."

Peter nodded. "That's how they followed you to Greece. When a thief stole your purse in Venice, they made sure you got it back.

"I suppose so." I looked out the window at the red-roofed city slowly shrinking below us. "Who are they anyway?"

"I don't know. They sounded Swabian, from southern Germany. I certainly don't think they were from Dr. Nimolo."

"Why haven't they shown up in Trieste?"

"There's a train strike. It's hard to travel. But they'll probably be here soon."

A malicious thought caused me to smile. "And then the homing device in my purse will lead them to Nimolo down in his cave. You know, I think they deserve each other."

The tractor pushed our streetcar into the town of Villa Opicina at the top of the hill. The car slowed to a stop and we got out. We asked around in English until we found someone who could tell us where to find the train station for Slovenia. It turned out to be nearly a mile's walk on confusing back streets. There were no taxis, so we set off at a fast jog. When we finally found the station I was pretty well winded. But there was a rust-streaked Slovenian train waiting on the tracks. It had been sitting there for five hours, marooned by the Italian strike. Incredibly, it was heading back for Ljubljana in another five minutes. While Peter bought tickets, I quickly ran to call Harmony on the station's ancient pay telephone.

All I got was an answering machine, and the connection was so awful I couldn't be sure how much of my message Harmony would actually get.

"Harm! I don't have much time, but this is important. Dr. Nimolo's crazy. When I went to his laboratory he had his guards holding me at gunpoint, trying to get the formula."

A thought struck me. I checked my jeans pocket and was a little surprised to find that I still had the blue bottle. "They were the ones who stole Cloud Nine from you, but I've got it back. Anyway, I managed to make a mess of the laboratory and escape. You won't believe this, but I was helped by the cowboy detective, Peter Weiss. It turns out he's working for a baroness in Germany who might be a relative. He's taking me to Klingenstein, a castle outside of Ulm, in southern Germany. If I need help, Harm, I'll try to let you know, but I might not get a chance to call you again for a while. The train to Slovenia is about to leave, and Nimolo's guards are still out looking for me. You were right not to trust Gilberto. Take care, Harm. Bye."

Peter was waving at me frantically from the door of the train car. I hung up and ran to join him. The train was nearly empty. We had just settled into facing seats beside a window when a conductor outside blew a whistle. An engine rumbled, and a series of clanks ran the length of the train as the cars began to move.

"We did it," I marveled. "We left them all behind. Nimolo's guards, the two German thugs, all of them! I'm safe."

Peter shook his head. "No you're not." The steely look in his eyes made my blood run cold. How much did I know about this man anyway? Had I made a mistake, switching my trust so quickly? What was I doing, alone with him in a train car to Slovenia?

"Look behind us," he said, nodding out the window.

I turned and looked. Three police cars with flashing lights had pulled up at the train station along with the black Mercedes.

"Nimolo's men know where we are," Peter said. "They'll be waiting for us in Ljubljana."

A CALL FOR HELP
(Harmony)

Jeez, nothing is more maddening than waiting for lawyers! By now everyone knew the protesters were innocent. The law was just mumbling around with paperwork before letting them go. After a long, pointless morning in a courtroom I finally just walked out onto the streets of Florence and turned on my cell phone to see how much of the real world I'd missed.

"Harmony - Ferguson - has - one - messages," a ditzy robot voice intoned.

I pressed a button, heard the robot announce, "11 - 43 - AM," and then found myself straining to hear snippets of Ana's voice, chopped up in a blizzard of static.

"Harm! I don't have much time, but this is important." A buzz saw cut the voice short for a moment. ". . . holding me at gunpoint, trying to get the formula." The buzz saw broke in again.

Alarmed, I held the phone closer. ". . . the cowboy detective, Peter Weiss . . . . He's taking me to Klingenstein, a castle outside of Ulm, in southern Germany . . . . I need help, Harm . . . . I might not get a chance to call you again for a while . . . . Trust Gilberto. Take care, Harm. Bye."

I replayed the message three times, trying to understand more of it. I was about to launch a fourth replay when the phone in my hand actually rang. I saw with relief that it was Ana herself, no doubt calling to explain.

"Ana!" I said, "Thank God. What's going on?"

There was a pause. Then a man's voice with an Italian accent asked, "Who is this?"

I rechecked the caller ID, but it really did say Ana Smyth. "No, who are you? You're using Ana's phone. Where is she?"

"Um, I don't know. I just pushed the redial to see whom she had called last."

"Are you that Gilberto guy?" I demanded.

"Yes. Would this be Signora Ferguson?"

"What's happened to my friend? How'd you get her phone?"

"She lost her purse in Dr. Nimolo's laboratory. I found her phone in the purse. There was an accident, and she's still missing." He cleared his throat awkwardly, apparently struggling with his emotions. "I'm afraid Ana may have been frozen in the cyclotron."

"What!" I sat down on the stone rim of a fountain, frightening a flock of pigeons. "How could Ana be frozen in a cyclotron if she left a message with my answering service fifteen minutes ago?"

"Fifteen minutes ago?" Gilberto's voice rose. "Are you certain?"

"Yeah. There was a lot of static, and she sounded like she was in trouble, but she definitely wasn't frozen."

"This is good news!" Gilberto said. Then he asked, "Just what kind of trouble was she in?"

"Well, the message was a little garbled, but she said something about being held at gunpoint by the cowboy detective, Peter Weiss. I think he's taking her to a castle in Germany. Does that ring any bells for you?"

"Bells?" He sounded a little lost.

"Hello? Gilberto? Ana's been kidnapped."

"I see. Where did you say she is going?"

"To a castle called Klingenstein. With a maniac. At gunpoint. You're supposed to be her boyfriend. Or is this not a problem for you?"

"No. I mean, yes—" he ran aground, groping for words.

"You mean you can't quite get off work to come help me rescue her? " I'd always thought Ana had given Gilberto too much credit. Every time she'd been in danger, he seemed to be somewhere else. He was like every other wishy-washy man in the world.

"No!" the voice boomed out of my cell phone with startling conviction. "I'm not working for Nimolo anymore. I'll be in Florence at three o'clock. Where can I find you?"

"Um—" Now it was my turn to grope for words. Was it even possible to get from Trieste to Florence in three hours? "I don't know. In front of the train station?"

"Look for an old white Saab," he said. And then he hung up.

STOP FOR LUNCH IN SLOVENIA
(Ana)

Peter Weiss and I watched gloomily out the window as our Slovenian train pulled away from Villa Opicina. The ancient railcar rattled and creaked as if some painful metallic arthritis had crippled its undercarriage. The forest of the Italian border began slowly creeping past the window. Although Nimolo's men had not managed to stop our train from setting out on its five-hour trip to Ljubljana, their Mercedes was obviously faster than our rickety train. They would be waiting for us with their pistols. To make matters worse, I couldn't shake a lingering suspicion that Peter might not really be on my side. As the cowboy detective, he had deceived me more than once.

I looked at him sideways. "Before you say anything else, I want to know why a baroness would hire a sculptor as a detective."

Peter ran his hand over his face. "I know it sounds strange. The truth is, the baroness of Hohensteuern is not a wealthy woman. She cannot afford a real detective. My parents are her only employees, other than a part-time gardener. My father works as secretary. My mother cooks. We all help with cleaning and repairs. Perhaps because she has no children, the baroness treats us almost like family. She helped pay for my art education. When she asked me to find out more about you, I couldn't say no."

"Do the German police know about this?"

He nodded. "They did their own investigation when the baron said Marthe von Hülshoff-Schmitt might have survived the war. They didn't find anything."

I was shaking my head. "Don't you have anything to prove what you're saying is true?"

He took a billfold from one of the pockets in his overalls. "I didn't think to bring much. Here is the baroness' card. Here is a picture of my parents at the castle. This other picture is my latest bronze installation."

The business card had a small embossed crest. The first photograph showed a stiff, sixtyish couple standing in front of an ordinary stone wall. The second photo showed a remarkable, expressionistic sculpture of a flock of geese, somehow mounted above a pond. None of this proved anything, of course. Anyone can have a business card printed with a crest. But then I thought about his feeble evidence. If he were really a spy—some sort of double agent, perhaps—wouldn't he have brought more convincing documentation?

"What's this?" I asked, pointing to a third snapshot of a small stone cross.

He flipped the billfold closed, frowning. "That's from my last visit to Slovenia."

"You've been here before?"

He looked out the window. "Nine years ago. I was nineteen. I did my military service with the blue helmets, the UN peacekeeping force in Maribor. Yugoslavia was falling apart in war."

"Then you speak Slovenian?"

"No. Only a few words. I had a translator."

I thought about this a moment. "Slovenia is part of the European Union now, isn't it?"

"Sort of, yes."

"If the Italian police ask, will the Slovenians arrest us?" What would they charge me with, I wondered? Sabotage? Vandalism?

"I don't know."

Suddenly our compartment's sliding door banged open. I jumped back, startled. A military officer was blocking the doorway. With leather straps across his beige uniform and a big silver badge on his military hat, the man looked like an actor playing a banana republic colonel.

"*Dober tek*?" Peter said.

I was impressed that Peter could come up with a Slovenian phrase so quickly.

The officer lowered his eyebrows. "Good appetite to you as well. May I see your passports?"

Peter flushed and took a green European Union passport from a pocket in his janitor outfit, Meanwhile I fished up the passport pouch hanging on a string around my neck. The officer opened our passports one at a time, looking from the photos to our faces. Then he flipped through the back pages, stopping to note the entry and exit stamps of the various countries we had traveled through.

"What is the purpose of your visit?" the officer demanded.

Peter glanced to me. "We're tourists?"

Why, I wondered, did Peter have to let his voice rise when he was nervous? It made everything he said sound like a question.

The officer asked, "May I see your hotel reservations?"

"We don't have any yet." I forced a smile, but my heart was in my throat. "You see, Slovenia is kind of a spur-of-the-moment fling for us."

Peter nodded. "Yes? A getaway?"

"I see. A getaway." The officer reached into a pocket that bulged ominously at his hip.

For a moment time seemed to stand still. I had already seen more than enough guns for one day. I was still trying to smile, but my mouth had gone dry.

The officer withdrew his hand and held out a brightly colored brochure. "Info Karta," he said.

I looked at the brochure. My heart was still beating very fast. A banner across the front read:

> *Why not stop for a moment in Slovenia? And discover the hidden treasures of our country, have lunch, and take a rest on the way to your destination?*

"All the best places to stay. Ten percent discount at the Hotel Jolly if you mention Jan." The official nodded once and closed the door behind him.

The man had hardly left us when the train began slowing for its first stop in Slovenia, a gritty station in an industrial town. Signs along the track announced *Sezana.*

"Ach, shit," Peter groaned, peering ahead with his cheek pressed

to the window. "There's the black Mercedes already, parked by the tracks. What are we going to do?"

I looked out the window and swallowed. "You're supposed to be the detective. Can't we hide in the bathroom or something?"

"That wouldn't help for long." Peter motioned for me to duck out of sight while our window slowly passed in front of the Mercedes.

When the train stopped I peered back out the window. "They have four men. Two are getting on the train. The others are getting back in the Mercedes."

Peter slid open our compartment door. "Come on, I have an idea."

I didn't have an idea, so I followed him. He hurried forward through the train to the first car, at the far end of the station platform. Then, just as the stationmaster blew a whistle and waved to the engineer, Peter stepped down onto the platform.

He held out his arm to me. "Would you like to stop for lunch in Sezana?"

"Why not?" I jumped down. The doors closed and the train clanked forward. We stood there, hidden from the station itself by a post, as the train rolled by. In the window of the next to last car I recognized Dr. Nimolo's two Italian thugs. They pointed at us, shouting and struggling with the window levers.

Peter waved to them as they vanished down the track toward Ljubljana.

I gave a heartfelt wave as well. "I hope they have a nice trip."

After the train was gone we waited, hiding behind the post. After a moment I peered out and saw the black Mercedes driving away from the station in the other direction.

I was so relieved that I planted a kiss on Peter's cheek. "That was wonderful, detective."

He beamed. "Wow. Thank you."

Perhaps Peter was a year or two young for my taste, but he was a good-looking man, and it charmed me that I could make him blush so deeply. "Of course Nimolo's men will be back, but we probably have half an hour head start."

"Perhaps we can catch another train?" Peter suggested.

I looked around at the shops facing the station square. "I'd rather rent a car. Let's try over there."

As it turned out, the man in the car rental shop knew almost as little

English as Peter knew Slovenian. After gesticulating and fumbling for words for several minutes, the man finally announced, "No car now. Two hour."

Even I could understand this. We didn't have that kind of time.

"*Mala* car?" Peter asked. "*Mala mala* car?"

The man thought about this a moment. "*Mala mala mala* car?"

Peter nodded.

I had no idea what "*mala mala*" meant, and I wasn't sure Peter did either.

The rental man motioned us out a back door and led the way across an oil-stained lot strewn with car parts. At this point I would have been happy with a goat cart.

Instead the rental men held out his hand toward a metallic-flake blue BMW motorcycle with gleaming chrome tailpipes. "OK?" he asked.

I had my credit card out of my passport pouch in a flash.

"Wait," Peter objected. "I don't have a motorcycle license."

I just laughed. For an instant I even considered leaving him behind. But he'd rescued me from the Trieste, so I'd owed him one. "Look, detective, if I'm paying, you're riding in back."

Minutes later Peter and I were roaring out of Sezana on the BMW, outfitted with helmets and a map of Slovenia that showed the locations of rental shops with stars. I wasn't entirely sure, but I had the impression that we could return the bike at any rental shop on the map. Actually I didn't care, as long as we left Nimolo's men behind.

"Keep going north through Nova Gorica," Peter shouted into my ear. "There's a back road that cuts through the Julian Alps to the Austrian border. I once had a skiing holiday there when I was with the blue helmets."

"Where did you stay?" I called back to him. "Maybe we can get that far by dark."

He paused a moment before answering. "It was called Kranjska Gora."

"Got it." I opened the throttle wide and blasted a dozen kilometers through green farmfields and forest, putting Sezana behind us. The smells of pine needles, manure, and new-mown hay hit us like rain-squalls in a hurricane. Then I slowed to zigzag past the white stone farmhouses of three villages. Each town had an onion-shaped bell tower sprouting from a stucco church. Modern tractors and surprisingly new Western cars stood parked along the narrow cobblestone streets. After that I hugged the speed limit, not wanting to alarm the police.

We filled the tank at a gas station beside a big river bridge in Nova Gorica. The only food the station offered was sausage. It was greasy and gross, but Peter bought one, and I was so hungry I ate almost half.

For the rest of the afternoon we traced the river up into the Alps, dodging one wall of snow-capped peaks after another. Finally the stream we were following petered out at a village in a box canyon. I was tired. I pulled into a white gravel parking lot for *Triglavske Narodni Park,* hoping the building here would be a visitor center with restrooms. Maybe even coffee.

Peter unwrapped himself from my back and groaned as he stretched his muscular legs. Watching him, I realized how much comfort his presence had given me since Sezana, with his chest against my back and his arms about my waist. Although we hadn't really spoken for two hours, it seemed as if we had communicated through our contact.

"Thanks for stopping before the pass," Peter said, taking off his helmet and shaking his wiry hair. "You know we're going to freeze up there?"

I looked up the mountain where the road vanished toward snow. I was still wearing jeans and a short-sleeved shirt.

"One thing at a time," I said. I followed a *WC* sign to a bathroom around the side of the building. When I came out again Peter was gone. With a twinge of fear I wondered if he had ditched me and taken the bike. But the motorcycle was still standing there in the parking area. And of course I had the only key. So I went into the visitor center's lobby. Peter wasn't there either—just racks of brochures. Beyond was a diorama of marmots, heather, and wrinkly white rock formations labeled *dolomite.* Beyond that was a gift shop. I went in and bought a plastic bottle of apricot juice. I also bought the only clothing they had—two large blue sweatshirts decorated with a silhouette of a hairy mountain goat in bluesy sunglasses. I had just gone back out the front door when I heard Peter arguing with someone in German. He was standing outside at a pay phone I'd overlooked beside the men's bathroom door.

"I don't believe it," he said angrily. When he saw me he switched to a calmer tone. "I don't care. Tomorrow night, then, if all goes well. I'll call again. *Tschüss.*"

"What was that about?"

He gave a nervous little laugh. "Parents! First they send you on an undercover mission to Greece. Then they're worried when you don't call home." He held out the receiver. "Anyone you want to call? Perhaps your mother?"

I knew he was hiding something about his telephone conversation, and I found it unsettling. As for calling my mother, I could only imagine waking her up in the middle of the night to let her know that her only daughter was escaping from armed Italian thugs in Slovenia. She wouldn't need to fake a heart attack at that news. For a moment I was tempted to do it, just to get back at her for telling Dad that I was dead.

"Or your friend Miss Ferguson?" Peter asked. "It's being charged to me."

I nodded and took the phone. My call to Harm that morning had been full of static, and a lot had happened since then. I dialed her cell, wondering if she'd be able to get out of Florence when the trains were striking. I also wondered where I'd say we could meet. At the castle in Klingenstein? Most of all, I wanted to warn her that Gilberto might try to contact her. He was trouble. And so was she, really. Harm has a mouth on her. The last thing I wanted was to throw those two together. Or no—the last thing I wanted was for her to lead Nimolo's thugs to me.

I tried dialing three times, but something was wrong, either with the Slovenian phone or with Harm's cell. I couldn't even get through to leave a message.

As I stood there with the phone in my hand I felt a sudden lonely pang, thinking how few other people I knew well enough to call. There were my colleagues at the high school, of course. I'd done many an education conference with Ed, the math guy across the hall, for example. But these weren't people you could rely on when calling from Slovenia, even if you did have their numbers. Likewise my chums from the library where I volunteered weren't up to this level of friendship. The only family members I had left in the world were an egocentric, hypochondriac mother and a reclusive, eccentric father without a telephone. Of course I knew the number of my ex-husband Randy, but calling that lecherous airhead was simply out of the question. How had I lived thirty years without building more bridges to people who cared about me?

Finally I gave up and went back to the motorcycle. I was glad to see Peter waiting for me there. "Surprise," I said, holding out my shopping bag.

He pulled out the matching baggy sweatshirts and laughed. We put them on, drank the juice, and climbed back on the BMW. Was it my imagination, or did he hold me a little tighter than before? What had he learned in his call to his parents at the castle that he didn't believe? And why had he not wanted to tell me? Somehow the fact that he was hugging me, and that he had saved my life that morning, made me a little less determined to grill him immediately. Plus, the road we had been following suddenly demanded all my attention. The pavement zigzagged crazily up into the sky like a rocket with a missing tail fin. It was all I could do to bank the heavy motorcycle around the hairpin curves without scraping the footrests. After forty turns my arms were aching, but we had shot up beyond the last of the forest. All around us was the rocky heather landscape I'd seen in the visitor center's diorama. Craggy snowpeaks loomed to either side, each capped with a cross—as if for a cemetery of mountain spirits. A roadside chapel flashed past, complete with Virgin Mary icon and votive candles. Then we crossed a pass and launched down into another giant slalom of switchbacks. Waterfalls tumbled off cliffs beside the serpentine road.

"Shouldn't we be in Austria soon?" I shouted back to Peter.

"No, this is still the Julian Alps," he shouted back in my ear. "We won't get out of Slovenia for a long time."

"Maybe we'll have to stay for dinner," I said. I thought it was a good joke, after the advertising brochure's ridiculous plea to "stop for lunch in Slovenia," but Peter didn't laugh, and he might have hugged me a little less tightly too.

Deep shadows gradually filled the valleys until only a few peaks remained, pink banners against the armies of the night. Finally we shot out of a forest canyon toward a little city amidst hayfields. A sign read *Kranjske Gora.* Concrete hotels, decorated with chalet roofs and ornate Tyrolean balconies, had washed up against a slope to the left, apparently marooned there when the tide of ski tourists had ebbed that spring. To the right, across a rock-banked whitewater river, a casino sign blinked colored lights.

I headed toward a pointy stone steeple on a clock tower. When I turned the bike down a cobblestone street, the handlebars almost jolted out of my hands. The street narrowed and turned sharply before opening onto a square beneath the tower. I parked at a *Zimmer Information* sign, pulled off my helmet, and gave my matted hair a shake, hoping in vain to revive it to its usual frizz.

"Has the town changed much since you skied here?" I asked Peter.

He nodded without looking at me. "Then there was a war. But the city was a sculpture from the baroque. Now there's tourist money. The city looks like a cheap imitation of itself. I think the soul is gone."

He still wouldn't look directly at me. I nodded toward the tourist office. "I'll see if they know where to find rooms."

Inside, a smiling receptionist greeted me in English. She made a phone call and sent us down the street a hundred meters to a door with a lit buzzer. The middle-aged woman who answered the door led us up the stairs and showed us a room with a double bed. "Is this OK?"

"Yes, but we need two rooms," I said.

"I have another upstairs. Here are the keys. I will need your passport."

I hesitated. My passport was the only documentation—the only baggage—I had left. I looked to Peter, hoping he would gallantly offer his passport first. But he just stood there, dazed and somehow distant. So I pulled out the pouch around my neck.

After the landlady had left us I told Peter, "Let's wash up and meet for dinner in half an hour." When he just nodded I took him by the arm of his goofy sweatshirt. "What's wrong, Peter? What did your parents tell you? Do they know if the police are looking for us?"

He sighed. "No, it's not that."

"Then what is it?"

He turned his room key over in his hands. "The baroness says I should leave you here in Slovenia and come home alone."

"What? Why on earth did she have you follow me all the way from

America? Just to ditch me in some Alpine village?" It didn't make sense—unless this mysterious noblewoman wanted me completely lost.

"Remember the hat I bought?" Peter asked.

"Hat? What hat?"

"Your great-grandmother's hat. At the garage sale."

The memory of that sale resurfaced slowly, as if from a deep sea. Had it really been only a week ago? "What about the hat?"

"I sent it to the baroness. She had a hair from the hat tested for DNA to see if your great-grandmother was related to the Hohensteuern family."

I nodded, my heart quickening as another piece of my family's mystery appeared ready to fall in place. "And was she related?"

"No." Peter lifted his shoulders. "The laboratory shows it is not a match."

This news hit me like a blow to the chest. After all I'd been through, piecing together stories from my father in Greece and Dr. Wenger in Venice, I had come to believe I was getting close to learning Margret's ancestry. Of course it was possible that Peter was lying about the test, or that the baroness had tested a hair from the wrong person, or that the test itself was faulty. How easy was it to extract DNA from a hair, anyway?

Peter went on. "The police say your great-grandmother may be a different missing woman."

My heart jumped. "Who?"

"I don't know. Someone from Böblingen, another small town near Ulm."

"If we go there, maybe we can find out."

"Maybe. But the baroness says I've been wasting her money. She says you've misled her."

I watched him closely. "And what do you think?"

"I think I need to prepare for dinner." He flushed, gave me the awkward smile of a teenager with a doomed crush, and withdrew to his room.

For the next half hour, as I quickly showered and washed my wilted hair, I jumped every time I heard a door slam or a motorcycle rev to life. Peter had been ordered to abandon me here. The embarrassed blush he had given me had been as easy to read as a billboard: He was conflicted. He was torn between loyalty to the baroness and an unspoken bond with me—not merely the camaraderie of those who have come under fire together, but real affection. Where were the disguises he had hid behind so easily in the past?

When I was ready I opened the door of my room, watching for Peter to appear in the stairwell. After forty-five minutes I began tapping my heel. Then I rubbed my little finger nervously. If I had ever been stood up for the high school prom—and I hadn't, because I'd gone with a group of six girls and four boys as a protest against exclusionist, gender-biased institutions—I imagine I would have checked my watch with the same self-deprecating anguish. Is there any torture worse than waiting for betrayal? Of course with my credit card and passport I might have found my way out of Slovenia without tripping over Nimolo's men, but I still let out a breath of relief when Peter finally looked up from the stairs.

"Sorry I'm late," he said sheepishly. His gray eyes met mine directly, without the moony numbness of that afternoon. "I used to know an excellent old restaurant near here. If it's still there, I'll treat." He held out his arm.

I hesitated, partly as revenge for my anxious wait. Then I took his arm.

The restaurant turned out to be a cellar of stone arches lit with sputtering candles. Peter ordered *eneloncnica brez mesa* and *pivo* with such confidence that I just nodded to the waiter and said, "I'll take the same, please."

Moments later we were brought big glass steins of heady beer and a cloth-lined basket of dark, thick-crusted bread. I was so hungry I ate two fat slices. Then the main course arrived: bowls of bland-looking, soupy stew.

"What is it?" I asked.

"The only thing I know how to order," Peter admitted. "Sort of a national specialty. Sauerkraut soup."

"Sauerkraut soup? You really know how to treat a girl."

"Yes, but *brez mesa,* without meat. That way it's actually not bad. Better than it sounds." Peter raised an eyebrow at me. "Will you never trust me again?"

I sipped a spoonful. Although it really was surprisingly good, I focused instead on what he'd said about trust. "Tell me, Peter. When you were in your room for an hour, were you thinking about leaving me here?"

He stirred his soup a moment and then looked at me frankly. "Yes."

"Why did you decide to disobey the baroness?"

He tilted his head. "Am I really disobeying? She told me not to waste any more of her money on a wild goose chase. Very well, then. I've stopped using her credit card. Instead I've switched to mine." He sipped his beer. "Actually it's very freeing. I never liked that cloak-and-dagger stuff. Now instead of dragging you to Klingenstein as some sort of suspect, I can invite you there as a personal guest." He looked at me over his beer glass. "Do you still want to go?"

I nodded slowly, appreciating this new, more honest relationship. I had a lot of questions about my family, and I didn't know where else to look for answers. "Do you believe the DNA test results?"

Peter shrugged. "It was nice to think you might be a Hohensteuern. It fit together with the time your great-grandmother turned up in Switzerland, and even with the air raid that wiped out the rest of the family. But I guess the police already have an idea about who your great-grandmother might really have been."

"What?" I leaned forward, eager to know more. "Who was she?"

"I don't know. Someone else who escaped the fires. The police in Klingenstein have been working on their own investigation." He looked down. "The baroness says they've been doing a better job. At least they haven't been blowing up cyclotrons."

The muffled wail of a two-tone siren echoed down into our cellar from the street. We both fell silent, waiting nervously until the sound had faded.

Peter caught our waiter's eye and made a motion of writing in the air. The waiter nodded and brought the check. I briefly offered my already stressed Visa card, but Peter solemnly refused. "Ana, I owe you much more than this. Besides, I want some new memories of Kranjske Gora."

Back on the cobblestone streets I tried to walk in the shadows. Peter shook his head and took my arm. "The best way to hide is to pretend you own the town."

As we strolled from streetlamp to streetlamp I said, "Something happened the last time you were here, didn't it?"

When he didn't answer I ventured, "You said you were on a ski vacation from the military. You weren't alone, were you?"

Again he said nothing, but I saw his head lower slightly, as if to duck a cold wind.

"Who was she?" I asked on a gamble.

He looked away and shook his head. "I thought I was supposed to be the detective, not you."

I remembered the photo I'd seen in his wallet, a white cross from his last visit to Slovenia. We had almost reached the stairway to our rooms. "I'm sorry. What was her name?"

He sank against a doorpost and closed his eyes. "Do you have to do this?"

I almost relented, now that it was clear I'd hit near the truth. "I know so little about you, Peter."

"Her name was Mira. She was a translator assigned to our unit by the UN." He took a deep breath. "She was Croatian. They speak almost the same language as Slovenians. But in World War II the Croats collaborated with the Germans. Someone must have thought she was still a spy. The day after we came back from Kranjske Gora they found her—"

He stalled, and I held up my hand. "I'm sorry, Peter." It was enough.

"It's been nine years and four months," he said, looking me in the eyes. "Don't let anything happen to you in Kranjske Gora." He squeezed my hand, turned, and climbed the stairs to his room.

I let him go, sorry that I'd opened such a painful wound and yet glad that I'd torn loose yet another mask from him. Had I seen the last of the cowboy detective's disguises?

At that moment a man in a long dark coat paused on the other side of the street. He struck a match and cupped it to a cigarette, briefly illuminating a face of angular features and dark whisker stubble. Either the man was practicing for a B-grade movie, or else he really was a spy. I ducked off the street and hurried up the stairs to my room.

After I closed my door behind me the room was pitch dark. With the windows shuttered I couldn't even see a light switch. While I waited for my eyes to get used to the dark, I put away my room key. But when I reached into my jeans pocket I was surprised to find something else there as well—the little glass vial of Cloud Nine. Somehow it was a comfort, this bottle of my father's most valued perfume. I felt my way to the bed, sat on its edge, and held the vial before me as if it were a sacrament to ward off the powers of evil that seemed to be swirling up after me like invisible poisonous gases. Why had my father prized this formula so highly? Was Harmony right that it held the key to the mysteries of gravity?

I uncorked the bottle in the darkness. I waited, but no sensual aroma overpowered me. I held it cautiously to my nose. Nothing. Had someone replaced Cloud Nine with water? Had this been my father's final prank?

And then I saw it. Or rather, I sensed it in the blackness of the room. A dim, glowing fog. As if an aurora borealis were dancing slowly across the bed. Why had I never experienced this before? Perhaps the phenomenon was so faint that I could perceive it only in total darkness.

Was it a light? Not really, but it did have a color that struck me with wonder—and with love for the father who had left this present for me so long ago.

The mysterious fog before me warmed the room with an astonishing, special hue.

It was *my color*. It was a shiny royal blue.

THE PERFECT TIRAMISU
(Harmony)

The whole time I was getting my backpack from the hostel in Florence I kept thinking: This is crazy. Okay, so maybe it was my fault that Ana had gotten mixed up in this mess in Europe. And now she'd been kidnapped by the cowboy detective. But how was I supposed to rescue her from a maniac in a German castle?

It's not just that I was scared, but I didn't like the idea of working together with Ana's boyfriend Gilberto. He'd gotten her into even more trouble than I had. Where had he been when Ana was being captured, or almost frozen, or whatever, in Trieste?

When I got to our supposed rendezvous point at the Florence train station at a quarter to three, I was amazed to find the trains running. A guy at the newsstand told me that a judge had freed the anti-globalization protesters and the transportation strike was over! I smiled to think my efforts had succeeded. Here was proof that nonviolent tactics beat confrontation, given time. Now I could leave Florence with a clear conscience. Maybe I'd eventually come up with some nonviolent tactics to help Ana too.

With ten minutes to kill I bought a map at the newsstand. It took a while because I'm not very good with maps, but I found a little black castle symbol labeled *Klingenstein* a few kilometers this side of Ulm. Then I added up the kilometers between Trieste and Florence and got 391. To cover that distance in three hours Gilberto would have to *average* over 130 kilometers per hour—more than 80 mph. No one could do that on Italian roads, even on the *autostrada*. Ana's boyfriend was full of hot air.

Nonetheless, when the city's countless church bells started tolling three o'clock I lugged my backpack out to the front steps. He wasn't there, of course.

But then, just as the last of the chimes was dying away, an ancient, dusty white Saab actually did pull up to the curb. The pear-shaped car had round fenders and small windows that dated back several decades—to the same 70ish vintage as my own Fury. Those were days when Americans built cars that looked like fruit crates and Europeans built cars that looked like fruit.

The man who stepped out of the Saab took off his sunglasses and swiveled his head with a single smooth motion, a dance step that so many Italians seem to know. His black hair was already receding from his high forehead, and his tawny features were not extraordinarily good looking. I wondered why Ana had fallen for him so easily.

When he saw me, I was surprised that he didn't smile. Men always smile at me. Especially Italian men.

"Signora Ferguson?" he asked with a formal nod. "I am ready to help you find Signora Smyth."

Then he actually looked down, as if the sight of me was somehow going to hurt his eyes. It was all very puzzling.

"OK," I said. "But, like, how did you get here in three hours? Does that Saab of yours fly?"

Finally a reluctant smile spread across his face, revealing a handsomeness that caught me off guard. His eyes were a piercing gray-green. "If you wish to fly, signora, all this car is lacking are the wings."

Gilberto tossed my pack in the backseat and held open the passenger door for me. By the time I had slid in and fastened my seat belt harness he was throwing the gear shift forward. We roared out into the mad Italian traffic with a speed that pressed me deep back into the white vinyl seat. A hula doll on the dashboard danced as if berserk.

"Do you know the Saab symbol?" Gilberto asked, pointing to a silver emblem on the steering wheel.

"I guess so." I recognized the logo's three circles, bisected by a horizontal line.

"It represents an airplane, you see? Seen from the front. Before this company made cars, it manufactured Swedish fighter planes. In that spirit I have made a few—how do you say?—modifications."

"I thought you were a physicist."

Suddenly he switched to Italian. "Is it so different? Trying to understand the spirit of an old car, or trying to understand the spirit of the universe?"

He pulled onto the northbound *autostrada* with a velocity that took my breath away. Or was it Gilberto's words that had stolen my breath? Perhaps it was his unexpected depth that had interested Ana as well. If he weren't already claimed, I might have enjoyed exploring those depths myself. Somehow his unwillingness to give me a second glance made him all the more intriguing.

"Maybe we should slow down," I cautioned, bracing myself against the dashboard as the Tuscan landscape flew at us. "Do you even know where we're going? Or what we'll do when we get there? Or why they took Ana in the first place? What happened in Trieste? And why aren't we calling the police for help?"

"Wait, signora. Let's answer your first question first," Gilberto said, looking straight ahead. "Didn't you say Signora Smyth is on her way to southern Germany?"

"Yeah, Ana mentioned a place near Ulm. I brought a map."

"Good. We'll study it at breakfast."

"Tomorrow?" I asked. "Why not now?"

"Because we cannot drive to Germany in half a day, signora, even in my Saab. My parents own a *rifugio* in the Alps at Livigno. If we press pedal to metal, we might arrive in time for dinner. Until then, please, feel free to ask me the rest of your questions."

"What about asking for help from the police?" The question ran against my nature. I'd just had a bad experience with the cops in Florence. But Ana had been kidnapped.

He gave me a sad smile. "Signora Ferguson, after one has blown up a cyclotron, the Italian police may not be as helpful as you think. My father is retired from the *carabinieri*. Tomorrow we can ask his advice. Today, I think, we need to try answering our own questions."

For the next four hours I grilled Gilberto over the hottest coals I had. As his souped-up Saab soared through narrowing roads toward the Alps I learned that Dr. Nimolo had an Einstein fetish, that his laboratory in Trieste was a hangout for old physics kooks, and that Gilberto was sorry he'd ever hooked up with them. I gasped at Ana's courage when I heard she had braved a hail of bullets to tip over a nitrogen tank with a crane. I was as puzzled as Gilberto that she had survived the icy blast of liquid nitrogen only to be abducted by that master of disguise, Peter Weiss. Everyone seemed to be after the same thing: the second half of Einstein's formula for quantum gravity. The clues all led to Germany. The only strokes of fortune in the entire debacle seemed to be that Gilberto had recovered Ana's purse—enabling him to contact me with her cell phone—and that Ana had managed to smuggle out a message encouraging me to trust Gilberto.

"But why should I trust you?" I demanded. "It sounds like you've been working for a mad scientist all along."

Gilberto sighed. "At first, all I knew was that Dr. Nimolo was a famous physicist. As soon as I found out about him, I quit. Like you, I want to help Ana."

I decided Gilberto would need to prove himself before I believed him entirely. The fact that he'd come to help so quickly was a point in his favor.

"At this speed we might not survive to help Ana," I commented. I looked out the little back window at the empty road. "At least no one will follow us."

"Follow us? Who would follow us?"

"Well, let's see. Dr. Nimolo might be curious about why you and Ana both vanished after wrecking his cyclotron. Then there's the guys he sent after me to steal the perfume. And maybe a few others."

"I see." He was silent a moment, and then brightened. "But I think Livigno is the safest place in the world. We have a saying, 'In the Alps there is no sin.' It is not like the rest of Italy, or like America for that matter, where you are always being watched."

"What do you know about spying in America?"

He shrugged. "When I was studying physics at Berkeley I joined a protest march against the Gulf War. After my picture was in the newspaper I lost the second year of my scholarship."

"Wow." I didn't know what impressed me more—that he'd studied at Berkeley or that he'd had the courage to protest the Gulf War. I too had joined No-Blood-For-Oil peace marches against the elder Bush's war, but the rallies had been small because the war had been popular with so many other people.

"That's so unfair," I said. "What did you do?"

"I spent a few months living with the hippies in Peace Park before the police told me my student visa had expired. Then they deported me."

"My parents are always saying how cool it would be to drop everything and go hang out in Peace Park."

He shook his head. "Mostly it wasn't cool."

I looked at him from the side. Who would have thought that this young Italian physicist could already have dived into—and resurfaced from—the bubble of rainbows and flowers I'd known as a child?

The sun had set behind ragged white mountains but the midsummer sky was still a deep purple when the road, now just a paved one-lane track, crested a treeless ridge and wound down toward a cluster of perhaps a hundred stone buildings. A dark lake filled the valley beyond the village. Beige cows looked up, clanging enormous bells about their necks. The houses had red-and-white striped shutters and shake roofs weighted in place with large rocks. A surprising number of the buildings had signs advertising cameras and perfume.

"What's with all the perfume stores?" I asked.

"Livigno is a duty-free zone between Italy and Switzerland. Some tourists come here just to shop."

I said nothing, but I wondered if Ana's father might have once visited Livigno in his travels as a perfume buyer. Perhaps the ingredients for Cloud Nine had come from a place like this, close to the clouds. I couldn't help thinking perfume might be part of the puzzle we were trying to solve. I was glad that Ana had retrieved her father's vial.

Gilberto drove past a sign for *Pensione Montale* and parked at the back of a two-story building made of squared gray rocks. We got out and he led the way past plastic crates of beer bottles into a kitchen with a ceiling of low wooden beams.

"Berti, what a surprise!" a short, gray-haired woman exclaimed in Italian. "And look what my boy has brought. Such a beauty! Does this mean you are finally, finally to be married?"

Even in the kitchen's dim light I could see Gilberto flush red. "No, Mama. This is Signora Ferguson, a friend of a friend. We are traveling to Germany tomorrow on business."

I held out my hand. "Pleased to meet you, Signora Montale."

The woman wiped her palms on her apron and shook my hand. "Here we are all family. Please, call me Maria."

I shook her hand, charmed by this breezy Italian mother. "My name is Harmony. In Italian, *Armonia.*"

"Armonia. Che bella!" She admired me a moment as if I were a marvelous sculpture she had just created. Then she turned abruptly to Gilberto. "Berti, I have thirty-two Dutch tourists, a whole busload, just sitting down for dinner, and Paolo is in Milan. Please tell me you can wait tables."

Gilberto glanced to me. "Mama, I have a guest."

I jumped right in. "Maria said I'm family. I waited tables for two years in college. Where are the menus?"

For the next half hour "Berti" and I shuttled orders and plates between the Dutch tourists and his parents in the kitchen. What a hoot! By the time the four of us had settled down to our own plates of lasagna at a rickety table behind the woodstove I really felt I was part of this family. And what divine lasagna!

Gilberto's father, Marco, had a big white moustache and dark, twinkling eyes that danced all over me. *"Allora, Signora Armonia,* I would hire you on the spot. You would make our little *rifugio* famous in all of Italy. They would make movies here for the beautiful scenery, and I'm not talking about the Alps."

Marco winked at me, and we all laughed. Then he asked, "So what is this business that takes you and my son to Germany?"

I faltered. Gilberto had said we'd talk about the police tomorrow. "Well, it's research, you know? About a physics formula."

Gilberto's father nodded sagely. "Physics. I never did understand it."

At that moment the Dutch tour guide leaned his head in the kitchen doorway. "Dessert?" he asked in English.

The elder Montales both looked at Gilberto. Maria said, "Berti, could you?"

Gilberto held up his hands. "No, no, no. Not for thirty-two people. Not in so little time."

"But I have nothing else," Maria pleaded. "Please. You are the only one in the world who can do it right, without letting it sit overnight."

Gilberto sighed. "Do you have what I need?"

"Yes, everything."

He looked to me. "I would need your help."

I nodded, breathless with anticipation. "What are we making?"

"Tiramisu," he answered. "Tiramisu *perfetto.*"

For the next quarter hour I was in heaven—or rather, I was an acolyte for a ritual mass at the gates of heaven.

"First, you must arrange the *savoiardi* in the bottom of the dishes, like this, just like this." Gilberto carefully covered the bottom of a glass dessert bowl with a layer of ladyfingers—crunchy Savoy wafers. "Now you try. Yes, do all the bowls like that. Good."

While I laid out the wafers he followed behind, anointing each dish with a mixture of coffee and Marsala wine, an amber fluid from a dusty bottle. As soon as I was done he said, "Now we must walk on water."

"How?"

"It's an old kitchen miracle. Others call it whipping egg whites until they are firm."

I helped him separate three dozen eggs and whip the whites to stiff peaks. Then he folded in sugar and a white cheese that looked like yogurt.

"Is this *mascarpone?*" I'd seen Italian triple-cream cheese in America, but this stuff looked a little different.

"Here in the Alps it is made from special milk, from cows that are fed on grasses filled with herbs and flowers."

Just when I was expecting he would ladle the white mixture into the dishes he turned to me somberly. "I am sorry, signora. But now you must look away. There is a final step none may share."

"But—"

"Please, turn away."

I turned to face the wall, hardly able to contain my curiosity. For several long minutes I heard the creak of mysterious cupboards, the clank of mysterious bottles, and a stirring of silver on glass. Finally he let out a long breath, as if he had solved a complicated mathematical equation.

"It is nearly finished, signora."

When I turned back to him he had already started grating a block of dark chocolate into tiny curls onto each dish.

He gave me a silent nod to indicate I could carry the first tray of tiramisu in to serve the Dutch tourists. By the time I returned with a second tray several of the tourists were already moaning with pleasure. My own hands were trembling when I was finally back at the kitchen table. Before me stood my own dish of Gilberto's tiramisu. I dipped in my spoon, took a bite, and closed my eyes.

I might have been swimming in honey and sweet cream. This was a tiramisu that lifted me ten feet off the ground and spun me around in the air. What dark secret had made this possible?

When I opened my eyes and saw Gilberto, the archbishop of this sweet sacrament, he was quite simply the handsomest man I had ever known. Ana had been a genius to find him for me.

But then the thought of Ana brought me back to earth with a jolt. Ana was still kidnapped. And Gilberto was *her* boyfriend, not mine. Somehow I would have to stop myself from falling in love with him.

In fact, how had I let myself get so distracted by Ana's boyfriend at all? Sometimes I think there's another person inside of me—perhaps the flower child I tried to leave behind years ago when I drove off to college in my Fury.

With an effort I stopped gazing at Gilberto like a star-struck roadie. But when I looked down I realized that I had somehow unfastened the top *two* buttons of my blouse while working with him in the kitchen. Blame the flower child, I guess. Anyway, now I couldn't redo the buttons without looking like a dork.

Incredibly, Gilberto didn't appear to notice all the curves exposed by my button problem. Tight-lipped, he was studying the lettering on the back of his spoon handle, as if "Stainless Italy" were some inscrutable lost poem by Dante. I'd never met a man like this. Was he really this nonchalant, or was he struggling not to look at me? I found myself flailing about for something to say.

"So I guess tonight's the solstice," I finally blurted.

"The what?" He looked up, catching me with a little smile. Then he quickly looked back down at his spoon.

"The longest day of the year, June 21. Or is it June 22? I forget. Anyway, back home in Eugene we celebrate the solstice by building a bonfire and jumping through the flames."

"Isn't that dangerous?"

"Not if you jump fast." I laughed a little, more at ease now that we were talking. "My mother says it's an old pagan tradition from the

Druids. The flames catch all the evil spirits that might try to follow you into the new season."

He set his spoon aside. "Maybe that is what we need. I feel as if we've been followed by evil spirits ever since Dr. Nimolo bought the violin case. Ana, me, you—all of us."

"But not here," I objected. "In that amazing old car of yours we just flew away from trouble. And this alpine hotel really is a refuge." Just being with Gilberto made me feel safe.

For once he smiled at me without restraint. "You liked these things? My Saab and my parents' *rifugio?"*

"Oh, very much. Very, very much." I was gushing again like a ditz. Why do I keep doing that? To backpedal a bit I asked, "Don't you have a tradition like that here?"

"What kind of tradition?"

"You know, the bonfire thing on the solstice."

"No. Why?"

I shrugged with one shoulder. "It's just I've been watching this flickering reflection in the window, so I thought—"

I stopped short, suddenly overcome with dread.

Without another word Gilberto unlatched the window, opened it inward, and swung back the wood shutters.

There was indeed a bonfire behind the hotel. With a horror that knotted my stomach and drained the blood from my face, I realized that the flames were coming from the blackening frame of Gilberto's beloved Saab.

IN ULM UND UM ULM HERUM
(Ana)

Rags was much older in this dream, his gait stiff and his once brindled snout now bristling with distinguished white whiskers.

"Thanks for getting me out of that cave," the old dog said.

"What happened down there?" I asked. "Where's Dad? Did we stop the dust?"

"Not so fast." Rags pulled the covers off my bed with his teeth. "Put on the wet suit."

"But—"

The dog looked at me steadily. "Your Dad's doing better. But yes, the dust is still out there, about to make the world fall apart. That's why you need to put on the wet suit."

I held up the black rubber outfit that had somehow materialized at the end of my bed. "A wet suit? Like for diving underwater? I don't know how to do that."

"Ana, this is a dream. Trust me, you can do it. Just put on the suit."

I pulled on the stretchy black pants without even taking off my nightgown. "Where are we going?"

"Deep sea treasure hunting," Rags said. "Inside your closet. Neat, huh?"

I pulled the suit's top over my head. "There's no ocean in my closet."

"Well, there is now. And it's full of shipwrecks." Rags opened the door with his paw, revealing a shimmering wall of shiny, royal blue water. He dog-paddled ahead into the blue.

I stepped in after him and found myself swimming in a sea of murky shadows. Somehow I wasn't surprised that I could breathe normally, even without a facemask or tank. "Where are we?" I asked.

"Somewhere between now and next week." Bubbles rose up with his words as if in a cartoon.

"I don't understand."

"You've got to start figuring stuff out for yourself, Ana. Dreams open the dimension of time."

"Like attics and black holes?" Brightly colored fish darted past as I breast-stroked ahead, my hair waving back and forth like frizzy brown seaweed.

"Yeah, maybe. After you sold the violin case you got a couple free visits to the past. In Venice you saw your Dad in the present. Here's your chance to swim into the future for a look around."

"What kind of treasure are we looking for?"

"Not what you expect."

Ahead, looming from the seafloor, I could see the black hulk of a battleship. Its hatches and railings were crumbling with rust. Starfish and barnacles encrusted useless deck guns.

"Why did it sink?" I asked.

Rags paddled about to face me. "Look around."

I turned my head and noticed with a jolt of fear what should have been obvious all along: The sea in all directions was full of mines. The bombs surrounded me like spiny, deadly sea urchins, tethered by chains to the seafloor.

"But how are we supposed to find the treasure with all these mines?" I asked.

Rags shook his grizzled head. He paddled past the rusting derelict, narrowly missing several of the mines. In the mud beyond lay the half-buried wreck of an even older ship, a wooden galleon of the sort you see in old pirate movies. Cannons and broken masts littered the seafloor nearby. Here, instead of mines, there were sharks. I shivered as the gray monsters glided past, their toothy heads wagging left and right as they swished their tails. I recalled from somewhere that sharks hunt by smell. In these deep, royal blue waters they seemed to be ignoring me.

Then I spotted the treasure chest. The size of small picnic cooler, it was sitting right there on the deck in plain sight. I swam down to the deck, grabbed a grappling hook, and smashed the lock. When I pried the chest open, the rusty hinges gave way and the entire lid floated aside.

I looked inside, my heart pounding.

Of course I'd feared the treasure box would be empty. But it was more than empty. As I watched in horror, the water about me began pouring into the chest as if toward an unplugged drain. A passing school of small red fish slipped backwards into the darkness, sucked down as brief streaks of color. Somehow I seemed unaffected by the current, but Rags was already spiraling into the vortex.

"Rags!" I grabbed him by his shaggy paws and held on tight. "How do I stop the hole?"

The old dog shook his head. "Simply let go."

"What?"

"I'm old, Ana. Let me go home." He looked up at me from the void, his shaggy ears streaming behind as if from a gale.

"But I need you!"

"Not if you let me go."

"No! Don't leave me now!"

"It isn't now yet, Ana. But that time is coming."

"Rags!" I cried. I felt his paws slipping from my grasp. "Rags!"

I awoke with a start. It took me a moment to realize I was curled on the seat of a train compartment.

"Gut geschlafen?"

Had I slept well? I rubbed my eyes and focused on the voice opposite me. This was Peter Weiss, the cowboy detective who had helped me escape from Trieste. Now he was speaking to me in German instead of English. Presumably because we were in Germany.

"Yes—I mean, no." It takes me a minute to shift languages, even though I am a German teacher. "I guess I didn't sleep much last night. I kept thinking Nimolo's men were going to find us." That much was true. But I had also lain awake thinking about my father. Before he was a monk he had created a secret formula of his own—Cloud Nine—and had left it in the attic shrine for the day his little girl would be a woman.

"It's good to be together with you, Ana, instead of merely chasing you," Peter said. His knee brushed mine, sending a sort of warm electric shock up my thigh. His eyes held mine until I looked away and blushed. Why am I so susceptible to these simple romantic gestures? No doubt I'd have more resistance if I were Harmony, and good-looking young men were bumping my knee all the time.

I recalled that morning, when Peter tapped at my door to tell me we should be leaving Kranjske Gora as early as possible. There may still have been a whiff of Cloud Nine in the air when I opened the door. I'd seen him stop as if momentarily confused. He went on to tell me he would wait for me outside by the motorcycle, but something made me think the perfume may have affected him after all. I would have to be more careful about releasing the genie in my father's bottle.

Now when I looked out the train window, tidy German houses were rolling past like so many Monopoly tokens, all with the same white stucco walls and red tile roofs. Next came a tidy farm field, neatly striped in yellow and green. Even when the train ducked through a forest the landscape was strictly ordered, with tree trunks standing at attention in rows. No fallen logs were left to rot here. The world was *zack zack,* as they say in German: ship shape. To all appearances, this is a country with no mysteries and no confusion. But sometimes the deepest secrets are hidden in plain sight.

"Have you been to Ulm before?" Peter asked.

I shook my head. The closer we got, the more I worried about my reception at the Klingenstein castle. The baroness had apparently uninvited me because my great-grandmother's DNA didn't match up with the Hohensteuerns'. So I would be Peter's guest. How would that work? And what was I supposed to wear to a castle? All I had were the jeans and shirt I'd been sweating in for two very long days. I would definitely need to buy clothes.

"Ulm isn't much, I'm afraid," Peter said. He nodded to the window. "The best part is the view from across the Danube."

We had left the forest and were slowing down through an industrial area. Then the train ventured out onto a long iron bridge. Across the blue river stood a medieval-looking walled city, guarded by an ancient, leaning watchtower. Rising above the jumble of tile rooftops was an improbably tall black stone church spire.

It was such a calming scene that I wasn't prepared for the sudden return of fear. When our train curved into the city, I saw the flashing blue-and-white lights of the police ahead.

"What's wrong?" Peter asked.

I pointed ahead. "There's a police car waiting for us at the station." I glanced to Peter. He didn't look as worried as he ought to be. That's when my fears took an even darker turn.

"You knew about this, didn't you?" Perhaps he'd been working for the police all along. "Were you the one who called them?"

"No!" His eyes widened in surprise.

"Then why aren't you suggesting we sneak out the back or something?"

He shook his head. "This is Germany, Ana. You don't run away from the police here. Besides, it's just Rosi."

"Rosi?"

"Everyone from Klingenstein recognizes her. It's not a big village, so we don't have a lot of policewomen. Come on, we might as well see what she's doing in Ulm."

Part of me wanted to bolt—to run away from another trap. But this wasn't a black Mercedes. It was the local police. I took a deep breath and followed him down the train car's corridor to the door.

As soon as we stepped onto the station platform a youngish, short-haired policewoman in a crisp green uniform swept Peter and me toward the patrol car. "Quick!" she whispered, gripping my upper arm firmly. She rushed us into the car's back seat, glancing about nervously. Then she slammed the door, got into the front seat, and drove around a barricade to a busy street.

After a block or two she seemed to relax a bit, but my heart was still thumping. I didn't know if I'd been arrested, abducted, or rescued.

"So you must be the famous Ana Smyth," she said over her shoulder. "Welcome to Ulm. I'm Rosi Meyerhof, *Bundespolizei*." Almost in the same breath she said, "Peter, your parents are worried. We all are. Yesterday I got a bulletin that the Italian police want Miss Smyth for questioning. This morning a car full of Mafia types showed up in Klingenstein, looking for her. What the hell have you been doing?"

Peter and I exchanged a grim glance. Somehow Nimolo's men had gotten ahead of us. Maybe they'd traced our telephone calls or our train tickets. Obviously we hadn't been as clever as we thought.

"Peter?" It was Rosi again. "You shouldn't be getting mixed up in trouble like this."

Something in the policewoman's tone raised a warning flag for me. Than I realized that she'd been calling Peter *du* instead of *Sie*. She was addressing him with the familiar form—something you do with small children and sweethearts. Just how intimately did she know him?

Peter cleared his throat. "Well, Ana sort of blew up an Italian cyclotron. By accident, of course."

"Of course," Rosi said. "It could happen to anyone." From the back seat I could see her in profile. She had a cute little nose. Her brown hair was short but full. The uniform included a men's tie that draped over her snappy green shirt.

Peter went on. "Anyway, it turns out Ana knows half of a missing Einstein formula from her great-grandmother. An Italian physicist threatened her at gunpoint because he wants the other half. Ana broke a nitrogen tank while she was running away. Then I helped her get here."

"Am I under arrest?" I asked. "Where are you taking us?"

"We're just driving in circles," Rosi replied, "trying to keep you out of the Italians' gun sights until we decide where to land. Now tell me what else I should know."

I sighed. "I think I need to find the other half of that formula before Dr. Nimolo and his men get it."

Peter looked at me uncertainly. "Now you want the formula too?"

"I guess if Margret kept it safe for all those years, it seems like my responsibility now. And I certainly don't want Nimolo to have it."

"Why?" Rosi asked. "He's a physicist and you're not."

"Oh, because he's got an old grudge. He wants to use a miniature black hole to build a gravity bomb or something."

"And that's bad?"

I nodded, even though she couldn't see me. "Possibly very bad. End-of-the-world bad."

"Why would Dr. Nimolo want to build a bomb?" Peter asked. "If the world ends, doesn't he go with it?"

"Nimolo's pretty old." I thought back to laboratory in Trieste. "He talked a lot about immortality. I think he wants to make a big discovery about gravity, and he doesn't care if everything blows up in his face."

"That sounds crazy," Rosi said.

Peter nodded. "That's the picture I'm getting too."

I went on, "If I'm going to find the rest of the formula, I think I have to figure out how and why my great-grandmother left Germany. If I could talk to the baroness—"

"Don't go near her." Rosi cut me off. "Your family doesn't have anything to do with the Hohensteuerns. The baroness thinks you're trouble."

"What about me?" Peter asked.

Rosi shrugged. "Your parents are looking forward to having you back home. The Italians didn't seem to care about you. You should be OK, but as a police officer I have to tell you, Ana Smyth isn't safe in public."

"Are you going to turn me over to the Italian police?" I asked.

She tilted her head. Did she know her short haircut turned this into a suspiciously cute gesture? "They don't actually have an arrest warrant out yet, so I can close one eye if I want. Still, the safest place for you really might be in the Ulm jail."

"But I've got to trace my family. Isn't there anything we can do?"

Rosi pulled up at a stoplight. She turned to look at me. "Listen. I'm putting my job on the line by suggesting this. There's a man, Herr Schlanger, who says he may know your family. I mean your real family. He's got a place for you to stay here in Ulm. It's not pretty, but it's safe. Actually, it may be the same place your great-grandmother stayed. If you want, I could take you there."

I turned to Peter. "What do you think?"

He looked down. "I don't like the idea of splitting up."

I appreciated his concern. Still I said, "Maybe this way you can look for information at the castle while I learn what I can from this Schlanger guy."

He didn't look at me. "Maybe."

I turned back to Rosi. "Let's go meet Herr Schlanger."

Rosi drove us to a city park with lawns and trees. Beyond a colonnade of elms I could make out the pink stone blocks of a gigantic, overgrown wall. I asked Peter if it was the Klingenstein castle.

He shook his head. "This is part of Ulm's old fortifications. I don't know why Rosi's taking us here."

"Because this is where Herr Schlanger runs his museum," she said over her shoulder.

"What museum?" Peter asked.

"I just found out about it myself," Rosi admitted. "It's only open a few days a week, and no one seems to visit."

She pulled up in front of a dark, gated archway in the wall. The place was as eerie and unwelcoming as a bat cave. A small enameled sign read *Fort-Oberer-Kuhberg-Museum.* As we got out of the patrol car, Rosi looked behind to make sure we hadn't been followed. Then she unlatched the gate and led us across the shadowed entryway to a large wooden door.

Inside was an echoing stone hall. Banks of miniature halogen lamps spotlighted posters and photographs along the walls.

A balding man with a bow tie strode toward us, his fingers outstretched as if he were about to present us with an invisible beach ball. I think he said, "Oh, and to think that history so often comes full circle," but he spoke so fast, and the hall echoed so much, that I wasn't sure.

Rosi introduced us all round.

I got straight to the point. "Herr Schlanger, what can you tell me about my great-grandmother, Margret Smyth? I hear you think she might be a missing housewife."

The man leaned back, ricocheting a peal of laughter off the vaulted ceiling. "A missing housewife indeed!" He clenched his hands and leaned forward. "Or a missing heroine of the resistance? Do you know of the White Rose?"

I shook my head.

He filled me in. "The White Rose was an underground movement in World War II, based in Ulm. They passed out leaflets against the Nazis."

"What happened to them?" I asked.

Rosi answered this time. "The Gestapo caught them. They were tried and hanged."

"But not all of them," the curator said. "No one was sure about one of the prisoners, a divorcee named Margrethe Semmel. A mysterious person, really. They kept her here while they tried to find out more."

"Here?" I looked about the room. "In an old fortress?"

The curator held out his hand to the photographs on the wall. "The fortifications were built in the 1840s, but by World War II the government was using it as a prison, a holding place for undesirables on their way to the death camp at Dachau. Then came the Allied air raid."

The black-and-white photograph he showed me next was startling. Dead people and horses lay piled beside a smoky street where buildings must once have stood. Here and there a remnant wall staggered from the rubble. The gray ghost of Ulm's gigantic church spire, miraculously unscathed, haunted the horizon.

"It was December 17, 1944," the curator said. "That evening a fleet of English airplanes dropped more than 96,000 bombs on Ulm. Of course the city's air raid shelters were inadequate. People stormed the bunker here, trying to get in. In the confusion, Margrethe Semmel and a handful of others disappeared. Everyone assumed she had died—until we heard about you, Miss Smyth."

The story gave me goose bumps. "Could Margrethe have taken a small child with her? And an old Jewish man?"

The curator shrugged. "There were several Jewish detainees here at the time. As for the child—that's part of the mystery about Frau Semmel."

"Tell me."

"We know her husband divorced her because of an affair. He claimed their young son wasn't his. No one has ever identified the biological father. In any case, the boy vanished before Frau Semmel was arrested. We don't know what happened to him, but we suspect he went to stay with the true father. The boy was never seen again."

"Unless she took him to America," I said quietly. If she had escaped on the night of the air raid, her first thought would have been to find her son. Of course, that meant Margret was neither my great-grandmother nor my great aunt. She was my grandmother. And who was my mysterious grandfather? It was all so confusing that it made my head hurt.

"I know there's a lot of information here you'll want time to study," the curator said. "Frankly, I'm excited too. I've been working on a family tree of Margrethe Semmel's parents."

Rosi added, "Half of Böblingen claims to be related to the lost heroine of the White Rose. So far we haven't made anything public. Do you want to meet some of these people?"

I should have been thrilled to hear I might have an entire village full of distant cousins. Perhaps because I was so tired from a long and bewildering trip, I just shook my head. "Let me think about it. I'm not ready yet."

"Wait a minute," Peter put in. "What about Einstein's violin case? If Margret escaped from prison here, how did she end up with an Einstein formula?"

The curator leaned back and fired another staccato burst of laughs into the air, although I couldn't understand why. Then he bent forward and said, "Zeppelin."

"What?"

"Ask the family of the late Count Zeppelin." He took a card from his shirt pocket and wrote an address on the back. "A great niece by the name of Ulrike Landenburger lives across the river in Neu Ulm. She comes in here every once in a while with her ideas. She'll be glad to fill your ear about Einstein."

"Yes, I'll want to meet her." But by this time the weariness and tension of the day were starting to overwhelm me. I was fading fast. I blinked to keep my eyes open. "Peter, maybe you could help me get in touch with this Landenburger person?"

"Sure." Peter took the card. Then he asked the curator, "Did you say there was someplace safe Miss Smyth could stay?"

"It's been a long day," I agreed.

"Well, this is a little unusual for us, but Officer Meyerhof explained the situation. Because you're a guest with such a strong historical connection I'm willing to make an exception." The curator led the way through a second, smaller exhibit room to a doorway marked *Staff Only*. Beyond was a corridor lit by bare bulbs. Cots lined the wall.

My stomach knotted. The corridor reminded me of Nimolo's *Sincrotrone*—a windowless cave from one of my nightmares.

Peter was shaking his head. "This is no place for you, Ana."

"It's safe," Rosi said. "That's the most important thing."

Herr Schlanger handed me a key. "Margrethe Semmel stayed in the room to the right, but I'd rather you used one of the cots here in the corridor. Toilets and washbasins are down the hall."

"I didn't bring anything for overnight," I managed to say. "Not even a change of clothes."

The curator nodded. "Our facility was used as a civil defense shelter until the end of the Cold War. The cupboard here has extra blankets, food rations, even disposable jumpsuits. You're welcome to use what you need, but only from this one cupboard."

I unfolded one of the disposable paper uniforms. Long German words were stenciled across the front, but by this time my eyes were too tired to read them. How had I ended up here? This wasn't what I'd imagined in Ulm.

"Everything we know about Margrethe Semmel is in the displays," the curator confided. "Good luck with your research, Miss Smyth. Take care of my museum. And please, don't answer the door until I'm back to open it up at ten."

Peter ran his hand through his hair. "Look, we'll think of something. I'll come back tomorrow morning. This isn't—" he faltered. "Tomorrow, Ana."

Herr Schlanger was already using his outstretched arms to herd Peter and Rosi toward the exit. Along the way the curator turned a knob on what appeared to be an alarm system. "All the light switches are by the door. The city makes us pay for electricity so shut off any lights you don't need. Am I forgetting anything?"

I stood before him, open mouthed. What could I say?

"It's been an honor to meet you, Miss Smyth. Until the morning, then. Sleep well." The curator shook my hand, nodded, and closed the door behind him. For a moment I dimly heard their voices—Peter arguing, Rosi insisting, and Herr Schlanger laughing like a broken machine gun. Then the patrol car growled off into silence.

Alone in the prison of the brave woman who may well have been my grandmother, I sank to my knees and cried like a lost child.

BORDER PATROL
(Harmony)

The flames licking the skeleton of Gilberto's Saab seemed like a force of pure evil, some incomprehensible vortex of violence. He backed silently away from the *rifugio's* shimmering window, his eyes wide with the same hot fear I felt.

No one had outraced his Saab on the *autostrada* from Florence. We both knew that. But if we hadn't been followed, what caused the fire?

The rest of that night slid into a blur. Eventually we sent everyone to bed with a fairy tale about a leaky fuel line. Gilberto's dad, Marco, obviously wasn't buying that story. He's a retired policeman, and the guy could sense when his son was talking loopy. Anyway, because the *rifugio* was full of Dutch tourists, Gilberto and I wound up on cots in the basement, on either side of a glowing wood furnace. Talk about putting a fire between us! I could hear Ana's boyfriend breathing uneasily all night, right there, so close. This was the man who had cooked me the perfect tiramisu—a man I was struggling not to love. Part of me really did want to leap over there and kiss the devil out of him.

"Enough nonsense, Berti," Gilberto's father said after breakfast. We had just finished serving pears, croissants, and cappuccinos to the Dutch tourists. Now we were sitting with cheese and bread at the rickety kitchen table as if for a summit. "I logged onto the *carabinieri's* secure site this morning. What the hell's going on?"

Gilberto winced. He obviously hadn't slept well either.

Maria kept slicing mozzarella. "Really, don't be so hard on the boy. He's here with a beautiful young woman and they're both helping out." But then without missing a beat she added, "What are the *carabinieri* saying?"

"They've alerted the border stations not to let Berti's white Saab leave the country."

"I guess that's not an issue anymore," Gilberto said gloomily.

"Did the police say anything about me?" I asked.

"No, not you, Armonia," Marco said, "But they want my son for questioning. They're also interested in an American woman named Ana Smyth."

"Why on earth do they want to talk to Berti?" Maria asked. "And who is Ana Smyth?"

"This is all my fault," I admitted. "Ana's my friend. I talked her into coming to Europe to look for her father in Greece. I guess Gilberto went to help her because he speaks Greek, but then there was an accident in Trieste, and she was kidnapped by a detective from Germany. So that's where we're going."

Gilberto's parents looked at me, nodding very slowly, as if they were having trouble absorbing this all at once.

"We haven't done anything illegal or wrong," Gilberto assured them. "And I really don't know why my car caught on fire. Maybe it has to do with Dr. Nimolo. He might be angry because I left my job at the physics institute."

"You quit your job?" Maria asked, concerned.

"I should have told you about it last night. It turns out Dr. Nimolo has been working on a dangerous project. A project I don't like. That's why there was an accident, Mama, and that's why I left." Gilberto looked from his mother to his father. "I'll look for a better job later. Right now I need your help. Signora Ferguson and I have to get to Germany to rescue Ana Smyth."

Marco leaned back. "You say this Smyth woman was kidnapped. Why?"

"Some people think she can find a lost Einstein physics formula." Gilberto let out a long sigh. "I don't know. I'm afraid maybe she can."

"A formula? For what?"

"For quantum gravity," Gilberto said.

I said, "It's what holds the universe together. If Nimolo gets the formula he might build a bomb that makes everything fall apart."

"Why would he do that?" Maria asked.

Gilberto shook his head. "Nimolo's old. I think he's frustrated that he never made discoveries as important as Einstein's."

I said, "I think Nimolo wants to go out with a bang."

A long silence hung over the breakfast table.

Finally Marco placed both of his hands on the table. "Pack us lunches, Maria. I'll call Catarella. We'll leave in twenty minutes."

Soon Gilberto, Marco, and I were bouncing up a rugged mountain track in an old Fiat.

"Smugglers have been using this route for centuries," Marco shouted to me over the whine of the engine. "I never thought I'd use it to smuggle my own son."

"So that's Germany up there?" I asked.

Marco held up a finger. "Switzerland first, my dear Armonia. Italy doesn't share a border with Germany."

When the road ended at a rocky slope we parked and got out our backpacks. Gilberto had borrowed a pack from his parents. It looked heavy with all his stuff in it. My own backpack was already so full that I had to put our lunches in Ana's old purse and tie it on outside. We climbed for two or three steep kilometers on foot. Then we reached a broad pass where there was an old green tractor and a little wooden trail sign: *Passo di Cassana 2694 m.*

Behind us dark storm clouds had begun boiling up over Northern Italy. Stretching ahead, however, was blue sky. A jumble of distant mountains filled the horizon. A few lumpy white lakes of morning fog lingered at the bottoms of the valleys.

"This is it?" I asked. "We're out of Italy?" The trip had seemed too easy. I was hardly winded. We hadn't been stopped by fences or dogs or guards or anything.

"This is it." Marco fished a set of keys out from a hole in the tractor's bumper. "My Swiss friend, Catarella, says we can use his tractor all day."

Gilberto looked at his father skeptically. "So, do you and he do this smuggling thing a lot?"

"Just for visiting friends. He has a cousin in Livigno. This route saves time."

"What would your colleagues in the *carabinieri* say?"

"Berti, I'm retired. I don't have to tell them everything."

"I'm glad," Gilberto said.

"So where's the nearest train station?" I asked.

"The best connections to Germany are in Klosters," Gilberto's father said. He climbed up to a bucket seat in the tractor's glassed-walled cab. "That's sixty kilometers, *bambini*. Let's get going." He turned the key and the engine cranked to life with a pop-pop-popping sound.

Gilberto and I scrambled onto a little fold-down seat at the back of the cab. Of course there were no seat belts, so we bounced all over as the tractor jolted down the track on the Swiss side of the pass. I laughed, Gilberto laughed, even his father grinned. Hey, we'd escaped from Italy! After the tension of the previous night it felt good to be jostling against Gilberto for a while. He had nice narrow hips, and they jostled well.

When we reached a paved road, however, Gilberto grew serious again, focusing his attention on the traffic outside. Our tractor was just slow enough that we backed up cars. A gray rental with German plates got stuck behind us for ten minutes while we wound through a narrow valley. From my seat up in the glass cab it was funny watching the fat German driver argue with his passenger.

It was a little less funny, however, when I noticed the same German car coming back toward us five minutes later. "Look, that's the gray car that used to be behind us."

"Tourists are always getting lost out here," Marco said. "Klosters is just ahead."

Gilberto turned to watch as the car passed. The passenger was still arguing, pointing to one side as if he thought the driver should have gone a different direction.

Gilberto frowned. "That man looks familiar."

"He does?" I asked, getting worried. "How could he be familiar?"

"I don't know."

Behind us the German car slowed down, pulled off the road, and backed around.

"Holy shit. They're coming back again. It's like they were arguing about whether to follow us."

"Greece," Gilberto said suddenly.

"What?"

"That's where I saw them. They were hanging around the hotel where Ana and I stayed on Milos."

Marco looked at us in the mirror. "Would you like to meet these gentlemen again?"

"No way," I said. "Ana was almost killed in Greece."

The German car was gaining on us. The man on the passenger side rolled down his window and held out something that looked suspiciously like a handgun.

"Dio mio!" Gilberto turned to his father. "Did you bring your service revolver?"

"I'm retired, Berti."

I swallowed hard. "We've got to do *something*."

"Here's the train station," Marco said.

"Papa! These must be the guys who burned my car. They might be coming to kill us. We can't just sit at a train station."

His father glanced in the mirror again. By now the German car was hardly a hundred meters behind and closing fast. "All right, *bambini*. Then you'd better hold tight."

Marco spun the steering wheel to the right, swiveling the tractor sharply uphill onto a village street. Gilberto and I landed together with our backpacks against the glass wall of the cab. Wood-planked chalets and balconies of red geraniums jolted past. The tractor's cab bonked a hanging signboard for a tavern. A dog barked and a woman on a balcony yelled. Marco twisted the wheel back and forth, dodging up through a maze of alleyways for several disorienting minutes.

Where the pavement ended at the upper end of the village he finally stopped at an overlook. Beside us stood some kind of roadside chapel where a fountain from a stump poured into a trough made from a hollowed log.

"Sorry about the ride," Marco said.

"That's OK." I was glad he'd driven so wildly. Nobody could have followed us through all those turns.

But then I saw the gray rental car venturing out from the village below. The two men still seemed to be pointing and arguing, but they had in fact turned up the correct road to reach our chapel.

"Dio!" Gilberto shook his head. "How do they do it?"

I looked up at the dirt road ahead. It appeared to end at a wall of mountains. "Now we're trapped."

Marco shifted gears and floored the accelerator. "Not quite, *bambini.* There's still the old trail to Gargellen."

"Gargellen?" Gilberto asked.

"In Austria. The wrong country, maybe, but it'll do. Those Germans look too fat to catch up with you on a mountain path."

We drove over a rise and suddenly came face to face with a herd of a hundred milk cows blocking the road. They blinked at us, banging bucket-sized bells as they chewed their cud. Marco swerved off through a meadow, churning up chunks of turf with the huge rear tires. By the time we clambered back onto the road I could hear the Germans honking, trying in vain to rouse the drowsy cows.

Five minutes later we were parked at the end of the road, beside a stone dairy shed with red and yellow arrows marking hiking trails. The German car was nowhere in sight.

Marco lifted my pack down from the cab. "Armonia, take care of my son. Once he trained for the *carabinieri,* but now he's a physicist. What can I say? He needs a strong, beautiful woman like you. If I weren't already married, I'd want you for myself."

He planted kisses on my cheeks—once, twice, three times. His moustache tickled. When he stood back to look at me his eyes were damp.

I couldn't resist giving him a hug.

Gilberto looked to one side as if he were embarrassed—or maybe jealous?

Marco pointed straight up the hillside. "Follow signs for a pass. I think it's called *Schlappinerjoch.* I haven't been there since I was courting your mother. I remember it was like climbing to heaven. After that—well, after that it's all downhill to Gargellen."

"I'll call when we get to Germany," Gilberto promised.

The old man blinked away a tear. Then he nodded, climbed up into the tractor, and drove back down the mountain valley.

Gilberto and I hefted our packs. We climbed in silence a few minutes up the trail. At the third switchback we had a view back down the valley. Far below, the green dot of Marco's tractor was just being passed in the opposite direction by a gray dot. Each of the vehicles kept going.

"Dio mio!" Gilberto breathed. "How the hell do those Germans keep following us? Who are they?"

Fear crawled up inside me, tightening my throat. "I don't know. I guess they don't want us to help Ana."

He looked at me—really looked at me for the first time since I'd met him. It made me shiver all over. "You're right. Whatever trouble we have, Ana is in worse trouble." He cinched his pack's straps tighter over the muscles in his shoulders. God, how I wanted him to hold me reassuringly right then!

By the next switchback we could see the Germans had started hiking up our trail. Each of them carried what looked like a gun. Gilberto and I shared a frightened look and set off up the path faster than ever.

For the next two hours we climbed at an exhausting pace, passing mountain brooks and heather. At every switchback we'd look back to watch the Germans. Incredibly, they were keeping pace.

Lunchtime came and went without any thought of stopping. At first I was glad when clouds rolled in, blocking the hot sun. But then a cold wind blew down from the mountains and the clouds lowered around us. The trail set off across a vast snowfield. We had to chip steps into the snow with our shoes. Gilberto stopped to cough. He obviously wasn't used to this kind of climbing. I had to catch my breath too. Our shirts were soaked with sweat.

Finally the clouds became so thick there was nothing left to see but gray sky, gray boulders, gray snow, and two small gray dots behind us—the impossibly relentless Germans.

Then the windstorm doubled in fury, ripping across the mountain slopes. At the same time the air bloomed with snowflakes. In June!

Gilberto sank to one knee in the snow. "I'm sorry," he said, his words almost lost in the wind. "Sorry for Ana and for—"

"We're almost to the pass!" I shouted against the wind. "Listen, do you hear the bells?"

He lifted his head. "My father said it would be the gates of heaven."

"Oh, don't be silly. Look, there's a herd of goats up at the pass."

"Goats?"

"Yeah, come on." I dragged him to his feet and helped him ahead to a frosted iron signpost. On one side it read *SCHWEIZ*, and on the other side, *ÖSTERREICH*. By now the goats were all around us, nuzzling our legs and clanging the bells on their collars. I noticed some of them seemed to be coming from a slope to one side.

"This way! Maybe the goats have some kind of shelter up here." Just because I said this, I didn't believe it would be true.

But it was. Fifty paces from the pass was a rustic stone shed that some compassionate goatherd had built into the face of a rock cliff. Despite its open wooden door and a single small window, the place was so well camouflaged in the storm that it was a wonder we had found it at all.

Gilberto staggered inside, dumped his pack on a pile of straw, and leaned against the back wall, panting. "Thank you. signora. They—"

I laid my hand on his shoulder. "They won't find us here."

"Yes they will." He wiped a hand over his face. "Those Germans—they couldn't have followed us alone. They had to have help."

"Like what? Helicopters? Pixies? Second sight?"

He shook his head, catching his breath. "In Venice. Remember Ana's purse? It was stolen on the Rialto bridge."

I recalled Ana's phone call from Venice. It seemed like months ago. "Ana said two big German tourists gave it back to her." My eyes widened. "These must be the same guys!"

Gilberto looked out the open doorway. "Here they come."

"Oh—my—God." Panic gripped me as never before. The dark shapes of two men had in fact reached the pass. Each man held one hand outstretched with a gun. I wished I could use my martial arts training against them, but how? Aikido doesn't stop bullets.

"What can we do?" I whispered.

"The purse."

"What?"

Gilberto nodded to my backpack. "Ana's purse. They must have planted a locator in it."

I tore Ana's purse off my backpack and dumped the lunches onto the straw. Then I ripped out the lining and turned the purse inside out. A thumbnail-sized metal disk clung to the leather like an alien leech.

Gilberto reached for the transmitter. "Throw it out the window."

"No." Suddenly inspired, I plucked off the transmitter and grabbed the nearest goat. The animal fidgeted while I held her against my chest and pressed the tines of the transmitter deep into the underside of her leather collar. Then I spanked her hard out the door.

At that moment a clap of lightning from the storm smashed into the rocks outside. The goat kicked her heels and streaked across the pass into the mountains of the border.

Hardly twenty steps from our door the German shadows stopped.

The guns they had held in their outstretched hands were not guns after all. They were little black boxes with antennas.

Buffeted by the swirling snow, the two fat German men slowly began turning away from our stony refuge. They argued, shouting at each other in harsh syllables.

Finally, like clumsy marionettes pulled by a hidden string, the two big goons stumbled away from us. Then they disappeared into the storm, apparently unaware that they were now following a goat.

I collapsed backwards into the straw, laughing with relief.

"That was genius." Gilberto beamed at me.

I rolled across the straw, grabbed him, and kissed him hard on the mouth.

He looked up at me, gasping. "Armonia – "

"Yeah?" I looked back into his eyes, my heart beating like a snare drum. Even then I knew that this wasn't me, that this was the wrong Harmony. But I was exhausted and the passionate flower child was going strong. "Tell me exactly what you're thinking."

"Are you sure you want to know?"

"Yes, tell me the truth. Now!"

He looked so helpless there in the straw. His lower lip trembled. "The truth is that I have wanted to kiss you every minute of the past two days. Armonia, you are the most beautiful woman I've ever known. It has been killing me, trying not to look at you all the time, but I've been worried about— "

"About Ana? Oh God, Berti."

"If you ever kiss me again, Armonia, I will be lost forever."

Did he know the battle raging within me? The old Harmony had thrown back her head, laughing with delight, confident that she had already won. She was ready to rip open Berti's shirt and smother him with the kiss of no return.

But I had learned something from Ana, a woman with a black belt in the dark art of overpowering her own emotions. I gathered my strength, threw a body block, and sent myself reeling with a kick to the heart.

"Let's hike down to Gargellen," I said.

COUNTING ZEPPELINS
(Ana)

Peter didn't show up when the museum opened the next morning. But to my bewilderment, Peter's parents did.

"Herr Weiss, Frau Weiss." I could hear the curator's voice echoing from the front hall. "I've heard about you from my colleague in the Klingenstein museum. Yes, I believe our celebrity American guest is in back."

No, I didn't rush out to greet them. What was Peter thinking, sending his parents? Because the museum had no shower, I'd been forced to wash up in a bucket from the lavatory. The disposable civil defense suits were almost as stupid as hospital gowns, so I'd had to put my smelly old clothes back on. Not quite the thing for meeting the folks.

"Hallo?" a woman's voice sang out. A black pillbox hat leaned into my corridor. The woman's face was mostly hidden by oversized sunglasses and a red silk scarf. "Peter's told us all about you. We're his parents."

Why, I wondered, was she wearing sunglasses inside? In the background, the curator gave a little wave and retreated. "I'll be in front if you need me."

Herr Weiss shuffled up behind his wife and cleared his throat. "Good morning, Miss Smyth." Although his face was in shadow, I could tell he had Peter's good looks, but with white hair, spectacles, and wrinkles around his eyes.

"Welcome to my humble prison," I said—not the friendliest thing, I'll admit.

"Very nice," Herr Weiss replied in his gravelly voice, obviously unfazed. "I wish we could stay."

"Yes, we're just stopping by on our way to town." His wife hid a smile with her hand.

What was going on? Now even Herr Weiss had broken into a grin. I looked at him more closely. Were those wrinkles real?

"Peter?" I asked.

He winked. "*Gut geschlafen?*"

The master of disguise was back. "Peter, what the hell are you doing? And who is this woman?"

"Oh, I really am his mother. Isn't this exciting? Peter's talked me into trading places with you so you can interrogate a suspect about Einstein."

"Well, that's—" I stalled, trying to grasp this twist. Peter had shown up after all, and he'd found a way for me to visit the Zeppelin relative without being spotted by Nimolo's Italian henchmen.

"I've brought some knitting to keep me busy," Frau Weiss went on. "There's extra clothes in my bag for you, I just hope they're your size. Here, go ahead and try on my hat."

I held the black hat in my hands. Peter's mother was offering to take my place in the prison so I could venture outside. My own self-centered Mom would never have agreed to such a scheme. "That's very generous of you, Frau Weiss. Thank you."

She took my hand in hers. "You speak German so well. Have fun in the city. Just don't do anything I wouldn't. And for heaven's sake avoid my hairdresser, she'll gossip to everyone about my new younger style."

Fifteen minutes later Peter and I were outside in the park, walking into town as Herr and Frau Weiss.

"You might try to look a little less like a fugitive from the Italian police," Peter whispered. "Remember, we've been married thirty years."

"Time flies."

He clicked his tongue. "Just slow down, hold my arm, and *stroll*."

It felt strangely reassuring to stroll through the park with Peter. Pigeons strutted slowly out of our way. Kids on skateboards detoured around us. The breeze of an approaching storm shivered the leaves overhead but we strolled on, an old couple in the long coats that old German couples seem to wear all year. I'd always thought Peter looked too young for me. Now, with his white hair and a slight stoop, he had the dignity of a general retired from distant wars.

"So are we going to look for the Zeppelins in Neu Ulm?" I asked.

"I called Frau Landenburger last night. She's working today at a booth for the Summer Festival downtown. We can meet her there."

"Perfect. What else did you find out while you were at the castle?"

Peter sighed. Perhaps because he was playing the part of an old man, he stopped to lean against a railing. Across a sluggish green creek, ducks were paddling past a half-timbered house. "The baroness wanted to hear everything—about my trip, you, and everything. She still suspects you might be up to something."

"Like what?"

"She doesn't know. She's curious."

"And what do you think?"

"What do I think?" He held out his arm. We continued our stroll, crossing a small bridge to a street of antique shops. "I think you're honest, contemplative, and very attractive. Unfortunately, Frau Weiss, that means you're not even slightly convincing as my mother."

I lowered my head to hide a smile. "Sorry."

"What about the research you were going to do in the museum?" Peter asked. "Did you learn anything else about Margrethe Semmel by looking at the displays?"

"I found some pictures of her."

"Does she resemble your grandmother?"

I lifted my shoulders. "It's hard to tell. The photos were black and white, and they weren't very sharp. Just a schoolgirl in pigtails, you know. Riding a bicycle, sitting on a stump at a picnic. She had a kind of dark expression that struck me as familiar. I also noticed that her age doesn't quite match."

"Oh?"

"If Margrethe Semmel is Margret Smyth, then my grandmother was ten years younger than we thought."

"Is that possible?"

"I suppose Margret could have been eighty-six when she died instead of ninety-six. It's hard to tell when people are that old. But women usually lie about their age to make people think they're younger, not older."

"That's true."

"It also means my father is a year older than he claims. He must have been two when he left Germany." I recalled talking with my father in the Greek monastery. He'd told me about his earliest memory—a night of flames, before he had words. That really might be how a two year old would remember an air raid.

"I wonder how the Zeppelins are involved in all this," Peter said.

He led me to a plaza dominated by the gigantic stone spire of Ulm's central church. Most European cathedrals have two towers in front, but this one gathered all its Gothic tracery and flying buttresses into one single colossal point, like the prow of a monumental spaceship poised for takeoff.

Only when we were crossing the square did I notice that a carnival of white tents had been set up on the far side, dwarfed by the tower. The first booths we passed had commercial vendors, selling everything from flashlights to socks. Closer to the base of the church, however, the booths were selling food.

Suddenly I realized how hungry I was. One tantalizing booth offered fresh-baked pretzels. This was the genuine article, too, as thick as twisted bagels and speckled with rock salt. At another stand a woman was glazing roasted almonds with caramel. The sweet, nutty aroma weakened my knees. A third booth displayed giant gingerbread hearts, iced with sentimental phrases like *Immer Dein* and *Ich Liebe Dich.* Perhaps it was best that Peter led me straight past this German junk food to a restaurant tent.

"I'm looking for Frau Landenburger," Peter told the woman at the counter. "My name's Weiss."

"Really?" The woman was perhaps fifty, but she did a pretty good job of packing herself into a tight little dirndl with a puffy lace blouse. "You sounded so young on the phone."

Peter coughed lightly, like an elderly man. "We're traveling incognito today. This is the American I told you about, Miss Smyth."

"Oh! It's a pleasure." She reached across the counter and shook my hand. "I might as well go on break so we can talk. With this storm coming it'll be dead here anyway. Is there anything I can get you to eat?"

A few minutes later I was sitting at a folding picnic table inside the tent, shamelessly forking down a serving of potato salad with *curry-wurst*. I felt as if I hadn't eaten in days. That morning I'd looked at the bomb shelter's ancient rations and skipped breakfast.

Frau Landenburger brought each of us a schooner of *Königsbräu,* a pale yellow beer with a two-inch head of foam.

"This is awfully nice of you," I said.

"Prosit," she replied, clinking her glass against mine. "Now tell me, is it true that Einstein cooked up a recipe for gravity?"

"Well— " I hesitated, not sure how much I should tell her. "I guess I did learn part of a formula from my grandmother—if that's who she was. So yes, I think he might have."

"I knew it!" Frau Landenburger thunked down her glass. "My family has believed this for years."

Peter sipped his beer. "Herr Schlanger tells us you're a descendant of Graf Ferdinand von Zeppelin."

"No, I just married a great nephew. But somehow I'm the one who's wound up researching family history."

"I hope it's not been as hard for you as it is for me," I said.

"I think we've got the same problem—a big blank during the Nazi years." She leaned forward. "The Zeppelin family hated Hitler. They almost convinced our company director, Hugo Eckener, to run against Hitler for president in 1929."

I raised an eyebrow. "Imagine how that would have changed history."

"Eckener was so famous back then, he really might have won. But he wanted to stick with what he knew—building airships. Eventually the Nazis declared our whole family 'non-persons.' The press wasn't allowed to mention our names."

"Didn't the dirigibles keep flying for a while?" Peter asked. "I mean, until the *Hindenburg*— "

Frau Landenburger cut him short. "That wasn't our fault. The Zeppelin family had a perfect safety record, a million miles without an accident. We flew the first airship around the world. All the problems started when the Nazis nationalized our factory in Friedrichshafen. They cut corners to save money. They switched the design of the *Hindenburg* from helium to hydrogen. Of course it blew up. The Nazis ruined everything they touched."

Rain had started to pelt the tent. A man hurried past outside, his head covered by a newspaper.

"Here, let me show you a picture." Frau Landenburger searched the apron pocket of her dirndl. "The count died just before the war ended. I found this in his files when I was working on the genealogy." She. wiped the table with a rag and laid a photograph before us. "What do you think of that?"

The picture showed a desk with a metal model on a wooden stand. At first I thought it was a model of a dirigible. But then I noticed decks of gun turrets underneath. "I don't know. It looks like an upside-down battleship."

"That's exactly what I thought." She tapped the picture with her finger. "A flying steel battleship."

Peter wrinkled his brow. "How would that work?"

"It wouldn't, of course. Unless you knew the formula for gravity." She took a long drink of beer.

I exchanged a skeptical glance with Peter. "A flying battleship?"

She narrowed her eyes. "Our family specialized in lighter-than-air machines. Back then the underground was full of rumors about a lost Einstein formula. Count Zeppelin worked with the resistance. I think they found something here in Ulm. I think they found a gravity formula he thought could end the war."

"Still, a dirigible with an anti-gravity device sounds pretty far-fetched."

Outside, the rainstorm was sagging the awnings. High above, where the church walls disappeared into the gray sky, a row of dark stone gargoyles had started spouting water—monsters spewing into the air.

"So it sounds far-fetched, does it?" Frau Landenburger emptied her beer glass and set it down with a thunk. "Well, you know the rumor. Einstein's formula was supposed to be hidden in a violin case. Talk about crazy, huh? But isn't that exactly what your grandmother was trying to smuggle to the Allies?"

Perhaps it was the beer, or the Zeppelin story, or the sudden end of the rainstorm, but I did not behave like a reserved old lady on the walk back through town. To be sure, I still wore Frau Weiss' ridiculous pillbox hat. But I grabbed Peter's arm like a teenager and pulled him from one window to another along Ulm's pedestrian shopping street. I bought shoes, jeans, a dress, and underwear totally unsuited to a matron of my age. I don't know whether Peter or my Visa card suffered more.

Then I found an Internet café with telephone booths and I called Harmony's cell. Still no answer—and her message service wasn't working either. What on earth was Harm doing? I came out and complained about her to Peter.

"Maybe you should phone home, Frau Weiss."

He was right, of course, but I didn't want to hear it. "You mean call Harmony's parents? I don't have their number."

"No. You should call your mother."

Peter waited just outside the booth. Through the glass door I could see him watching the café entrance, as if he was worried the Italian police might suddenly show up. I was more worried about what I'd say to Mom—the woman who had lied to me all my life.

The phone rang in Eugene, Oregon for a long time. I could picture my mother in a bubble bath, ignoring the phone. She was probably still mad at me for visiting Dad. She had tried to erase all memory of him. She probably thought the troubles I'd faced in Europe were my own fault, and I might just as well—

"Uh, hmm. Um, hello?"

"Monty?" My stepfather's mumbling monotone is unmistakable. In a way, I was relieved to talk to him. "This is Ana. Where's Mom?"

"Um, she's out. Did you, uh, find your father?"

"Yeah, I did."

"Oh, uh, good. We've been, um, wondering, you know?" I heard a meow. Then the telephone clunked. There was a pause, followed by the sound of tiny bells. It took me a while to realize that Monty must be pouring dry cat food into Einstein's glass bowl. Only Monty would stop to feed a cat during an international phone call.

"Uh, Ana, are you still there?"

"Yes Monty. Listen, Harmony's here in Europe, but I've been having trouble getting in touch with her. For some reason her cell number's not working. You haven't heard from her, have you?"

"It's funny, but you know, Harmony's parents just called, right before you."

"They did? What did they say?"

"They asked the same thing."

"You mean about Harmony?" Now I was really getting worried about her.

"Um, yeah. They said all the protests and strikes and things in Italy were over, but Harmony hasn't been answering her phone for two days. They sort of hoped we'd know why."

I gave Peter a frantic wave through the glass.

He opened the door a crack "What is it?"

I covered the mouthpiece. "Harmony's missing. No one's heard from her for two days."

He pushed up his spectacles, frowning. "You don't think this has to do with the formula, do you?"

"She's been attacked once because of it. I'm worried."

"If Nimolo thought she can lead him to the formula, he might have sent Gilberto to kidnap her. But what can we do to help?"

"Everything comes back to the formula." I uncovered the phone. "Listen, Monty? I'm in Germany now, and—"

"You're where?"

"In Germany. I'm working on a project. Maybe it will help Harmony too."

"Uh, Ana? Did you know your cell phone doesn't work either?"

"I lost it. I'm sorry. Look, I'll try to call you again tomorrow. Let me know then if you've heard anything about Harmony, OK?"

"Oh, OK. Bye, Ana."

As soon as he hung up I dialed Harm's cell again. Nothing.

Damn it!

Back on the street I checked my watch. We'd been away from the museum for two hours. The real Frau Weiss had probably knitted an entire bedspread by now. But after learning that Harmony was missing, I wasn't ready to return to my solitary confinement until I'd done a little more detective work.

"We know Margret Smyth came to America with a violin case and a fur coat," I told Peter. "The coat was from a shop in Ulm at Bahnhofstrasse 29. I want to find it."

"Yes, and I want you to see it," Peter said. "It's on our way back to the museum."

He led me down the pedestrian promenade. One of the storefronts had its doors open to a display of television sets. Twenty identical weathermen were pointing to twenty maps of a swirling white octopus-shaped cloud over Northern Italy. "More high winds and high water today on the Adriatic coast," the voices warned in unison. "The low-pressure system is spreading rain as far north as Germany."

A couple of blocks from the train station the shopping promenade turned sharply to the right and changed names to Bahnhofstrasse. I counted down the street numbers as we walked. The metal digits for 29 were bolted to a modern concrete building—the Dresdner Bank.

"Another dead end," I said, disappointed.

"This whole district was destroyed in 1944. Even the streets have been realigned." Peter pointed to a monument down the street. "There's something else I'd like you to see. It's the place where most of the Hohensteuern family died."

I approached the stone sculpture as hesitantly as a visitor in a cemetery. Square granite beams had been stacked fifteen feet tall in the middle of the street. The monument looked like a giant, dismantled Rubik's cube. A German inscription on the base read, "In a house on this site, on March 14, 1879, Albert Einstein came into the world."

I turned to Peter. "I don't understand."

"The twenty-four blocks represent time," Peter explained. "The hours of the day. The sculptor arranged them to suggest the original house."

"That's not what I meant. You said this is where the baroness' family died."

He looked at me uncertainly. "That's right. They were killed in the air raid."

"Here? In the house where Einstein was born?"

"I thought you knew that. It's why your eBay notice caught my eye."

If I'd known, I'd forgotten. "Tell me about the Einstein house."

"It was just an ordinary house. The Hohensteuerns bought it during the war."

"From Albert Einstein's family?"

"Some of their relatives, I think. When the Hohensteuerns bought it the old baron's niece moved in with her husband and their one-year-old son."

CHAPTER 33 ~ ANA

"Wait. Who was the one-year-old son?"

"The baby's name was Moritz. His grandmother was Marthe von Hülshoff-Schmitt, the old baron's sister."

"It's all a little confusing."

"Not really," Peter said. "Everyone in the family was invited to a party for the baby's first birthday on December 17. During the air raid that evening a bomb went straight through to the air raid shelter in the basement. That was it. Everyone died."

"What about the baron?"

"You mean the old baron? He died here too, but his son Gerhard was stationed in France with the *Luftwaffe*. After the war Gerhard came back. He was the only Hohensteuern left, so he became the new baron."

"But later he said some of the others might have survived."

"Yes, his aunt Marthe and a baby boy. I really did tell you about all this."

He had told me most of it. I remembered now. But seeing the actual site, hardly a hundred feet from the shop where Margret had bought her fur coat, brought the story to life. Could Marthe have survived an attack that leveled the entire neighborhood? And if she had, might she have changed her name to Margret?

"I want to talk to the baroness."

"We've taken enough risks for one day." Peter took my arm and led me down the steps of a pedestrian underpass. "We shouldn't even be here, so close to the Einstein monument. It's where anyone would look for you."

"Tomorrow, then," I insisted. We climbed a set of steps to a sidewalk and headed past the train station toward a row of parked buses. I noticed one of the buses had the word *Klingenstein* in blinking lights up front. "You said the baroness was curious about me. Well now I'm curious about her too."

"Maybe tomorrow if—"

Suddenly we were knocked backwards by a man staggering across the sidewalk from the bus stop.

"*Scheisse!*" The man spat and turned to face us.

He was big. He was dirty. He smelled of liquor and of barnyards—as if he'd spent a night with a herd of goats. And yet I knew I'd seen him before.

Peter clutched my arm, backing away. "Careful," he whispered to me in English, "I think this is the man who broke my ribs in Greece."

Yes, and he was the same suspicious tourist who returned my purse in Venice. Already a second drunk German man was staggering up to squint at me. My heart was pumping pure fear.

"Run!" I whispered back.

So we ran.

That night, in the darkness of my museum prison, lying on a stiff cot, I kept turning questions over in my mind.

How had we been followed by two stumbling drunks? Even if they had planted a locator device in my purse, I'd left my purse in Trieste. Here in Ulm, the men hadn't even appeared to recognize us. Our disguises had worked. But what must they have thought when the elderly Herr Weiss and his wife suddenly sprinted down the street toward a park? If we wanted to arouse suspicion, we'd done a good job of it.

I also found myself haunted by an unlikely image—the swirling storm I'd happened to see on television. To my knowledge, Italy didn't have hurricanes. And yet there it was, a giant low-pressure system centered over Trieste, with clouds spiraling into a central void.

What happens when you damage a cyclotron? Dr. Nimolo had talked about capturing a miniature black hole—a singularity that swallows matter. Could a miniature black hole create a low-pressure storm?

As my fears crept closer, I found myself wishing Rags would curl up on my cot and guard my dreams.

BESIEGING THE CASTLE
(Harmony)

"We're interested in old buildings, you know, like castles?" I flashed an innocent American smile to the girl at Ulm's tourist information counter.

Well, what was I supposed to do? Neither Gilberto nor I could speak German. It's not so easy, rescuing a kidnapped friend when you're in a strange country.

Our whole mission had become more difficult since I kissed Berti. Yes, I had succeeded in overpowering the giddy girl who wanted nothing more than to jump into bed with him. Gilberto and I had managed to hike down to Gargellen and order separate rooms at a mostly empty ski hotel. It's not like I could forget what had happened—I was pretty hopelessly hooked on Berti. But I was supposed to be helping Ana, not stealing her boyfriend.

"You'll want to visit our church." The girl tore a city map of Ulm from a pad and began drawing a line from the train station. "The *Münster* has the tallest church tower in the world. It's—"

"No, no," Gilberto stopped her. "We want castles."

"Castles?" She thought a moment. "Well, I suppose there's a museum in the old city wall. Let's see—oh, it closed at two o'clock."

"What about this castle here?" I pointed to the little black square on my German road map.

"Schloss Klingenstein?" She frowned. "No one goes there."

"Why? Is it haunted?"

The girl laughed. "No, it's just small. I think it's private, too. They don't have tours."

"That's OK. How do we get there?"

The bus was sitting near the train station with a sign blinking *Klingenstein.* I took out a handful of euros to pay the driver. But everybody else had some kind of ticket thing. Where did they get that? Improvising quickly, I offered the driver a big smile. "Can I buy a ticket here?" I shook my ponytail and shrugged my backpack with one shoulder, wiggling things all around. The driver gave me a goofy look, said something in German, and waved us on.

"Is it free?" Gilberto asked, concerned.

"Yeah, it's magic."

Everyone on the bus was watching us—I mean, really watching us. Old ladies with string bags. Turkish men with UCLA sweatshirts. Teenage boys with spiked hair. It made me want to shout, "Hi, everybody—we're not just weird, we're on a secret rescue mission!"

For the next half hour the bus fooled around through commercial streets, shopping centers, and industrial backwaters. Finally Gilberto and I were the only passengers left. The driver swung around in front of a sign for the *Hotel Alte Post,* looked in the mirror, and said pointedly, "Klingenstein!"

We got out and stood there with our backpacks, looking like the most clueless tourists on the planet.

The castle was up on a hill. Anyone could see it, an old stone house with a little tower. It certainly wasn't the fairy tale palace from Disneyland. It made me wonder if I'd misunderstood Ana's call for help. Was she really being held in a dump like that? And how exactly were we supposed to slash our way in to rescue sleeping beauty?

Berti read my thoughts. "Maybe first we should see if they've got rooms here in the hotel."

They didn't. At least not two rooms. And it was the only hotel in Klingenstein.

"There's a convention in town this week," the receptionist apologized. "We have cement contractors here from all of Europe."

"Cement contractors?"

The receptionist nodded. "You don't know of Klingenstein's fame?"

We shook our heads.

"Cement," she said. "It was developed here because of the limestone. All we have left is one room with a double bed."

"Oh, we'll make do," I lied, thinking quickly. A night in a double bed would be a painful test of our fidelity to Ana, but the option was to have no room at all. "Mr. Ferguson and I shared a bed for the first five years of our marriage."

The receptionist smiled as she ran my Visa card.

We were pretty nervous about our rescue mission, I admit. Gilberto and I took our backpacks up to the little room. We decided we might have more luck spying on the castle after dark, so we went out to buy groceries. Then we sat on the balcony with brie and merlot, watching the sun go down. We didn't say much, but my thoughts were split between the kidnappers in the castle and the perhaps equally dangerous proximity of a double bed.

That evening we put on our darkest clothes and set out in the twilight. I found a bike path across a field and then headed cross-country through the brush, climbing straight up toward the castle.

This was tricky work. We had to scramble around a stone wall, shimmy up a chute of rough rock, and make our way through a jungle of trees to the base of the castle. When we crested a rise, out of breath, I saw an old Volkswagen beetle pulling into the castle courtyard.

"Shh!" I motioned for Gilberto to crouch behind a rock where we could watch.

The driver who got out of the Volkswagen was a white-haired man with spectacles.

"Is that Peter Weiss?" Gilberto whispered. "I don't know what the cowboy detective looks like."

"He wears disguises," I whispered back, "But there's something familiar about this guy."

The white-haired man opened the car's back door and took out a laundry basket.

"Those are Ana's clothes!" Gilberto whispered.

The geeky striped shirt definitely belonged to Ana. It made me shiver, thinking that this violent, unpredictable kidnapper had taken her clothes.

"She must not be at the castle after all," I whispered.

"What do you mean?" Gilberto looked puzzled. "He's got her clothes."

"Yes, but where did he get them? If Ana were at the castle, why would he take her clothes away and then bring them back? He's probably keeping her somewhere else."

Gilberto nodded slowly. "This is logical thinking, Armonia. So how do we find her?"

"Follow him. It looks like he's staying here tonight. Maybe he'll go back to check on her tomorrow."

"Good. In the morning we'll rent a car."

We had a plan. Ana was not far away. Against all odds, we really might slash through the haunted thickets and wake our princess. For extra luck, I took a stick from the forest floor and tossed it over my left shoulder.

Instantly an electronic alarm went off, whooping like a sick duck.

"Oops."

A big brown-and-black dog came barking out of a shed, held on a leash by a very old man with a saggy beret. *"Vamos, Golfo!"* the man wheezed.

Gilberto and I frantically scrambled back downhill. Somehow we ended up on a terrace with an overgrown tennis court. The dog followed us, barking like crazy. We were trapped against a cliff and a stone wall at the far end of the old court.

Gilberto crossed himself. Yeah, like that was going to help.

The dog's handler backed us into a corner of the court. The dog was going nuts, obviously eager to jump up and rip out our throats.

I was terrified. But then I recalled what the old man had said: *Vamos, Golfo*. That might be German, but somehow I doubted it.

"Hola," I said, switching gears at top speed. I flashed a huge smile. "Do you guys speak Spanish?"

The old man stopped. The dog still growled.

"Español?" I repeated.

The old man tilted his head. *"Español?"* He squeezed the word out with difficulty, one syllable at a time.

"Si," I said, still smiling like a goodwill ambassador at the United Nations.

"Mushrooms!" Gilberto said suddenly.

"What?"

"Ask if he likes mushrooms."

Now I knew we were doomed. Gilberto had gone bonkers. Still I kept smiling and asked in my best Spanish, "So, do you like mushrooms?"

Incredibly, the man nodded.

I guess Berti's magic is subtler than mine.

A ROCKY REUNION
(Harmony)

I didn't get much sleep much that night, knowing we would face Ana's kidnapper in the morning. It was also really difficult to lie on a double bed a few inches from Berti without touching him.

I think I was even more enamored of Gilberto since he'd saved us at the castle. The old Spanish groundskeeper had not only accepted the idea that we were hunting wild mushrooms, but when he heard Gilberto had an Italian truffle recipe he wanted me to translate a copy for him. How had Berti known?

We turned restlessly all night, jumping whenever a toe strafed the other's knee. By dawn I had managed to get perhaps an hour of fitful sleep.

After breakfast we rented a little Opel Kadett and were back on Ana's case, lurking on a side street near the castle gate.

The VW bug drove by around eleven. This time the cowboy detective's hair was dark and his spectacles were gone, but I'd learned to spot the elusive Peter Weiss. I put our Opel in pursuit and followed him back to the edge of downtown. When the VW stopped we parked a hundred meters away to watch. Weiss got out with a laundry bag and walked across a park lawn to a big iron gate.

Gilberto and I left our car and crept from tree to tree toward the gate. It turned out to be the entrance to some kind of underground war museum.

"Ready?" he asked, looking at me.

"We can't just walk in," I objected. "The kidnappers are in there."

"Exactly. They must be trying to get the second half of the formula from Ana. That's why we're here."

"But what if they're armed?"

"What if they're hurting her?"

"I—"

I stopped short when the door opened. A bald man with a ghastly green bow tie stepped outside. He sat on a bench by the door, took a pack of cigarettes out of his tweed jacket, and said something incomprehensible to us in German.

Gilberto and I stood perfectly still, as if caught in a game of freeze tag. I swallowed hard.

"You're Americans, aren't you?" The bow-tied man lit his cigarette and took a hungry drag. Then he narrowed his eyes at us. "Go on inside. It's free today anyway."

We hesitated. He waved his fingers at us, as if to dispel the cigarette smoke. "Go on, go on."

So Gilberto and I went in. The first room looked like a cave. Everything was dark except for a row of display boards with tiny spotlights. I couldn't see people, but there was a distant, echoing voice.

I reached for Gilberto's hand. Too late! He was already stalking ahead into a second, smaller room, toward the voice. I didn't dare call out to stop him. All I could do was follow.

Practically the only light in the museum's back room was coming from a doorway. Silhouetted against the open door stood the cowboy detective, his arms crossed. He looked like the shadow of evil itself.

A voice was quietly crying, out of sight beyond the door.

The voice was Ana's.

Gilberto and I exchanged a pained glance. Ana was speaking in German. Although I couldn't understand her, the despairing tone was chilling.

Slowly Gilberto lifted an ammunition shell casing from one of the displays. About the size of wine bottle, the antique steel shell must have weighed five pounds. Gilberto took a long, slow breath. He looked to me and nodded.

I didn't want him to do this. But I couldn't think of another way.

Gilberto crept forward to the doorway. Then he rose up and whacked the cowboy detective on the back of the head.

Peter Weiss went down like a sack of potatoes.

Ana screamed.

Gilberto turned to me with a look of surprise, pride, fear—all of that, mixed together, in a single second.

Then Ana swung something dark and heavy behind him. There was a thud and Gilberto slowly sagged into a heap on top of Peter Weiss.

This time I was the one who screamed.

Yeah, so there we were: Ana and I, facing each other over two unconscious men.

"Ana!" She was wearing a hot little black skirt and a snappy white blouse. Nice outfit for a hostage, I thought.

"Harm! What are you doing here?"

"Trying to rescue you, what does it look like?"

"Rescue *me?* Didn't I warn you about Gilberto?"

"Oh, for—" I gave up and turned my attention to Berti. She'd clubbed the poor guy pretty hard with some sort of sandbag. He was breathing all right, but his eyelids wouldn't even flutter. He was out cold.

And here's the amazing thing: While I was checking out Berti, Ana got down on her knees to stroke the bump on the *cowboy detective's* head.

"OK, Ana, what's going on?" I sat back and crossed my arms. "First you clobber Berti, and then you start pawing over the cowboy detective."

"Berti?" Ana stared at me "So now he's *Berti?* Just where has he been keeping you for the last two days?"

I don't blush easily, but my face was hot. "We've been on our way to help. You said you'd been kidnapped. Of course the phone message you left me was pretty confused."

Ana put her hand on her forehead, as if to stifle a migraine. "Harm, I don't know what you heard. But Peter Weiss is on our side. He's a good guy, understand? He's trying to help me find my family here in Ulm."

I frowned at the two men lying before us. "So Weiss didn't kidnap you?"

"No. He's the only reason I got out of Trieste alive. Dr. Nimolo had people shooting at us. There was this black Mercedes—"

"Gilberto told me all about the black Mercedes. He told me everything. You see, Ana, he's on our side too."

"No, he's working for Nimolo! All Gilberto wanted was the Einstein formula."

"Ana! Gilberto quit his job because of you. He's risked everything to come here." I looked at her askance. "I thought you liked him. That's what you said from Greece."

Now it was Ana's turn to blush. "Gilberto and I had a fling, I'll admit. But things never really clicked between us. He's not quite my type. Too much like Randy."

"Randy! Berti's not at all like your ex."

"Listen to you, Harm. I remember in Greece you told me I shouldn't be trusting Gilberto so much. How did you let him get to you? You of all people."

I took a breath and confessed. "Actually, it was the other way around."

"Wait a minute. Explain that."

"He's a better man than you think, Ana. He saved my life in the Alps. He smuggled me across two borders. And yet all the time he was worrying about you. He wouldn't even look at me. Honestly."

"Until?"

I looked down, embarrassed. "He has this thing when it comes to cooking."

"That's true. The man is irresistible in a kitchen."

"He made tiramisu for me, Ana."

"You're kidding. Tiramisu?"

I gave her a one-shouldered shrug.

Ana started to smile. "And it was *that* good?"

I nodded.

We looked at each other and broke out laughing. I'd missed Ana so much, and I'd been so worried about her. We hugged each other, tears in our eyes. I think the greatest relief was that we were still friends.

Finally Ana dried her eyes with her sleeve. "All right, Harm. If you think we can trust Gilberto, you can have him."

"Are you serious?" Inside me, a fifteen-year-old girl was doing cart-wheels.

"Yeah, he's yours. But you have to promise to let me have Peter."

Her tone was so earnest that it caught me by surprise. I looked at the boyish face of the cowboy detective, sleeping peacefully beneath Gilberto's arm. "Is that what you want? I thought he ransacked your apartment in Eugene."

"That wasn't him. Peter's been looking out for me all along."

"Are you sure?"

Ana nodded. "He's not really a detective. He's a sculptor. His parents work for a baroness in the Klingenstein castle. He thinks my family is somehow connected with the people here. I think he really cares."

"Wow. You've fallen for him pretty hard, haven't you?"

"I'm not sure. We've both been hurt before. And he's so shy. It's not like for you, Harm. You can jump into a relationship with both feet." She stroked the dark, wiry hair from Peter's temple. "This guy may never be able to tell me what he really feels."

Peter groaned. *"Ach, das tut weh."* He lifted his shoulder, rolling Gilberto to one side.

Gilberto's head bonked on the floor. Suddenly he jerked upright with a howl. *"Dio!"*

The two men caught sight of each other and began scrambling unsteadily to their knees. Ana grabbed Peter by the shoulders. I pulled Gilberto back.

"You!" Peter exclaimed, pointing at Gilberto.

"Stop! Stop right there." I held up my arms between them like a referee. "No more violence."

"That's right," Ana said. "Peter's been helping me and Gilberto's been helping Harmony. We'll explain it all later. Right now we need to stop fighting and start working together."

The two men rubbed their heads, obviously disoriented.

"Together?" Gilberto muttered, rubbing his neck. "How can we work together when he's keeping Ana locked up in a cave?"

"I'm not keeping her locked up," Peter protested. He touched the lump on the back of his head and winced.

I latched onto Gilberto's question. "Yeah, Ana. Why are you in a cave?"

"Actually it's an old prison."

"All right, why are you in an old prison?"

Ana looked to Peter uncertainly. "It seemed like a good idea at the time. The Italian police wanted me for questioning, and for a while Nimolo's men were looking for me too."

"But now we've decided she might be safer at the castle," Peter said.

"Why's that?" I asked.

"Yesterday we ran into two big German men not far from here," Ana said. "I'm pretty sure they were the ones who broke into my apartment in Oregon. They've been following me ever since. At first I thought they'd put a locator device in my purse. But then I lost the purse and they still showed up here."

Gilberto covered his face with his hands. "Not them again."

I put my arm around Berti's shoulder. Even I could hardly believe that the two relentless Germans had made it to Ulm.

Ana raised her eyebrows. "You mean you know them?"

Gilberto nodded. "I found your purse in Trieste. I used your cell phone to call Harmony. We drove up into the Alps. You were right about the transmitter in your purse. The Germans followed us, burned my car, and chased us into the mountains."

Peter frowned. "That sounds like a worse trip than the one we took through Slovenia."

"We finally found the transmitter at the Austrian border," I said. "I stuck it on a goat's collar. The German guys walked off into a snowstorm. That was fun for a while, watching them follow a goat."

Ana thought a moment. "But that doesn't explain how they found us here."

"No," I said. "There's something about those guys we don't understand."

"There's nothing about them we understand," Peter objected. "Who are they? What do they want? All they've done is follow us and cause trouble. It doesn't make sense."

Ana said, "I think we're getting closer to the answer all the time."

The museum guy looked puzzled when we all walked out together. Ana and Peter stopped to talk with him in German. Gilberto was still so pale and shaky from the blow to his head that I had to help him stagger along.

When we got to Peter's car, Ana took charge. "Harm, I think you should take Gilberto back to your hotel. He looks like he needs to lie down. Peter and I will call if we need backup at the castle." She stopped for a moment. "By the way, do you still have my cell phone? And what happened to yours, Harm? Nobody's been able to reach you for days."

Gilberto and I both dug phones out of our pockets. He handed Ana's phone to her. "I used it only once, the day I called Harmony."

My own cell phone was displaying a long, annoying message from the phone company. "Oops. I had a free one-week trial for cell service in Europe. It must have run out. I guess I'll have to pay up."

Ana got in the driver's seat of the VW. "We'll call each other whenever something comes up, OK? And Harm?"

"What?"

"Call your parents. They've been worried."

After I helped Gilberto to the Opel I punched Visa numbers into my cell phone until it worked again. Then I got in the driver's seat, pulled out into traffic, and called my parents. I guess they were glad to hear from me, but they didn't exactly jump up and down. It was 4 am in Oregon, and they seemed to be having a hard time understanding what I was doing in Germany.

When I stopped at a light beside a big cement mixer, Gilberto leaned forward with a groan. The poor guy looked like he was going to be sick. Head wounds can have that kind of delayed effect.

"Gotta run, Mom. Bye." I turned off the cell and asked, "Berti, are you all right?"

"The truck driver!" Gilberto moaned, keeping his head down. "Don't let him see you."

I sneaked a look out Gilberto's window. For a moment I thought I might be sick too. The driver of the cement truck next to us was the same big German guy who had driven the rental car in Switzerland. Only now he was tapping the wheel of a cement truck and singing along with the radio.

"Holy shit. He doesn't seem to know we're here. Should I follow him or what?"

The light turned green. The truck growled forward, its gigantic oval tank slowly turning. I pulled behind it and punched Ana's button on the phone.

Gilberto reached a pale hand toward the plastic bag that held our car rental contract. "Armonia? I don't feel well."

"Peter Weiss," the cowboy detective's voice came from my phone.

"Quick, let me talk to Ana."

"I can't. There's a law against using cell phones while you're driving. You aren't driving now, Harmony, are you?"

I rolled my eyes. "Just tell her we've found one of the German men who've been following her."

"Really?"

"Yeah, he's driving a cement truck."

"I see." Peter didn't sound very surprised. "What kind of cement truck?"

"The letters keep turning around. It starts with *Kling*, and then ends with something about *fabric.*"

"The *Klingensteiner Zementfabrik,*" Peter said.

"You know the place?" I was still a little suspicious of Peter Weiss. "Look, I want to talk to Ana."

There was a pause. Meanwhile Gilberto barfed into the contract bag.

"Harm?" This time it was Ana's voice. "Is the German guy still chasing you?"

"No, I'm chasing him. He's singing along with his radio. Gilberto's throwing up. We're having a great time."

"Maybe you should just try to get back to your hotel."

"What about the thug? What's he planning to do with the cement truck? Pour concrete boots for us?"

Ana sighed. "I don't know. Let me think about it. Somehow a guy singing in a cement truck is not quite as threatening as gunmen in a black Mercedes."

"Whatever you say. Toodle-oo." I turned away from the main highway, leaving the cement truck to fend for itself. A minute later I was pulling in front of the Hotel Alte Post. A bellhop waved me toward a sign for parking around the back.

Gilberto was just lifting his pale face above the dashboard when we drove into the parking lot behind the hotel.

The only empty slot was in the middle of a row of five cars. Three of the cars had Italian license plates. Two had tinted windows.

But all five were black Mercedes.

Berti took one look and threw up on the dash.

MEET THE BARONESS
(Ana)

"Maybe this isn't such a good idea," Peter said, frowning as I drove up a hill toward the castle.

We had just gotten a second call from Harmony, this time informing us that a fleet of black Mercedes was parked behind her hotel. She and Gilberto had locked themselves in her room. She'd called the receptionist on the hotel phone and had been told that the hotel was full of cement contractors, not criminals. Maybe Italian contractors like black Mercedes. Maybe German spies drive cement trucks in their spare time. Maybe Peter was right—Klingenstein was not the safest place to be.

I fought back my fears and drove on. "Running away won't solve anything. The sooner we find out what's going on, the better."

Peter sighed. "That's what the baroness said."

"Wait—I thought the baroness said I was trouble."

"Yes, she said that too. But I think she has something planned. Tomorrow's her birthday."

"What's that got to do with it?" I slowed at a switchback near the top of the hill. Ahead was the castle's arched stone gate.

"I don't know," Peter said.

I drove the VW into a white gravel courtyard overgrown with grass. A rock face rose up to the left, topped with scraggly trees. To the right stretched a two-story stone building with peeling gray stucco and an uneven red tile roof. At first glance it looked more like an ancient barracks than a castle. But it did have a handsome square tower with a banner-shaped weathervane. Statues of armored knights flanked the front door.

Then I noticed a very old man with a beret. He was waving hedge clippers at me. I parked where he was pointing and got out.

Peter introduced us. "Ana Smyth—Ramon Diaz, our gardener. And our chief of security."

I held out my hand, but the old man merely grunted and returned to his hedge. It didn't make me feel very welcome, or very secure.

As Peter and I walked to the castle entrance he told me quietly, "Ramon's been here so long that the baroness lets him stay out of charity. He's really not much for gardening, or guarding, or even talking. He came here from Spain and never learned much German."

The castle entrance was an ordinary double door at ground level. The stonework framing the doorway was fake, painted onto the gray stucco. But the statues of swaggering knights on either side were wonderful. They had detailed visors, crests on their shields, and a saucy stance that suggested ballet dancers under the armor.

Peter said, "They're only concrete. Most sculptors won't touch the stuff. But Klingenstein is famous for cement, so I've learned to work with it."

"You made these?" I asked, impressed. "They're beautifully done. Who are the knights?"

"Some Hohensteuern men I saw in an old engraving." Perhaps out of embarrassment he turned aside and opened the front door.

The castle's foyer was small, dark, and a little shabby. A wooden staircase to the left had been crudely modified to accommodate the metal rail of a wheelchair lift. A doorway to the right revealed a narrow laundry room with clotheslines. Ahead was a hall with an arch that opened into a kitchen.

"Peter, you're back! And look, it's Miss Smyth." Peter's mother came out, smiling. She took my hands. "Oh, I love your new skirt outfit. It suits you so much better than my old dress. I've just fixed a stew. Have you had lunch?"

"Not yet." I squeezed her hands, grateful for the warmth of her welcome.

"Mother," Peter said. "Ana would like to meet the baroness."

"She's lunching with Wolf Meyerhof now. They're planning things for tomorrow. Maybe later when your father serves coffee—" she stopped suddenly, concerned. "Peter! What happened to your head?"

"I bumped into something. I'm fine."

"Now you just sit down and let me take a look."

For the next half hour we sat at a kitchen table opposite a big gas range, eating chicken vegetable stew while Frau Weiss bustled about us. I learned that the baroness would be celebrating her eighty-fifth birthday tomorrow evening with a dinner for close friends and staff. Frau Weiss had already started cooking some of the courses.

We had just finished the stew when Herr Weiss came down the stairs with a tray of dishes. He bowed slightly toward me. "It's a pleasure, Miss Smyth. I've heard a great deal about you." He was smaller than Peter and had a broader head with thin white hair. The wrinkles around the eyes, however, were exactly as Peter had drawn them for our stroll through town as Herr and Frau Weiss.

"You can show Miss Smyth to the blue room," Herr Weiss told Peter. "I'll call when the baroness is ready for an audience."

Peter led me down the hall to a small room—just plain walls with a casement window and a cheap bed. Still, we were alone, and as we stood there looking at each other, I was ready for Peter to make a pass at me. Honestly, why didn't he?

Instead he blushed and stepped into the closet.

"Peter?" I called after him.

"Oh, it's a feature of the blue room. The priest's escape passage."

I looked in the closet. Peter was opening a panel in the back wall. I followed him through a little wooden door into a huge room lit by arched windows.

"A fire damaged the old chapel long ago," Peter said. "I repaired it for use as a studio."

"Impressive work! This is a beautiful space." Although the pews were gone and the windows had been replaced with plain glass, he had obviously worked hard to restore the room. White sculptures of people, animals, and windswept shapes stood on either hand, as if frozen in place. "It's generous of the baroness to let you use the old chapel for your art."

"The Weiss family has been loyal for generations. My grandmother started here as a maid in the 1930s."

I touched the neck of a stone swan and noticed with a twinge of childish fear that my fingertips were white with dust.

"Is something wrong?" Peter asked.

"No, it's just—" I scoffed at my old anxiety. "When I was little I used to worry about dust. I was afraid it was a sign that things were falling apart. That the world was slowly coming unglued." I felt silly telling him this. I hadn't talked about it for years.

"Interesting." He sat on a bench where the altar must once have been. "Klingenstein is built on white limestone like that, you know. It is a weak rock. The castle walls have many cracks. When I sculpt limestone for my statues I collect the chips. Then I grind them into powder."

"You make dust on purpose? Why?"

"How did you say it—to hold things together."

"What do you mean?" I joined him on the bench.

"I've learned to mix a special cement from powdered Klingenstein limestone. It's as solid and white as marble. Even dust can become the hardest stone, if you have the right formula."

I thought about this. "Yes. The right formula."

Suddenly the creak of a door made me jump.

"There you are, Peter." Herr Weiss stepped from the shadows of a balcony at the back of the chapel. "Coffee is served. The baroness will see you now—both you and Miss Smyth."

My stomach tightened at the thought of finally meeting the baroness. I felt certain she could help unlock my family's past. Perhaps she even knew where to find the other half of the Einstein formula.

My heart beat faster as I followed Peter up a spiral staircase to the balcony. A door opened into an office with filing cabinets and a desktop computer. A bay window overlooked treetops to an ugly quarry and cement factory on the far side of the valley.

We continued down a hall. The corridor had a higher ceiling than the one downstairs, but it was just as poorly lit. I assumed that the closed doors on either side led to the baroness' private rooms.

I whispered to Peter, "Should I call her 'your highness' or 'your grace' or something?"

"No, just 'baroness.'"

At the end of the hall Herr Weiss tapped twice on a double door. Then he stepped inside and announced, "Peter and Miss Ana Smyth."

I straightened my skirt self-consciously. The last time I'd been this nervous I'd had to speak in front of television cameras, defending the foreign language requirement at a Eugene school board meeting.

"Come in, Miss Smyth," an elderly woman's voice barked in English. "I won't bite you."

Her taunt gave me the courage I needed. I strode into the dining hall, nodded, and replied in German, "Thank you, baroness. I've been looking forward to talking with you."

The hunched old woman who sat across from me in a wheelchair drew a withered hand to her lips and studied me carefully. I noticed she had wispy white hair. The wrinkled skin of her face clung to high cheekbones. Her eyes were dark and intelligent. Beside her an equally old man had risen stiffly from a straightback chair. He acknowledged me with a guarded nod. His wire-rimmed spectacles perched between bushy white eyebrows and a bushy white moustache.

"Astonishing," the baroness said, slowly lowering her hand. "I don't believe I have ever known an American to speak German without an accent."

"I teach German, baroness." What struck me as odd was that the baroness herself seemed to have an accent—a faint French lilt.

"I thought young people only bothered to learn English these days." She held out her hand to the gentleman on her left. "This is Wolf Meyerhof, a family friend and a retired police commissioner. Wolf has taken an interest in your case, Miss Smyth. I believe you have met his granddaughter Rosi. She is an officer in the local force."

"Yes, baroness." I glanced to Peter. Why hadn't he told me the policewoman was a granddaughter of the baroness' close friend? Is that why she and Peter were on a first-name basis? "Fräulein Meyerhof has been concerned about my safety. She's also helped me start researching my family here in the Ulm area."

The old gentleman nodded again. "So I've heard."

The baroness was still eyeing me critically. "Peter has told me of the difficulties you experienced in Greece and Italy. You have seen many dangers, Miss Smyth. Frankly, you don't look like an adventurous person. But apparently you are."

I felt my ears redden. Even when the baroness offered praise, it seemed to come with a backhanded dose of criticism. Obviously she had prepared herself not to like me. Peter had said she could be generous and charitable. I suspected her gruffness was just a shell. Somehow

I needed to reach the gentler woman beyond that shell.

"I think everyone can be more daring than they think possible," I suggested, looking at her steadily. "Have you ever had adventure forced upon you, baroness?"

She leaned back, meeting my gaze. She looked like a giant tortoise deciding whether to snap at a bug.

When she finally snapped, however, it was not at me.

"Herr Weiss! Where's the coffee? Our guests are standing here with empty cups. I honestly don't know why I keep you on."

I felt sorry for Peter's father. He turned to fetch a silver coffeepot from a sideboard. Peter and I sat down. From the way Peter had tightened his lips, I could tell this was not the first time his father had endured humiliation. When our coffee cups were full, Herr Weiss set the pot on the table near his son and withdrew from the room.

In the silence that followed I had a chance to look around me at the hall. It was larger than the chapel but it seemed smaller because the ceiling wasn't arched. Glass chandeliers with dim electric lights hung at either end of our long wooden table. Copies of Peter's knight statues stood against the windowless inner wall. Behind them, painted on wooden panels, was a family tree with twining branches and illegible names on shields. The other walls had deep casement windows. An alcove in the far corner of the room was evidently the square tower I'd noticed from outside.

"You ask about adventure, Miss Smyth," the baroness said at length. She set down her coffee cup. "I am not really a Hohensteuern, you know."

"You're not?" I asked.

"No. It appears the baron was the last. Still, it is possible that the story of my own adventure with this family will allow us to reflect on your history as well."

Peter sipped his coffee as if he had heard this story before, but I sat on the edge of my chair, silently encouraging the baroness to continue.

She sighed. "I suppose you can hear it in my voice as well as anyone. I grew up in Paris. I trained for the theater, a naughty profession at the time. During the occupation I sang chansons in cafés. I'll admit I learned some German and English in those years. I had to live too."

"So you met the baron in Paris?"

"No. Gerhard was with the air force in Marseilles." The baroness raised her cup toward the bespectacled gentleman beside her. "Wolf can tell you about their war years."

Wolf cleared his throat. "Gerhard and I served together with the German Condor regiment in the Spanish Civil War. I didn't have the eyesight for a pilot, so I did guard work. Later I was left to serve with the home guard in Ulm. When we heard the British had shot Gerhard down over the Mediterranean, well, we all assumed he was dead. Then the Allied air raid took the rest of his family."

The old gentleman shook his head "That was a terrible night, with chaos everywhere." He took a deep breath. "I organized the castle staff to keep up the building. But what was I to do when the Americans marched in? They took it over and turned it into a lieutenant colonel's headquarters."

"I still don't see how the baroness got involved with the Hohensteuerns," I said.

The baroness explained. "After the war I was entertaining the American troops as a singer. My tour brought me to Klingenstein for a week. On the second night, Gerhard came back. That was a scene to remember."

Peter leaned forward to refill our coffee cups.

The baroness smiled wistfully. "The poor man had been in a prison camp in the Algerian desert when the war ended. Somehow he'd gotten a ride on a steamer to Marseilles. Then he'd walked all the way back across France alone, with rags on his feet. He was thin and dirty. But you should have seen him when he found the Americans in the castle!"

She chuckled, and for a moment I could see her as a beautiful young French chanteuse. "Gerhard was so angry they had to lock him up in the burnt-out chapel. Of course I felt sorry for him. He'd just found out he was an orphan—and that he was the new baron. I stayed another week to nurse him back to health. Then I stayed another week, and another."

I cradled my coffee cup. "It sounds as if you haven't just waited for adventures, baroness. You've made them happen."

"What?" She looked at me sharply, as if she had just noticed I was still there. "Oh yes. And do you know how all of this connects with you, Miss Smyth?"

"No. How?"

"It doesn't." She laid her bony hand firmly on the table. "The police did a scientific test that shows you're not related to the Hohensteuerns. Your people were with the underground."

Wolf interjected, "That's not completely certain at this point."

"Nonetheless." The baroness appeared to gather her thoughts for a moment. "My point is that Gerhard's aunt, Marthe von Hülshoff-Schmitt, may have sympathized with the underground movement, so she might have known your grandmother."

"Really?" I set down my cup.

"Yes. The German aristocracy didn't get along well with the Nazis, you know. Gerhard always suspected that his aunt had been involved with the resistance. We know she was interested in Einstein. She bought the old Einstein house for her daughter. That's why the entire family died. They were all celebrating the first birthday of Marthe's grandson Moritz. Personally, I think Marthe had been in touch all along with that housewife person, the one who escaped from prison."

"Margrethe Semmel," Wolf said. "On the night of the air raid, after Semmel escaped, there was a break-in here at the castle. The Hohensteuern family treasure was stolen."

"Treasure?" Immediately I thought of my father's words—that he hadn't seen a formula, but rather money and jewelry in the violin case. "Where did you keep this treasure?"

The baroness released the brake on her wheelchair, spun to one side, and rolled across the room toward the paneled wall. She stopped just short of the two concrete statues. The armored knights stood there, barring her way with a battleaxe and sword. "Peter, could you move them, please?"

"Of course, baroness." Peter reached under the head of the table. He explained to me, "I put a switch down here. Just for a bit of fun. There."

I heard a click underneath the table. A motor whirred and the two concrete knights pivoted aside.

I stifled a smile at Peter's lordly whimsy.

The baroness rolled past the statues to the wall. "I'm afraid it isn't very well hidden." She pulled open the central panel of the family tree painting. It swung out to reveal a rectangular metal safe. She tapped the cover and it bounced open. The shelf inside was empty. "I don't even bother to lock it. The Hohensteuerns have nothing left to hide. All we have are debts and an old castle in need of repair. Our treasure, it seems, has gone to America."

Now I understood why the baroness had wanted to see me—and why she had sent Peter as a detective to Oregon. She hadn't merely been looking for a possible heir. There was very little left in Klingenstein for anyone to inherit. She'd been trying to track down stolen property. Did she really think the treasure would be intact after all these years?

"There's a lot we still don't know," I said cautiously. "Almost anyone could have taken the treasure in the confusion after the air raid. Certainly if it ended up with Margret Smyth in America, it's been spent long ago. We don't even know for sure who Margret was."

The baroness asked, "Would you like to know, Miss Smyth?"

"Yes. In fact there are three mysteries I'd like to solve—Margret, the treasure, and Einstein's formula. All three of them may have answers in Klingenstein."

The baroness raised her eyebrows. "I am beginning to like you after all, Miss Smyth. I too am ready to clear away mysteries." She rolled her wheelchair back to the head of the table. "Tomorrow is my birthday dinner. Traditionally it is a time for family and staff to discuss the year ahead. This time, I want it to be a forum on the puzzling events behind us."

"Sounds like a good idea," I said.

"Of course it's a good idea. I've already invited Wolf, Rosi, and the castle staff. Am I leaving anyone out?"

Wolf said, "I think it would be politic to invite Rosi's fiancé."

I shot a glance to Peter, but he didn't flinch. That was a relief. Whoever was engaged to Rosi, it evidently wasn't him.

"Yes, I suppose we'll have to," the baroness said, frowning. "I've never cared much for factory owners and politicians, and Dieter Braun qualifies on both counts."

"Nonetheless, baroness," Wolf said.

The baroness turned to me. "Is there anyone you would like to bring, Miss Smyth?"

"I have two friends who've come to help me with my investigations. Harmony Ferguson and Gilberto Montale."

"Fine. Now I want everyone to go out and look for answers." The baroness leaned back. "Tomorrow night each of us should bring at least one family secret to share."

Wolf adjusted his spectacles. "Baroness, this sounds overly dramatic."

She smiled. "My dear Wolf, it's no use accusing me of drama. I trained as an actress."

Peter objected, "What kind of information can we come up with in one day?"

She tilted her head. "You might talk to Frau Werther at the Klingenstein museum. I remember Gerhard saying that his aunt Marthe had collected some Einstein things there. Maybe Miss Smyth will be able to make sense of them."

"What about security?" Wolf asked. "Rosi has been concerned about Miss Smyth's safety. You remember the Italians?"

"They haven't been back," the baroness said.

I hesitated a moment. Then I said, "We heard there are some black Mercedes with Italian plates parked behind the Hotel Alte Post."

"You see? I'll ask Rosi to check, but I don't like it." The old police commissioner took off his spectacles and cleaned them with a handkerchief.

"We've also been followed by two German men," Peter said. "They broke into Ana's apartment in America. Later they tried to hit her with a speedboat in Greece."

The baroness said, "Yes, you told me about them. You said they spoke with a local accent. That's another puzzle, isn't it?"

Peter nodded. "We saw them yesterday at the train station in Ulm."

"In Ulm?" Wolf frowned. "They followed you here?"

I said, "They followed me as far as Italy by putting a locator device in my purse. But I left the purse in Trieste. I'm not sure what they're up to now. I'm not even sure they're after the formula like everyone else."

"Ana's friend spotted one of them today in Klingenstein." Peter gave the retired police commissioner an oddly direct look and added, "The man was driving a cement truck."

"A cement truck." Wolf set his spectacles on the table and ran his hand over his eyes. "We do have a lot left to investigate."

THE EINSTEIN ATTIC
(Ana)

"What's going on with you and Meyerhof?" I asked Peter when we'd closed the door of the dining hall behind us. "You knew he'd be interested in the cement truck. And how did you get on a first-name basis with his granddaughter?"

"You mean Rosi? We went to school together."

We started walking down the corridor. I said, "There's more to it than that, isn't there?"

He paused at the top of the stairs and sighed. "We dated for a year or two in school. It didn't work out."

"Why?"

He shook his head and went down the stairs. I followed him outside. After he'd closed the castle's front door behind us he said, "I never really trusted Rosi. The day I left to study art in Cambridge she admitted she'd been seeing someone else. She said she wanted a man who would have more money than an artist."

"So now, years later, she's engaged to marry somebody rich."

He nodded. "Dieter Braun. His family owns the cement factory."

"I see." In Klingenstein everything seemed to revolve around cement. Despite Rosi's engagement I suspected she still had a crush on Peter. I'd felt it from the first, when she met us at the train station.

I asked, "So it's not just a coincidence that the German who followed us was driving a cement truck?"

"I don't know. Nothing makes sense, Ana."

"No, but we're collecting a lot of puzzle pieces, aren't we?" I wasn't sure how to find out more about the cement truck driver. The German thugs were dangerous men. My instincts told me to stay as far away from them as possible. Maybe it was best to leave them to Herr Meyerhof and the police for a while.

I suggested, "Let's start by checking out the Klingenstein museum, like the baroness said. Where is it?"

"Next door, in the old factory."

We went to the castle gate and peered out to the street. No black Mercedes and no cement trucks were in sight. So we took our chances and walked up the sidewalk. A hundred yards up the hill the view opened up all the way to the distant spire of Ulm's church. Dark storm clouds were swirling up from the south. I was reminded of my fears from the night before—that the storm from Italy might somehow be connected to the cyclotron we'd damaged in Trieste. By the light of day the idea seemed pretty far-fetched.

I turned to look at the old factory. The barn-like building stood at the top of the hill, with four tiers of crooked windows and a great, sloping roof of brown and red tiles. A small sign read *Heimatmuseum Klingenstein*.

"What kind of factory was it?" I asked.

"A harpsichord factory," Peter said. "The Hohensteuerns became wealthy by building them. Until pianos came along."

"Margret had a clavichord," I mused. "She taught me to play."

"Aren't clavichords different?"

"A little. They tap the strings. Harpsichords pluck them. Still, it makes you wonder." Margret's DNA might not match the Hohensteuerns, but her interest in early keyboard instruments obviously did.

"I haven't been in here for a while," Peter said. "I guess the baroness has been talking about renovating the place. She wants to rent out space for shops and offices."

"Sounds like a good idea. Why doesn't she do it?"

"All it takes is money." Peter opened the museum's door.

Inside we met Frau Werther, a thin woman who reminded me of a librarian, perhaps because she wore half-lens reading glasses on a chain about her neck.

"Herr Weiss, it's good to see you again. And Miss Smyth. A

colleague of mine said you might visit."

I paid our five-euro admission fees. "I'm particularly interested in the family history of the Hohensteuerns."

"Well, we have a lot of that here." She led us past glass cases of stone age pottery, bronze spears, and Roman coins to a framed engraving of two knights in armor. "I suppose it starts with Konrad and Lorenz von Klingenstein, the brothers who built the first castle here in 1254."

"Those are the knights you used for your statues," I said to Peter.

He gave an embarrassed shrug.

"You've seen his sculpture?" the curator asked. "I've been trying to get him to make copies of his knights for the museum. He makes concrete look like marble."

"Miss Smyth asked about harpsichords," Peter said.

"Oh. Well, they're back here." She led the way to a large back room with workbenches, hand tools, and half a dozen harpsichords. Curled wood shavings littered the floor. "We've kept this workroom just as it was."

"When did they stop building harpsichords?" I asked.

She wrinkled her brow. "It's curious you should ask. Officially the factory closed in 1939. National defense was a priority by then, not harpsichords. The few employees who were left became soldiers or went to work in the armament industry. But two of the harpsichords here—in my opinion, the best ever built—are dated 1941 and 1943. Look at the inlay on this soundboard, and the carved scrolls on the ends of the keys. These are works of genius."

The harpsichords were indeed beautiful. I wanted to play them, but I was afraid that might be frowned on in a museum. Instead I asked, "Do you have any other family effects? The baroness said her husband's aunt Marthe may have collected mementoes of Albert Einstein."

"Albert Einstein? I don't know about that. But we have stored quite a few uncatalogued items in the attic. Some of them are from the Hohensteuern factory. Others are old exhibits we've retired. I suppose you could take a look if you like."

"Could we?" I recalled how eagerly Dr. Nimolo had searched for Einstein memorabilia. I hoped he hadn't been here first.

Frau Werther unlocked a door and led us up a crooked wooden

staircase that switched back and forth with each flight. The floors we passed had vast, dusty rooms with exposed, sagging beams. The windows were small, but had spectacular views of the valley and the distant silhouette of Ulm.

"It's interesting you should mention Einstein," Frau Werther said over her shoulder. "The factory used to employ one of the Buchau Einsteins. It's a different branch of the family than Albert Einstein's, but he helped them all escape before the war anyway."

"Really?" I asked.

"Yes, after Albert Einstein got a job with an American university, he sent letters to help even his distant relatives get visas out of Germany."

After four flights of stairs, Frau Werther led us up a ladder through a trap door to the attic. The garret's slanting ceiling exposed the undersides of ceramic roof tiles and crude rafter poles. Saucer-sized circles of hand-blown glass let in light from little gables. A plank pathway led between rows of boxes.

I think it was the smell that took me back so forcefully—dust, wood, and old paper. Suddenly I felt I was back in the attic of my childhood home in Eugene. Margret had said it was a portal to the fourth dimension, to time itself. In her will she had left me the contents of her attic. Perhaps she really had wanted to give me a kind of time machine, a ticket back to a world of dusty memories.

"Ana, are you all right?" Peter put his hand on my shoulder.

"Sorry, yes." I gave him a flustered smile. "Daydreaming, I guess."

"So, what are you looking for?" Frau Werther asked.

"I don't know, exactly," I admitted.

She put her hands on her hips—just the sort of impatient, imperious gesture that matched my image of her as an old-fashioned librarian. "I shouldn't be leaving the front desk unattended."

Peter said, "The baroness asked us to look for some family things. I'll take responsibility for Miss Smyth."

"She hasn't even seen the rest of the museum," Frau Werther objected.

"Give us half an hour to look around here first." Peter smiled. When he smiles, he's hard to resist.

"Half an hour, then." Frau Werther descended the ladder, watching us as she went.

I really wasn't sure what were we looking for. Peter and I walked the plank pathway, peering into the boxes on either hand. Books, tools, old clothes—the sort of stuff you'd find at a flea market.

Peter echoed my thoughts. "If some of this really was Albert Einstein's, how would we know?"

The plank ended at an old museum display—a dusty diorama beneath a gable's circular window. I was about to turn back when Peter chuckled.

"What is it?"

He pointed to the diorama. "Oh, it's just the old Klingenstein legend. No wonder they hid it up here."

The scene of soldiers and tents was laughably amateurish. Still, something about it struck me as familiar.

"What's the legend?" I asked.

"Every town in Germany has invented some story like it. Back in the Hundred Years' War the French and the Swedes were always marching through, threatening to burn down the villages they passed. Then some hero would step forward."

"In this case, a Hohensteuern?"

Peter shook his head. "The town's mayor. He walked into the French camp and challenged the general to a drinking duel. The French laughed at him, of course. But the general was amused. He said he'd spare the town if the mayor could drink a giant bottle of wine in one draught."

The centerpiece of the diorama was a two-foot-tall statue of a fat man, grinning victoriously as he held up an enormous beer stein.

That's when it hit me—the mayor was a gnome. Whoever had built the diorama hadn't created a special statue for the mayor. They'd just bought a big garden gnome with a beer stein.

I turned to Peter, my mouth open. I didn't know whether to laugh or cry, so I just gaped. I must have looked like I'd gone mad, but I didn't care. I was a little girl again, playing make-believe in Margret's magic attic.

"Ana! What's the matter?"

In reply I simply hugged him, burying my face in his shirt. He had a warm, wonderfully reassuring smell. When I came up at last he looked puzzled and worried, and yet somehow happy at the same time.

"It's the burgermeister of the gnomes," I managed to say.

Peter bit his lip. "Ana, are you OK?"

"Yes, yes. It's just—" I stopped and took a long breath. "It's what Margret always told me to look for. When I was a girl and she taught me the rhyme about Einstein's formula, she said I should only tell it to the burgermeister of the gnomes. And now, here he is."

"All right," Peter said slowly, as though he wasn't sure whether Margret or I—or both of us—were crazy. "Then what is that supposed to mean? Even if this is the burgermeister she was talking about, how would you tell a secret to a statue?"

"I don't know. Maybe the statue's supposed to tell me a secret in return." I bent over and picked up the mayor. He wasn't very heavy. I blew the dust off his painted, ceramic grin. He wore a short white beard, a red cap, and dark green lederhosen. He held the giant stein in front of him with delight, as if he were embracing a beer barrel. If he had a secret, there were no obvious clues.

"Try shaking it," Peter suggested.

The gnome was so large I had to use both hands. Was there a faint rustling inside? I turned the figure upside down. The words "Made In Germany" had been stamped into the ceramic. But what gave me a zing of excitement was a coin-sized hole in the base. The hole had been plugged with some kind of white gum.

Peter and I exchanged glances. I could tell we were thinking the same thing. Maybe you're not supposed to break things in a museum—even a seal on the bottom of a gnome—but we were far too curious to stop now.

I used my thumb to press the white gum. It crumbled easily. Then I reached my fingers inside the gnome and fished out a tightly rolled notebook.

By now my heart was beating dangerously fast. I set the gnome to one side and unrolled the booklet. Penned on the yellowed cover in an ornate, old-fashioned script were the words *Tagebuch – E. Einstein.*

"Einstein's diary?" Peter asked.

"But not Albert Einstein's," I pointed out.

"Who is E. Einstein?"

Shoulder to shoulder, we leafed slowly through the notebook. There were only about forty pages, with short entries every month or so from November 8, 1938 until December 12, 1944. The last few pages were blank. At first glance there were no mathematical formulas.

Finally Peter shook his head. "Do you suppose it could be the Einstein relative who worked here at the harpsichord factory? Frau Werther said he left Germany before the war. But these entries go right up to the week of the air raid."

"Maybe he waited too long to get a visa out of Germany. He could be the one who built the harpsichords from 1941 and 1943 that we saw downstairs." Some of the entries did appear to be about harpsichords.

"If this Einstein relative really was hiding here in a boarded-up factory," Peter said, "he had to have help on the outside."

"Someone at the castle." My mind was racing. "Marthe. The one with connections to the underground."

"You're jumping to conclusions, Ana."

"Then let me jump one more time. I'm willing to bet that the E stands for Ephraim."

"Ephraim?" Peter looked skeptical. "Where did you come up with that name?"

"In Venice. Gilberto and I went to see the Swiss doctor who published *The Red Cross and the Broken Cross*."

"The book about the war? You found the author?"

"Yes."

"And he remembered the day Margret showed up in Switzerland?"

"He also remembered the old man she'd escaped with. The old man couldn't talk much because he'd been shot in the lungs. But the old man said his name was Ephraim."

"Ephraim." Peter thought about this. "Did the Swiss doctor learn anything else from him?"

I nodded. "Ephraim told him the lady with the violin case was going to save everyone. She was smuggling a lost Einstein formula for quantum gravity to the Allies. He said it would allow the creation of a gravity bomb."

Peter sat down on a wooden crate. "I guess that explains why so many people have been looking for the formula. If Ephraim Einstein leaked word that it was that important, every physicist in the world would want to see it."

I sat down beside him. "But where is the formula? It's supposed to be written on a piece of Brahms sheet music. Margret gave me a clue about the burgermeister, but all we've found is a diary."

Peter picked up the gnome, tilted the hole to the light, and looked inside. "Maybe that's not all the burgermeister knows."

I grabbed the gnome and looked. A small wad of paper was stuck in the beer stein. Quickly I searched around for something to pry out the paper. I found a coat hanger in a nearby box, bent it into a long hook, and worked the paper loose. The wad dropped out of the hole and rolled across the plank floor like a ball.

I caught the paper just as it was about to fall into a crack between the planks. For a moment I just held it in my hands, taking deep breaths to steady myself. Then I sat beside Peter and smoothed the paper out on my skirt.

It was indeed a Brahms sonata for violin and piano. There were indeed scribbled physics notations in the margin. But the page had been torn in half.

"Oh, shit," I whispered.

"What?" Peter asked. "Isn't this the right formula?"

"It's the right formula, but the paper's ripped down the middle. Only half of the formula is here."

"Which half?" Peter asked.

"The part I already know." I pointed it out on the page.

$$F = \frac{Gm_1m_2}{r} +$$

"The wrong half." Peter thought a moment. "At least it proves Margret was here. I wonder why she left only half of the formula?"

"Wait." I closed my eyes and let myself whirl back through time, trying to imagine myself as Margret. I knew her—a haunted woman, suspicious and secretive.

"Maybe I know why," I said, opening my eyes.

Peter looked at me uncertainly. "Why?"

"I think she was afraid to leave the entire formula in one place. She memorized the first half and left it here with Ephraim's diary. The second half she took with her in the violin case."

"If Margret took it to America, why didn't you find it in your attic there? Where would she have hidden half a sheet of music?"

I looked at him, wide eyed. "In the gnomes!"

"What gnomes?"

"She collected garden gnomes. She'd been keeping them in her attic for years. They were part of her shrine to Einstein."

"That does sound suspicious. What happened to her gnomes?"

"Harmony and I put them up for sale on eBay. Nobody bought them. Then we tried to get rid of them at the garage sale. Nobody wanted them then either."

Peter nodded. "So when the German thugs searched your apartment, the gnomes weren't there."

"That's right. They were at the garage sale. And the formula was probably stuffed inside them all the time."

"And now?" Peter asked. "If the gnomes really do have the secret of the gravity bomb—where are they now?"

"They're in a cardboard box in my apartment in Eugene."

We sat there for a moment, thinking about what to do.

Finally Peter said, "Maybe you should call your mother and tell her to open them."

I shook my head. "She'd flip out if she knew what's in there. She's unpredictable. Besides, she's always hated the gnomes."

"Maybe you should tell her to destroy them."

"I think she'd like to," I admitted. "But I don't think that's right either. Most of Einstein's formulas have been used for good. Even $E=mc^2$ has given us more than atomic bombs. Space travel, research, I don't know. I want a real physicist to look at the formula before we destroy it."

"A physicist you trust? Who is that?"

I shrugged. "Gilberto?"

"Gilberto." Peter appeared to consider this a moment.

"You don't have to like him. I think Gilberto's proven he's on our side." I reached into my purse and took out my cell phone.

"You're calling him now?" Peter asked.

"No. I'm calling my mother." The phone rang in distant Oregon. While it was ringing I figured out that it was six in the morning over there. Too bad, Mom.

"Gah," a voice croaked from my phone. "If this is anyone but my daughter, go to hell."

"Mom?" Obviously this was the right thing to say.

"Jesus Christ, baby. I've been so worried about you. I haven't heard a peep from you for ten days, and then Harmony's parents tell me you're in some German castle with a baroness, surrounded by killers."

"I'm OK, Mom." I'd been bracing myself for days to make this call. I was still pretty angry that she'd lied both to my father and to me. I hadn't expected her to show such concern about me.

"Ana sweetheart. Where are you?"

"Well, I'm not exactly in the castle. Right now I'm next door with the cowboy detective—you know, the guy who dressed up as an Australian missionary?"

"Jesus, baby. Is there anything I can do?"

"Actually, there is. You remember that box of ceramic gnomes no one wanted at the garage sale? They're in my apartment. I'd like you to pack them up real well and ship them here by overnight express—that's right, overnight. I'll pay whatever it costs. The baroness is having a dinner tomorrow and everyone's supposed to bring a surprise. This will be mine."

I asked Peter the address of the castle and relayed it to my mother, letter by letter. When I was done, there was a long pause.

"Baby? I'm coming."

"What?" I held the phone closer to my ear. "I'm sorry Mom, what did you say?"

"Monty and I will be there tomorrow, sweetheart. I've been thinking about it since the Fergusons called. I'm worried about this formula thing. There's a Lufthansa flight that gets to Stuttgart at 2:05 in the afternoon."

"Mom! What are you talking about?"

"Ana honey, I know when something's wrong. I've got to be there."

"No you don't! Just send the damned gnomes."

"I'll bring them on my lap, I promise. If we don't see you at the Stuttgart airport, we'll rent a car and find the castle on our own."

"No, Mom!" In desperation I handed the phone to Peter. I whispered, "My mother wants to fly here tomorrow. Tell her she's crazy!"

Peter took the phone, frowning. "Mrs. Smyth? Yes, this is Peter Weiss. I believe we met in Eugene."

For a long time Peter merely nodded. Then he said, "Of course, Mrs. Smyth. I understand. Tomorrow then, at the airport."

He punched *END* and handed the phone back to me.

I stared at him, dumbfounded. "What the hell did she tell you?"

He looked down. "She is your mother, Ana. If I ever hope to love you, I think I need to respect her too."

Now I couldn't even get mad at Peter. How can you throw a phone at a gentleman who admits he might hope to love you?

"Halloo?" a voice called up from the trap door. It was Frau Werther, returning to see if we were done prowling in her attic.

Quickly I stuffed the diary and the sheet music in my shirt. I whispered to Peter, "We'll talk about this later."

He replied, "In the meantime, we need to call Harmony."

AN APPROACHING STORM
(Harmony)

I'll admit Ana's call caught us at an awkward moment.

I'd been frightened by the black Mercedes, and Berti was still woozy from the whack to his head. I'd laid him out on the double bed and sat beside him, giving him water to sip. We talked for a long time like that. He asked about my kindergarten job, my family, and finally my divorce. Reluctantly I told him about marrying Leo, the hunk every girl in college wanted. My handsome husband had been part of my youthful rebellion. Leo had been the opposite of my free-rein parents. Leo had controlled everything. Like an idiot I'd waited to divorce him until I was practically a prisoner in my own house.

Confessing this humiliation brought me to the edge of tears. But my history also seemed to bring the color back to Gilberto's face. He sat up beside me on the edge of the bed. He dried my eyes.

When I looked up at him we exchanged a look that had enough voltage to blow up a substation. Powering that charge was the knowledge that Ana no longer stood between us. She hadn't been kidnapped. She'd dropped her claim on Gilberto.

I was leaning in for a fateful kiss—the one Berti had said might doom him—when the Mamas and the Papas burst in singing from my cell phone.

So yeah, it was bad timing. But I figured the kiss could wait. It turned out that Ana had a lot of news from the castle. Gilberto and I were invited to a birthday dinner with the baroness the next day.

Guests were supposed to share a family secret, whatever that meant. Ana's mother was flying in from Eugene with a box of garden gnomes that might contain the rest of the gravity formula. Ana herself had found a diary by an Einstein—not Albert, but some distant cousin. Confusion still reigned about who Margret Smyth had been and what had happened when she left Germany.

"And then there's the formula," Ana said on the phone. "Now that I think we might really find it, I'm getting worried. Could I talk with Gilberto?"

I handed the phone to Berti. Soon he was lost in conversation, his brow furrowed. For some reason he even went to the television and turned on a weather station. The romantic mood was definitely gone. Besides, Ana had gotten me thinking about family secrets, and I couldn't help myself from hatching a plan of my own. Perhaps there was something I could do to help after all.

When Berti finally flipped the cell phone closed he took a piece of hotel stationery from the desk and began writing numbers.

"What are you doing?" I asked.

He hardly glanced at me. "Armonia, I'm sorry. I have a mathematical problem about miniature black holes."

"Well, I guess that's your specialty." I sighed. There were definitely drawbacks to a relationship with a physicist. "What does this have to do with Ana?"

"Ana asked if a black hole could have caused the low-pressure system over Trieste."

"You mean the storm in Italy?" I frowned. "Could a black hole do that?"

"Not usually. Miniature black holes are subatomic. They're so small they almost never run into an atom. But if Dr. Nimolo really had one in the cyclotron he could have pumped it full of protons. Who knows how large it could get?"

"Large enough to create a storm?"

"I don't see how. He'd have to contain it in a magnetic field or it would suck in the whole city. Even then, to create an atmospheric disturbance it would have to be the size of an apple."

"That doesn't sound very big."

"Armonia, a black hole that size would weigh as much as India."

"India what? An Indian elephant?"

"No. The subcontinent."

"Oh."

"I know. But look at the news."

He turned up the television. An announcer with a blue blazer was pointing to map of the Adriatic hurricane's path. The storm had hung over Trieste for days, whipping the region with rain, wind, and floods. Now the spiral's center was moving steadily northwest through the Alps.

Even I could see the storm was heading straight toward Ulm. Whatever was powering the storm was coming our way.

THE EINSTEIN DIARY
(Ana)

Dreams engulfed me that night in the Klingenstein castle.

A tornado of black dust was snaking its funnel through Ulm, disintegrating entire blocks of houses. As I watched helplessly from a hilltop, the buildings below would rumble, puff apart, and join a stream of black dust spiraling into the sky. Terrified people in the streets suddenly froze, turned black, and whirled away as thin clouds. The church tower in the middle of town blew apart with a flash. Then the ground itself began to crumble. Soon only a crater remained where the city had been.

When the tornado began to lift, I could sense a dread shape in the clouds where the dust had gone. Slowly the curve of a giant black Zeppelin emerged. I felt a chill run through me. This was a ship that could destroy entire cities with gravity. Portals along the riveted metal sides were sucking in the last of the dust. Something thumped inside the death ship, three times. As the dirigible turned I could just make out the shadow of a person at the window of the pilot's cabin. I wanted to run, but somehow my feet had been buried in the ground. When the ship stopped in front of me, I recognized the pilot—

"Ana?" A voice came from my closet.

I opened my eyes with difficulty. The closet thumped three times.

"Is someone in there?" I asked.

"It's me, Peter."

"What are you doing in my closet?"

"Trying to wake you for breakfast. Can I come in?"

Finally I remembered that the closet in my room had a back door to Peter's studio. I also realized that I wasn't wearing pajamas. All I had on was the rather racy underwear I'd bought in Ulm. I wasn't in the mood to model it yet.

"Go away," I said. "I'll see you at breakfast."

"I want to show you what I found in the diary."

"At breakfast, OK?"

I don't know where the baroness breakfasted, but I found the Weiss family eating eggs and muffins at a table by a window at the back of the kitchen. I managed to give Peter's parents a quick *Guten Morgen* before asking Peter if he'd found the formula in the diary after all.

We had struggled through twenty pages of the diary the night before, trying to decipher the scrawled handwriting. Finally my eyes had become so tired I'd gone to bed. Most of the diary entries were tedious descriptions of harpsichord construction methods. But even in the first few pages we had learned several important facts about E. Einstein. For one thing, "E" really did stand for Ephraim. The last employee at the harpsichord factory, Ephraim had stayed because he felt he was too old to start over in a new country. He had no wife or children. When it became clear that the authorities were likely to arrest him because of his Jewish background, he had boarded up the factory and set up a secret apartment for himself in the attic. As I had suspected, it was Gerhard's aunt Marthe who brought him food and supplies from the castle.

Peter spread the diary out before us on the breakfast table. " I didn't find the formula, but at least now we know where Ephraim found it."

Herr Weiss kept eating his breakfast, but Frau Weiss stood up to join me as I read the entry.

January 21, 1942.

It has been two weeks since the Südwest Presse announced the city was selling Rudi's building in the Bahnhofstrasse. I'm sure they didn't know he had been preparing to turn the house into a museum. Perhaps in a different world? I told the lady what was hidden in the attic. Rudi had bought most of the things from Albert's apartment in Berlin. I remember how hard it was for him, bidding against foreigners and keeping the reason secret.

Yesterday the lady bought the house at auction. She said she wanted a place in town now that Monika was pregnant again. The lady didn't say more, but she has always been concerned about my family. She met Albert when she spent a summer in Switzerland as a girl.

Today she drove her car back with clothes, books, a violin case, and a typewriter. She thought it would be safer here.

"When Ephraim writes about 'the lady,' he means Marthe von Hülshoff-Schmitt?" I asked.

"At this point, yes."

"OK. So far he's explained how Marthe got the violin case, but he doesn't mention the formula."

Peter turned to a page near the end of the diary. I read on.

February 13, 1944.

I am cold all the time, afraid to show smoke from the chimney. The lady comes to visit at strange hours. Sometimes she forgets to bring food. She has changed since she learned about her husband at Stalingrad. Always now she wants to see the violin case. She has told two people about Albert's notation, Z and the lady from Böblingen, but she is afraid to tell them exactly what it says. She thinks it might help end the war. I don't understand her.

"I didn't know Marthe's husband died in the war." I sat back, thinking. "She really did lose everyone."

Peter said, "I find it confusing that Ephraim starts referring to two different people as 'lady.'"

"Not really. The 'lady from Böblingen' has to be Margrethe Semmel, the woman who worked with the resistance. And I suppose 'Z' might be Count Zeppelin. Judging from the model he had of a flying battleship, he seemed to know about the gravity formula too."

"I'm still not sure. Here, look at the final entries." Peter flipped to the back of the diary.

November 29, 1944.

I am frightened. They have arrested the lady from Böblingen. She knows about me. The police could come at any time. That's not what scares me most. Sometimes I think I have already lived too long. But what if they find the formula for the gravity bomb? The lady was going to take it out of Germany. Who can do that now?

December 12, 1944.

Still no word. I have even considered doing it myself. But I am too old. How could I avoid the patrols? What would I do with myself in a new country?

The nights have become so terribly long. I managed to move the harpsichords downstairs where I have a little more light. Still I cannot tune them, for fear someone might hear. In this cold they wouldn't hold their pitch long anyway. They are my children, silenced by the war. I pray that someday we all will be able to speak again.

I was so touched by Ephraim's last entry that I pushed the notebook back and looked silently out the window. A distant bell rang. Herr Weiss got up, gave me a slight bow, and left with a tray.

At length Peter asked, "Do you see why I'm confused? When he says 'the lady' was going to smuggle the formula out of Germany, it could be either Marthe or Margrethe."

Frau Weiss brought me a glass of orange juice. "I think it's intriguing. One of these two women must be your relative. But which one? The baron's aunt or the heroine of the White Rose?"

I turned to her. "The first, I think. A woman escaping from prison isn't likely to wear a fur coat. That would mean Marthe is my great-grandmother."

"But what about the DNA test?" Frau Weiss objected. "I thought it showed you aren't related to the Hohensteuerns."

Peter closed the diary. "I'd like to find out more about that test. Lots of things can go wrong when they're sampling a single hair."

"I agree," I said. "How do we go about checking it?"

"I think the police run their tests at the university in Ulm," Peter said. "I know some people at the lab, but they're surrounded by a big bureaucracy. I may have to knock on quite a few doors to find out anything."

"You're probably needed here, to help your parents get ready for the dinner tonight," I said.

Frau Weiss shook her head. "Your friends from the hotel called. They've volunteered to help with the cooking."

"Harmony and Gilberto called?" I asked.

"Yes, apparently they've done restaurant work before. They suggested a dish with wild mushrooms, and some secret Italian dessert."

"But they don't speak German," I said.

Frau Weiss smiled. "I think everyone at the castle speaks enough English to get by."

Peter looked at his watch. "I'd better get started if I'm going to bicycle over to the university."

"Wouldn't it be quicker to take your car?" I asked.

"Ana, you're going to need my car today. Remember? You have to meet your mother."

By the time I set out in Peter's Volkswagen the wind was rising and clouds were darkening the sky. I wasn't keen on driving to Stuttgart alone, and not just because of the weather. I looped around the back streets of Klingenstein like a crazy woman, trying to shake any black Mercedes or cement trucks that might be lurking about. When I decided no one was following me I headed for the *autobahn*. Of course the German drivers on the freeway were even crazier than me. With no speed limit, little dots in my rearview mirror suddenly turned into fire-breathing BMWs, blinking their lights to get me out of their way. I gripped the wheel, slowing down traffic at a frightening 130 kph. Gusts of wind kicked the Volkswagen from side to side.

I made it to the airport intact, left the car in a garage, and found an *Ankunft* TV monitor. Mom's flight was delayed. That left me an hour to fret about what I'd say when she actually showed up. I leaned against a wall in a carpeted hallway, watching travelers straggle out of the customs hall with their bags.

I felt as uneasy as I had in Greece when I'd been waiting to meet my father. Somehow both my parents had become strangers. For the first ten years of my life they had been infallible gods. Then Dad had faded to a sepia-tone saint, the mystery man who guarded my dreams. Mom had become Mom—the solitary sun who sometimes flared too hot and sometimes darkened in eclipse, but was always the center of family power. Now everything had changed, and I wasn't sure about my new role.

CHAPTER 39 ~ ANA

"Here's your formula, sweetheart." My mother's voice startled me. I hadn't spotted her at first because she was dressed like a visiting head of state. She wore an elegant burgundy pants suit with a form-fitted jacket, a silver brooch, and a white Lady Diana hat. Monty trailed alongside her in a princely navy blue suit with broad shoulders and French cuffs. A blue tie set off his tanned face, making his teeth glow even whiter than usual. Monty pulled a suitcase on wheels. Both he and my mother carried black book bags that bulged suspiciously.

"Mom." I stood in front of her with my arms crossed. "What do you know about the formula?"

"Oh, we figured it out right away." She looked at me more closely. "You've gotten some sun, baby. It looks good on you."

Monty cleared his throat. "Hm, don't worry, Ana. Einstein's OK."

"Einstein?" I turned to my stepfather.

"The cat," Monty explained. "We, uh, left him with Harmony's parents."

I confronted my mother again. "What did you figure out about the formula?"

Mom patted her book bag. "That the gravity formula is in the gnomes, of course." She took my arm and kept on walking. "Honestly, why else would you ask us to bring them on the next plane?"

"I didn't ask you—" I began, but then I shifted gears. "Is the formula really in the gnomes?"

"Sure, we opened one. There's just plaster plugging the bottom hole. Here." She set her book bag down, right there in the middle of the concourse. She'd wrapped the gnomes in newspaper, but they still clattered. She took an envelope from the top of the bag and handed it to me. "See for yourself."

Here at last was Margret's secret. I knew I should take it to the privacy of the car before looking, but I couldn't resist. I opened the envelope.

Inside was a small, triangular slip of wrinkled paper. It had been cut from the edge of a piece of sheet music. In the margin was the same handwriting I'd seen on the paper from the gnome in Klingenstein. But the fragment on this scrap was just an illegible part of a word.

"This isn't a formula." I reached for the rest of the gnomes.

"Not yet, honey." Mom quickly picked up the book bag. "We'll open the other gnomes when we have dinner with the baroness."

I looked at her, amazed at her audacity. "You're not invited to the dinner."

"Oh? You said everyone at this party is supposed to bring a family secret. These gnomes are my ticket in."

I couldn't help laughing at my mother's audacity. I shuttled Mom and Monty outside to the car. The first fat raindrops of the storm were starting to smack the windshield when I turned onto the *autobahn*.

Finally I said, "Mom, do you realize how arrogant you sound, coming all this way to crash a party at a castle?"

"What on earth?" She turned in her seat harness to give me a hurt look. "Here I am, worried that you've gotten yourself mixed up in something dangerous. All I'm trying to do is help."

"Oh, you're great at helping. Just like you helped by telling me Dad was dead."

She adjusted the bag of gnomes on her lap. "I've had some time to think about that, baby. I still think what I did was right."

"Are you serious?" I gave her a quick, angry glance. Then I had to turn my attention back to the blurry German racecars jockeying for position on the rainy *autobahn*.

"Of course I'm serious. You must have found out about it when you talked to Max."

"Found out about what?"

"You know, that he'd already signed up as a monk before he left for Greece."

"That's not what he told me."

Mom sighed. "I guess I'm not surprised. Max wouldn't want to bring up the ugly part. The truth is, he fell apart when Margret left him out of her inheritance. He enrolled secretly as some kind of monastic novice. Then he told me he was taking off on another of his perfume-buying junkets. Later he called me to say he wasn't coming back. He said he'd given everything he owned to the monastery, including his return plane ticket."

"Whoa."

"Whoa is right. What was I supposed to do? Tell you he'd abandoned us? Sweetheart, you were ten. I thought it was better if you thought he'd died. At least then you'd have good memories of your father." My mother turned away. "Of course that didn't work for me.

I was so mad I burned all my pictures of him."

By now I was matching my mother's story against what I'd heard from Dad. It wasn't a perfect fit. "Wait a minute. Dad said *you* were the one who asked him not to come home. He said you told him he was crazy, and that he was making me crazy too."

"I don't know what all we said back then. It's true, you were seeing a counselor. His bedtime stories had given you nightmares. But he'd already made his decision by then. He'd already left us."

"What about the letters Dad wrote me? You never let me see them. He said he kept writing letters until you told him I was dead. You told him I'd committed suicide, and that it was his fault. How could you do that?"

"Is that what he said?" My mother rolled her eyes in disbelief. "You were fifteen when he sent his first letter. Fifteen! By then he'd been dead to you for five years. That's a little late to start feeling remorse, don't you think? Besides, you were having this really difficult time in your sophomore year, coming home in tears, blowing up about little things. Those letters were confused and depressing, not the sort of thing you needed then. I couldn't do it to you, I just couldn't. I had to tell him something to leave you alone."

There are two sides to every story. Now that I'd heard both sides of my parents' divorce I found I didn't like either one. I could also see how badly mismatched they had been as partners. Without Dad's Cloud Nine perfume, they might never have married. In me they had blended a new concoction of their absurd dreams and strange fears. Grappling with their history meant grappling with myself.

I turned the windshield wipers on high. The blades slashed at the rainstorm, revealing the red running lights of a large, rounded truck ahead. A cement truck?

"I've always tried to do what's best for you," Mom said. She held the bag on her lap a little closer. "That's all I've ever wanted, sweetheart."

"Please don't call me sweetheart." In the rearview mirror I could see the dark hood of a car closing in through the storm. The hood ornament was a silver star.

"I'm sorry, baby."

"Don't call me baby either." I turned the wheel hard to the right, swerving toward a freeway off-ramp at the last possible moment.

"Ana!" my mother exclaimed. "Are you sure you know where you're going?"

"Nope." I glanced in the mirror. Neither the truck nor the Mercedes had managed to follow us. I kept the pedal to the floor. The little Volkswagen coughed and rattled, trying to accelerate down a paved lane between cornfields.

THE BIRTHDAY DINNER
(Harmony)

Wind roared about the castle. Rainsqualls pelted the windows. When the lights blinked off I was terrified, alone with the flickering candles I'd been sent to light. Even when the power returned the dining hall was full of shadows. All day as Gilberto and I helped prepare for the birthday dinner, we had speculated about the secrets the baroness wanted revealed. I had already learned more about this family than I thought was safe. I was beginning to fear the storm brewing inside the castle as much as the one battering the walls outside.

I had just finished lighting the forest of candles on the dining table when the baroness rolled her wheelchair through the doorway, followed by a very old man in a tuxedo—evidently the retired police commissioner Ana had talked about. His white eyebrows and moustache poofed out as if he were part sheepdog.

"You see, Wolf?" the baroness said, turning her chair toward him. "This is why you must practice your English. Here is Miss Ferguson, Ana Smyth's very attractive American friend."

I felt so awkward, introduced by a German aristocrat, that I did a little curtsy—a goofy maneuver when you're wearing black jeans and a rainbow-colored long-sleeve T-shirt. Hey, I didn't pack for a castle event.

"It is a pleasure, Miss Ferguson," the commissioner said with a nod. Then he addressed the baroness. "You have invited very many Americans, I think."

The baroness laughed. "You still wonder about the mother? I understand this woman exactly. She arrives with a secret and a handsome husband. Of course she is invited. How many do we have now, Miss Ferguson?"

"Thirteen," I said, setting out another napkin. Yes, I'm superstitious. This didn't bode well.

"Perfect. I will sit at the end. Then we have six on each side, alternating man and woman. Wolf, you will be to my right."

The other guests began to arrive. The first in the door was Ana, followed by her mother and Monty. They carried book bags that bulged with ceramic gnomes. Ana's mother goggled about the room, exclaiming at the china, the crystal glasses, the knight statues, and the painting of the family tree on the wood-paneled wall. Still, something about her tone suggested that she had been expecting a much grander banquet hall. The baroness seated them at the far end of Wolf's side of the table, leaving two empty chairs between Ana and Wolf.

Next came the Weiss family. Herr Weiss landed on the baroness' left, the closest seat to the door, where the baroness said he could "fetch anything we need." His wife and Peter got the seats beside him.

Gilberto and the gardener Ramon came in next, their hands full of saltcellars. The baroness placed me between them at the far left-hand side of the table, near the knight statues. She apologized that this arrangement left two men side by side. "But Peter and Gilberto, you are old friends from your trip to Greece," she said. The two men gave each other a tense smile. They had been enemies on that journey. I think they were having a hard time adjusting to their new role as allies.

The last to arrive were Rosi Meyerhof and her fiancé Dieter Braun. They didn't look like a cop and a cement factory owner. Rosi wore a sequined black gown with a plunging neckline. She carried a jeweled purse. Dieter was a square-faced, clean-shaven man. He wore a spiffy white tuxedo with a white bow tie that would have been appropriate at the Academy Awards. I wanted to crawl into my rainbow-colored T-shirt and die.

The baroness tapped her crystal water glass with a butter knife. "Thank you all for coming to my birthday. Because we have so many American guests, I would like to ask that our common language tonight be English. Dieter, is that a problem?"

"Yes, a little."

"I thought politicians could speak everyone's language."

"We try, baroness, but I am running only for mayor."

Everyone laughed. I could feel the tension in the room ease a bit. The baroness knew what she was doing.

"Tonight will be a birthday without my beloved Gerhard." The baroness lowered her head a moment. She blinked her eyes, obviously struggling with her emotions. "As you know, the baron left many questions. Tonight I hope to find some answers."

"Let us begin with a toast to the baron's memory," Wolf suggested. "I see we have his favorite wine, *gewürztraminer*."

"Yes, let's drink it while it's still quite cold." The baroness waved her hand at the wine bottles arranged down the middle of the table. "I'm afraid we must serve ourselves tonight. Please."

We filled our glasses with a wine that shimmered like gold.

"To the baron," the baroness said, clinking her glass with Wolf's. "*Prosit.*"

I clinked mine with Gilberto's and we sipped, watching each other. The wine had a strange, intense flavor that somehow reminded me of Christmas cookies.

"I had planned nine courses for nine people," the baroness said, setting down her glass. "With each course, one of us would reveal a secret. Now that we are thirteen, the secrets must come faster. What is our first course, Herr Weiss?"

"A wild mushroom soup. The recipe is from our Italian guest, Gilberto Montale," Herr Weiss stepped to the buffet, uncovered a tureen, and began ladling servings into flanged china bowls.

The baroness took the moment to lean back and reflect. "Mushrooms. They are both of death and of life. That fits the secret I wish to reveal. You see, this is not my eighty-fifth birthday.

"Really?" Wolf asked. "We have always celebrated it on this day."

"Yes, but I'm older than you thought. Today I am ninety."

Peter began to applaud, and we all joined in. Then we dipped our spoons into the soup. It was wonderful—buttery and earthy at the same time.

"Because I am old," the baroness said, "I worry about what will become of my castle. Schloss Klingenstein needs much work, and I have no money for it. Dieter has given me an answer. If I leave the castle to the city, the government will preserve it."

"The government?" Peter looked doubtful. I could guess what he was thinking. If the government took over the castle, Peter would lose his studio. His parents would lose their jobs. Hadn't the baroness considered that?

"This is my plan," the baroness said, "unless I find an heir, or my lost treasure."

"What's this about a treasure?" Ana's mother asked Ana.

Ana explained it quietly. Her mother frowned as she heard about the empty wall safe behind the wood panel. I wondered how much Ana's mother knew about the money Margret had brought to America. Ana's father had said he'd seen Margret's violin case filled with treasure, and that she'd used the money to buy their house and perfume shop. Had all of that wealth originally come from the Hohensteuern safe?

When we finished the soup, Herr Weiss collected the bowls and served delicate little crab cakes. He said, "I think my secret is a match for the fish course. Crab is not quite a fish, and what I have to tell is not quite a secret."

The baroness nodded. "Go ahead, Herr Weiss."

"My mother once told me the old baron gave dinners like this before the war. Everyone from the castle and the harpsichord factory came here on the second day of Christmas. The old baron opened the safe and gave presents to everyone."

"This is not Christmas, Herr Weiss," the baroness said, her voice betraying an edge. "Do you have something else?"

"I found the accounting records for the war years."

"And?"

Herr Weiss served himself the last crab cake. "Today the treasure missing from the safe would be worth about 150,000 euros. It would be enough to repair the castle foundation and begin renovation of the factory."

"Does this matter?" Frau Weiss asked. "What's gone is gone."

The baroness studied her. "If we are going around the table, you would be next, Frau Weiss."

"Me? I spent the day cooking with Mr. Montale." Frau Weiss gave Gilberto a flustered smile.

I would have been jealous, but I understood. When Gilberto is in a kitchen, women tend to melt a little from the heat.

Frau Weiss turned to the baroness. "Still, I did remember something the baron once said. When money was short after the war, he sold the vacation house on Lake Constance. He said his boat there had been stolen during the war. I think he wondered if his aunt Marthe had used it, and was alive in America."

The baroness waved this information aside. "We know Marthe is not related to our American guests. I've finished my crab. What's next?"

I found myself liking the baroness a little less for the abrupt way she was treating the Weiss family.

Frau Weiss lowered her eyes and said, "Peter has a salad."

"And a secret." Peter pushed back his chair. He rose to his feet and left the room. A moment later he returned with a tray of glass bowls. Sprigs of fresh basil topped brightly colored chopped tomatoes and cucumbers.

"A Greek salad," the baroness said. After she had sampled a cube of cucumber she said, "Is your news also from Greece, Peter?"

Peter set down his fork. "No, it's from Ulm. I went to the university lab today. I found out there was no DNA test." He paused and looked directly at Rosi. "The Klingenstein police did not check the hair I sent from America."

Everyone began talking at once. Rosi raised her voice to be heard. "The sample you sent was not suitable for testing, Peter. Besides, these tests are very expensive. The department followed correct procedures."

Ana cut in, outraged. "But you lied to us. You told the baroness the test was conclusive. You told me I was related to a woman from Böblingen."

"No," Rosi objected. "I told you an expert at the museum has a theory about your grandmother. That is true. I told the baroness that the DNA test settled everything because I wanted to calm her. She is an old family friend, and deserves peace."

The baroness propped her hands on the table. "Rosi Meyerhof, I will decide when I need peace. Tonight I want truth. Was Miss Smyth's grandmother a Hohensteuern?"

"The museum expert thinks not, baroness," Rosi replied. "Of course, now that Miss Smyth is here, we could test her DNA."

"That would take several days," Peter said.

I glanced around the table, trying to read the faces. Rather than resolve a mystery, we had actually deepened one. Now we had no solid evidence about Ana's ancestry.

The wind outside gusted, rattling the windows.

Herr Weiss stood up. "I think, baroness, it is time to serve the roast duck."

"Yes, and I need more wine." The baroness had us open bottles of a Moselle riesling while Herr Weiss brought a platter from the kitchen. He served slices of duck breast with an orange glaze.

It was Wolf Meyerhof who spoke next. "Baroness, you have already heard from my granddaughter. Now it is my turn. I'm afraid this secret is something Rosi should have discovered on her own."

Rosi looked at him uncertainly.

The old police commissioner sat with military stiffness, his tuxedo hanging from his shoulders as if from an old coat rack. "I have identified the two German men who followed our American guests."

Ana gave a small gasp. "The men who tried to kill me? Who are they?"

"Employees of the Klingenstein cement factory," Wolf said. "They were sent by my granddaughter's fiancé, Dieter Braun."

Rosi's face flushed red. She turned to Dieter. "This can't be true."

Wolf looked steadily at the factory owner. "Tell her."

"Well," Dieter said, straightening the lapels of his white tuxedo. "The factory has many workers. I can't watch what they all do."

"Then they did come from the factory?" Rosi demanded.

Wolf nodded. "Dieter hired them to frighten Miss Smyth. Their assignment was to keep her away from Klingenstein."

Dieter was shaking his head "No, no. Not to frighten. When the baroness sent Peter as detective, I thought, I will send detectives too."

"Detectives!" I couldn't stop myself from joining in. "Those guys tore up Ana's apartment in Eugene. They burned Gilberto's car and chased us through the Alps. They're not detectives, they're gangsters."

"Ah, well," Dieter spread out his hands. "I told them, find out things. Don't hurt people. There is no proof of damage."

Rosi shook her head. "Why didn't you tell me about all of this?"

"You didn't want to know," Wolf said. "You wanted a rich husband. This is how he became rich."

"*Opa*, please," Rosi said. "I know you've never liked Dieter. It's not fair to think everything he does is for money."

"Then why did he hire the men?" Wolf asked.

Dieter shrugged. "I wanted only to help."

Peter touched his hands before him in a tent shape. "I may not be a detective, but I think Herr Braun had another reason."

Ana looked at him. "What are you thinking?"

Peter said, "We all heard the baroness. She said she was giving the castle to the city of Klingenstein—unless she found a Hohensteuern heir. Obviously Dieter does not want the baroness to find one. He sent those two men to keep you away from Germany, Ana. Their job was to frighten you and Harmony enough that you'd stop asking questions about your family."

"Why doesn't he want the Hohensteuerns to have an heir?"

"Because everyone knows the Klingenstein cement factory is running out of white limestone," Peter said.

"So that's it," Wolf said.

I still didn't understand.

Peter continued, "Once Dieter is mayor and the city controls the castle, he can turn over the castle's land to his company. The castle would be preserved, yes, but it would be an island in a big white quarry."

The baroness drew in her breath. "That is not what I wanted."

"Wow," I said. "You'd think a guy that clever would hire smarter thugs."

"This is all of it wrong." Dieter stood up, smiling broadly. "Rosi and I need to talk. We will explain everything later. Now we must leave."

But Rosi did not stand up. "I think I need to stay."

Dieter's smile faded. "Rosi, come with me. Now."

She shook her head. "No, Dieter. I'm learning a lot at this dinner. If you leave, you leave alone."

"I see." Dieter threw his napkin on his chair. "*Guten Abend,*" he said, and walked out the door.

As Dieter Braun's footsteps echoed down the hall, I think we all suspected he might not marry Rosi. Enough issues had been raised that he might not become mayor of Klingenstein either.

The baroness frowned. "This is most disturbing. I don't like losing guests. We are no closer to answering the baron's questions than when we started. I'm not sure how to continue."

"Asparagus?" Frau Weiss suggested.

I spoke right up. "I love asparagus. And I think it's my turn to reveal a family secret."

The baroness nodded vaguely, no doubt wondering what secret I could contribute.

When the asparagus came it wasn't what I expected. Instead of tender green shoots Herr Weiss brought us platters of tough white stalks. They had been peeled and covered with a ghastly white sauce. I pushed it aside and announced my own little bombshell.

"I'm not part of your family," I said, "but I know how important families are, and your big mystery seems to go back to World War II. So I asked myself, who's been at the castle since the war?"

Ana looked at me blankly. She wasn't expecting this either.

"Your gardener, Ramon," I said, holding out a hand to the man in a beret beside me.

Peter gave me a pained look. "Ramon understands German, but he doesn't talk."

"He doesn't talk in German," I said, correcting Peter. "Ramon does speak Spanish, and even a little English."

"I," Ramon started, and then stopped. He lowered his head. "I like Harmony."

Everyone stared at the big Spanish man beside me. With this short speech he had taken a step out of the cage he'd built around himself for sixty years.

"You can talk?" the baroness asked him, obviously taken aback.

Ramon looked down. "No."

I explained, "Ramon's parents died in the Spanish Civil War. That's when he stopped talking to people. But the other night I heard him talking to his dog Golfo in Spanish."

Peter asked, "How on earth does he know English?"

"His mother grew up in Gibraltar," I said. "His father was Spanish. After he was orphaned the baron took him to Germany and got him a job at the castle."

Ana asked, "Then he was here during the air raid?"

I nodded.

"Does he know what happened that night?"

"He told me about it this afternoon."

"And?" Ana asked.

I took a breath and launched ahead. "Ramon told me he was afraid when the airplanes came. It reminded him of the attacks in Spain. He ran through the forest to a place that overlooks the valley. He watched as the bombs exploded. Later, when he got cold, he came back to the castle. He found a strange car here, and Wolf's motorcycle."

"I don't see how the motorcycle could have been mine," Wolf said. "I was down in the city that night, fighting the fires."

I started to translate this for Ramon, but he held up his big, callused hand. "No. Wolf was here."

Ramon switched back to Spanish. I translated the rest of his story, sentence by sentence.

"Ramon says he heard a gunshot inside the castle. He hid in his gardening shed. Marthe came running outside with a boy and a violin case. She wore her fur coat and a hat with a widow's veil. She put the boy and the case in the car. Then she ran back inside. A minute later she helped a bloody old man into the car. Then she drove off."

Ana asked, "Was he sure the woman was Marthe?"

"He says it was dark, but yes, that's who he saw."

"Then the Smyths may be related to the Hohensteuerns after all," Peter said.

Ana asked, "Did he see Wolf?"

I asked Ramon in Spanish. "Wolf came out a few minutes later, rubbing his head and checking his gun. He drove off on his motorcycle. Ramon went inside and found the safe open. Someone had tried to wipe up bloodstains, but he could still see the drips."

Wolf shook his head. "He must be mistaken. That evening I was in Ulm."

Ramon spoke to me in a low voice.

I looked to Wolf and explained. "Ramon says he was afraid of you. Now he is old and has nothing to lose. He says you were with the Nazis."

"That's a lie!" Wolf insisted.

"That's enough, everyone." The baroness held her wrinkled hand to her forehead. "This is difficult for me. And also confusing."

"I may be able to fill in the gaps," Ana said. "Finally I think I have enough puzzle pieces I can tell you what really happened that night."

"Not yet," the baroness said. "I need *Müller-Thurgau* first."

Ana looked at her uncertainly. "Who?"

The baroness pointed to the table. "The green bottles at the end. I believe it goes with the *spätzle,* Herr Weiss."

"Yes, baroness." Herr Weiss went to the kitchen while we opened the last two bottles of wine. The electric lights flickered out a moment, but then came back on. Herr Weiss returned with a platter of handmade noodles, baked with cheese and onions.

When he had served the *spätzle* and the baroness had taken a deep drink from her wineglass, she nodded to Ana. "All right, Miss Smyth. I'm ready. What happened on the night of the air raid?"

"First let me share my family secret." Ana took out an old, curled notebook. "Yesterday Peter and I found this diary in the attic of the old factory."

The baroness raised an eyebrow. "Whose diary is it?"

"It belonged to Ephraim Einstein, a relative of Albert Einstein." Ana passed the book to the head of the table.

The baroness flipped through the pages. "What have you learned from this?"

Ana said, "I think I may be your husband's great niece."

"How can I know? Start at the start and tell me everything."

"Ephraim Einstein was a harpsichord builder at the factory here," Ana explained. "He was Jewish but didn't want to leave Germany, so he boarded up the factory and hid upstairs. Marthe brought him food and news. She had always liked the Einstein family. In 1942 she bought the house where Albert Einstein was born. She wanted to preserve it as a museum. One of the artifacts she found in the house was a piece of sheet music with Einstein's formula for quantum gravity. She thought if the Allies had the formula it might help end the war. They decided to have a woman from the resistance movement smuggle it out of Germany. That woman was Margrethe Semmel. After Semmel was put in prison they needed another plan."

"Does the diary say all of this?" the baroness demanded.

"Yes, but that's where the entries stop," Ana admitted. "Still, I think I can piece together the rest of what happened."

All eyes were on Ana. This was the story we had come to hear.

"Go on," the baroness said.

"The night of the air raid," Ana said, "the entire Hohensteuern family met at the Einstein house. They had come to celebrate the first birthday of Marthe's grandson Moritz. Somehow Marthe and the baby were the only ones to escape the bombs. They drove out of the burning city to the castle. She went to see Ephraim, and they decided to deliver the formula to the Allies themselves. They went to the castle to get the treasure from the wall safe. They weren't stealing it—Marthe thought she was the surviving heir. Then Wolf arrived on his motorcycle. He thought Ephraim was a thief and shot him. Marthe must have hit Wolf on the head. Then she escaped with the baby and Ephraim.

"After that night, Marthe's mind was never the same. She'd seen Ulm go up in flames. She'd lost everyone she cared about except the baby. She became Margret Smyth, the woman who called herself my great aunt."

The candles had burned low, flickering in a draught.

The old police commissioner drew in a long breath. "Well, some of your story is true."

The baroness looked at him sharply. "You admit to this?"

Wolf shook his head. "Not all of it. I was at the birthday party in the Einstein house. They invited me because I was Gerhard's best friend. His airplane had just been lost in the Mediterranean."

The old commissioner tightened his lips. "It was not a happy party. The baby was sick. It cried. Marthe left to walk him on the street, trying to calm him. Then came the air raid alarm. I volunteered to go outside and bring Marthe back. I couldn't find her. The bombs started falling. Everywhere was fire and noise. The Einstein house was hit. No one survived."

Wolf lifted his spectacles and rubbed his eyes before he could continue. "Eventually I took my motorcycle back to Klingenstein. I was worried about looters. Sure enough, I found an old man opening the wall safe. I ran at him. He fought back. Somehow my police revolver went off. Then Marthe came out of the shadows and hit me. When I woke up she was gone. So was the treasure."

"You should have told me this long ago," the baroness said sternly.

"I'm sorry, baroness." Wolf looked like a skeleton in a tuxedo. "It was a night I have tried to forget."

Peter leaned forward. "But you told Rosi, didn't you? That's why she lied about the DNA test. Both of you knew Marthe had survived. You wanted to cover up the past. You didn't want people to know that a police commissioner had shot an innocent man."

"I was not a Nazi!" Wolf retorted. "I was a private in the home guard. The shot was an accident."

The baroness put her hand on his arm. "I know. Now at last we understand what happened in those dark days."

"No way," I blurted before I could stop myself. What was I doing, contradicting a baroness?

"No way?" the baroness asked, drilling me with her dark eyes.

"I'm sorry, it's just—" Now I was getting flustered, trying to fit something together that wouldn't fit.

I put my hand to my head. "It's just I think you've got the whole story backwards."

THE BIRTHDAY DINNER
(Ana)

Everyone looked at Harmony. She sat there, holding her head as if she thought it might explode. Even I wondered if she had gone off the deep end. "Harm, what's up?"

"You'll say it's a small thing," Harmony said, "But if one part of the story's wrong, everything's got to be wrong."

"What small thing?"

"Ramon said he saw Marthe with a boy."

"So?"

"He used the word *muchacho*. The word for a baby boy is *niño*."

I didn't understand, and my expression must have shown it.

"Marthe's grandson was celebrating his first birthday, remember?" Harmony turned to the gardener and asked him something in Spanish.

"What did he say?"

"The boy was at least two years old. Ramon knew Marthe's grandson, and the boy he saw was someone else."

This was puzzling news. "Why on earth would Marthe have a stranger's child with her?"

"She wouldn't," Harmony said. She leaned toward me across the table. "Don't you see, Ana? All of the baron's family must have died in the air raid. The woman at the castle wasn't Marthe. You're not related to these people."

"But both Wolf and Ramon saw her. It had to be Marthe."

By now Peter was raising his hand like a student with an answer. "Maybe Harmony's right. Why would Marthe have driven to the castle in a car no one recognized? Why did she wear a veil? Why did she hit Wolf instead of talking to him?"

Finally I understood. "Because she was really Margrethe Semmel in disguise."

At this point the baroness groaned and sat back in her wheelchair.

"Are you ill?" Wolf asked.

"Just dizzy," the baroness said. "This is all so fast. Perhaps Herr Weiss should bring the next course. Then I want to start over. I want Miss Smyth to explain everything again."

Herr Weiss brought two platters of little meatballs in a dark brown sauce. I gave them a pass. I was busy rethinking what had happened.

The baroness stabbed a meatball with her fork and said, "Well, Miss Smyth? Do I have an heir or not?"

I shook my head. "Probably not. I guess Marthe must have died on the streets of Ulm. In the confusion of the air raid, Margrethe Semmel escaped from prison. She did have a two-year-old son hidden somewhere in the city. She must have gone to find him."

"Semmel was divorced, wasn't she?" Wolf asked.

"Yes. Her husband said the boy wasn't his. Margrethe never told the name of the real father, but he probably worked with her in the White Rose, the resistance group."

The baroness took another meatball. "Remind me, what do these people have to do with the Hohensteuerns?"

"The baron's aunt had been in contact with them for months. Marthe wanted Margrethe to smuggle the Einstein formula to the Allies," I said.

"Oh yes. Go on."

"I don't know exactly what happened when Margrethe Semmel found her son," I admitted. "The boy's father must have persuaded her to go ahead with the plan and take the boy with her to safety. She drove to the harpsichord factory and got the Einstein formula from Ephraim. To keep the formula safe, she memorized it, tore the paper in half, and hid half in a museum statue. Ephraim put his diary in too and sealed it up."

Wolf stroked his chin. "Semmel was wanted by the police. To escape she needed a new identity. That must be why she put on Marthe's fur coat and veil."

I nodded. "She also needed money. Ephraim went to get some from the castle safe."

Harmony asked, "How did they know the combination?"

"He must have picked the lock," I said. "The baroness said it's not complicated, and he was a skilled craftsman. Still it must have taken him a while. That's when Herr Meyerhof showed up. The gun went off. Ephraim was wounded and Margrethe hit Herr Meyerhof on the head."

Wolf added, "Then the two of them stole the treasure and went to Switzerland."

"I don't think that was their original plan," I said. "In his diary Ephraim wrote that he didn't want to leave Germany at all. I think he just wanted to get Margrethe enough money to help her out of the country. But after Ephraim was shot, Margrethe must have panicked. She couldn't take him to a doctor in Germany, so she had to take him with her to Switzerland. To make sure she had enough money, she simply emptied the safe into the violin case."

Peter looked thoughtful. "That explains things better than your first version of the story. The one thing I don't understand is what happened to Margrethe Semmel afterwards. Instead of giving the Einstein formula to the Allies she kept it secret. Why did she change her name to Margret Smyth and go to America?"

My mother spoke up. "I can tell you what happened. Margret went crazy."

"No, I think what she did was brave," Harmony countered. "She'd seen the Allies destroy a city. Who knows what a gravity bomb could do? The right thing was to hide the formula from everyone."

"Certainly she'd been through a lot of trauma," Peter said. He looked to me. "What do you remember about her, Ana?"

"Margret was eccentric," I admitted. "And secretive, too. That's pretty much how the museum in Ulm described Margrethe Semmel. She refused to tell anyone about her past. But I also remember Margret as imaginative and kind. When I was a child, we used to pretend we were princesses, dressing up for a castle ball." I could feel my face reddening. Those fantasies had turned out to be only partly true. In fact, neither Margret nor I were princesses. We were both just single women trying to survive.

The baroness rapped the table as if her hand were a gavel. "So what should I do? Pay for one of these scientific tests?"

Rosi shook her head. "A DNA test won't help. The Smyths are not your relatives."

"Well, I don't want to leave the castle to the government." The baroness looked around the table. Her gaze stopped at me. "What about your father?"

I almost choked. "My Dad? He's a Greek monk. He gave away all his possessions."

"Oh, that's right."

Struck with sudden inspiration, I suggested, "What about the Weiss family? If you want someone to take care of the castle, give it to them."

The baroness dismissed this idea with a short laugh. Then she turned to the white-haired secretary. "Herr Weiss, what is our next course?"

"*Haricot verts* in an almondaise sauce, baroness."

"Bring it." She gave him the command as if he were a slave rather than a servant.

The secretary nodded, stood up, and left the room, heading toward the kitchen.

The room was silent, but I could feel the tension that this painful display of duty had created. Harmony, for one, seemed about ready to jump up and strangle the arrogant old woman right there in her wheelchair. Peter kept his eyes lowered, but I felt the burn of his anger.

To my surprise, the first to speak was Wolf.

"Paulette," the old police commissioner began, suddenly shifting to a more familiar tone. "There is another family secret you should know."

She looked at him sharply. "What?"

"When the baron was ill, he spoke of family members who might have survived the war."

"Of course. His aunt Marthe and her grandson."

"No, his words were, 'Aunt Marthe and *a baby boy*.'"

"It's the same thing."

Wolf paused. "Gerhard wanted to protect you, Paulette. I think he was talking about a different child. Someone closer to you."

At this point Herr Weiss walked back into the room, carrying a large silver tray of sauce-covered green beans. All eyes turned to watch him—almost as if the elderly secretary had suddenly been illuminated by a spotlight. Even the baroness studied him from the side while he served her the beans.

When Herr Weiss stepped around the table to serve Wolf, the retired police commissioner thanked him. Then he asked, "By the way, Herr Weiss, how long did your mother serve here at the castle?"

"Six years, commissioner. From 1938 to 1944."

"If I recall, she found other work after the air raid."

"Yes, commissioner. With the Hohensteuerns gone, the castle had no need for a chambermaid." Herr Weiss moved on to serve Rosi. "My mother married a bookkeeper and helped with his work."

The baroness asked, "How long after their marriage were you born?"

Herr Weiss stood up straight. "I'm sorry, baroness?"

"I asked you a question, Herr Weiss."

The old secretary stood his ground. "It was a personal question, baroness." Then he turned to me. "Beans, Miss Smyth?"

"Yes, please." After a moment I asked him, "Don't you wonder why the police commissioner is interested in your mother's work?"

Herr Weiss glanced back to Wolf. "Yes, I do."

Wolf cleared his throat. "Gerhard and I were very close friends. Before he was sent to France he told me he had been meeting with a maid at the castle. A month later he was shot down. Then came the air raid, and the rest of his family died. The poor girl quickly married a bookkeeper. Still, I'm afraid her son was born quite early."

"*Gott im Himmel,*" the baroness breathed.

Even the unflappable Herr Weiss seemed taken aback. "Are—are you saying my father might have been Baron Gerhard?"

"That's exactly what I'm saying, Herr Weiss."

The old secretary dropped his tray, splattering beans and sauce across the floor at the far end of the table.

Rosi looked at Peter with wide eyes. "Then would you be the next baron?"

"Enough!" The baroness raised her voice. "Gerhard had no children."

"A DNA test would tell us if he did," Rosi suggested.

Was it possible that Peter could be in line to become baron, I wondered? What a marvelous switch that would be from his family's role as servants! Still, I felt suspicious about Rosi's motives for suggesting the DNA test. She had blocked a test for Margret. Now she was jumping at the chance to prove Peter was a Hohensteuern. The way the policewoman smiled across the table at Peter made me more than a little jealous. Had she forgotten her fiancé Dieter so quickly? And was it my imagination, or had she dipped her shoulders to make her gown's plunging neckline a little plungier?

Wolf told his granddaughter, "Herr Weiss cannot become baron, Rosi. The title of baron can be inherited only by a child born within a Hohensteuern marriage."

The old police commissioner paused a moment. Then he turned to the baroness. "Still, I think Gerhard always wondered if Herr Weiss was his son. He found Herr Weiss a job at the castle. Later he paid for Peter's education at Cambridge. I think Gerhard would have approved if you left the castle to the Weiss family instead of to the government."

The baroness shook her head, "I want proof. Rosi, order a test. Then I'll decide what to do with the castle. Now the real problem is money. Herr Weiss?"

The secretary had started cleaning up the spilled beans with a napkin. "Yes, baroness?"

"Please, leave that for now." The baroness' tone had softened a little. "Join us at the table, Herr Weiss."

"Shall I bring dessert? Mr. Montale has prepared something special."

"Not yet. First I want to know what happened to my treasure." The baroness turned her dark eyes toward me. "Miss Smyth, you ended your story too soon. You stopped when your grandmother was filling a violin case with money. What happened to the case?"

"The violin case." Would I ever escape from it? If Harmony hadn't persuaded me to sell it on eBay, I might still be in Eugene, spending my summer vacation trying to write a mystery. At least now I had a real mystery to write. I just didn't know how it would end.

"Well?" the baroness asked.

"I asked my father in Greece about the violin case," I admitted. "He remembered seeing it full of money and jewels."

"Just as I thought," the baroness said.

"But my father said Margret spent it all in Oregon," I went on. "She used it to buy a house and a perfume shop. By the time I saw the violin case, it was empty."

The baroness raised an accusing finger. "Everything was stolen."

My mother rose to her feet. "It wasn't stolen. Haven't you been listening? Margret was sent on a mission. When she got to America she needed that money. It's been gone for years."

"Mrs. Smyth," the baroness said, eyeing my mother. "Did Margret leave anything in her will?"

My mother hedged. "She didn't leave anything to Max. That's what he wanted. He's a monk."

"Margret gave the house in Eugene to my mother," I explained. I wished Mom hadn't come to the dinner. Everything she said seemed embarrassingly self-centered.

"The house is legally mine." My mother crossed her arms. "I checked with a lawyer. Everything except for the stuff in the attic. Margret gave all that to Ana."

The baroness considered this a moment. "What was in the attic?"

"Junk," my mother said. "It all turned out to be junk except these." She took one of the garden gnomes out of the book bag and put it on the table. The white-bearded gnome tipped over, poking his pointy red cap into a butter dish.

"Garden gnomes." The baroness covered her eyes with a hand.

"Margret thought they were important." I unfolded the torn half-sheet of music Peter and I had found the day before. "We found half of a formula for quantum gravity in the museum. I think Margret hid the other half inside the gnomes."

The baroness asked, "Why is an old formula important now?"

I looked to Gilberto. He cleared his throat. "The formula is historic. Of course, physics has advanced since Einstein. Still, no one has successfully defined quantum gravity. Many physicists are interested to see what he thought."

Rosi said, "The Italian men who came here were interested in it too."

"Yes, the Italians," the baroness said. Outside, the storm roared louder than ever. The lights flickered three times, and then went out altogether.

Harmony gave a small cry of alarm.

The candles that remained had burned down to stumps. I could see Harmony looking around anxiously at the shadows, her eyes large. Behind her, the light flickered on the looming statues of the two Hohensteuern knights. The sword and battleaxe almost appeared to twitch in their hands.

"I'll bring more candles, baroness," Herr Weiss said. He took a candelabrum from the table and set off down the hall.

"So this is what remains of the treasure," the baroness said, looking at the fallen gnome. "Perhaps there is more inside these gnomes than just a formula. Open them!"

"OK." My mother picked up her table knife and whacked the gnome on its beard. Chips flew.

"Don't break them!" I objected. "Margret really liked gnomes. Every birthday she asked for them."

"And I always hated them." Mom took off the broken head and pulled out a scrap of paper.

Herr Weiss returned with the candles. He handed me an empty page from a photo album. "I thought this might help to put the papers together."

I laid the torn half-sheet of music at the bottom of the album page. Then I placed the new scrap above it. It fit perfectly, filling in part of a bar of music. Next I took out the scrap Mom had given me at the airport. It didn't match yet, but I set it on the page where I thought it might eventually fit.

"Puzzle pieces," I said. "Now all we need are the rest."

"Uh-hmm." My stepfather Monty lifted the book bag onto the table. He began carefully setting out the rest of the gnomes. "You can open the holes in the bottoms."

Everyone joined in, picking up gnomes, opening the plaster seals, and taking out the paper scraps.

Gilberto and I hunched over the table, sorting the bits of paper. At first the puzzle went slowly. But by using the bars of music as a guide, we began fitting the pieces together. Finally, the puzzle was complete. Not one piece was missing.

Thunder rumbled outside.

Gilberto stood there as if stunned.

The entire formula lay before us in Einstein's own hand.

The long-missing second half of the equation was not complicated.

It consisted of a series of scrawled letters over the notation "r^3".

Before I could make out the letters, however, a clap of thunder exploded just outside the front windows, shaking the walls. But where was the lightning? There was no flash.

Suddenly I feared that something else was outside—something unimaginably worse than a thunderstorm.

ATTACK OF THE GNOMES
(Harmony)

Ana almost knocked over her chair on her way to the rain-streaked window. "There's a white truck outside. It has a picture of an ice cream cone on the back."

The baroness asked, "Is this Mr. Montale's surprise dessert?"

Berti was still studying the formula, lost to the world. I went to the window and looked over Ana's shoulder. "It really does say *Gelato Italiano.*"

"An Italian ice cream truck?" Peter asked.

Ana said simply, "Nimolo!"

Three ominous shadows were pulling up behind the truck. A wave of fear swept through me.

"Here come the black Mercedes," Ana said. "What do we do?"

Rosi stood up to take command. "OK, I'll call for backup." She reached into her sequined purse and pulled out a makeup kit. Then she reached in again. This time she took out a pair of handcuffs. Finally she dumped the purse on the table.

"Dieter must have taken my cell phone when he left. Does anyone have a phone?"

I'd left my phone in my room. Ana shook her head too.

Heavy footsteps resounded up the entry stairs. By then I knew we were toast.

"We can't let Nimolo find the formula," Berti said.

Peter opened the hidden panel in the wall. He thrust the formula into the safe and spun the dial.

A moment later the door to the banquet hall banged open. A man in a black suit stepped into the room with a submachine gun. He opened fire over our heads, spraying plaster across the table. Everyone scrambled for cover.

"Tutti seduti!" the man shouted, ripping a dozen more bullets into the ceiling. By this time five burly men in black suits had come in behind the gunman. They stood on either side of him, casually crossing their arms or straightening their cuffs.

Trembling, I translated the gunman's demand. "They want us all to stay seat— "

A third burst of machine gun fire smashed the glasses beside me on the table.

Rosi stifled a cry. When I dared to look she was glaring at the gunman. She didn't seem to notice that a red stripe was running down her bare arm from her sequined shoulder strap. I closed my eyes and took a shaky breath. I don't do well with blood.

The door opened again. This time an elderly man in a green lab coat walked in. He was carrying the same rectangular violin case I remembered from Ana's attic. He might as well have worn a nametag: Hi, my name is Dr. Enrico Nimolo.

"Buonasera, baroness," he said, tilting his bald head slightly. "Forgive these simple men, please. This is a formal dinner. I told them to leave the guests sitting."

The baroness spun her wheelchair to face Nimolo. "Get out of my castle."

"Soon," Nimolo said. He pressed the clasps of the violin case. It flopped open, revealing an empty interior of plush green velvet. "All I need is the formula that belongs in this case."

"We don't have it," Gilberto said.

Berti really isn't a very convincing spy.

Nimolo aimed a withering glance at him. "Signor Montale, it has been amusing to watch you and Peter Weiss travel through Europe. Both of you led me here. I waited until you found the second half of the formula. Now it is time. The formula, please."

Ana said, "We thought the formula would be in the gnomes, but it turned out they were empty."

Nimolo looked at her a moment. Then he broke out in laughter.

"*Brava!* Miss Ana Smyth, your performance is the best of all. So let me think. Where did you hide it?"

Nimolo squinted about the room. "Don't tell me you put it in the safe? This is so obvious." He motioned for the gunman to follow him to the wood-paneled wall. Without so much as a pause, Nimolo swung open the hidden panel. Then he nodded toward the lock. "*Un colpo.*"

The gunman rattled a few bullets into the lock. The safe's door swung free.

"No!" Gilberto cried, springing forward. Two of the Italian thugs grabbed him and threw him back to his chair. My heart went out to Berti for his courage.

Nimolo took out the page of Einstein's sheet music and held it before him, studying the formula. I wished there was something we could do to stop him, but the gunman was standing right there, covering us with his machine gun.

"So simple, so elegant." Nimolo looked up at Gilberto. "I see you are unhappy, Montale. Your string theory was too complicated, after all? It has been wrong for twenty years. All along, Einstein had the key to my doorway."

"Doorway?" Ana asked.

A dog barked outside. Nimolo walked to the window and looked out. "Although you destroyed one electromagnetic containment unit in Trieste, Miss Smyth, I have another. And you know? Police do not question ice cream trucks, even if there is a miracle inside."

"What you are talking about?" the baroness demanded.

"I have brought you a birthday surprise. A little hole in space-time. Quantum black holes are not easy to keep. They are even harder to unlock. Einstein's key will open a dimension beyond time. It is the doorway of the Immortals. This is my one last chance to know the infinite."

Gilberto ran his hand through his hair. "You're mad! If there's a quantum black hole in that truck, it could be enormously dangerous."

"Is it causing the storm?" I asked.

Nimolo laughed. "Not from its containment field."

Gilberto said, "You don't seriously expect to go through a black hole and survive?"

"I am an old man. Who knows what consciousness exists in the dimension beyond? True science always comes with risk."

"Risk?" Gilberto shook his head. "If you have a black hole out there and it collapses, it could release enough energy to disintegrate everything."

"Everything?" I asked.

Berti considered this. "Just one planet."

The baroness rapped the table firmly. "I refuse to allow this!"

"No?" Nimolo motioned for the gunman to aim at the wall. *"Un colpo di più."*

Bullets splintered the panels with the Hohensteuern family tree.

"Baroness, the future is in the stars," Nimolo said. "The Earth is tired. Your family line is dead."

Maybe it was the challenge—maybe it was because Nimolo had simply gone too far. Herr Weiss straightened his shoulders and looked around the table. Then he turned to Nimolo.

"Perhaps the family is not entirely dead, doctor." The secretary pressed his knee against an electric switch beneath the table.

Suddenly the two concrete statues of the old Hohensteuern knights came to life, swinging to either side. The gunman ducked, but a battleaxe caught his machine gun. A sword whacked him from behind.

At the same time Peter launched himself at the man's knees. The five Italian men came forward, but Gilberto, Ana, and the others were there to meet them.

Peter pinned the gunman against the wall. The machine gun flipped loose and skittered across the floor to my feet.

I picked up the gun.

Everyone froze.

Yeah, so I think I might have been holding the gun upside down or backwards or something. I don't really know much about guns, and this one was covered with strange clips and levers. Anyway, all five of the Italian thugs decided to come after me.

I didn't have time for target practice, and you know what? I'd rather defend myself with Aikido anyway. So I dropped the gun and dealt with the Italians one at a time.

The first thug tried to bowl me over. I stepped aside and propelled his head against a stone wall. The next guy swung at my chin. I ducked, helped him into the air, and convinced him to come down on his neck. The third tripped over my knee in a way that must have hurt his testicles a lot, judging from the way he screamed.

I recognized the last two Italians guys—the big stupid man and the crewcut kid who had tried to mug me in Florence. They seemed to recognize me too, perhaps from the way I'd damaged their colleagues. Anyway, they stopped where they were. Rosi came up behind them and clicked on her handcuffs.

Wow.

I mean, we'd gone from losers to winners in thirty seconds, and we'd let the bad guys' violence work against them. It was perfect.

Except that Dr. Nimolo had picked up the machine gun.

I noticed this because everyone else was looking at me in a very strange way. When I turned around, I saw an obviously insane Italian physicist pointing a very ugly barrel at me.

"*Stupendo, signora,*" Nimolo said. "A wonderful show. Now, however, I must leave."

"All by yourself?" It wasn't much to say, but it's all I had.

"No, I need a hostage."

This wasn't what I wanted to hear either.

"Come!" The submachine gun he aimed at me gave everything Nimolo said a certain weight. It was strange, but my fear had begun to harden, crystallizing into a source of strength. Perhaps he'd pushed me beyond some ultimate threshhold of terror. I couldn't save myself, but at least I could hope to save the others.

Emboldened with this new courage I led Nimolo out of the room and into the corridor. As we went down the stairs I glimpsed Gilberto following cautiously at a distance. At the door Nimolo stopped.

"Your beauty is not immortal, Signora Ferguson." Nimolo held the gun's muzzle to my throat. Anything I said might make Nimolo pull the trigger. Fear would have made the old Harmony blurt something dangerously inane. But now I looked Nimolo squarely in the eye. Then I gave him a silent smile and a one-shouldered shrug.

Nimolo squinted and lowered the gun. "Wait on this side of the doorway. You and everyone else. *Capito?*"

Then he slipped out the door and was gone.

"Armonia!" Berti hurried down the stairs and held me in his arms. "Thank God you're all right. Where did you learn martial arts like Ana?"

"Get away from the door," Rosi said. "I'm calling for backup." The left side of her gown was spattered with blood. She went into the baroness' office and began dialing.

"Upstairs, quick," Ana called. "We can watch from the windows."

Gilberto and I followed Ana back to the banquet hall. Soon everyone had clustered around the windows. Even the Italian thugs managed to crawl to a window to watch.

Through the rainy glass I could see the back door of the white van standing ajar. My heart was hammering. What could Nimolo do with a hole in space?

A bolt of lightning crashed onto the hillside behind the castle with an ear-shattering boom. Somewhere a dog howled as if berserk. A dozen more flashes lit the courtyard – unearthly, blinding lights that made me turn aside.

When I looked again, blinking blue lights and two-tone sirens were coming up the hill from town. Three green police cars barreled through the castle gateway, swerved around the black Mercedes, and surrounded the ice cream truck. Half a dozen officers jumped out with their guns drawn. They scrambled for cover behind their cars. Then they shouted something I couldn't make out.

The truck just sat there. After a minute, lightning struck somewhere across the valley. Thunder rumbled.

A policeman shouted again. The rain slowed to a drizzle.

Finally something small and brown appeared near the bottom of the back door. I tensed. The policemen aimed their guns.

The door opened a fraction wider. Slowly a shaggy brown head emerged, sniffing cautiously to either side.

"I've got to go down there," Ana said, heading quickly for the hall.

This was the stupidest thing I'd heard in a long time, but I wasn't about to let her go alone. I set off after her, followed closely by Peter and Gilberto. We caught up with her at the bottom of the stairwell, where Rosi was peering out the castle's front door.

As we watched, a big brown-and-black dog jumped down from the truck's back bumper. The dog lifted a shaggy ear in our direction, gave a single low woof, and then began lapping up water from a puddle among the cobblestones.

Rosi held us back with her arm. "It could be a trick."

Peter said, "No, it's the gardener's dog."

Now I recognized the dog. "It's Golfo. He can be vicious if he wants."

"He looks like – " Ana began.

"Like what?" Gilberto asked.

Ana shook her head. "Like a dog I knew long ago."

"Wait here!" Rosi commanded. "I'm going in." Crouching awkwardly in her gown, she ran to the nearest police car. She whispered a moment with the policemen there. Then she took a revolver and edged around to the side of the truck. The dog came up to sniff her legs, wagging its tail. She pushed past it and sprang behind the truck.

"Halt!" Rosi cried, aiming her gun with both hands toward the truck's back door.

I held my breath, expecting machine gun fire to erupt from the truck.

Rosi pushed the doors wider open. She waved her gun around. Then she said something in German to the policemen. They began making radio calls.

"What did she say? I asked.

"Nimolo's gone," Ana said. "The police are launching a search."

"Dio mio!" Gilberto walked boldly out across the courtyard toward the truck.

We followed. A strange smell hung in the air—a mixture of the sharp ozone tang from an electrical short and the sweet scent of apples. Although a policeman kept us back from the truck's doors, I saw right away that no one was inside. Ice encrusted the walls. Dangling from the ceiling was what looked like a large metal cooler chest with its lid open. Frost on the floor showed scuffed footprints.

"What happened in there?" I asked.

"I don't know," Gilberto said. "If Nimolo had a quantum black hole, there is no precedent."

"Could it really be a portal, like he said?"

"Black holes take matter through a point of infinity, yes, but—" Berti faltered.

"I thought you said it could explode," Peter said.

"The mathematics are complicated. Maybe it still will. Maybe it was never there."

"The violin case is gone," Ana said. "Does anyone remember the formula?"

"Dio mio!" Quickly Gilberto searched his pockets. He found a pen but no paper, so he started writing frantically on the palm of his hand.

CLOUD NINE
(Ana)

The police stayed past midnight, asking questions and searching the castle grounds. Ramon took in his dog and fed it leftover *spätzle*. By the time the police finally cleared the vehicles from the courtyard we were so dazed that everyone just stumbled off to their various rooms. I slept without dreams for the first time in ages.

When I finally woke up the sun was high. The castle was silent. A single dust mote hung in a sunbeam above my bed, as tiny and white as a distant star. I put on my jeans and the black blouse. The difficulties of the last few weeks must have whittled away the ten pounds I wanted to lose, because my clothes were fitting looser. I brushed back my hair as best I could. Then I went out to see if the world would make more sense than it had the night before.

The smell of fresh-baked bread drew me straight to the kitchen.

Frau Weiss stood up in a cloud of steam and laughed. "We'd almost given up hope. Breakfast was four hours ago."

"I'm famished. What's cooking?"

"A picnic for your Independence Day."

I looked into the pot before her. "I didn't know you could buy corn on the cob in Germany."

"The baroness wants us on the veranda. Can you give me a hand?"

We carried fresh buns, bratwurst, and a platter of hot corn down the hall to a door beside the tower. When we went out onto the terrace, everyone began to applaud—as if we were the stars of a Fourth of July parade.

Peter put his hand on my shoulder. "My sleeping beauty wakes."

He could have kissed me right then, in front of everyone. He was looking into my eyes. Why didn't he dare to do it?

Harmony was arm-in-arm with Gilberto, glowing as if she'd been wakened by a princely kiss.

The baroness rolled her wheelchair to a table beside the veranda's railing. Someone had put little American flags in the geranium flowerpots. Behind her the green crowns of a beech forest curved away down the valley slope to a meadow with a silver river.

"Americans are not of our family," the baroness said. "But they have become our friends. In their honor, let us eat hot dogs. Afterwards, there is a dessert left over from last night."

"Tiramisu is better on the second day," Gilberto said.

Harmony beamed.

The baroness held out her hands. "Please, *bon appetit*."

My stepfather isn't shy about food. Monty stepped right up, putting a bratwurst in a bun and slathering on some mustard. We followed his example.

My mother pulled me aside. "Harmony's changed her plane ticket so she can fly home with us. You'll want to be on the same flight, won't you?"

"When?"

"Tonight. Harmony's driving her rental car to the airport."

"But I need more time than that." I couldn't believe Harmony was ready to leave yet either.

"Why? You've done what you came to do. You saw your father. You found out how Margret came to America."

What could I say? There were other questions left. Besides, the only thing waiting for me in Eugene was a messy apartment.

"Another week, Mom. I still have some problems to sort out."

A few minutes later one of my unsorted problems drove a silver BMW into the castle courtyard. The door of the sports car opened and a long pair of legs slid out.

Rosi Meyerhof stepped out as if she had been practicing her entrance all morning. She wore a sleek red business suit that clung to her curves. Her brown hair bounced with pointy curls. Any damage from the night before must have been light, because it sure wasn't slowing her down now.

She made straight for Peter. "I only have a moment," she said, "but I thought you'd like a report from the police station. There's good news and bad news."

"Have they found Dr. Nimolo?" Peter asked.

"That's the bad news. He's still missing. But we'll get him soon enough. The *Bundespolizei* has expanded the search."

"How far?" Gilberto asked. His tone made me wonder if his real question was 'To how many dimensions?'

Rosi replied, "To the entire European Union."

"What's the good news?" I asked.

She touched her finger to the front of Peter's shirt. "We had Peter's DNA test on file. The United Nations had taken a sample after they lost a translator in Slovenia."

"What did you learn?" the baroness asked.

"Peter is a match," Rosi said. "He really is the baron's grandson."

Peter moved Rosi's finger aside. "Are you telling the truth this time?"

"Of course, love," she said.

I was so jealous of the way she was fawning on him that I wanted to slug her.

"We'll keep in touch." Rosi walked back to her car and opened the door. "*Tschüss*."

As she drove away everyone was quiet. Then Harmony raised a bottle of fruit drink toward Herr Weiss and Peter. "Cheers to the latest Hohensteuerns."

The rest of us joined in, lifting our paper cups and bottles.

"Congratulations, Herr Weiss," I said.

The old secretary responded with a tired smile. "Thank you, Miss Smyth."

The weariness in his tone suddenly reminded me of my own father. Learning the truth about one's family can be a mixed blessing. Still, it's a first step toward moving on with your life. I decided right then that I would return to Greece to tell Dad what I'd found out about our ancestry. He'd asked me to wait, so I wouldn't go right away. But I knew I'd be hiking the trail out to his monastery soon. I wondered how our relationship would change once we both knew the truth.

The baroness rolled her chair closer to her secretary and studied him with her dark eyes. "What does this mean, Herr Weiss? You can't inherit the title of baron. What will change?"

Herr Weiss said, "I hope to serve you for many years, baroness."

"Good." She thought a moment. "Since you appear to have Hohensteuern blood, I suppose I will leave you the castle. But don't expect more than a ruin. I have no money for repair. I can't save Schloss Klingenstein."

I looked up at the castle tower. At first glance it was impressive, with its decorative red window shutters and its banner-shaped weathervane. But the stucco was peeling and an ominous crack ran diagonally for two stories. Peter had told me the castle was slowly slipping off the edge of its limestone cliff. Now I could see it was true.

"Uh, hm," Monty cleared his throat "I, uh, talked with Winona."

"Winona?" The baroness turned her wheelchair, examining my stepfather as though she had never really paid much attention to him before. "Who is Winona?"

"My wife." Monty took a checkbook from his pocket, wrote a few lines, and tore off a sheet. "I didn't have a surprise last night, so now, uh, anyway."

The baroness stared at the paper. "Two hundred thousand dollars!"

"What!" My mother turned to Monty. "That's not the amount we talked about."

Monty smiled—such a disarmingly handsome smile. "I think it's about right."

I hadn't appreciated my stepfather properly until that moment. His check was roughly the value of the treasure Margret had taken from the Hohensteuern safe.

Monty put his arm around my mother. "We'll manage, Winona. Let it go."

That afternoon while my mother was packing the rental car I dragged Harmony into my room to talk.

"How can you just go home like this?" I asked.

"Like what? I've already stayed an extra week."

"But what about Gilberto? You've been getting along with him so well."

Harmony sat on the edge of my bed. "This isn't about Gilberto, is it? It's about you and Peter."

"Harm! It is not." I leaned against the end of the bed and folded my arms. "Well, maybe. But what about you and Gilberto?"

"I'm going to teach kindergarten in Eugene. He's going back to the institute in Trieste."

"I thought he quit his job."

"They want him back, with a promotion. Now that Dr. Nimolo's missing, everyone's curious about what he was doing. Berti thinks he might be able to figure it out. He has to think about his career."

"But how can you just walk away from him? The man makes tiramisu, for crying out loud."

"Ana, it's not forever. He needs some time to publish a paper about the formula."

"Then the formula really is important?"

"Maybe. Berti says string theory has run into a dead end. Physicists are beginning to look at quantum gravity instead, and he's got a head start. If he publishes an important paper he can get a job anywhere. Even at the University of Oregon."

I should have known. Harmony is not as impulsive as she seems. In the months since we met at the divorce support group I'd watched her confidence grow. Now she knew exactly what she was doing, and I was the one at loose ends.

"Maybe you need to take a break too," Harmony suggested. "Everything's happened so fast. Two weeks ago Peter was a cowboy detective. Now he's some kind of semi-baron."

"He's neither of those," I objected. "He's a sculptor. He's shy."

"Where is he now?" she asked.

I nodded toward the closet.

She raised her eyebrows. "Peter's in your closet?"

"No, in the next room. He's making concrete geese in his studio. There's an art competition for the new Berlin airport. If they like his statues, they'll want hundreds."

"That sounds promising," Harmony said. "Why don't you give him some time to work on his art? I thought you wanted to write a book."

"I do. I will. It's just—"

"What?"

I looked out the window at the lights across the valley, unsure how to answer. Harm is such a powerful force on men that I wasn't sure she could understand. When she smiles, men remember. Even if she left Gilberto for years, he'd move heaven and earth to find her again. I don't seem to have that kind of pull.

"I don't know," I said. "Maybe I belong here for a while."

"In Germany? You're kidding."

"I could take a sabbatical. You know, to freshen up my language skills."

Harm nodded slowly. "Is that what you want?"

"Klingenstein is the kind of place Margret and I used to dream about. I think Peter feels it too, but he can't say it. It's like there's a barrier neither of us can break through."

"Maybe that barrier has a name," Harm suggested.

"Like what?"

"Like Rosi."

I looked at her from the side. "You figured out that Rosi used to be Peter's girlfriend?"

"Cops are pretty transparent."

I sighed. "If I leave Klingenstein, it's goodbye Peter."

"Then go the other way. Grab him! "

If anyone had experience at grabbing what she wanted, it was Harmony. "What worked with you and Gilberto?"

"Gilberto? I pretty much tore off his clothes in a goat shed."

We looked at each other and broke out laughing.

After Harmony settled back down she said, "Naw, I wouldn't recommend it."

"Then what?"

"I don't know." Harmony unfolded her legs and scooted off the bed. "I've got a flight to catch."

"Just like that, you're leaving?"

"Ana. You'll find a formula that works."

Even before Harmony left I'd thought of Cloud Nine. The memory loomed up in the castle room like a dangerous ghost. I dug out my old purse, the one with the cut shoulder strap. The little blue bottle was still there.

Here was the mysterious perfume my father had invented long ago. My mother had thought it made her feel five pounds lighter.

Harmony had said it had no effect on men. Dr. Nimolo had wondered if it might be the trigger of a gravity bomb. But I knew it matched the color my father saw in me.

I turned out the light. Then I pulled out the vial's stopper and waited.

Nothing. The lights from the window were too bright.

I opened the closet and sat on a blanket inside, against the wall. For a long time the darkness was absolute. Then slowly a glow began to emerge—maroon at first, and then a deep royal blue.

I felt as if I were adrift between worlds. Dark galaxies of split wood, summer rain, and apples pulled me on. Blue shimmered on all sides, amazingly beautiful against infinity.

Was I nine or ninety? Margret's attic was beyond time.

Somewhere far away, a dog was barking.

I looked to either side. There were two portals that led from the darkness of my past. Both ways glowed in the unearthly blue of my father's potion.

I could do it now.

I could do it on my own.

I put the stopper back in the vial and set it aside.

Then I took a deep breath and opened the door to Peter.

William L. Sullivan

is the author of a dozen books about adventure, Oregon, and history. This is his second novel.

Sullivan completed his B.A. degree in English at Cornell University under Alison Lurie, studied linguistics at Germany's Heidelberg University, and finished an M.A. in German at the University of Oregon. He reads in half a dozen languages, plays the pipe organ, and enjoys backcountry ski expeditions. After backpacking more than a thousand miles across Oregon's wilderness in 1985 he published Listening for Coyote, *a journal that has since been chosen one of Oregon's "100 Books." In summer he writes at the log cabin that he and his wife Janell Sorensen built by hand in the wilds of Oregon's Coast Range, more than a mile from roads, electricity, and telephones. The rest of the year they live in Eugene, Oregon, where he volunteers to promote libraries and literature.*

A list of Sullivan's books, speaking engagements, and favorite adventures is at www.oregonhiking.com.